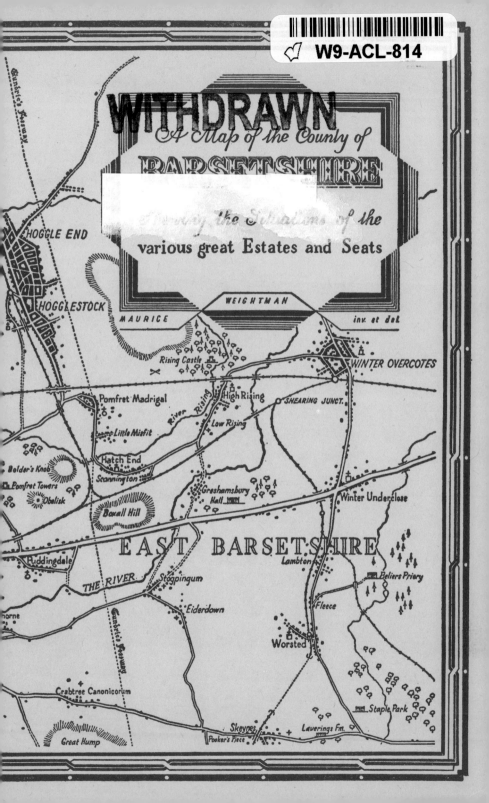

The Novels of ANGELA THIRKELL

LOVE AT ALL AGES   CLOSE QUARTERS
A DOUBLE AFFAIR
NEVER TOO LATE   ENTER SIR ROBERT
WHAT DID IT MEAN?
JUTLAND COTTAGE   CORONATION SUMMER
HAPPY RETURN
WILD STRAWBERRIES and HIGH RISING
THE DUKE'S DAUGHTER
COUNTY CHRONICLE   THE OLD BANK HOUSE
LOVE AMONG THE RUINS
PRIVATE ENTERPRISE
PEACE BREAKS OUT   MISS BUNTING
THE HEADMISTRESS
GROWING UP   MARLING HALL
NORTHBRIDGE RECTORY
CHEERFULNESS BREAKS IN
BEFORE LUNCH   THE BRANDONS
POMFRET TOWERS
SUMMER HALF   AUGUST FOLLY

THESE ARE BORZOI BOOKS PUBLISHED IN NEW YORK BY

ALFRED A. KNOPF

THREE SCORE AND TEN

THREE SCORE AND TEN

by
Angela Thirkell

AND

C. A. Lejeune

NEW YORK: ALFRED·A·KNOPF

19  62

L. C. catalog card number: 62-11048

THIS IS A BORZOI BOOK,
PUBLISHED BY ALFRED A. KNOPF, INC.

FIRST AMERICAN EDITION

THREE SCORE AND TEN

CHAPTER 1

🙷

IT WAS one of those delightful English summer days so well de-scribed by Lord Tennyson. The cuckoo of a joyless June had far too long been calling out of doors, making all bird-lovers think and in some cases say aloud: "Oh, shut UP." But they might as well have kept their breath to cool their porridge, for joyless June had now gone by and, as Lord Tennyson so truly wrote two verses further on, The cuckoo of a worse July was now call-ing through the dark. It is all very well for poets and musicians to rhapsodise about the cuckoo, but he is just as bad as Brown-ing's wise thrush who will sing each song twice over, Lest you should think he never could recapture, The first fine careless rapture, till you could willingly shoot him if you had a pistol and knew how to use it.

But people who live in the country have to take the weather as it comes, and a good many of them really do not notice it much unless it is a question of The Asparagus, Those new chick-ens, or The Strawberries will rot if we don't eat them all now ripe or not. At any rate Mrs. Morland, the well-known writer, had given up trying to grow strawberries for, as she so truly said, they were never so nice after they were picked, but she didn't like to eat them straight from the strawberry bed because one had to stoop and one wasn't so young as one was. These com-plaints she was unloading onto her old friends, the George Knoxes, who had come to tea, together with George's daughter and son-in-law, Sybil and Adrian Coates, and her much older friend Lord Stoke who had been driven over in his dog-cart by an elderly groom, bringing some odds and ends of garden and orchard produce with him.

"Never pick your own strawberries," said his lordship, who was looking more than ever like a character from a Caldecott picture-book, with a kind of rather flat truncated light brown top hat and a cutaway coat with the much coveted buttons of the Rising Hunt, which, owing to the increase of young pony-riders, was in a better position than anyone could have hoped. "If you do, your man won't take a proper interest in them and then there will be trouble when he brings them up to the house."

Mrs. Morland said, with a fine simplicity, that she never picked her own strawberries now because she hadn't got any and hadn't a man either.

Lord Stoke said everyone had strawberries but old Lord Pomfret's were much the best.

"Well, I haven't any," said Mrs. Morland, "because Stoker would keep them for jam when I had a small bed of them and usually my boys used to pick them first and there were dreadful rows. So I just Put the Strawberry Bed Down."

Mrs. Knox asked how you put one down.

"Simply," said Mrs. Morland, pushing her garden hat back on her forehead in a very unbecoming way, though it must be admitted that it was just as unbecoming when it was straight, "by telling the gardener—at least he wasn't a real gardener because he was the boy from Brown's garage who comes round after his tea to do a bit of work here, only Stoker *will* give him another huge tea in the kitchen—to dig them all up. Since when that bit of ground has never looked the same."

"Couldn't, if you had all the strawberries dug up," said Lord Stoke. "Needed *properly* digging and sowing and then the roller over it. Must roll grass and turf to keep them down."

"I know exactly what you mean," said Mrs. Morland. "A pony with four leather shoes, only they were more like boots. And a man pushing the mowing machine."

"What the dickens does he push it for?" said Lord Stoke. "If you have a horse to pull it you don't want to push. You just keep your hands on the handle and the other man leads the horse. Used to do it myself, but it's all electric mowers now."

"Not here, Lord Stoke," said Mrs. Morland. "My grass isn't big enough. I mean there would hardly be time for the mowing machine to get to the far side of the lawn before it had to turn round again. Besides," she added, evidently with a lively picture in her mind's eye, "if I had an old mowing machine the horse would get to the end of the lawn before the machine did and if the machine has to go right to the edge to cut the grass the horse would be in the laurel hedge, which is, I believe, poison to animals. Or is it something else that poisons them? There is one of Thomas Hardy's depressing little *contes*——"

"Thomas Who? Never heard of the feller," said Lord Stoke. "And what's a cont? Never heard of one."

George Knox, with a general feeling that he represented Literature far better than Mrs. Morland, said he was a Wessex poet.

"Wessex? That's all old history. Alfred and the cakes and all that," said Lord Stoke.

George Knox said that Hardy had also written novels about Wessex. Perhaps, he said, Lord Stoke knew Tess.

"Tess?" said his lordship. "That's not English. It's a black girl, isn't it? *Uncle Tom's Cabin*. Runs away from her owners across an ice pack or something. Eh?" which last word—or rather noise —his lordship exploded to that extent that some of his listeners nearly had the giggles.

"Now *Nelson's* Hardy was a fine feller," said his lordship, speaking in a way that made his hearers feel that the gap in time was almost negligible. "Nasty business that, when the Labour Government took the Nelson pension away—a good many years ago now, but a dirty job. Spend millions of pounds on factories and things and cut Nelson out. Bah!" which expletive gave his hearers considerable pleasure. "Do you know what the Nelson place was called?"

After a dead silence Mrs. Morland suddenly said: "Trafalgar."

"Quite right," said his lordship approvingly, and evidently wishing to pat her hand in recognition, if he had been near enough. "Only it was called Trafal*gar*. And Browning made praise and pray rhyme with Africa. You can't do it. Have to say Prah and Africah—or Pray and Africay. But Browning wasn't at Oxford. If I'd made a howler like that when I was at The House, my tutor would have told me off and made me write it out fifty times."

"Wasn't that *Eton*, Lord Stoke?" said Mrs. Morland.

"Daresay you're right," said Lord Stoke. "Things get a bit mixed when you get older. Now, I can remember the pattern of my nursery wallpaper as if it was yesterday. If Nurse put me in the corner I used to lick my finger and rub it up and down the wallpaper. I got quite a lot off that way till Nurse told my mother. I miss them both, you know," and his lordship was silent, in a kind of looking-backward dream.

His hearers, who were themselves beginning to think of a youth when every goose was a swan and every lass a queen, didn't quite know what to say and perhaps some of them—certainly Mrs. Morland—would have found utterance difficult. For Nelson is still a word to stir the blood and to bring back the tears of things which a Roman poet knew so well more than two thousand years ago; and to deprive his successors of the Nelson pension was an ugly and not to be forgotten deed, when far more is spent on unnecessary things.

"Well, well," said Lord Stoke, expunging as it were any previous remarks, "that's that. How are your boys, Mrs. Morland? Never remember how many you have."

"Considering that Gerald is nearer fifty than forty now and the others are all getting on," said Mrs. Morland, "I think you ought to know. Even Tony is a middle-aged man. And I may say that I shall be seventy next birthday."

On hearing this, Mr. and Mrs. Knox looked at their hostess with some respect.

"Will you have a party?" said Mrs. Knox.

"I have been thinking about it," said Mrs. Morland. "But I think not. I mean people might think I wanted birthday presents and they might feel they ought to be rather expensive ones, because of course one is only seventy once in one's life."

"That, my dear Laura, is irrelevant," said George Knox. "One is only the age one is—whatever it may be—once."

"Except that dreadful Mrs. George Rivers," said his wife. "She goes on being the age she thinks she is but she doesn't look like it. Have you read her last book?"

"I don't quite know," said Mrs. Morland. "I mean she writes the same book every time, all about wives having romantic affairs and apparently their husbands don't mind, which must be very comfortable but a bit depressing."

"I have often wondered," said Mrs. Knox, "what I would do if a middle-aged man of great attraction and very rich fell in love with me."

"You would ask my advice at once," said her husband.

"So I should," said Mrs. Knox, evidently much struck by this loophole. "And I am sure you would give me very good advice, darling."

"I know what I *would* say," said her husband. "I should say: Please yourself."

"My husband used to say that," said Mrs. Morland. "But he died a long time ago," which *non sequitur* left her friends slightly addled, a state in which they not infrequently found themselves when in her company.

"Lots of them did," said Lord Stoke. "Join the majority and all that."

Mrs. Knox said that phrase used to puzzle her when she was young because she thought it meant always living with majors, and she would rather live with captains because majors sounded so old.

"But more permanent—I mean *safer*," said Mrs. Morland. " 'The captains and the kings depart,' which is a quotation, but it doesn't say anything about majors."

"It's a funny thing, but there aren't any majors in the Bible," said Lord Stoke. "Captains, yes; and kings. But no majors."

Mrs. Morland said she supposed they weren't invented yet.

"I daresay, I daresay," said Lord Stoke, not very patiently.

"I have a copy of *Cruden's Concordance, 1875*," said George Knox, "with the front cover missing. There's practically nothing you can't find. *Right*, together with *Righteousness*, take up almost the whole of seven columns of small print. But no majors. I daresay there weren't any, or they didn't count."

"I have never known," said Mrs. Morland, who had obviously put her learned sock on, "why majors, which after all means greater than something else, are less than colonels."

Mrs. Knox said she used to think majors were the greatest because there was Major, Minor, and Minimus, at which point everyone might have gone mad if Mrs. Morland's faithful and very trying old maid, Stoker, had not come round the side of the house pushing a large tea-trolley.

"Here you are," said Stoker. "I made a cake special for you, Mrs. Knox. I'll never forget the night you was here when your por mother died and Mr. Knox carried you up to Mrs. Morland's bedroom. As good as Marleen it was," which tribute nearly made Mrs. Knox have the giggles, but she managed to restrain herself.

With a benevolent look, such as Nannie might give to a nursery tea-party where the children were still behaving like nice little ladies and gentlemen, Stoker tripped away to her kitchen. And when we say tripped, we mean it, for quite often people of considerable bulk are far more agile than one would suspect. We remember in our far-off callow girlhood how at small dances there were one or two cavaliers who, clasping one to their very stout, stiff-shirted bosoms, would whirl one round quite delightfully and hardly ever trod on one's toes. And no reversing either, for that was still a little fast. *O tempi passati!*

"You are in fine form, Stoker," said Mrs. Knox when that Hebe reappeared with a tray of glasses and various bottles and a large jug of lemonade with ice floating in it. "How are your symptoms?"

"Opening and shutting all down my back, same as those wooden blinds," said Stoker, putting the jug down with a hearty good-will that slopped the lemonade over the tray. "Dreadful it is. Old Doc Pepper's Pick-Me-Up, that's what I take for it. It clears the liver, so they say. My mother used to give it us when we were kids and we had to swallow it. If we didn't, she pinched your nose the way you had to open your mouth and down it went."

"And did it do you good?" said Mrs. Knox.

"Good?" said Stoker. "It cleared the blood. Look at *me*."

Everyone obediently turned his or her head in that direction.

"Look at my arms," said Stoker, stretching them out for observation, bare to above the elbows and of portentous size. Everyone looked, some with interest, some with faint loathing.

"It reminds me of the Princess," said Mrs. Morland.

"What Princess," said Lord Stoke. "Not that dreadful old Princess Louisa of Cobalt—one of the Hatz-Reinigens?"

"No, no. I mean *The* Princess," said Mrs. Morland. "Or if you must be up-to-date, Ther Princess. Tennyson."

"Oh, The Princess," said Lord Stoke. "My dear mother used to read it aloud to us, with expression. You don't get expression now."

"But you *do*, Lord Stoke," said Mrs. Knox. "That woman who recites and has a different coloured shawl for every poem and bare feet."

"Don't know her," said Lord Stoke. "Nobody ought to have bare feet—except children, of course. My dear mother used to let us go barefoot in the summer. I remember that feeling of nice warm squelchy mud coming up between one's toes. And then one day I looked at my feet and saw they were grown-up."

"Do you mean ingrowing toe-nails?" said Mrs. Morland.

"Of course I don't," said Lord Stoke. "I mean grown-up feet."

"Oh, I *do* know what you mean," said Mrs. Morland. "When your big toe joint begins to get bigger and your little toe squasheder."

"That's right," said Lord Stoke in a satisfied voice. "And when I looked at them I never took my socks and shoes off again."

"Did you *sleep* in them?" said Mrs. Morland, thus giving much pleasure to her other guests, who were longing to hear all.

"Sleep in them?" said his lordship indignantly. "Of course not. My man would have given notice if I'd slept in my shoes and socks."

"Then what *did* you do?" said Mrs. Coates, rather lost now in his lordship's divagations and short cuts.

"Do?" said Lord Stoke. "I didn't do anything. But I never went barefoot any more. Why people go barefoot on pebbly beaches, or in the country where you'll always get some thistles —especially those nasty little flat ones you find on the downs—I don't know. So I said to my bootmaker—you know, Catt in Bond Street; Puss-in-Boots we used to call him because his bespoke boots and shoes were so well made, and of course Puss stood for Cat as well. You can still have boots made to order there, but they stock a lot of ready-made stuff too. Same with my Tailor— feller in Savile Row—name of Cutt. I've always had my suits made to order, and he still knows how to dress a gentleman, but a lot of young fellers can't be bothered with the fittin's now.

Cutt wouldn't work for the Prince of Wales himself unless he came in for at least three fittin's," and Mrs. Morland could have embraced her old friend for his Victorian manner of speech. So few of us drop "g's" now—once almost a mark of rank and blood.

"So, as I was sayin'," Lord Stoke continued, after not listening to anything anyone else said, "I never went barefoot again."

"It reminds me of Tony," said Mrs. Morland.

"Tony? That's that youngest boy of yours," said Lord Stoke. "You brought him over to Rising Castle once. There was cherry pie for lunch and your boy kept all the stones in his mouth and when he had finished he spat them all out onto the plate."

"I do remember that," said Mrs. Morland. "I was never so ashamed in my life. I was so sorry for Albert."

"Albert? You don't mean the Prince Consort. He came to Rising Castle in my old father's time—long before your day," said Lord Stoke. "What Albert?"

"Well, really, Lord Stoke, you might remember who your own servants were. He was the footman then and when Tony spat out all the stones Albert couldn't help laughing and your butler gave him a nasty look," said Mrs. Morland.

"Quite right," said his lordship. "My dear mother wouldn't have cherry pie unless all the cherries were stoned first. She said half the appendicitis in England was caused by people swallowing cherry stones. What would you say, Mrs. Morland?"

"I don't think I'd say anything," said the gifted authoress after a moment's thought. "I mean I always put the stones on the side of my plate, but sometimes one does escape and they go down quite easily and that's that," and she looked round for sympathy.

"When I was a little girl," said Mrs. Knox, "we used to do Tinker, Tailor with our cherry stones."

Her husband asked what she meant.

"Well, George! if you don't know, you did had ought," said Mrs. Knox, to which her husband's unsympathetic reply was what on earth did she mean.

"I mean you did had ought to," said Mrs. Knox firmly. "And that is good plain English."

> *"Of all sad words of tongue or pen*
> *The saddest are these: 'It might have been!'*
> *But sadder far are those to me*
> *'It is, but it hadn't ought to be,' "*

said Mrs. Morland.

"An excellent sentiment," said Adrian Coates, "and new to me. Where does it come from?"

" 'Out of the everywhere into here,' " said Mrs. Morland.

Adrian Coates asked her what she meant.

"You generation of vipers," said Mrs. Morland, though without heat. "It is a well-known misquotation from I can't at the moment remember whose works. Probably George Macdonald. And now I have suddenly remembered that what you were asking about is in a very well-known poem by, I think, an American poet whose name I can't remember, called *Maud Muller*. I mean the poem, not the poet. At least, it is a kind of parody of it," which very clear explanation left her hearers much where they were.

"What on earth were we talking about?" said Mrs. Coates.

Everyone was at a loss by now, as indeed Mrs. Morland's friends were, more often than not, when that distinguished writer had said what she thought was what she meant to say.

"Maud Muller," said Mrs. Morland firmly. "The judge was in love with her, but he didn't think his mother would like it. 'So closing his heart the judge went on And Maud Muller was left in the field alone.' "

"Don't think much of that poem," said Lord Stoke. "Who wrote it? Mark Twain?"

There was a dead silence.

"Don't know what we are all talkin' about," said his lordship. "Mrs. Morland, you began all this. What's it all about?"

"Well, really nothing," said Mrs. Morland. "I mean the first two lines are in the poem, but of course the two last ones are a kind of joke—a parody."

"Now, there was a feller called Swinburne when I was a young man," said his lordship. "I didn't read him but my dear old mother did. He wrote some parodies, too. Don't know why he did it—came of a good family and went to the dogs at Putney. Oh well!"

"But I have got his parodies, and they are very funny. And he parodied himself too. I wish I could parody people. Myself perhaps and then you, George," said Mrs. Morland.

"You couldn't parody yourself, Laura," said Mrs. Coates.

"But I do—every year," said Mrs. Morland indignantly. "That's why people buy my books. I mean if you read a book and you like it, then you like to read another book like the one you liked. Now Dickens is always different."

"Therefore, my dear Laura, you do *not* wish to read another one," said Mr. Coates, rather unkindly.

"Don't be silly, darling," said his wife. "You don't know what you mean when you talk like that."

"Dickens," said Mrs. Morland, assuming the air of an eminent Q.C., "is always different because he was a genius. And what is more, Edwin Drood was never finished, so we shall never know."

"And you are never finished, my dear Laura," said George Knox, who had been trying to get into the conversation for some time.

"But I AM," said Mrs. Morland indignantly. "When I have said what needs saying I stop talking. I shall now stop."

She took up a curiously shaped piece of knitting, extracted two knitting needles from a ball, picked up a number of stitches, and began to knit. Mrs. Knox asked what she was making. Mrs. Morland came to the end of the row, dropped the loose needle, and picked it up again.

"Just swabs," she said.

"For the Cottage Hospital?" said Mrs. Knox.

"Oh, not *that* kind," said Mrs. Morland. "I mean *swabs*."

"I don't mean anything to do with the Navy," said Mrs. Knox.

"Nor do I, Anne," said Mrs. Morland. "I mean for swabbing things like basins and the bath when you get a dirty streak round it far too high up, which always happens if any of my sons are at home, which they mostly aren't. This very thick cotton yarn is excellent for swabbing except that it comes to pieces very soon, so I really don't know why it was invented."

"You are really *impayable*, Laura," said George Knox, who from his French mother, now long dead, had inherited a number of useful words which he spoke with an excellent accent. "Do explain yourself."

"But I just have," said Mrs. Morland.

Lord Stoke, who, as was more and more his habit, was apt to go off into a kind of private dream, now came to suddenly and said his mother used to get all her house linen at the Army and Navy Stores. No nonsense about knitting. The Army and Navy Stores, he added, *was* the Army and Navy Stores then.

"But, it still is," said Mrs. Morland. "I mean in Victoria Street. And a very good shop."

"Ah, in my mother's days you had to be a shareholder to shop there," said Lord Stoke. "My mother had a ticket—everyone had a ticket—with their number on it. Hers was 17801—can't think why one remembers things like that. And if she forgot to take her ticket with her she used to give the assistant her visiting card. They all knew her. Now it's free to all," a fact which his lordship appeared to find highly derogatory to that excellent firm. "But she did it once too often," and his lordship chuckled —a word we hardly ever use now, but it combines laughing with a slightly malicious tinge.

As it was obvious that Lord Stoke had by no means said all he wished to say, Mrs. Knox very kindly enquired what happened next.

"Happened? Nothing happened," said Lord Stoke. "When she was interviewing the cook that morning she had to ask the woman why four plates had been broken and why there were six empty beer bottles in the scullery. And the cook said the bottles were a mistake, and as for the plates, it wasn't the drink but the worry. Of course my dear mother didn't believe her, and she was a good cook and it didn't often happen. But my dear mother made a note of it on one of her cards so that she could tell my father about it. Then she went to the Stores and when she had ordered what she needed she handed that card to the shopman so that he could take her name and address and what he read was 'Lady Stoke. It's not the drink but the worry.' "

He then looked round for applause. Everyone was mildly amused by his anecdote and perhaps exaggerated their amusement a little to give him pleasure.

"Long time since my dear mother died," his lordship went on. "I sometimes wonder if she would know me now. I've changed a lot since then. Daresay she has too, but I expect they look after all that. Keep young. Nothing else to do."

Mrs. Knox said in her usual calm, competent way that one did not know.

"But I hope people don't stay young for ever in heaven," said Mrs. Morland. "I mean if I went to heaven and met my mother whom I was very fond of and she was about twenty-five in a muslin dress and a large floppy hat which was what I remember when I was very small, I expect I wouldn't know her. And probably she wouldn't know me as I am now, especially since I had my false teeth. I always hope that when I am dead and find myself somewhere else I shall have my dentures with me. I mean if one puts them in a glass of water by one's bed and dies in the night by mistake, you wouldn't be able to talk to St. Peter or *anyone*. At least not comfortably, because when you take your teeth out it feels funny and you really can't say much except thith, thith, thith. But I expect one will be understood all the same, though," she continued thoughtfully, "I daresay they would say understanded in heaven."

Lord Stoke, who had been straining at the leash while his old friend delivered herself of one of her rambles and excursions, said he knew a man once who cut a third set of teeth.

Everyone said how marvellous and they wished they could, if and when a time came when they needed them.

"Nasty ones too," said his lordship, ignoring this interruption. "All black and decaying. Had to have them all taken out."

Mrs. Coates asked if he grew a fourth set.

"If he did, it wasn't down here," said Lord Stoke. "He died a week later. Great friend of mine. Hadn't seen him for years. He lived up near Welshpool."

Mrs. Knox said she supposed he liked sailing.

"Not a piece of water near his place," said Lord Stoke. "There was a waterfall, but it all ran away under the ground and you don't sail in waterfalls."

Mrs. Morland said: Not even a pond? One could go on a pond in a rowing boat, she said. An old uncle of hers who was President of the S.C.T., which they must have heard of—Society for Correcting Translations—had a large square pond in his garden in Sussex, and one day when he was going up to London for an important meeting of the Society he fell into the pond by mistake. Luckily, she added, it was only about two feet deep, but his striped trousers and frock-coat were wet through and his top hat was ruined and he had to change and go up to town in his second-best trousers and a jacket and a bowler.

"Like the time Adrian fell into the river when they were cutting the rushes," said Mrs. Coates, with a voice of proud adoration.

Her husband said, though not unkindly, that he hoped he had lived that down and would hear no more about it now.

"But one thing we *must* hear about," said Mr. Coates. "That birthday of yours, Laura. I mean seventy is a kind of turning-point—or do I mean a landmark?"

His wife said not to be silly. Seventy was seventy and lots of people lived to eighty. Like her father's old mother, she added, looking proudly at George Knox.

"She just missed her ninetieth birthday," said Mr. Knox. "I was going to give her a new television set, but she died, so I didn't."

There was a subdued murmur of What a pity.

"Well, I don't know that it was," said George Knox. "She used to have the old set on all day long, but she hardly ever looked at it. Said it was too small and no one need tell her that people in the studio as they called it, though she couldn't think why as there weren't any painters there, were only a few inches high and trembled like a jelly all the time."

"Well, you don't *know*," said Mrs. Morland. "Perhaps they do. I mean one would. I should certainly tremble all over if I had twenty cameras barking at me."

"Without holding any particular brief for the B.B.C., that ravager of our noble English tongue," said George Knox, "I must raise an objection to what you have just said, Laura. Cameras do not bark."

"Nor do all dogs," said Mrs. Morland. "But they can be very disagreeable. I mean when they suddenly run across the road in front of your car and you have to pull up and your teeth nearly come out."

"Much as we love, nay, respect our dear Laura——" George Knox began.

"You *don't* respect me, George," said Mrs. Morland indignantly. "You never have. And I don't respect you. We are just friends."

"Well, friends the merest Keep much that I resign," said George Knox with a voice rather unlike his own.

"I know why you are talking like that, George," said Mrs. Morland. "You've been reading Browning. But I am *not* your Lost Mistress."

There was a moment's silence from her slightly stunned audience.

"And I have never been *anyone's* mistress," the gifted writer continued. "Nobody ever asked me and I should have been furious if they had. Stoker would have given notice. And it would have been *most* awkward for my boys; especially the married ones. I mean my boys wouldn't have taken much notice but my daughters-in-law, whom I am devoted to, would think it not a good thing."

"Certainly not a good thing," said Lord Stoke. "I won't say that I didn't fling a leg when I was young. But in a quiet way. Then I met someone whom I admired and would have loved if she would let me. But she didn't. You know whom I mean, Mrs. Morland."

There was a brief silence. Mrs. Morland had never forgotten how Lord Stoke had once told her of his young love for Edith Thorne, who had married the old Lord Pomfret—all so long ago now.

"Well, there we all are," said Lord Stoke. "Coates and his wife, Knox and his wife. You and I, Mrs. Morland," which was so true that no one knew what to say.

Mrs. Morland, who knew Lord Stoke better perhaps than any other of his friends, went back in her mind to the day when she had taken that pretty Edith Graham, now Lady William Harcourt, to Rising Castle and Lord Stoke had given Edith a little pearl necklace which he had hoped many years ago to give to Edith Thorne who had married old Lord Pomfret. Her heart felt a mixture of compassion for the young man that Lord Stoke had been and the old and rather lonely man he had become. But her head pointed out to her that those of us who live to be old must necessarily become lonely as our contemporaries drop out. For many of us there are our children of course and our delightful exhausting grandchildren; but one has to accommodate oneself to them, not they to you. The River of Life flows on, much as Blake painted it; coming whence we do not know, going whither we know even less.

"Time, like an ever-rolling stream . . ." she said half aloud to herself.

George Knox, ever anxious to be first in the fray, cleared his voice.

"If you are going to make a speech, George dear, don't," said his wife; and before he could so far recover himself as to ignore what she said Mrs. Morland continued more or less what she had been saying.

"It is *so* true," she said. "So often husbands die before wives, because the wives have stamina. I don't exactly know what stamina is, or ought I to say are—because neuter nouns in Latin I seem to remember do form their plural in *a*, at least in one of the declensions, I think, but I never know the difference between a declension and a conjugation."

She then looked round for approval or criticism, but for a few seconds her audience were too bewildered to speak. George Knox, as usual, was the first to leap into the breach.

"I am no true Latinist," he said, "but enough was knocked into me at school for me to value—to deeply value——"

"No need to split infinitives, George," said his son-in-law rather impertinently.

"To value, as I was saying . . ." George Knox went on, but he was again interrupted by Adrian Coates, who said he was dodging the issue, at least that was what he was doing if what he had said meant what he thought it meant.

"How eagerly," said George Knox, who had remarkable powers of switching off any conversation he did not approve and turning it to his ends, "do the young debunk—I believe that is the word—their elders. The splitting of infinitives is a moot question. The late lamented H. Ward Fowler in his *Dictionary of Modern English Usage* puts the case very clearly in some half-dozen closely printed columns. Would that I had it by me."

"Well, George," said his wife, "*I* wouldn't. I know you. You would read it all aloud to us with your own comments and we should all go mad."

There was a brief pause and Mrs. Morland had to suppress her increasing desire to have the giggles.

"So be it," said George Knox. "My helmet has become a hive for bees."

"If you mean that awful old hat of yours, Daddy, that has been hanging on a hook near the garden door for ages, no bee would look at it," said his undutiful daughter. "I shall use it for a Guy Fawkes next November. Is that all right, Anne?" she added, turning to her stepmother, with whom she was on excellent terms in the Monstrous Regiment of Women—not that the Regimentation was unkind, but it could deflate George Knox and thus keep him within bounds.

"I had half promised it to the odd man who comes to give a hand," said Mrs. Knox. "He is rather mental and he says he can think much better if he has something on his head to stop his mind running away."

Some stepdaughters might have taken mild offence, but Sybil Coates and her stepmother were on excellent terms, not seldom banding together against Man as exemplified in their respective father and husband; but as he had a habit of ignoring anything he didn't like, no harm was done.

During this conversation or argument, whichever it was, Lord Stoke had sat quietly listening, or at any rate appearing to listen, and had not made any contribution to the discussion. This had not passed unnoticed by Mrs. Morland, who suddenly said: "What do *you* think, Lord Stoke? You are older than all of us."

Lord Stoke, rather flattered by this invitation, began to get his opinion under way (for under weigh we never write since studying Mr. Fowler's words on the subject), and the rest of the party kindly waited while he wrestled with himself.

"I see it this way," he said. "A promise is a promise. Let's have him here and thrash it out."

"That would be lovely," said Mrs. Coates. "He's really awfully kind. He used to make Skipjacks for me when I was small and he could charm warts. I'll run down in the car and fetch him, Daddy," and away she went.

On hearing these words George Knox became a philosopher, pondering the riddle of the universe, remote from everyday affairs. To his slight mortification no one seemed to notice his new role, so he retired into the sulks, which also remained unobserved by the party: except his wife, who often had the lowest opinion of the husband she adored. We believe this is quite usual.

"I say, Mrs. Morland," said Adrian Coates. "Where is Lord Stoke?"

Everyone looked round. His lordship's chair was also empty and no one had noticed him go.

"Probably in the kitchen with Stoker," said Mrs. Morland calmly. "They get on very well and tell each other about their past and neither of them listens to the other."

This might have surprised an outsider, but his lordship's peculiarities were well known to his friends, who were quite used to his coming into their houses via the stables, the kitchen, the cowshed, or the boot and knife room. And so various were his methods of approach that even the front door had to be counted with.

The Knoxes had often discussed this peculiarity of his lordship, with no result at all. We think that the late Lady Pomfret could have explained it, for if a most eligible peer has loved you in your youth and you have, in all kindness and friendship, told him that you love Another, your heart may still remember him even if your head does not. But as the generations pass and everything imperceptibly changes in the diurnal course of not only rocks and stones and trees but also human lives, much is lost as each generation passes away. With the partial break-up of the social system after two wars, more has been lost than we can count as the big house, or the well-endowed rectory with a squarson, quietly vanishes. The house will be made into flats for those who can afford them, with a small part reserved for its owners, who, it must in fairness be said, are mostly very comfortable and can now afford to go to London, or abroad. As for the rectory, it also will often be divided, if not let as a whole, and the incumbent—though rather shorn of his glory—be lodged in a smaller house where his wife and family can be warm and there is a proper bath and an up-to-date kitchen; as Mr. Parkinson with his nice wife and children found when he was moved to Greshamsbury New Town and had a new house with a garage built onto it so that he could get into and out of his car without having to face rain or snow, not to speak of a good dry basement with the newest type of water-heater which supplied really hot baths and kept the linen-cupboard warm.

In less time than it has taken us to write the preceding and rather lengthy paragraph (with frequent intervals to look out of the window and watch the workmen painting the house opposite a most revolting shade of shrimp-gamboge, which we could describe far more accurately in one word, borrowed from our formerly lively neighbours the Gauls, if it were not rather too French) Mrs. Coates had driven to her father's house, collected the odd man and the hat, and brought them back to Mrs. Morland's side door.

We may here say that the odd man was the pride of High Rising. In earlier times he would have been called—without malice —the village idiot, a person without whom no community is complete. His mother, who was a nice girl though distinctly wanting, had listened once too often to the advances of a small commercial traveller known to her simple mind as "the gentleman" and the odd man had been the result. Like so many of his kind he was only mildly half-witted, and had a passion for animals of every size, from horses who appeared to understand every word he said to birds who would perch on his hat or his hand, not to speak of a vixen who allowed him regularly to inspect her cubs, and spiders who were apt to nestle between his neck and the collar of his shirt. He could make whistles out of the stalks of various plants, tickle and catch (quite illegally) any fish that he found in the little river Rising, take an egg or two from a sitting hen, was in request for miles round for the *accouchements* of cows and sows and washed as seldom as possible. George Knox had once consulted Dr. Ford on the subject of washing. Dr. Ford's answer was that in his long experience of people who never washed they were perfectly healthy—in the country at any rate. In fact, he said, a bath would probably first frighten him into dangerous idiocy as against his mild half-wittedness and then give him pneumonia, which would be the end of him.

"Well, here's Daddy's hat," said Mrs. Coates, coming triumphantly into the garden. "Isn't it *ghastly*? Come on, Alf."

Alf, a gangling not-so-young man, shuffled forward and to the joy of all present pulled his forelock—or rather gave what we can only call a token pull to his very short hair.

"You've been cutting your hair off again, Alf," said Mr. Coates accusingly.

"Ah!" said Alf, looking cautiously round.

"What did you cut it with?" said Mrs. Coates.

"Ah!" said Alf, assuming an expression of extreme cunning.

"Come on, Alf," said Mrs. Coates. "Was it the garden shears?"

"Nice old shears," said Alf. "I took her and I sharpened her with the whetstone and I spat on her just for luck and she cut fine, she did. Here it is," and he pulled from the pocket of his shabby jacket a dirty piece of paper. This he unfolded and offered to his audience with an angelic smile.

"That's my hair as the old shears cut off," said Alf.

"And what are you going to do with it, Alf?" said George Knox.

Alf said Ah.

"Ah's all very well, but it isn't an answer," said George Knox, which was an ill-advised move, for Alf evidently took his words as a kind of threat or insult, and looked wildly round for help.

"Out with it, Alf," said George Knox.

"Mother she said she'd have it," said Alf, "but I didn't let her have it. She might have pixied me."

At this unexpected influx of Cold Comfort Farm the audience were stunned to silence.

"Come, come, Alf," said George Knox. "There aren't any pixies now."

"Old Alf knows all about it," said Alf. "That old hat" (or as Mrs. Morland afterwards insisted, "Thiccy old hat," but no one believed her) "I'm keeping her for the horse when we mow the lower meadow. Alf'll cut two holes in it for his ears. Horses they do get the staggers, if it's too hot, same as people."

This conversation might have gone on for ever had not Lord Stoke rejoined them.

"Sensible woman that cook of yours, Mrs. Morland," said Lord Stoke. "Knows what she's talking about."

"And what," said George Knox, "was she talking about?"

"Old times," said Lord Stoke. "What we old uns all talk about now if we can find anyone to listen."

"But I *always* listen to you, Lord Stoke," said Mrs. Morland, "even if I'm not listening. I mean I know what you mean."

"So you ought by now," said his lordship. "You are a very good listener. No, I don't mean that. I mean a very kind listener."

"I take you, Stoke," said George Knox, an affected archaism which infuriated some of his friends, made others laugh and a few say that Knox was breaking up.

"We were talking about ranges," said Lord Stoke.

"Let me hear of them," said George Knox. "Ah! those snow-capped ranges of Kinchinjunga—its first syllable now cropped, mutilated, I gather, to Kitchen. Kinchinjunga, twin guardian with Everest of our far-flung frontier. Were I younger I should join those gallant, those intrepid climbers who among ice and snows and moraines—whatever they are but the word itself is beautiful—reach the summits that guard the springs of great rivers."

"Now do come down to earth, Knox," said his son-in-law, who felt, not unfairly we think, that as a very successful publisher and Mr. Knox's son-in-law, he was not presuming too far if he tried to keep his wife's father down a little. "Now I come to think of it, Kinchin is English too. In *Oliver Twist* the boys who work for Fagin are taught to be kinchins and prig people's wipes. And how we have got to petty theft from kitchen ranges via Stoker, don't ask me."

"And may I say," he added, hauling himself out of his deck chair, "that the canvas on the chair I've been sitting in is sagging to that extent that my heels were nearly as high as my head."

"I *am* sorry," said Mrs. Morland. "I'll tell Stoker to get some more canvas at the Stores. I know they have plenty because I was in there this morning and I saw them unpacking it. It's that rather thick sort that is green. I like the old ones that were an ordinary colour with some stripes on them but one can't have Everything. And this canvas is all ready."

"Ready for what?" said George. "*Précisez*, my dear Laura."

"We all know, George," said Mrs. Morland, "that your mother, who could be very alarming but was always kind to me when I went to see her in Rutland Gate, was half French, but you are only a quarter French—a quadroon, I suppose one would say."

"No, Laura, one would *not*," said George Knox.

"Alexandre Dumas," said Adrian Coates, who had been listening to this conversation, "was a quadroon and his son used to

say of him that his father was so conceited that he would get up
behind his own carriage to make people believe he had a Ne-
gro servant. But I do not think that my respected father-in-law
would do that."

"He couldn't," said Mrs. Morland. "At least I mean there are
hardly any carriages now and you couldn't get up behind a car
because there isn't anything to stand on except the bumper bar.
Of course there are those dreadful new cars with a kind of coupé
in the middle and a huge front and behind sticking out in front
and behind, which is tautology, I believe, but you couldn't stand
on the behind because it is shiny and slanting."

She then came to the end of whatever it was she was trying to
say and looked round for comment.

"I'd like to have the cleaning of one of them big cars," said
Alf, whose presence had been rather forgotten. "I'd clean them
till their own mothers wouldn't know them. Crool it is not to
clean a car. She needs it, same as a lady does. Alf he seed some
cars on the road on Sunday, stuck they was at Hoppers Corner
because there was sheep going along the road to Mr. Knox's field
and they was as mucky as anything. If Alf had had his nice old
rags he'd have given the cars a proper shine."

All were silent and held their countenances intently.

"Out of the mouths of babes and sucklings," said George
Knox.

Everyone felt that Alf was so far removed from being either
that George Knox's words had better be ignored.

"Well, I must be getting along," said Lord Stoke. "Here, Alf,
can you go along to the kitchen and tell my man to bring the
dog-cart up to the front door?"

"Alf knows," said the owner of the name. "Lord Pomfret he
gave Alf a shilling to hold Master Giles's pony when he come
here."

"All right, Alf. A shilling it will be," said his lordship. "Cut
along to the kitchen and tell him."

"Alf likes the kitchen," said Alf. "Mrs. Stoker she gives him some nice bits and pieces. But Alf doesn't like the man."

"All right," said Lord Stoke, "then he needn't have the shilling."

This conversation in which both parties had scored then came to an end. Alf went off to the kitchen where Stoker and Lord Stoke's groom were peeling potatoes. The wireless was on at full blast, so that Alf's entrance was not heard till he said loudly the Lord had sent him.

"Now, none of your Salvation Army rubbish here," said Stoker. "I'm busy."

"The Lord said to tell the man to come," said Alf.

"Por thing he's not right in the head," said Stoker. "You'd better go and see what his lordship wants. I'll see to Alf."

The groom went away and Alf stood in the door, first on one leg and then on the other.

"I did tell the man Lord Stoke wanted him, Mrs. Stoker, didn't I?" said Alf anxiously.

Stoker, who was quite used to Alf having an occasional fit, told him he had done it very nicely and to sit down and she'd give him a nice cup of tea. The kettle was on the boil, the nice strong cup of tea set before Alf, and then Stoker gave him two large slices of bread and a hunk of cold fat bacon.

"You eat it up," she said. "Do you good. You're not a bad sort, Alf," but we much doubt whether Alf heard her last words, as he was already gorging himself with the bread and bacon and greedily drinking the tea.

By now the groom had brought the dog-cart round to the front door. Lord Stoke, with the help of a little hoisting from Adrian Coates, got up beside him. The equipage rolled away and Adrian went back to the party.

"Lord Stoke is remarkable," he said. "If I live to his age I hope I'll be even half as alive as he is. He must be a bit lonely sometimes. I wonder he never married."

Mrs. Morland could have told him why, but saw no reason to do so, and the talk turned to other things.

The sherry being finished, the party began to disperse, aided by Stoker, who almost wrenched the deck chairs from departing guests before they had made the final heave that gets one out of them. And anything more calculated to show off one's legs to the worst advantage than getting up from a deck chair we do not know.

"I gave Alf a nice tea," said Stoker to her nominal mistress when the guests had gone. "There's nothing wrong with Alf, he's just a bit of a natural. My old auntie at Plaistow she had a boy like that, all along of an organ with a monkey in a red jacket and he broke his chain and ran up her arm and grinned at her he did. Then the organ grinder he took him off and my auntie she gave him sixpence, but she was carrying and it was a seven months' boy and that's about all he is now. In a Home he is and nearly killed the nurse—what they call a male nurse— and it took two men to pull him off. I'm going down to the village and I've left your supper all nice and ready and there's something in the oven."

Without waiting for an answer she went back to her kitchen and peace fell upon house and garden.

CHAPTER 2

IT HAPPENED a few days later that Dr. Ford, who was going over to Rising Castle, asked Mrs. Morland if she would like to come too, as Lord Stoke was an old friend of hers. She was quite capable of driving herself over whenever she wished, but company is always pleasant and Dr. Ford was an old friend, so she accepted.

The day was bright and warm. Stoker proposed to wash some of the rugs with carpet soap and let them dry in the garden. This would mean that the kitchen would be full of Stoker's village friends with endless cups of tea and much local gossip, so it was just as well for her employer to be out of the way.

All of us who have inherited carpets or rugs known roughly as Oriental will remember how they respond to kind treatment, how their colours glow for a week or so. We also know how much repairing has to be done; the ragged ends of worn fringes gently trimmed, pieces of some mysterious sticky-backed material applied on the underside of badly worn places and then eased into place with a warm iron; not to speak of cutting the carpet's hair and nails as it were and giving it a good shampoo. There is also the chance of finding such objects as a bent safety-pin, an elastic band, or even a halfpenny under the carpet and the hope—rarely if ever realised—of finding a stray sixpence or a loose stamp.

By eleven o'clock or so Stoker's friends, having done their own cleaning and washing and shopping, were gathering in force in the kitchen quarters. Not yet would work begin. First there were elevenses—which were movable feasts and might

equally have been called tenses or twelveses—or, more nostal-
gically but now rarely used, beavers or noonings. Stoker had
laid in a packet of Tupman's Tasty Tips, which had the double
advantage of making a strong black brew of tea and promising
the buyer a four-ounce packet free if she (for we doubt whether
the stronger sex took any notice of Tupman's product, prefer-
ring a pint at the local) bought eleven more packets and sent
the labels to the Tupman headquarters. As we all like the hope
raised by any kind of lottery, though most of us have never
won more than a badly made needlebook, Tupman's Tips were
doing very well.

Mrs. Morland was trying to tidy her papers so that if she
were killed on the way to or from Rising Castle her executors
would know what to do with them. This she frequently did,
though her efforts usually ended in the papers being more
muddled than they were before she began to sort them. From
time to time Mrs. George Knox, who had in the past done a
good deal of typing for her, would come over and try to deal
with the muddle, but she had hardly got things straight before
Mrs. Morland—rather like the old woman who lived in a shoe
—had got her literary children muddled again and beat them all
soundly and put them to bed. When we say bed, it was a large
cumbersome cupboard whose upper shelves could only be
reached by standing on a chair and as Mrs. Morland was terrified of standing on chairs (though she was even more terrified
of the kitchen step-ladder) she was apt to tie her manuscript
into a bundle and throw it towards the shelf where she thought
it ought to be, and where she mostly could not find it on account of its having alighted on a higher or lower shelf. Then
Dr. Ford was at the door and Mrs. Morland, after finding that
she had brought down two left-hand gloves and having to go
up and find the right-hand one, got into his rattle-trap of a car.

Rising Castle, as most people know, is on a slight eminence

above the confluence of the River Rising and Rushmere Brook. It had originally been a Norman castle and part of the walls and the keep were in fair condition under the National Trust, while his present lordship lives in a more modern mansion built partly by his great-grandfather from the stones of the ruins. His nephew, son of his redoubtable sister Lucasta and the late Lord Bond at Staple Park, will inherit what is left of the property.

There was a pleasant friendship between his lordship and Mrs. Morland. Each could speak openly to the other and to her he would sometimes talk about his one great love. The older inhabitants of that part of Barsetshire remembered hearing say that his lordship did once go courting old Lady Pomfret— the one she was a Thorne—and they were quite right. Lord Stoke had bound up his wounds and gone about his county duties, but Edith Thorne was never far from his mind, and because of Edith Thorne he had taken a liking for Edith Graham, her connection and namesake. Edith was now Lady William Harcourt, sister-in-law to the Duke of Towers, with a very nice baby and every hope of more to come, and could not often get over to Rising Castle.

Mrs. Morland was one of the few people who knew about Lord Stoke's far-off romance and when she went to Rising Castle he liked to talk to her of his younger days, knowing that she would not make capital out of it. Once, some years previously, he had, rather shamefacedly, said something which might or might not have been a proposal of middle-aged marriage. To his great relief she had—in the words of Lord Tennyson—smiling put the question by. He had never mentioned it to anyone. So their peaceful friendship went on very comfortably and Mrs. Morland continued to write exactly the same book year after year, never being a best-seller but remaining what was to her much more to the point, a regular seller.

"Do you want to go to the front door?" said Dr. Ford to Mrs. Morland. "I usually go to the back door to get the lowdown on his lordship's health, but just as you please."

Mrs. Morland said she would like to see the back door, but as she didn't know Lord Stoke's staff very intimately she thought the front door would be better.

"I expect you are right," said Dr. Ford. "Protocol and all that. Just as well. So few people can afford a front door now or anyone to open it that I've got into a back-door habit," and he turned his car onto the still well-kept gravel sweep in front of the house, got out, and rang the bell.

As Mrs. Morland and Dr. Ford knew Lord Stoke's establishment, it was not a surprise to them that the door was opened by a real butler, even if he was only Albert, the George Knox's housemaid's brother.

"How are you, Albert?" said Mrs. Morland. "And how is the whitlow?"

There are few better ways of making easy conversation than asking after a person's leg, or bronchitis, or that nasty cough. Also Mrs. Morland was an old friend and much liked by Lord Stoke's staff because she had taken pains to remember their wife, husband, children, or bad leg as the case might be. Albert's whitlow had been an Open Sesame for some time.

"Nasty things, whitlows," said Dr. Ford. "We had one last week at the Barchester General Hospital. I don't know when I've seen a finer one. A good patient too. He said he'd always wanted to see a whitlow lanced and he was damned if he wouldn't now he had the chance and he wasn't having any anaesthetic because it stood to reason they might take your hand off as soon as look at you."

Albert looked alarmed. Mrs. Morland said she was sure they would give him all the anaesthetics he wanted. Much relieved, Albert took them to the morning-room, where Lord Stoke spent much of his time. Why it was called morning-room no one knew, unless it was because Lord Stoke's mother, dead now some forty years ago, had used it as what she called a boudoir.

His lordship was reading the *Barchester Chronicle* and at once got up to greet his guests.

"Glad you could come, Mrs. Morland," he said. "And Ford. He comes to see this old buffer and brings me all the news. What happened about that drain down at Grumper's End, Ford?"

Mrs. Morland asked where Grumper's End was.

"Far side of Pomfret Madrigal," said his lordship. "No drains. Can't think what the County Council is thinking about."

Dr. Ford said the County Council appeared to be incapable of thinking at all, but no drains were better than defective drains and the cesspool had recently been cleaned, and in any case the rates were high enough to stop any ideas about draining.

Drains are one of the really interesting subjects and the party were well away on them when Albert came in and said could his lordship speak to Lady Bond on the phone; old Lady Bond he said he meant.

"Oh, all right, all right," said Lord Stoke. "Will you excuse me, Mrs. Morland, if I answer it here."

Mrs. Morland, of course, excused him at once and took up a copy of *Punch* while his lordship, deliberately deaf, was being at cross-purposes with his sister on the telephone and Dr. Ford melted away towards the servants' quarters. After a conversation which—at that end at any rate—consisted almost entirely of Lord Stoke not being able to hear his sister and not trying to, he slammed the receiver into place and came back to his guest.

"Sorry, Mrs. Morland," he said. "Lucasta *will* ring me up about nothing."

Mrs. Morland said What kind of nothing.

The Palladian Bridge at Staple Park, Lord Stoke said, and his half-sister Lucasta was as trying as they make them and that in any case the Palladian Bridge was no concern of hers as she was only the Dowager and her daughter-in-law was a very capable woman.

"She doesn't know her place," his lordship added. "I suppose Dr. Ford will tell me about Albert's whitlow when he has done gossiping. I like Ford."

"So do I," said Mrs. Morland. "He is so reliable."

"Ought to have married," said Lord Stoke. "People do like a doctor who has a wife. Makes 'em feel safe," at which view of that body of generous, self-sacrificing men, Mrs. Morland began to have the giggles, but managed to turn them into a cough.

"Well, he did *try*," said Mrs. Morland.

"Try? What do you mean? Was he—I mean couldn't he——" and his lordship might have gone on stumbling.

"Nothing of the sort, Lord Stoke," said Mrs. Morland severely. "It was a long time ago—but it wouldn't interest you."

"Interest me?" said Lord Stoke. "What would old buffers like me do if they couldn't be interested in their old friends?"

"Well, he did care for Anne Todd when she was my secretary—a long time ago—" said Mrs. Morland. "But Anne married George Knox and that was that. And I *think*—but you won't repeat this, will you," which is one of the silliest things you can say, for you obviously are yourself going to say something you should have left unsaid and are only passing the buck—or in simpler though longer phrase said something you felt you oughtn't to have said, even as you say it and hope the hearer will not make use of it. "I *think* he didn't marry because of that. There was a kind of idea about one of the Vicar's daughters but it fizzled out."

"Oh, well," said his lordship, who, to tell the truth, had lost interest in the whole affair. "That's how things go. All for the best, I daresay. Must be a devil of a nuisance being a doctor's wife with the telephone going off every half-hour just as you are getting comfortably to sleep."

Mrs. Morland said she thought some doctors had a buzzer on their night telephone instead of a bell, but on being pressed said perhaps she had heard it all wrong and it wasn't a buzzer.

His lordship said it must be a damned nuisance anyway, adding in a kind of soliloquy that it was a wonder doctors had any family at all if that was the way things were managed. Mrs. Morland could easily have had the giggles at this point, but suffocated them and tried to look calm and uninterested.

Dr. Ford then came back.

"Nasty finger your man has, Stoke," he said. "If I had more time—and he had—I'd like to get him into the Barchester General and have a good overhaul. How did he get it?"

Lord Stoke, who beyond a very sensible conviction that a whitlow was a whitlow and broadly speaking an Act of God confined mostly to the lower orders, knew little or nothing about such freaks of nature and said so.

Mrs. Morland, her ear caught by the repetition of the word whitlow, suddenly remembered a song—one of her nurse's songs when she was a child—with the words, "Swing high, swing low, Swing to and fro, That's how the wedding bells go, don't you know," and tried desperately to fit whitlow into it, without much success.

Lord Stoke said—and we think correctly—that roughly speaking it was white flaw, a nasty kind of tumour near a finger nail and his old nurse used to spit on hers.

"Quite right," said Doctor Ford. "There's a lot to be said for spittle. Hair of the dog that bit you, eh?" at which point Mrs. Morland nearly laughed.

But Lord Stoke—quite rightly we think—took the subject more seriously.

"When I was a little boy," he began and both his hearers suddenly had a vision of the kind of little boy he might have been, kept in frocks far beyond the age when knickerbockers are now worn, "if anyone in the village was bitten by a dog they always cut off some of its hair and burnt it and put the ashes on the bite."

Dr. Ford, who was quite truly interested in such things, asked if one had to spit on the bite too.

Lord Stoke said Of *course,* and when his old father was stung by a grass adder when out with his gun, he had some difficulty in getting the keeper not to spit on it. He, Lord Stoke's father, knew the thing to do was to suck the place where the bite was and then spit it out. *Then,* he said, you could spit on the place of the bite and tie it up and forget all about it.

"But grass adders aren't poisonous, are they, Lord Stoke?" said Mrs. Morland, to which his lordship replied: "Better safe than sorry."

Lord Stoke pressed Dr. Ford to stay for lunch, but he had too many visits to make and so went away, saying that he would pick Mrs. Morland up round about three o'clock, or thereabouts.

Lord Stoke then took Mrs. Morland to see some of the work that the Society for the Preservation of Ancient Buildings had been doing on the old parts of the castle. Except for the fact that the stonework was now very clean, Mrs. Morland could not see much difference, but she was careful not to show her feelings in case Lord Stoke wanted her to go up a repaired stone winding staircase with several steps still missing, or marked DANGER, and look out of an unbarred window onto a sheer drop to the bank of the Rising.

The booming of a gong, loud and long, called them back to their sole selfs (or selves), much to Mrs. Morland's relief, for if you are sixty-nine you do *not* want to rush up and down rather decrepit winding stone staircases with any pleasure at all.

Lunch, except for the butler brooding over the scene, was as usual very pleasant. Lord Stoke, if besieged, could still have held out against Roundheads, Sputniks, or even a mass attack of Boy Scouts. Owing to the ferocity of his excellent cook he

had installed every kind of Deep Freeze and Frigidaire that
money could buy and was making quite a good profit from
them, while always causing the best things to be kept for himself and his friends. Pheasants and partridges, rabbits and hares,
even large portions of pigs and cows went into what Mrs. Morland called The Ice Hell of Pitz Palu. And in case our younger
readers (if any) ask what Pitz Palu was, it was a film about
snow-topped peaks and a gentleman allowing himself to be
frozen to death alive (if our reader sees what we mean) for
some reason that we cannot remember, but all extremely noble
and unselfish, and the heroine was able to marry the Other
Man. And if this synopsis of a successful film is incorrect we
can only say that it is exactly as we remember it many years
ago.

Presently Lord Stoke heaved himself up and, saying to the
butler: "Coffee in the morning-room," led his guest away.

The question of what name to give a room is always interesting. Dining-room is fairly straight. Hall is hall, except
that one must remember that The Hall is the servants' hall,
if one has a large oldish house and some kind of staff. When
Lord Stoke's parents were alive his mother had a very pleasant
sunny sitting-room, which she called her boudoir, looking across
a well-kept stretch of grass to the old castle. After their death
their son had taken over the boudoir as a kind of retreat for
himself and his old friends. The large rooms were shuttered
and dust-sheeted except when people of rank or importance
were staying in the house, but those occasions had become
rare of late years. We think that the last time the rooms were
formally opened was when Princess Louisa Christina, daughter
of old Prince Louis of Cobalt, had paid a semi-royal visit to
Lord Stoke's sister Lady Bond, who had brought her over to
see the dilapidated glories of Rising Castle.

On this visit Lord Stoke was apt to expatiate at some length.
Not that he had the least respect for minor German princelings,

knowing in his bones that an English barony of respectable
age was far better than any foreign title, but protocol must be
observed and some of his other guests were impressed by the
faded glories of what was once Germany and briefly the German Empire and titles which could claim to have the Holy
Roman Empire in their past.

So Mrs. Morland and her host went to the morning-room
and drank their coffee.

"Now, tell me all about everything," said his lordship. "Will
you mind if I smoke?"

Mrs. Morland said if it was one of his special cigars she
would like it.

Lord Stoke got up and rang the bell. Not by pulling down
a brass or china handle by the fireplace, or pressing an electric
pusher, but by seizing a large brass ring attached to a long
piece of embroidered canvas which in its turn was attached
at the top to a kind of rather triangular brass contraption; an
arrangement which our older readers will remember. By a
cross-country system of wires this rang a bell in the servants'
quarters, where a kind of flag or round sign fell down so that
any servant who didn't know which bell it was could see if
it was the Pink Bedroom, or the Blue Dressing Room, or the
Estate Room, or what used to be called Her Ladyship's Boudoir,
that needed attention. As the kitchen quarters were at a considerable distance from the reception rooms, no one expected
the immediate arrival of a servant and more than once old
Lady Bond had forgotten why she had rung long before the
footman or butler arrived. But as they were excellent well-
trained servants, one or other of them was usually able to help
her ladyship to remember what she was thinking about before
she had entirely forgotten what it was.

The butler came in, carrying a wooden box as if it were
the Holy Grail.

"I brought the cigars in, my lord," said the butler, "because

I remembered that your lordship had said you wanted to try that fresh brand that Mr. Wickham brought over last Thursday. They were placed rather too near the hot pipes, my lord, doubtless in error, so I moved them to My Pantry."

"So that's why I couldn't find them," said his lordship, not unkindly, but as one who measures his adversary before crossing swords. "Don't take them away again."

"Certainly not, my lord," said the butler. "Shall I place them in the Cigar Cabinet?"

"Leave them on the table," said his lordship. "That's all."

"Perhaps," said the butler, pulling a small bunch of keys from a pocket, "your lordship wishes to have the key of the cabinet."

Mrs. Morland, feeling as if a thunderstorm were blowing-up, wished she could get under the table, whence she could hear, if not see, and so escape the thunderclap which seemed imminent.

"All right, all right," said Lord Stoke. "I've got my own key here. That's all, I said."

The butler moved with dignified speed to the door, shut it behind him with infinite precaution against noise, and went away to his own quarters.

"Makes me think of the *Corsican Brothers*, that man," said Lord Stoke.

Mrs. Morland asked if it was because he was a twin.

"Not as far as I know," said Lord Stoke. "But he comes gliding in. Why can't the feller walk like anyone else."

"Oh, I know what you mean," said Mrs. Morland. "I did see Irving in the *Corsican Brothers* when I was a girl and when he was the other brother who is dead he did seem to glide. Your man is rather like Littimer too."

"Which Littimer? Fred or Algernon?" said Lord Stoke. "Fred went out to Australia and no one ever heard of him again. Algernon's dead, I think. Everyone's dead now. Be dead myself soon."

"Of course you won't," said Mrs. Morland indignantly. "You'll see us all into our graves. Littimer is in *David Copperfield*—the man-servant who moves like a cat."

"Well, I hope my man won't move like a cat," said Lord Stoke, "nor mew like one either," at which piece of his own wit his lordship, who was not much given to joking, laughed so much that Mrs. Morland laughed too.

"Do you remember when I brought Edith Graham over here a few years ago?" said Mrs. Morland. "Albert was so nice about it. He had got orange juice and lemonade for Edith because he thought she wouldn't want wine. And she really didn't."

"Yes, I do remember that," said his lordship.

"And you gave her the little pearl necklace with that lovely diamond clasp," Mrs. Morland went on. "She still wears it though she has got some more important jewels now she is Lady William Harcourt."

"I remember the necklace," said Lord Stoke. "And tell her that I am glad she wears it. Pearls need wearing. Yes, it was the pearl necklace that I gave to Edith Thorne, hundreds of years ago, but when she was engaged to Pomfret she gave it back to me. I nearly threw it into the Rising, but I'm glad I didn't and that it is being worn—and loved. Yes—Edith. When I am in my grave perhaps Edith Harcourt will remember me as the old buffer who gave her an old necklace."

"I am sure she often remembers you," said Mrs. Morland, telling a noble lie, for she had not the faintest idea whether Edith Harcourt remembered the day when Edith Graham had paid her one brief visit to Rising Castle. We think she had rather forgotten it, for one cannot remember everything, but if Mrs. Morland gave her the message—which she certainly would, being a reliable creature—it would all come back to her.

There was a silence, but a comfortable one without any embarrassment, broken by Mrs. Morland who said how nice it was that the old castle was in good repair and under the protection of several societies, antiquarian and otherwise, who while seeing to it that the staircases were safe and the stone mullions of the empty windows in good condition, did not scrape and shave and pumice-stone it to excess.

"Well, it has lasted my time," said Lord Stoke, rather hoping to impress Mrs. Morland, who took the wind out of his sails by saying cheerfully that the castle would be alive and kicking as long as there was an England, adding as a rider that unless there was another war and bad air-raids it would still be there in two thousand and sixty.

"That is, if everything hasn't been blown up," she added. "But what worries me, Lord Stoke, is what on earth will people say when it is twenty hundred."

"Twenty hundred? No one says twenty hundred," said Lord Stoke. "Two thousand, that's what it will be."

Mrs. Morland, with vague recollections of something she had learnt at school, or read at some period, said What did people say in the year one thousand.

"Wasn't there and can't tell you," said Lord Stoke. "All I do know—at least that's what the history books say—is that lots of people thought it would be the end of the world and there was some kind of trouble about a comet—or if it wasn't then it was some other time. It's all in the books somewhere. Worst of books is you never can find the one you want. The man from the Barchester Public Library came out to look at my books not long ago. I kept an eye on him."

Mrs. Morland, not unnaturally, asked why.

"Never know with those fellers," said his lordship. "Might have taken a book and slipped it in his pocket."

"But librarians don't do that, Lord Stoke!" said Mrs. Morland. "They'd lose their job if they did, and talking of libraries, you are a member of the London Library, aren't you?"

"Of course I am," said Lord Stoke. "My old father was one

of the first life members and I've always carried on. The subscription keeps on going up, but it's well worth while. I remember there was a meeting some years ago about putting the subscription up—when the local Council first showed signs of sticking a lot on the rating. Some of the younger members were saying it was a bad thing to put the subscription up a guinea and books were the life-blood of a master spirit or something-or-other. Then someone got up and said the extra subscription was a guinea a year and how often did the younger members buy a bottle of gin. You could have heard a pin fall and they piped down. But the rates went up. Then Councils all have the same idea; Down with Private Enterprise and Civilisation. Oh well, I'm an old man and I'll soon be dead."

"So shall I," said Mrs. Morland, who felt that her old friend was presuming too much. "I shall be seventy in September."

"Do you read Dickens?" said Lord Stoke.

Mrs. Morland said with some indignation that of course she did.

"Then you must remember Jonas Chuzzlewit's remark," said Lord Stoke, "about how a man with any feeling ought to be ashamed of being eighty, let alone more, flying in the face of the Bible," at which Mrs. Morland had to laugh and so did his lordship, though laughter was very rare with him, and they agreed that a world without Dickens would be unbearable.

"Of course there were a lot of people who died before he was born," said Mrs. Morland, "so they wouldn't have minded."

Lord Stoke said aloud to himself *fortunatos nimium si sua bona norint* and Mrs. Morland said What was that.

"Only an old Roman poet," said Lord Stoke. "And now I come to think of it, it isn't particularly applicable. Quotations mostly aren't. My dear mother used to keep a book of quotations, one for every day in the year. A biggish book it was with violets or something sticking up on the cover."

Mrs. Morland said Perhaps embossed.

"I daresay, I daresay," said Lord Stoke. "Words are queer things. My mother had north-country blood and she used to put two pieces of thin bread and butter, together with hundreds and thousands between them, and called it Matrimony. I daresay there aren't any hundreds and thousands now," but this Mrs. Morland indignantly opposed, saying that the children at the village school bought them regularly.

"Not what they were in MY young days," said Lord Stoke, determined to be a *laudator temporis acti.*

"But they *are!*" said Mrs. Morland indignantly. "It's the toffee and barley-sugar and sugar-candy that aren't what they were. When I was a little girl the sugar-candy was *raw.* I mean it was like stalactites or stalagmites, whatever they are, or a swarm of bees, all clustered on a piece of string. And the toffee and barley-sugar is all wrapped up now and the Dreadful Children are given far too much money by their Dreadful Silly Parents and they throw the sticky wrappers all over the street. It needs Seven maids with seven mops to clear up the pavement when the dear little kiddies come out of the cinema."

"Dear, dear," said Lord Stoke. "I didn't know that. I never go to the cinema. Now, when I was a boy, there were photographs that moved. Nothing new about it."

"I know what you are thinking of," said Mrs. Morland. "The Egyptian Hall in Piccadilly. Pulled down years ago."

There was silence for a moment.

"Good Lord, yes!" said Lord Stoke. "Do you remember the train coming into the station and then they reversed it and all the passengers got into the carriages backwards and the train moved out backwards."

"*Hin und zurück,*" said Mrs. Morland, remembering an amusing one-act musical play by some German in which, at the middle, everything goes backwards and the character who has come in by the open window exits backwards out of it, and all the conversation goes backwards too. Nothing to do with *Le Spectre de la Rose.*

Lord Stoke asked what the dev— he meant the dickens she meant.

"I can never think," said Mrs. Morland, "why the dickens should be an equivalent for the devil. He wasn't ever called Richard, was he?"

"Don't ask me," said Lord Stoke. *"I* don't know him."

"And," Mrs. Morland continued, following her own line of thought, "there's Deuce too. Thackeray has a Captain Deuceace somewhere," at which point Lord Stoke gave up altogether.

"By the way," he said, "do you remember, quite a long while ago, how your boy Tony and a school friend of his went exploring the Stokey Hole?"

Well did Mrs. Morland remember it and how the two little boys had, against the distinct commands of the grown-ups, gone into the cavern on the river bank which was popularly but quite erroneously supposed to communicate with the Tower of London and how her son on emerging had rolled down the steep bank and then picked himself up with battered knees, a small cut on his forehead and a suspicion of tears in his eyes.

"I don't know why one has children," said Mrs. Morland thoughtfully.

"All depends if you're married," said Lord Stoke. *"I* never was," and there was a silence while each one thought of the past.

"But my sister Lucasta married," said Lord Stoke, "and now *she's* a widow," which last words he uttered with some contempt for people who could so far demean themselves to be widows. "Just as well. Her son and his wife are carrying on nicely at Staple Park. Lucasta thought she would be the Dowager and live with them, but it wouldn't have done—wouldn't have done at all."

Mrs. Morland said Then what was she going to do.

"A very sensible thing," said Lord Stoke. "I couldn't have thought of a better one myself. She's going to Cheltenham."

"But why?" said Mrs. Morland, who had a kind of feeling that one only went there if one wanted to be an invalid.

"Nice bit of country," said his lordship. "Some handsome streets and squares. Lucasta isn't badly off—her husband made a good settlement on her and it will go back to the young couple when she dies. And another thing, I needn't go and see her. Too far at my time of life," and his lordship looked steadily at Mrs. Morland as if defying her to contradict him.

"By the way," she said, "when does your sister go? I should like to say good-bye to her. Not that I know her well, but——" and her voice trailed off as she realised that she hadn't the faintest idea what she was going to say next.

But rescue came, even as she spoke, in the shape of Albert, who opened the door and stood aside, saying: "Lady Bond, my lord," and in came her dowager ladyship. Mrs. Morland had not seen her since Lord Bond's death and was much impressed by her Dowager look, which at once made her friends think of The Importance of Being Ernest, so deeply in black she was, or of Queen Victoria in her later years, though not quite so stout and a good deal taller.

"Well, Lucasta, I'm glad to see you," said Lord Stoke. "You're looking well. Been putting on weight, eh? Much better at your time of life. I've been the same weight for the last twenty years. When I was up in Town a few weeks ago I got myself weighed at the Club and the footman—he's an old friend—said there weren't many like me."

"I daresay," said his sister. "But there are plenty of people to tell you things if you want to listen."

At this point Mrs. Morland would have liked to escape through the window or get under the table, for to be the unwilling audience of a family row is no pleasure to most of us. But as it would have been too marked and also too difficult to do, she gave up the idea.

"So you're going to Cheltenham, eh?" said Lord Stoke. "Nice bit of country about there, but it's all built over now. Where are you going to stay?"

His sister said she hadn't quite decided. Lord Stoke at once recommended a hotel at which their mother had stayed several times, but his sister said it had gone down a good deal of late years.

"Lady Norton—I mean old Lady Norton—has asked me to stay with her at the very comfortable hotel where she has a private suite," said Lady Bond, "and I can then look about for a suitable permanent home. The young people quite agree that I am doing the sensible thing. I need more social atmosphere than I can get at Staple Park. I shall, of course, take my maid and the car and my chauffeur."

Mrs. Morland, when describing this interview to the Knoxes, said that at this point she had distinctly heard Lord Stoke say: "And a partridge in a pear tree." No one believed it, but it was generally considered that she had the root of the matter in her.

"Well, that's that," said Lord Stoke. "Sensible thing to do. You don't want to live with your son and his wife and they don't want to live with you. Can't think why."

"Of course you can't," said his sister. "You don't know what a family is."

His lordship said he supposed his sister meant that he wasn't married, but plenty of people had families without being married. Look at old Bunce down by the river near Northbridge, he said, and his daughters and grandchildren. All born out of wedlock, he added, to Mrs. Morland's delight, and a fine healthy lot and doing well at school.

"Can't think why I never did anything in that line," said his lordship thoughtfully. "Plenty of chances if I'd wanted to."

His sister made a sound which was uncommonly like a sniff.

"There was that nice girl over Chaldicotes way," Lord Stoke continued, "and that widow out Trumpington way when I was at King's and that little French girl in Paris when I was attached to our Embassy—my memory isn't what it was. But they all got married. I didn't."

"Mother wouldn't have let you," said his sister.

Mrs. Morland wondered if she ought to go out quietly, or pretend not to hear; so she began to turn over the pages of the Visitors' Book which lay on a side table. None of your ordinary books that might as well be a diary or an exercise book, but bound in red leather, now faded and crumbling at the corners, with a baron's coronet (or whatever barons wear) stamped in gold upon it and a dirty frayed bit of red ribbon to mark the page now in use. Mrs. Morland opened it at the ribbon page. There were three entries; the first the secretary of the Barsetshire Archaeological Society, the second The Dean of Barchester and Mrs. Crawley, the third illegible.

As there was a momentary lull in the family wrangle (which we may say left the participants unharmed and indeed refreshed), Mrs. Morland took advantage of it to ask whose name that was in that rather illegible writing that looked clear but wasn't.

Lady Bond came over to look at the signature.

"Of *course*, it is Denis Stonor," she said. "I expect Bond brought him over."

Lord Stoke said he didn't know anyone called Toner.

Lady Bond said Denis Stonor in a rather louder voice.

"All right, all right, Lucasta," said Lord Stoke. "I heard you, but I don't know anyone called Toner. Said so before."

"You couldn't, if you didn't know him," said Mrs. Morland to her host. "He's a musician. *Not* with a barrel-organ and a monkey in a red jacket," she added firmly. "He writes *real* music. Symphonies and things. You can hear them on the wireless. His father was a soldier and he died and his mother married again—I mean Denis's mother. And Lord Bond," she went on, almost making a slight bow in Lady Bond's direction, "took a liking to Denis and put up some money for him to get his music properly published and played and now he is very famous. And his name is Sssstonor—not Toner."

Lord Stoke, who had been gradually passing from complete misapprehension to a vague feeling that he might at some future date begin to understand what it was all about if he didn't go mad first, graciously said that he would tell his butler to let him know when Denis Stonor was on the wireless. Did Mrs. Morland, he said, know which programme Stonor would be on.

Mrs. Morland said she didn't know, but probably it would be the Third.

"That's the high-brow one, isn't it?" said Lord Stoke. "Now give me the Home Service every time. They've been giving some very good talks on birds. When I was a boy there were plenty of owls in the castle, but nobody knows where they've gone. If my ruins aren't good enough for them, they can go where they like," his lordship continued, rather venomously. "Now those magpies I told you about, Mrs. Morland—you remember?——"

Mrs. Morland said she was frightfully sorry but she had forgotten exactly what it was that Lord Stoke had said about magpies.

"Building nests, if nests you can call them, all over the castle," said Lord Stoke. "We tried shooting them, but it didn't have much effect. I'll have to try getting one of the local boys to go up. They're always wanting to climb the ruins, so I've given orders that they are *not* to climb unless one of the men is about, and if any of them go past any place where we've got DANGER on a notice they won't be allowed here again. I had a good idea.

I thought I might electrify some wires in the dangerous places. If the boys get a shock perhaps that will put them off."

"Well, if any of them are killed, don't blame *me*," said Lady Bond.

Mrs. Morland averred afterwards that she had distinctly heard his lordship say: "No business of yours, Lucasta. *You* won't have to pay for the funeral," which was evidently his lordship's way of reproaching his sister for her celebrated parsimony, but she either did not hear her brother or determined not to show that she had heard.

Mrs. Morland, with a view to promoting harmony, asked after the Dowager's son, his wife Daphne, and their children. This red herring at once made an improvement in her ladyship's attitude.

"Oh, they are doing splendidly," said the Dowager. "Do you remember the central hall at Staple Park?"

Mrs. Morland said, very untruthfully, that she did.

"You know how dark it was," said her ladyship, "because all the light came from a lantern in the roof and we had to paint black all over the outside of it in the war and it would have cost so much to scrape it off that we just put up with it. But Daphne had a very good idea and when the Dean was having the roof of the Cathedral scraped and cleaned she asked if the men could do Staple Park. It was most interesting to watch them. We thought they would have to put scaffolding up everywhere, but they got out on the roof and scraped all the black paint off. It makes such a difference. Now one can see the pictures."

Mrs. Morland remembered the pictures, which were mostly bad but highly varnished copies of second-rate Old Masters and said How nice.

"Of course my son and his wife have made a good many alterations," said Lady Bond. "I think they were quite right.

If you never move the pictures and the furniture in a house
it turns into a kind of museum."

"I only saw Staple Park once," said Mrs. Morland. "I went
with the Barsetshire Archaeological Society."

"You would find it much changed now," said Lady Bond
graciously.

"I am sure I would," said Mrs. Morland, and then wondered
if what she had said was tactful. She would like to have explained that she only meant that any change in that over-
furnished mansion must be for the better, but Lady Bond
took her words as a tribute to Time Was and there the matter
must rest.

"It has been such a pleasure to meet you," said Lady Bond.
"If you are ever in Cheltenham, do let me know."

Mrs. Morland, who had only once been to Cheltenham a
long time ago and while admiring its residential quarter felt
no particular interest in it, said she most certainly would let
Lady Bond know when she was there. If, she added, she ever
was, because the friends she had in Cheltenham had mostly died
or moved elsewhere, but one never knew.

"That is *so* true," said Lady Bond, more graciously than
ever. "By the way, Mrs. Morland, have you been writing lately?"

It was at this moment that Mrs. Morland decided never
again to try to like Lady Bond.

"Oh, just scribbling," she said airily. "My publisher is quite
a slave-driver. I expect you know him—Adrian Coates. He
married George Knox's daughter. He hasn't a very large list,
but all distinguished names. If you are going to write your
reminiscences, Lady Bond, I would like to introduce you to
him."

We must admit that this was a deliberate slight on Lady
Bond and Mrs. Morland almost regretted it even as the words
left her mouth. But she could not quite regret it.

We do not know whether Lady Bond realised how uncivil

Mrs. Morland was being. We think not, which was perhaps just as well.

Lord Stoke who had not paid much attention to what his guests were saying, and had indeed retired into one of the large, shiny illustrated weeklies, put it down and said those photographer fellers certainly made a good job of it. There was an article about Omnium's place with some very good photographs. He didn't know, his lordship continued, why they didn't do Rising Castle. If they wanted ruins, well the ruins were there.

"My late husband," said Lady Bond, putting on what her irreverent children called A Voice, "would never let photographers into the grounds. If my son and his wife allow them, it is not for me to raise any objection."

"Of course it isn't," said her brother. "Any fool could tell you that, Lucasta."

As another Scene from Domestic Life appeared to be boiling up, Mrs. Morland said she thought her publisher, Adrian Coates, knew the editor of one of the best and shiniest weeklies with serious articles on the English Country House and would Lord Stoke care to consider allowing him to see the castle.

Lord Stoke said Allow who?

"I suppose you mean Allow whom," said Mrs. Morland, much to the unwilling admiration of Lady Bond, who rarely got the better of her brother.

"Never mind what I meant," said his lordship generously. "If that editor-feller likes to come here, he can. Has he a good head?"

Mrs. Morland said his articles in the magazine in question were the work of a scholar and a gentleman.

"Funny idea to get a scholar *and* a gentleman to write your articles for you," said Lord Stoke. "I suppose one writes one bit and the other does the rest."

Mrs. Morland was quite capable of producing mild idiocies

herself, but this *aperçu* of Lord Stoke's left her in a state of bewilderment as to what to say next.

"Do pull yourself together, Stoke," said Lady Bond, addressing her brother. "Mrs. Morland said A Scholar And A Gentleman."

"All right, all right, Lucasta; I'm not deaf yet," said his lordship. Lady Bond, wisely we think, made no answer. "If the feller likes to get a gentleman and a scholar to write for him, that's *his* business not mine. I daresay they'd like to see the castle too. Might get them all down one day. If they come by train I'll send in to Barchester to meet them. Perhaps you'll come and do the hostess for me, Mrs. Morland. My sister will be at Cheltenham then," he added, with what Mrs. Morland afterwards spoke of as a fiendish grin. But that worthy creature was apt to see life in terms of the novelist's art.

"Well, Stoke, you will do as you think fit," said Lady Bond.

"Always did, Lucasta," said his lordship. "I hope you will have a comfortable time in Cheltenham. If you come across Admiral Prout, tell him he still owes me ten shillings. If you can get it out of him you can keep it."

To this, Lady Bond made no answer at all. This was not from cowardice, but from her ladyship's knowledge of her brother and the delightful certainty that her silence would annoy him far more than any amount of arguing. Meanwhile Lord Stoke had rung the bell. Albert answered it and received orders to see if her ladyship's car and chauffeur were there.

"The car is at the door, my lady," said Albert, "and your ladyship's chauffeur will be there almost at once. He has had some tea in the housekeeper's room, my lord. I thought this would be agreeable to her ladyship."

"Quite right," said Lord Stoke, who approved of hospitality whether in the baronial hall or the baronial kitchen quarters. "Feed a cold and starve a fever; that's what my old nurse used to say."

Albert said, deferentially, that he didn't think her ladyship's chauffeur had a cold, nor a fever neither, and he would tell her ladyship's chauffeur that her ladyship was ready to go home.

This he did with such zeal and celerity that he was back almost at once. Lady Bond said good-bye to Mrs. Morland, expressing a hope to see her at Cheltenham, and after kissing her brother in a perfunctory way, followed Albert to the front door.

Lord Stoke sat down heavily and made the noise described on the opposite sides of the Channel as Phew! or Ouf!

Albert came back to say that her ladyship had gone and Dr. Ford had come to fetch Mrs. Morland.

"My compliments to Dr. Ford and ask him to come in, if he isn't in a hurry," said Lord Stoke, "and bring the sherry," so Albert went away and shortly returned with the sherry and Dr. Ford, who was always glad of a pretext to talk with his lordship. But as Lord Stoke only wanted to say exactly what he thought of his sister, Dr. Ford gratefully drank the sherry and didn't listen. When he had drunk it he said he would have to be going back for his surgery patients if Mrs. Morland was ready, which she was.

"Well, how did you find Lord Stoke?" he said, when they were out of the castle grounds.

Mrs. Morland said In very good form.

"Has he ever asked you to marry him?" said Dr. Ford.

Mrs. Morland said: "Good Gracious No! What on earth makes you say that?"

Dr. Ford said Pure curiosity. Elderly bachelors and widowers often thought of marriage.

"As you did," said Mrs. Morland, remembering how—a good many years ago now—Dr. Ford had more or less proposed to one of the Vicarage daughters but it had all come to nothing.

"Touché," said Dr. Ford laughing. "Well, You Have Been Warned."

Then they came to the railway line and the level crossing and were held up till the local train had slowly huffed and puffed itself out of the station and they could get across. Dr. Ford deposited Mrs. Morland at her gate. Stoker came out to say there was a nice young fowl for supper and Dr. Ford had better stay. But he knew some patients would be waiting at the surgery and Mrs. Morland said Of course he must go.

"Had a nice time?" said Stoker. "The bath water's hot. There's a nice little chicken for you and some nice soty potatoes and some nice french beans."

Mrs. Morland thanked her devoted tyrant, had her bath, enjoyed her supper, and went early to bed with a new thriller called *I'll Grind His Bones.*

CHAPTER 3

IT IS an interesting fact that elderly women are much more apt than men to "have a leg." Not in the sense of Mrs. Mountstuart Jenkinson's description of Sir Willoughby Patterne, but—to use a very old expression for limping—dot and carry one. Going as we do up and down the main shopping street of the pleasant suburb of Riverside where we live, most of us—that is, the elderly—are furnished with a stout stick, or, as in our own case, the tall parasol of one's grandmother. This sounds like a French exercise but happens in our case to be the truth. It is a fine upstanding creature with a strong crook handle and each rib had an ivory tip. One, alas, was missing when the parasol came into our possession, and though we invoked all the Great Names of umbrella makers, not one of them could find among their old stock an exact replica, so we have to be content with a substitute which looks very much of a poor relation among the original rib-tips. And now the ex-parasol, re-covered with black, supports our rather rickety footsteps when we aren't using it to shelter us from unexpected rain.

"What can't be cured must be endured," said the proverb. Mrs. Morland began by enduring, but heaven directed her, leg or no leg, to go through her box-room. When we say room, it was really an attic, reached by stairs so low and so narrow that tall people bumped their heads and stout people were almost stuck there for good. In the attic were kept a good many things that Mrs. Morland didn't want, or meant to give as wedding presents to people she must give something to because of old Aunt Florence or old Uncle Harry. Her sons had of course thought it the most romantic place in the world, although it had only one small window stuck fast with paint and the dust of many years and one could only stand upright in the middle. More than once had Mrs. Morland, with the aid of one son or another when on leave or holiday from their various avocations, tried to clear it out, to sweep and garnish, but—and with this all owners of a loft will sympathise—there were so many things that one couldn't decide whether they should be got rid of or not, that things had accumulated, and were known to the family as Salable Offal, an echo of the Edible Offal of war years—also known personally as Eddie Beloffel.

It is well known that it is not safe to have books in the house as they marry and have children, so producing over-populated neighbourhoods; but attics are just as bad. So, if one comes to think of it, is one's own desk or writing-table, on which letters answered and unanswered, cards of invitation to various meetings, a Christmas Card that one can't bear to throw away because it is so pretty, a notice of a concert which took place two months ago, one or two newspaper cuttings, a newspaper which one kept because one meant to cut some-thing out of it and then forgot what it was, all get mixed up with one another, all lie in confusion; and old bits of furniture and other odds and ends do certainly increase and multiply.

This divagation is partly Mrs. Morland's and partly ours. The reason for her excursion into the attic was to see if the moth had got into anything, which it occasionally did. Luckily she had a very large tin trunk, into which she put her few furs and some extra blankets after the spring cleaning and so far no harm had come to them. Also there was, in a corner of the attic, one of those majestic dress stands on which, in long-ago days, the visiting dressmaker who came twice a year would put the gown she was making for one's mother and then go round it snipping bits off, putting pins in here and there, opening a seam, and in general ravaging the work she had already done. But in the end it nearly always came out right. This stiff body with a knob for a head, no arms or legs, and a kind of wire cage hanging from its ample hips, had always been known to the family as Mrs. Grabham, because Grabham was the name of her maker as advertised on her stand. And now Mrs. Morland bought all her dresses off the peg and Mrs. Grabham stood alone in the attic, the joy and terror of any visiting children. More than once her owner had thought of sending her to a Jumble Sale, but there were two objections. The first that practically no one had a figure like that now, the second that she would have to be got downstairs and someone would have to get her to the Jumble Sale because Mrs. Morland felt that she simply could not drive her through the town, as it had almost now become.

So she moved things about and put them where she probably wouldn't ever find them again, raised a cloud of choking dust by vaguely sweeping such bits of the floor as were not occupied, rather meanly pushed several small objects into the obscure angle where the sloping roof met the unswept floor, went half-way down the steep stairs, pulled down the wooden flap, bolted it, and so emerged into normal life, dirty and not having accomplished anything worth mentioning. This is a very common method of attic-cleaning and can also be applied to the garden shed and even to the garage, though here Mrs. Morland had drawn the line from the day when she had found a dead rat behind some empty petrol cans that ought to have been taken back to the local garage some time ago. Since then she had left the garage to Stoker, who could always conjure spirits from the vasty deep in the shape of boys who enjoyed nothing more than getting very dirty, with the chance of seeing and killing a rat, and then having biscuits and hot sweet cocoa in the kitchen.

The question now was what to do next. Mrs. Morland knew

perfectly well that there was something she ought to do but could not for the life of her remember what it was and didn't want to.

"Sheer laziness, my girl," she said aloud to herself. "Duty is duty. Think of Nelson," so she thought very hard of Nelson, but even as she thought a great many other thoughts came cranking in (to use Hotspur's words)—as indeed one's thoughts usually do, being almost entirely beyond one's control.

"And that reminds me," she said aloud to herself, "that it's the Cottage Hospital Comforts Committee this morning. Though why," she added aloud to herself, "Nelson *should* remind me, I don't know."

She might have gone on like that even longer, but she heard the telephone and went to her bedroom, where she had an extension line.

This was one of her great joys. High Rising for a long time still had party-lines, than which nothing is more annoying. For a few weeks it may be amusing to hear what your neighbours are saying, but when this novelty has worn off it is a great bore to hear Mrs. Smith talking to Mrs. Jones when you want to talk to Mrs. Brown. Now each house had its own telephone and Mrs. Morland had managed to get one with an extension to her bedroom. On the whole she managed them very well, but was still far too apt to take a call in her bedroom, leave the receiver off while she went down to the drawing-room where her engagement book was, have a long talk, put the receiver down, and not think of the neglected telephone in her bedroom till very peremptory noises often repeated made her realise that something was wrong and she rushed upstairs to cradle the receiver on its celluloid bed (or whatever the black shiny stuff is that telephone apparatus is made of) and then rushed down again in case she had forgotten to put the other receiver back in its place.

This habit was now recognised by the local exchange as

only being Mrs. Morland, and the operator was very nice about it. What effect if any it had on the telephone bills we do not know.

Then Mrs. Morland tied her head up in a scarf, collected a pair of old gloves, put a light coat on because you never know, found her shopping bag where she had left it on the wrong shelf, picked up a sheaf of paper bags of various sizes and shapes, and went down the village street to the cottage hospital.

When we say hospital, do not let us make our readers think of a hospital with an operating table and hundreds of eager young surgeons looking like the *Femgericht* or mediaeval lepers all swathed and bandaged. Some dozen years previously money had been raised by a murrain, a tornado, an avalanche of Sales and Raffles and various games of chance to which the police kindly turned a deaf eye (and if Milton says blind mouths, may not we in our humble way follow his example), and a fair-sized house which had been for some time uninhabited had been repaired, repainted, and re-drained within an inch of its life. There was provision for a dozen or so patients, a special wing for children where the old nurseries had been, and a small maternity ward, though this last was only for emergency cases when it seemed dangerous to drive a very expectant mother who had miscalculated her date to Barchester in a hurry.

This useful institution was run on the domestic side by a Committee of Ladies, who in addition to their other civic labours knitted industriously everything a baby could need and once a week performed a ritual known as Taking the Trolley Round, which sounds rather like a Shakespearean drinking song, but was really a perambulating shop from which patients could buy every kind of small article from hairpins to handkerchiefs and sweets at cost price. There was also a book trolley, but many of the patients when they asked for a nice book meant a sixpenny paper novelette and much preferred the older ones, however tattered and mended and re-mended, with titles like *A Good Man's Love* and *Hearts Are Trumps* or—much in demand—*Girls of the Gutter* (which was about Salvation Army Rescue work and a great disappointment to hopeful readers). To Mrs. Morland's everlasting surprise several of her novels about Madame Koska in a paper-cover edition were being read and literally thumbed to pieces and it was one of her pleasures to replace those that were really past repair.

When she got to the hospital the cars parked outside the door showed her that there would be a good many helpers. High Rising itself provided a regular quota and various ladies in the neighbourhood were apt to come in on the Trolley Day and all enjoyed themselves vastly.

Among voluntary workers there must always be one or two who are born to organise other people. They are mostly recognised by their co-workers as Queen Bees, making decisions, doing the bulk buying of the biscuits and sweets and small articles of toilet, and standing no nonsense. There is no envy, for Worker Bees do not want to organise—merely to do their routine jobs as well as possible. The Head of this band of volunteers was, very properly, Mrs. Gould the Vicar's wife, to whom the buying and checking of the goods to be sold from the trolleys were her wash-pot and over the pricing and selling of them did she cast out her shoe. She it was also who could keep the accounts and could meet Matron on almost equal terms; nor had there ever been any disagreement.

The room used by the voluntary workers was what had been the kitchen, a large light room at the back with a row of hooks on the wall and one of those splendid old-fashioned built-in dressers with shelves and drawers and a range which many kitchen maids had been made to polish with blacking till it shone. There were also some large cupboards built right up to the ceiling, in which the Helpers' stores were kept. This meant having to get on the step-ladder to reach the topmost shelves and as most of the helpers, not being so young as they had been, were rather frightened of falling off, the top shelves were hardly ever used.

After the Women's Institute this was perhaps the most useful work in the village. The two bodies were on excellent terms, and pooled or exchanged a good many of their resources, such as a tea trolley (gift of Mrs. Gould the Vicar's wife) with one leg whose wheel was always coming off or sticking fast and a huge black mark where in earlier days someone had spilt a bottle of stove polish; a cash box where everyone meant to put a weekly subscription and usually forgot till next week; and from Mrs. George Knox a disused bookcase which she had filled with old magazines, bound and unbound, known by the patients as Nice Books. And when we say books, we are speaking in the strange language of those many good and worthy people to whom the word book means more or less an illustrated magazine with a nice story about a nice girl who married a nice man but he wasn't really nice—not really, if you see what I mean—but the Influence of a Nice Girl changed him and they had the *sweetest* baby and if you sent a stamped envelope addressed to yourself, together with a postal order (*not* stamps, please) for 1s. 3d. to Nurse Lovechild, c/o the magazine, you would receive a full description of how to knit an ever so dainty little jacket for baby and some blue or pink ribbon according to whichever it was, or if you preferred it, white, because of course one never really knew till Baby Arrived.

The Vicar's wife was already packing or loading the Trolleys when Mrs. Morland came in, closely followed by Mrs. George Knox with her stepdaughter, and several of the village ladies, all full of zeal and all talking at once.

"Good morning, Laura," said the Vicar's wife. "So glad you could come. I have to go to a W.I. emergency meeting, but I'll be back before you have finished. The only thing we are short of is hair-ribbon so they are sure to want it. Here's the key of the big cupboard. You'd better lock it as soon as the Trolleys have gone. One never knows," with which dark and ominous saying Mrs. Gould went away.

Meanwhile the two Trolleys had been packed with something of everything that patients might want, except that every week someone wanted something that wasn't there. Mrs. George Knox, who was a very good organiser, then got the helpers with the Trolleys out of the room, shut the door behind them, and sat down, saying: "Ouf!"

"I can't think," said Mrs. Morland, also sitting down, "why we haven't a word for Ouf. English is a much richer language than French, but they have some words we haven't got."

"But we've got much more that *they* haven't got," said Mrs. Knox. "I mean we have more *words* than they have, even if they don't mean the same thing."

Mrs. Morland was not often at a loss, but this time she felt completely stymied or stonkered—a word to whose derivation we have no clue and perhaps it isn't a real word, but we have always known it. Perhaps—if it is a real word—it comes from Golf, a language of which we are completely ignorant.

"What *do* you mean, Anne?" she said. "Oh, give me that big tin of acid drops, there's a love. I can be bagging them."

We must explain here that the bagging was nothing to do with "Bags I!" or the filching of acid drops from the patients, but simply meant putting an exact number of sweets—of whatever kind—into paper bags so that the patients could buy them.

Mrs. Knox lifted the tin of acid drops from the shelves to the table, and then standing on tip-toe extracted from a higher shelf a parcel of small paper bags.

"There you are, Laura," she said. "And that's the lot. You'll have to cut down some of the bigger bags if there aren't enough. I know Mrs. Gould has ordered a lot more from Barchester, but if they aren't here that's not much use to us. I'll just see if Sister knows anything about them," and she went busily away. Mrs. Morland settled to her usual job of counting so many acid drops, or toffees, or whatever was at the moment in stock, and putting them into small paper bags which would then go onto the Trolley and be bought by the patients. This may sound quite simple, but it was not so simple as all that for Mrs. Gould, who was the organiser. Possibly the easiest way of doling out the sweets would have been simply to put so many into each bag and have done; but each kind of sweet—acid drops, barley sugar drops, peppermints, toffees, and other brands—had a different weight and if old Mrs. Grubb, who would never rise again from her bed but had a mathematical mind, had thought her ten barley sugars were simply a cheat if old Miss Bunce got twelve peppermint drops—the two packets being exactly the same weight—there would have been Words. And no one could have explained nor would she have listened if they had.

So Mrs. Morland got the little weighing machine from the cupboard—the sort on which one's grandmother and even mother would weigh letters in the days when postage was postage and a penny stamp with Queen Victoria's head on it could travel in comfort over most of the world—and found how many sweets of each kind would make a quarter of a pound. She was then able to settle placidly to bagging them. In earlier and freer days she would have grazed among the various sweets like an unmuzzled ox, nor would anyone have noticed if she did exceed; nor would they now, but her conscience most annoyingly reared its head and said she must first fill *all* the bags and then—but only then—if a few sweets were left over, she could keep them for herself.

It was a peaceful way of spending the time and her mind could wander to such unrelated thoughts as what she would give her three sons, their three wives, and their numerous offspring for Christmas this year and to decide that if any of them asked her to visit them during or near Christmas she

would have influenza at once. Not that she did not love them
and help them in many ways, but when you have become
used to living alone it is not easy to hold your part in a large
family gathering in other people's houses. So every year she
decided to have mild influenza from the middle of December
till after the New Year, knowing that her daughters-in-law, of
whom she was truly fond (and they could not have been
nicer and kinder to her), would be only too glad not to have
a potential germ carrier in the house.

At this point she suddenly wondered if she had been putting
the right number of sweets into the bags, decided to open
some and re-count them, got horribly muddled, quickly put
them back again and hoped for the best. The other helpers
would be back soon with their Trolleys and there would have
to be a replacing of all unsold goods, each in its proper place,
in the big cupboard.

A bump against the door made her conscious that someone
wanted to get in and probably it was Matron. So she got up
and opened the door and there was Matron herself with a tray
of cups and a large pot of tea and milk, followed by a pleasant-
looking woman, no longer young but not looking old. Mrs. Morland, holding the door wide for Matron, looked at the stranger.
Suddenly the past began to surge up from the abysm of time
forgotten.

"It isn't Nurse Chiffinch!" she said. "I mean I ought to say
Sister Chiffinch. Oh, HOW nice to see you."

"There!" said Matron, who was looking on with the pleased
expression of a stage-manager who sees the characters make
their entrances successfully. "I knew you'd be surprised, Mrs.
Morland. I said to Sister: 'Mrs. Morland *will* have a nice surprise.'"

"Well, I really *am* surprised," said Mrs. Morland, feeling
quite idiotic as she said it, but also feeling with the queer
instinct of the writer who writes for her public that this was

probably what Matron would expect. "It's ages since I've seen you, Sister."

"That's just what I said," said Sister Chiffinch, addressing both ladies. "I was saying to Matron, only a moment ago. Well, I said, Mrs. Morland *will* have a surprise."

"Well, it *was* a surprise," said Mrs. Morland, her writing self again making her say exactly what it felt she ought to say. "But a lovely surprise. I do hope, Matron, that you aren't too busy to have a cup of tea and Sister Chiffinch too. I've got the kettle on and the other helpers will be back with the Trolleys quite soon."

Matron graciously gave her assent and sat benevolently watching.

"And how is that nice son of yours?" said Sister Chiffinch to Mrs. Morland. "He's quite a family man now, isn't he? And the other sons that I've never seen."

Mrs. Morland said Tony had four delightful children and expatiated on their beauty, good health, and intelligence—but not too much—and that her other boys were doing very well but mostly in jobs abroad so that she didn't see much of them or their children.

"Well, that's the way things go," said Matron, speaking *ex cathedra*, though whether what she said meant anything we do not know. Probably not.

"And you were with Lady William Harcourt, weren't you, Sister?" said Mrs. Morland, knowing that Sister dearly loved a title—and why not? "Have you heard of her lately? How is she?"

Sister Chiffinch said she had been to lunch with Lady William and a little bird had told her that if Lady William looked just a *tiny* bit tired there was a very good reason for it and she believed she—Sister Chiffinch—would be over in that direction again some months from now. Her audience conducted itself perfectly, both ladies saying how nice for the family. And as each of the three ladies knew exactly what was meant there was no need for any explanations.

A sound of cheerful voices with a good deal of bumping now became evident from outside and with a final bump against the door in came the priestesses and the Trolleys, all talking at once, saying singly or in chorus It was extraordinary that however many things you put on the Trolleys there was always something missing and who would have thought old Mrs. Brown, mother of Mr. Brown at the garage, could have wanted nut chocolate when everyone knew she hadn't any teeth and wouldn't use the dentures she had got free on the Health because the Bible said not to worship graven images; at which point breath failed them.

Mrs. Morland said she didn't want to seem captious, but *were* false teeth graven?

"I believe they *used* to be," she said, "because I was reading a book about someone called Harriette Wilson and when she had stopped being supported by the aristocracy she went to live in Paris with a kind of adventurer and wrote a book called *Clara Gazul* and someone in it wanted not to be engaged to a lady whose relations were determined that he should marry her, so he got a dentist to let him hire two complete rows of false teeth carved in ivory with a bill for fifteen guineas and dropped it on the carpet and then the lady's friends broke off the engagement."

Matron said Of course that sort of thing wouldn't happen today, with the Health Service.

By now the helpers had put away all the unsold goods and were thirsting for tea. Mrs. Morland poured out the tea up to an imaginary line in the cups, added milk and far too much sugar (which was what almost all the helpers liked), and offered Matron and Sister Chiffinch each a cup.

Matron accepted graciously and said there was nothing like tea.

Sister Chiffinch said she *did* so agree. There was something about tea, she said, that you didn't get in coffee. Not that she *disliked* coffee, she said, but there was a *something* in tea.

Everyone then spoke at once, saying that you couldn't beat tea; that coffee was very nice but it did keep you awake; that a nice cuppa before you went to bed seemed to settle you, like; and that there was some nice American coffee that hadn't got anything in it; with which everyone agreed. And rightly, for though the non-caffeine coffee is quite a pleasant drink, it is NOT coffee, be the other who he may.

In the middle of the talk Mrs. Gould, who had come back from her meeting and had been going through some of the stock, suddenly said: "Ladies! Please!"

Whether pleased or not, everyone stopped talking and looked round.

"I have said it again and again," she began. "When you put the unsold stock back in the cupboard, *please* try to leave everything in order. Those large handkerchiefs are for MEN and must *not* be put with the women's handkerchiefs. You can easily tell which is which as they are quite different," and she held up a large plain white handkerchief.

"This is for MEN," she said. "The largest size we can get at present, and must *not* be sold on the Women's Trolley. These are for women," and she held up some normal-sized handkerchiefs each with some kind of flower embroidered by machinery in one corner, "and there are a few coloured ones as well," and she mentioned the selling price of each, which was exactly the same as the cost price, for the Trolley Service was a non-profit-making affair, only hoping not to be out of pocket at the end of the year. It is hardly necessary to add that so worthy and philanthropic an institution always was out of pocket, but George Knox—who had once been there to be bandaged when he sliced a bit off a knuckle while showing the old hedger how a hedge should be cut, thus affording intense pleasure to the old hedger and his friends, who discussed it for several weeks in pure Wessex at the local—had not only made a donation in gratitude for the bandage, but had bullied some friends into joining and was himself a regular and generous subscriber.

When Matron heard about this she had insisted on thanking him warmly, which made him very uncomfortable, but as he never visited the hospital he was spared further gratitude and all was well.

The ladies thanked Mrs. Gould for her reminder and forgot it immediately, while drinking their nice hot well-sweetened tea and—by immemorial custom and right—eating such of the biscuits as were hopelessly broken. This was quite a considerable number, for as far as we can make out there is far less butter in biscuits now than there was before the Kaiser began creating (a nannie's phrase familiar to most of us elders) and the Brazen Age began; probably to be followed by Ragnarok and the end of everything. The cupboard was then locked by Mrs. Gould, who put the key in a very secret place which everyone knew, and the ladies began to go home.

"Come back to lunch, Laura," said Mrs. Gould.

Mrs. Morland at once split into two people—a phenomenon common to all of us. One was the gracious lady, slightly older than Mrs. Gould, with four married sons and many grandchildren. The other was Laura Morland, not so young as she was and rather tired after a morning of philanthropy. Though it may be better to give than to receive, it is doubtless more tactful to receive than to invent a reason for not receiving, so she said how nice and she would love to.

By this time everything was tidy and the helpers were swiftly melting away to get lunch for their husband and/or children, for some of the children had a school lunch, which can only be described in the words of the poet as "a dinner plain and hearty," rhyming, as all our well-read readers will remember, with Bonaparty (only spelt Bonaparte), and was described by the Dear Little Ones as Yesterday's Hotted Up And Cod's Eyes—this last being the accepted name for tapioca as far back as our remembrance goes. There was, we believe, an attempt to re-baptise semolina as Haddock's Eyes, but this was never really accepted. One can have enough of a good thing.

So Mrs. Morland went back to the Vicarage with Mrs. Gould, rather glad to be able to be out of the scramble and the noise of some six or seven well-bred, well-educated ladies all talking at once at the peacock tops of their voices.

We have not been to the Vicarage very often since we first met Mrs. Morland, some quarter of a century ago, so does time fly, when we were both much younger. Then did Tony Morland, now a heavily married man, argue and fight on equal terms with what Stoker called "those Vicarage Girls"—otherwise Rose and Dora Gould. Now Those Girls were grown-up. Our impression is that Dr. Ford did propose to their elder sister Sylvia, some years previously, but nothing came of it and as in any case he was rather too old for her, all was well.

The whole question of marrying and giving in marriage is too complicated. One can only say that it suits some and doesn't suit others. Some of the happiest and most usefully occupied ladies of our acquaintance remain Miss; on the other hand we know a number of very happy and usefully occupied Mrs.'s— if that is how one writes the plural. Some women are Born Aunts—and what a comfort and blessing they can be to their relations, and often they go on blooming. We have just been re-reading the early life of Tony Morland and find that in 1934 the Vicar's younger daughters were fourteen and twelve; so now they must be well into their thirties but, in the words of our formerly lively neighbours the Gauls, *cela n'empêche pas*. Older than they have been happy wives made—to parody the Count of Paris's remark—and he probably knew.

The Vicarage was like most other vicarages, rather too large for its incumbent. Several times there had been a movement to have it de-consecrated as it were and a nice house found to take its place, with all mod. con., a garage and c.h.w.; which last was now much easier since whoever is responsible for vicarages had installed a gas heater for water in the kitchen and the bathroom. But it still remained The Vicarage.

Mrs. Gould, coming from good clerical stock whose women-folk took discomfort for granted, had managed quite well with the aid of untrained girls from the village and had now— as happens to most of us—become quite happily accustomed to making the best of things, though not unwilling to consider a more modern home if the authorities responsible for housing the clergy could find one.

As Mrs. Gould and Mrs. Morland approached the Vicarage, they saw a very shabby car blocking the gate.

"It *is* annoying when people use one as a parking ground," said Mrs. Morland. "Luckily I have that little bit of a drive or whatever one calls it when it isn't really large enough to be a drive, which keeps me fairly safe."

"I expect it's one of the girls," said Mrs. Gould, "or one of their friends. I can't think why they have so many friends. That's the worst of girls, and they all have cheap little cars which have to be parked somewhere."

"But don't they go to *their* friends' houses, or their friends' mothers' houses too?" said Mrs. Morland. "You see," she added, rather apologetically, "having only sons, I don't know much about girls."

"Oh, yes, they do," said Mrs. Gould. "As far as I can make out all these girls spend their lives in and out of each other's parents' houses. It's enough to make one emigrate."

"I *do* so know what you mean," said Mrs. Morland in heart-felt accents. "But luckily all my boys are married and mostly go to their mother-in-laws' houses because the female of the species is more deadly than the male."

Mrs. Gould, who had now got out of her car and was putting the windows up, said what on earth did she mean and would Mrs. Morland get out.

"I wish," said Mrs. Morland, as she squashed, turned, and unwove herself from the car, "I wish I knew why the people who make cars can't make them easier to get in and out of. When I was at school a stout elderly lady with a black bonnet who taught dancing used to come and teach us how to get in and out of carriages; but no one helps one about cars."

Mrs. Gould asked how one ought to get in and out of carriages.

"Well," said Mrs. Morland, "I can't really explain, because I was always clumsy about dancing. But it was something about always putting one foot on the step of the carriage first."

Mrs. Gould said one would have to do that anyway, or else jump onto it with both feet together, in which case one would probably fall backwards onto the floor of the carriage or backwards onto the pavement, and so speaking gently pushed her guest into the house.

"Yes, but it mattered *which* foot," said Mrs. Morland. "I think it was the left foot, because then you put your right foot into the carriage. No, it wasn't. It was right foot on the step, left foot into the carriage, then pivot on the left foot while you pulled your right foot up and made it go one step forward. Then you sat down. No: you put the left foot on the step and then put the *right* foot in as far as you could and began sitting yourself down while you pulled your left foot after you. At least I can't quite *exactly* explain. Of course if it was a Victoria one had to sit on the little seat—the strapontin— with your back to the coachman and footman, and your mother or whoever the carriage belonged to sat on the comfortable seat with any friend or guest. If there wasn't another grown-up one was allowed to sit on the comfortable seat with one's legs sticking out, because one couldn't reach the ground. But people stopped having carriages after motors came in. Funny things they were, those early cars, very high off the ground, always needing water and breaking down wherever they went, like Kipling."

Mrs. Gould, who had been listening with all the patience that a hostess should show, said would Laura like to wash her hands, which she did. There seemed to be a good deal of scuffling downstairs, but other people's scufflings are nothing to do with one and Mrs. Morland washed her hands and dried them on the Guest Towel—a horrid example of buying things at bazaars and flower shows, but adequate, so long as it was only used by one person—and went down again. In the large, rather shabby, but gentlemanly drawing-room were the Vicarage Girls, as Stoker disparagingly called them, from whom apparently the scuffling noise had proceeded.

Mrs. Morland had known Rose and Dora all their lives, from children in pinafores through the flapper age, and now they were grown-up women with jobs and interests outside their home and Mrs. Morland felt rather shy of their competence. But manners are manners and she said how nice it was to see them and what were they doing now. Not that she cared in the least, feeling morally certain that whatever it was it would be (a) dull and (b) something she couldn't understand. There was a third person in the room; a tall, good-looking not-so-young woman whom she knew she ought to recognise.

"You remember Sylvia, don't you, Mrs. Morland?" said Mrs. Gould.

"Good gracious! Of course I do," said Mrs. Morland, suddenly realising that it was the elder sister of Rose and Dora, "but I haven't seen her for ages. What are you doing now, Sylvia?"

"Mostly secretary work," said Sylvia. "I'm pretty good at it, but it isn't life. One is That Reliable Miss Gould," which she said mockingly, though not with bitterness.

Mrs. Morland asked who she was secretarying for.

"Mr. Adams," said Sylvia. "You know, the one that runs all those works and has an office at Pomfret Towers. He has two or three secretaries and I was lucky to get the job."

"I went there once," said Mrs. Morland, "though I can't remember why. But one thing I *do* remember——" and she paused, in a kind of trance of remembering.

Mrs. Gould asked what it was.

"I know," said Mrs. Morland triumphantly. "It was Mr. Adams's secretary Miss Cowshay, because she used to be in one of the shops in Barchester before the war, but which I cannot think."

Mrs. Gould said it was the cashier's office at Pilchard's Stores.

"Of *course*," said Mrs. Morland. "And she always knew who one was, which is *so* useful. And she was in the Regional Commissioner's Office at Barchester in the war and now she is at Pomfret Towers. One does *miss* the war sometimes."

Rose and Dora looked at one another. Old people! Quite useful in their way, but not much sense.

But Mrs. Morland was speaking more truly than she knew. Or perhaps with the writer's peculiar sixth sense she knew without knowing. The Something that makes us write. But she was saved from further confusing her audience by Mr. Gould coming in and asking if lunch was ready, which Mrs. Gould countered very neatly by saying that it was no good starting lunch before he came because things got cold and had to be hotted up and everyone knew that hotted up was NOT the same as straight from the oven.

Everyone began to move towards the dining-room, so causing
a kind of small scuffle for not going before other people. Mrs.
Gould settled the party in a masterful way, her self at the
head of the table and her husband at the foot with Mrs. Morland next him. The girls sat wherever they liked and as there
were only six people and the table was round, it didn't much
matter where anyone sat. And if our Captious Reader says a
round table doesn't have a head or a foot, we can only quote
the old story "Wherever The Mackintosh (for which read Mrs.
Gould) sits *is* the head of the table." But as her husband usually
sat opposite her, no outsider would have known which was the
Head.

The conversation, as was but too usual, was at first monopo-
lised by Rose and Dora, who felt obliged to discuss several
very uninteresting subjects without any reference to the rest of
the party. This their parents appeared to take as a matter of
course. Mrs. Morland hated them inside herself but being a
good guest made no comment. Their elder sister looked at
them once or twice and then said a few searching words as to
getting on with one's lunch. A lovely silence ensued during
which the elders were able to talk comfortably about village
affairs while Rose and Dora looked at each other with pity-
ing glances—not for themselves, but for people who were so
wanting in intelligence or consideration for others as not to
know—or care to know—that *A Mistress of Voltaire* was at the
Barchester Odeon, starring that ageless vedette Glamora Tudor
with her new male support Hank Pilsener, whose make-up as
Voltaire had been highly praised by such authorities as Professor Pierre Boulle of the Académie française and Abner P.
Schreibfeder of Seattle, Washington, U.S.A., who owned six
cinemas and intended to buy at least six more and build a super-
cinema with a restaurant, a swimming bath, and a planetarium
on his own estate; not to speak of an article in the *Spectator*,
which gave the film six literary lines of scholarly approval—

enough to put off most readers; but as the readers of that valuable weekly are mostly intelligent at least seven of them went to the film and owing to the blessed darkness of the auditorium were able to slip out unnoticed.

However, the lunch itself was good and when it was over Rose and Dora said they must go to the cinema because there was a Travelogue about New Guinea. Everyone was glad that they should improve their minds so long as they did it somewhere else, so they went away and there was peace.

Mr. Gould said he had to go out, so Mrs. Gould with Mrs. Morland and Sylvia went to his study. There was a good fire, the sun had come out and was shining through the large window.

"This *is* a nice room," said Mrs. Morland. "I can't think why you don't have it for yourself," and then wondered if she had been untactful.

"Well, if I did," said her hostess, "my husband would be here all the time."

"Yes, I do see that," said Mrs. Morland.

"I'm always telling mother," said Sylvia, "that father ought to have his study in front, because then he could see who was coming and escape through the other door. I can't think why father ever became a clergyman," which she said more in a spirit of enquiry than with any denigration of her father or the clergy.

"I do so agree," said Mrs. Morland. "I mean about escaping. It is *quite* the most important thing in a house. One ought to have two doors to every room. Of course I am a little safer because though the drive is very short I can see people coming up it and tell Stoker to say I am out."

"But Laura," said Mrs. Gould, "what happens if they have seen you while they were coming up the drive?"

"If they are really nice," said Mrs. Morland, "they know what Stoker means and say Never mind, I'll ring her up later.

But stupid people sometimes almost *push* in, which annoys
Stoker very much and then she says I have gone down to the
village and she doesn't know when I'll be back—which is a
Noble Lie."

Mrs. Gould said it was just as well that her husband wasn't
there or he would have spoilt everything.

"I mean," she added, "he doesn't believe in social lies, because he says one is nearly always found out. And it's perfectly
true. The number of untruths I have told would sink a ship,
but they were all to save him."

"I'm sure you are right, Mrs. Morland," said Sylvia. "I tell
the most whacking lies for Mr. Adams."

"He ought to tell his own lies himself," said her mother,
rather indignantly.

"But he *can't*," said Sylvia. "He is too busy. And it's just
as well, because if he tried to invent a lie I don't think he could.
But I'm awfully good at lies—for other people, I mean. And
anyway it isn't lies—I mean not like being a Liar. It's only
helping the boss. I had a talk with Mrs. Adams about it and
she said I was quite right."

"Now, she was Lucy Marling, wasn't she?" said Mrs. Gould,
suddenly taking an interest in the conversation. "A very good
Barsetshire family. Her mother was a daughter of old Lord
Nutfield. The title is extinct now."

It was at such moments that Mrs. Morland felt her lack of
citizenship, as it were. True, she had lived in Barsetshire for
all her married life and peaceful widowhood, but she was not
of the county and never would be. She was much liked and
had friends everywhere, but though she had been among them
for some forty-odd years there were still a great many things
she did not know. One has to have deep roots in the part of the
country where one lives if one is to understand and to be
understood. Her sons had all done well, married happily, but
not in Barsetshire. She had remained in that pleasant county,

was happy there and expected to die there; but would always be what in the north is called an offcome.

"I say, Mrs. Morland," said Sylvia, "I liked your last book most awfully and I gave it to two friends. I mean I bought two more copies for them, because I hate lending books," and having so delivered herself she went rather red in the face and twisted her hands.

Mrs. Morland also felt rather red in the face at this sudden tribute, but her first reaction was that Sylvia must be reassured.

"That *was* kind of you, Sylvia," she said. "Such a lot of people tell me they have been waiting for ages to get my last book from the Public Library—at least what they *do* say is Libery. And of course I am delighted if the Public Libraries have some of my books, but one does write books to earn one's living. And if you would really help me, do ask your friends to *buy* one of my books."

Sylvia said she certainly would.

Mrs. Gould, who had been listening with interest to the foregoing conversation, asked Mrs. Morland if she had ever thought of writing something about that part of Barsetshire.

"Well, I have," said Mrs. Morland, "but then I didn't. You see when you begin to describe a place, whether it's a town, or a village, or anywhere where people live, you are bound to get something wrong however hard you try and if your book is reviewed probably the reviewer happens to know about that particular thing—which of course saves him or her trouble. And then sometimes people write anonymous letters—hate letters, I mean. I expect your husband gets an occasional poison-pen letter."

"Yes, he does," said Mrs. Gould. "Not as many as he might," which words she said almost regretfully as though her husband were a Deprived Person, "but some quite nasty ones. Of course writing about religious affairs *does* make people disagreeable, but perhaps it cheers them up, so one can't complain. He had

a very good one not long ago from someone who wanted him
to join a society for the clergy to have open pulpits—I mean
just like a high small platform—because it says in the book of
Nehemiah that he stood *upon* a pulpit, not *in* one."

Mrs. Morland said How fascinating and did Mr. Gould answer it.

"He always answers letters," said Mrs. Gould. "Once. But
if they go on writing he doesn't. But I don't suppose you are
bothered in that way because everyone loves your books," which
made Mrs. Morland go rather pink in the face.

"I don't mean to boast," said that worthy creature, "but I
do get a fair number of nice letters and I always answer them
and if they—I mean the writer—writes again I answer on a
postcard but politely and then, with luck, that's that. I did
once have a really horrid poison-pen one," on hearing which
words Sylvia begged to know what she did about it.

"Well, there wasn't much I *could* do," said Mrs. Morland.
"You see there is a very pleasant Rhone wine called Montrachet
and I knew its name because I'd heard it talked about and liked
it, so I put it in a book and spelt in Monrachet, without the
first *t,* because I went by the *sound.* And what must have
been a very nasty old gentleman wrote me a most unpleasant
letter to say what an ignorant fool I was, but did not give his
name or his address, which was rather mean. But I never heard
of him again. If I ever do, I hope he will be an Author."

Mrs. Gould not unnaturally asked why.

"Because," said Mrs. Morland, "there's a great text in Gala-
tians——" and then stopped suddenly and laughed.

Sylvia looked surprised and almost alarmed.

"I didn't know *anyone* read Browning now," said Mrs. Gould.

"Oh, praise the Lord for *one* educated person!" said Mrs.
Morland. "It's all right, Sylvia. Your mother and I are just being middle-aged bores and you are neither, bless you."

"But what's it all about?" said Sylvia.

"If you ever tried to read Browning——" Mrs. Morland began, but Sylvia burst in, to say she simply adored him, only not the long poems.

"Well, what I was quoting isn't a long one," said Mrs. Morland rather severely. "It's called 'Soliloquy of the Spanish Cloister,' and it's all about how one monk hates another and he is talking aloud to himself about the monk that he hates and how he wants to get him muddled in his religion and one verse runs:

> *"There's a great text in Galatians,*
> *Once you trip on it, entails*
> *Twenty-nine distinct damnations,*
> *One sure if another fails:*
> *If I trip him just a-dying,*
> *Sure of heaven as sure can be,*
> *Spin him round and send him flying*
> *Off to hell, a Manichee."*

"How *lovely*," said Sylvia, which was perhaps not quite the *mot juste*, but expressed her feelings—and ours, though we have not the faintest idea what Manichees were, except a vague feeling that they are a peculiar kind of eastern fruit or nut.

"Oh lord!" said Mrs. Gould, who had been looking vaguely into the road. "It's the laundry, and a day too late."

"I'll go and see about it, Mother," said Sylvia.

"No, darling; I have been waiting for him for three weeks and missed him every time," said her mother, "and I simply MUST get it into his head that your father doesn't like so much starch in his collars. I shan't be long," and she went away with the light of battle in her eyes.

There was a short silence. Then Sylvia said she supposed Mrs. Morland thought she was a beast, to which Mrs. Morland replied that she saw no reason at all to think so.

"It's not that I don't like my job," said Sylvia. "They are

all awfully nice at Pomfret Towers and Mr. Adams seems to think I'm fairly good at the job, but it's—oh, I don't know. Sorry, Mrs. Morland."

"Not at all," said that lady politely. "I can't think how anyone can *bear* secretarying, but then I never tried. I can type, but very badly. I used to type all my own books and then I got better off and now I send them all to a delightful and *most* intelligent person who sees all the stupid things I haven't noticed and saves me from worse than death. I mean, if I make someone who is either thirteen or sixty get married when one really meant it to be someone of a suitable age, because I forget what I had said about them in another book."

We think that Mrs. Morland excelled herself in her snipe-flight but Sylvia took it calmly, merely remarking: "Oh, well! on we go."

"Well then, let's go somewhere amusing," said Mrs. Morland. "I'm going over to Rising Castle on Sunday. Come with me. I can pick you up after the service and we will have lunch with Lord Stoke. Do you know the castle? I mean the old part."

Sylvia said she had been there once on a public day and liked it very much, except all those steep, narrow, crumbling staircases.

"Well, we won't go up any of them or down either," said Mrs. Morland. "They frighten me too. Lord Stoke is very easy to get on with and not half as deaf as he pretends. The food is really good and he loves having people to lunch who appreciate it. So is the wine. Do you like wine?"

"I don't really know," said Sylvia. "I mean I do quite like it if anyone gives me some, but I am quite happy without it."

"That's all right," said Mrs. Morland comfortably. "I've known Lord Stoke ever since I first came to High Rising and I am very fond of him. He can be a bit brusque, but it doesn't mean anything," at which Sylvia laughed and said that after her

job at Pomfret Towers she could face *anyone,* and she was sure
Lord Stoke would be nice to her, especially as she came with
Mrs. Morland.

"Then that's all settled," said Mrs. Morland. "I suppose you
will be going to church," but Sylvia said she was anyway going
to the Early Service so she could be ready whenever it suited
Mrs. Morland.

"Then I will come about twelve," said Mrs. Morland, "unless," she added, seeing a faint shadow on Sylvia's face, "you'd
like to walk down to me."

This offer Sylvia gratefully accepted and though we cannot
quite explain why she preferred to walk down instead of being
fetched we think it was much the same feeling that prompted
Mrs. Gilpin to have the chaise drawn up two doors off, lest
all should think that she was proud. And then Mrs. Morland
went home.

CHAPTER 4

To Mrs. Morland, going to see Lord Stoke was a pleasure but no particular excitement. They were old friends and that was that. If he approved of Sylvia Gould—as she hoped he would— it would add one to the not very long list of people that he liked to see. He still kept up with a few hereditary old County friends such as the Pomfrets at Pomfret Towers and various connections of his family and—as we already know—his sister the Dowager Lady Bond.

It was not everyone who approached Lord Stoke with ease. His lordship, who was growing steadily more deaf, certainly got the best possible value out of this handicap. When he wished to hear, he heard pretty well so long as the speaker could find what we can only describe as the norm of his or her own voice. If he did not wish to hear, he managed to invent pre-texts for dropping his hearing apparatus, or beginning to talk rather overbearingly on any subject that came to his mind. For his sister Lucasta, Dowager Lady Bond, he had the affection of a brother who has known in far-off days what a useful ally a sister can be and what a meddling nuisance. We think that her lady-ship entirely reciprocated these feelings. People who got to know them for the first time, from one side or the other, found a certain malign pleasure in hearing them spar; but if anyone came between them with the mistaken idea of foment-ing irritation or—even worse—trying to soothe it, the adver-saries were apt to turn on the interloper and rend him or her. The only person who could deal with these domestic difficulties was Albert, the invaluable butler promoted from footman, who knew at what exact moment it would be tactful to come into the room to make up the fire, or ask if his lordship could see the man about the leaking gutter. As employer and employed the pair were pretty evenly matched.

Lord Stoke had, very properly, an eye for a good-looking woman. We must say on Mrs. Morland's behalf, who had no illusions about her own looks and mostly forgot to put on the very slight make-up in which she indulged, that it never occurred to her to speculate as to what effect her looks might have on her old friend. But they suited each other very well, each—in the well-known phrase of Mrs. Sam Adams—telling the other what with great freedom. To her, Lord Stoke had confided his early and hopeless attachment to old Lady Pomfret when she was Edith Thorne of a very good Barsetshire family. Mrs. Morland herself had nothing to confide, having lost her quite nice, very dull husband many years ago and never been asked to marry again. Nor had she wished to. But she was able to feed his lordship with small pieces of gossip from the village, which he vastly enjoyed.

When Mrs. Morland announced her intention of bringing Miss Gould, the Vicar's daughter, to Rising Castle, his lordship had merely grunted over the telephone. Mrs. Morland, very sensibly, took this as meaning "Do as you like, it's all one to me," and continued the even tenor of her way. And why people *will* say "noiseless" for "even" we do not know. An Oxford Book of Common Misquotations might be worth considering; we leave this to the Oxford University Press, together with our heartfelt thanks for their book of *Quotations*, to which we have made—in our own copy—several valuable additions, including "If pressed for time, omit Cambridge," though we cannot vouch for the phrase having occurred in a mid-nineteenth-century guide book, as we were brought up to believe. But we think it must have been somewhere, as no one now could have invented it.

The weather had so far forgotten itself as to be quite warm and Sylvia was looking forward to the drive almost more than the lunch, because the country was bound to be looking its best, whereas one never knew whom one might meet at Rising Castle and for all her courage she felt that if Lady Bond were to be there she could not possibly enjoy herself. She then told herself how silly she was and how nice the party would be; but another herself would go on whispering to her that when she was having the canteen lunch at Pomfret Towers among her co-workers she was in a better place. But as Shakespeare so truly remarks, travellers must be content.

The gravelled courtyard in front of the house was empty, but as Mrs. Morland knew that other guests would probably be coming she put her car into a place from which she could easily escape and walked with Sylvia towards the front door, stopping to lean on a balustrade and look over the ruins and the river.

"Of course this part of the castle isn't a castle at all," she said. "I forget who built it. Lord Stoke's grandfather, I think. It's a very nice house and if one wants ruins, which I really don't, here they are. But you've been over them, I expect."

Sylvia said she had been there fairly often when she was a girl and didn't much want to visit them again because she always felt giddy on corkscrew stairs.

"So do I," said Mrs. Morland fervently. "Especially when there isn't anything to hold on by. How people managed in those days I can't think."

Sylvia said Which days exactly, because the castle must be pretty old.

"Well, I really don't know the date," said Mrs. Morland, "because I never could remember any dates but I know Cromwell did a lot of damage in the Civil War, so the castle must have been there then, or he couldn't have besieged it. But we'll ask Lord Stoke all about it. He loves telling people things, though very often it's only the things he wants to tell and he won't tell

them the things they want to hear, like how many servants used
to sleep in one bed and whose business it was to carry hot water
up for baths. But that was in the new house, of course, not in the
castle, because there isn't any proper sanitation or draining or
anything there. And all those discolorations on the walls were
where they threw everything out of the windows into the moat,
to save trouble."

"It's awfully interesting about sanitation," said Sylvia, with
more animation than she usually showed. "Mr. Adams had to
do a lot of it when he took over Pomfret Towers for his offices.
It's really magnificent. Of course there were no real drains to
speak of in old Lord Pomfret's time. I mean this Lord Pomfret's
old cousin that he inherited from."

"No; nor nowhere else," said Mrs. Morland. "You children
don't know how restful that was. The big houses had lots of
servants—which is really the answer to everything. But they
weren't as drainless as you think, only the drains and things
didn't advertise themselves. And of course people didn't have
so many baths—I mean not so much water. Goodness knows how
many millions of gallons run away every day now."

"Do *you* remember not having bathrooms with a proper bath,
Mrs. Morland?" said Sylvia, hardly believing such a thing possible.

"Of course I do," said Mrs. Morland indignantly. "In the
house where I was born in London, just off Kensington Square,
there wasn't a bathroom and we all got on quite well. Nanny
brought hot water up from the kitchen for my bath and the
housemaid brought up water for my father's and mother's baths."

"It must have been an awful lot to carry," said Sylvia.

"Only one can at a time," said Mrs. Morland. "You can't ever
know how nice it was to sit in a large hip-bath with hot water
up to your waist in front of a blazing fire and Nanny waiting
with a big bath towel that had been warming on the fender and
then to sit on your little chair with your red flannel dressing-

gown and red felt bedroom slippers, in front of your own little table and having biscuits and milk for supper. Marie, Petit Beurre, Osborne and sometimes Animal biscuits, or Alphabet biscuits."

To the elderly among us these *échos du temps passé* are nostalgic almost beyond bearing, but Sylvia was not of the elderly. To her it sounded rather dull and indeed rather boring, but she had a kind heart and good manners and said how nice it must have been and what were Alphabet biscuits.

"Just letters of the alphabet," said Mrs. Morland. "I remember a cousin of mine cramming the whole alphabet into his mouth, just to show he could do it."

"But *could* he?" said Sylvia. "Not twenty-six."

"Well, he did," said Mrs. Morland. "He nearly choked, but he got them down and never did it again. We must go in."

She walked to the front door, which opened as she went up the steps, disclosing the butler Albert, whom she named to Sylvia as an old friend.

But Sylvia, a good daughter of the parsonage, had already recognised and placed Albert.

"But of course I remember Albert," said Sylvia. "It was you, wasn't it, Albert, that was so awfully sick when we had the village school outing to Barchester in a charabanc."

Albert went bright red: not from shame but from pride at being remembered.

"I wouldn't have known I had it in me, miss," said Albert. "Mother she said to me: 'Mind you don't drink too much ginger beer,' she said. But I didn't mind what mother said and the ginger pop—ginger beer, I mean—was that strong I felt quite queer."

"And you looked queer," said Sylvia. "I never saw anyone go green and yellow in the face the way you did. How is your mother?"

Albert shuffled his feet.

"Mother's fine," he said. "She won a prize at the Pally last week."

Rightly interpreting Pally as the Barchester Palais de Danse, Sylvia asked Albert to congratulate his mother and enquired what the prize was.

"Six serviettes, miss," said Albert. "Nice big ones and a nice flower embroidered at one corner. Mother was ever so pleased. She wrapped them up and put them away in the cupboard."

"Isn't she going to use them then?" said Mrs. Morland.

"They never do," said Sylvia in an aside to Mrs. Morland. "They *always* put things away. That's wonderful," she added, turning to Albert. "Tell your mother I was ever so pleased to hear about it. I think Lord Stoke is expecting us."

Albert, realising that his brief appearance as a public character was over, led the way to Lord Stoke's sitting-room and announced the guests.

As always, Lord Stoke was pleased to see Mrs. Morland, who said she had brought a friend with her, Miss Sylvia Gould.

"You know our Vicar at High Rising, Mr. Gould," she said to Lord Stoke, with a Look that told him he jolly well must, whether he liked it or not.

"Gould? Yes, of course," said Lord Stoke, looking with admiration at Sylvia.

"Well, this is his daughter," said Mrs. Morland. "She is highly intelligent and has given me a lot of help with my work and types some of my letters."

"Types, eh?" said Lord Stoke. "Thought you typed everything yourself."

"Well, I used to," said Mrs. Morland, "and very badly I did it, because I never learnt typing properly. I mean *real* typists just sit in front of their typewriter and do it all without thinking," which sketchy and inaccurate survey of a professional typist's work roused Sylvia to protest.

"But you *can't* type like that," she said. "One has to think awfully hard. One of our typists at Pomfret Towers came out in a kind of rash because she worried so much and Mr. Adams was awfully kind and paid for her to be treated and then she got married, so he might as well not have paid for her."

It was obvious by this time to Mrs. Morland that her old friend was completely at sea and not enjoying it, so she asked him what he had done about the Stokey Hole.

Sylvia asked what the Stokey Hole was, and by dint of repeating her question in a much louder voice, roused her host's attention.

"Bless my soul, young lady," said Lord Stoke. "Don't you know the Stokey Hole? I'll take you there after lunch. That was a nasty fall your boy had, Mrs. Morland, when he and his friend went exploring there."

"It was no more than he deserved," said Mrs. Morland severely. "He went into the Stokey Hole strictly against orders and fell down the bank when he came out and ricked his ankle, just in the middle of the holidays. I could have killed him."

"I remember that quite well," said Lord Stoke. "After your boy had that fall I had an iron gate put across the entrance to the hole so that no one would get hurt."

"But didn't people—I mean tourists and things—go in just the same?" said Mrs. Morland.

"Only if they pay sixpence," said his lordship. "And no half price for children."

"But that's not fair, Lord Stoke," said Sylvia, and Mrs. Morland wondered if Lord Stoke would think his guest had gone too far, but he was in a good mood and only laughed.

"If I'd had a little more sense, I'd have made it double for children," Lord Stoke said.

Mrs. Morland not unnaturally asked why.

"I know," said Sylvia. "It's because grown-ups *have* to let their children do what they want unless it's something really awful, because they don't want the other grown-ups to think they are being mean to their children."

Lord Stoke, who had, with an unusual effort, managed to follow this explanation, laughed and said the young lady was right.

As they were talking Albert came in and said in a confidential voice that Lady Bond was there and Lord Bond.

"Well, if it's Lord Bond bring him along," said Lord Stoke. "And tell Lady Bond I'm in Barchester. No, tell them both I'm in Barchester."

Albert looked surprised and rather worried.

"Wait a minute," said his lordship, "it can't be Lord Bond. Bond died some time ago—no stamina. And I do *not* want to see Lady Bond. She may be my sister, but enough's as good as a feast. Bond's dead. The woman's mad."

Mrs. Morland realised what the muddle was, but nearly had the giggles and could not speak. Not so Sylvia, who said clearly but kindly to his lordship that it must be young Lord Bond and his wife.

"Oh, well. Let 'em all come," said Lord Stoke. Albert, whose generation did not know this old fragment of a song very popular in its day, looked for help to Mrs. Morland, who quietly said would he show them in, which he accordingly did and so swiftly that there was no time for anyone to wonder why they had come.

"Well, it's you again, is it, Lucasta?" said Lord Stoke, crossly and determinedly looking in another direction.

"Good gracious no, uncle, it's me, not your sister," said a very pleasant voice, at which his lordship turned and saw his nephew, the present Lord Bond, with his wife Daphne.

"I'm sorry, my dear," said Lord Stoke, rather ashamed of himself for having greeted so cavalierly a lady whom he liked and admired. "I knew you were coming, but I forgot. One does at my age."

Mrs. Morland, anxious to cover her old friend's gaffe, at once began to talk to Lady Bond, whom she had known off and on for a long time, though she still found it difficult to remember that she had now been married for some twenty years. Time is a very rum thing, as Shakespeare knew—ambling, trotting, galloping, and sometimes standing still; though why Shakespeare had to add "withal" to these interesting facts we cannot explain. Perhaps he could not explain either, but wrote whatever came into his head, from what spring of Helicon we shall never know. Others abide our question, he is free. But it took another poet to put that fact into real poetry. As for a good many later poets, the less free they are, the better.

"But of *course* one forgets when one gets older," said Daphne. "My mother forgets like anything sometimes."

"Now your mother is a sister of Middleton's," said Lord Stoke. "He's a bit of a windbag, but his wife is good stock. I've been meaning to go over and see them. Got to keep up with old friends, or they die without letting you know and then if you go to the house and ask if they are in you make a fool of yourself. First thing every morning I read the first column on the front of *The Times* to see who's dead and the obituaries inside. Must pay attention to old friends. I used to go to the funerals but it's too much for me now, standing about in the rain without a hat. Well, one funeral makes more for us old 'uns. When I see any of them at a funeral I say: 'Don't be a fool. Keep your hat on. Old Tom—or Bill—or whoever it was—won't mind. *He* wouldn't have wanted you to get your death of cold just because someone else is dead.' That's the way that lawyer fellow got killed—what was his name? Oh, Keith, Lady Merton's father. He went to the Memorial service for old Lord Pomfret at Barchester and then he went to his son's house and then to the Country Club, where he had left his car. You know what the lighting was like in those war years. He walked straight in front

of a car without his hat and a lorry hit him—not the driver's
fault—and that was that."

If Daphne Bond felt that her host was rather long-winded
and the conclusions he had drawn rather muddled ones, she gave
no sign of her feelings. Mrs. Morland had told her who Sylvia
was, under cover of Lord Stoke's peroration, and now Daphne
came over to talk to Sylvia. We do not think that they had
met before, but there was good-will on both sides and—what is
almost as important—good breeding, and they were at once well
away into matters of common interest mostly connected with the
county and having to live in a house that was too big for one.
Daphne said they had shut up the biggest rooms at Staple Park
for the present and made themselves very comfortable in the
less magnificent part of the house, near the kitchen, whose excellent boiler also warmed the nursery above.

"Of course the Vicarage isn't *really* a big house," said Sylvia. "I
mean not really big, but it was built about a hundred years ago
when all the clergy had large families and luckily it was a well-
paid job and the man who was there before Father had private
means—I do like that phrase—and put in some good work with
baths and things. How people got on without them I don't
know, but they did. Mrs. Morland was talking about it before
lunch. And there are some rooms on the top floor that we don't
much use."

"Well, talking of lunch," said Daphne Bond, "are we ever going to have it? Perhaps Albert has murdered the cook," but even
as she hopefully uttered these words Albert announced lunch
and they all went across the hall to the dining-room.

Here Mrs. Morland, who was a kind of hostess for Lord Stoke
on occasion, quickly arranged the guests so that Daphne Bond
should be next to Lord Stoke and Sylvia on his other side with
Lord Bond next to her. As they were a man short and it was all
very informal, Mrs. Morland was quite happy to be next to

Daphne, when Albert came in with a face of importance and bent over Lord Stoke, to tell him that Dr. Ford was in the house-keeper's room, to which his lordship's reaction was to ask why the devil he hadn't come in.

"Well, my lord, it was really Mrs. Beeton he came to see because her leg's bad again, my lord," said Albert. "But I thought your lordship would like to know."

"Quite right," said Lord Stoke. "Tell him to come up here. There's plenty to eat, isn't there?"

"Very good, my lord," said Albert, ignoring his employer's last remark. "I will tell Dr. Ford what your lordship said," and away he went, to return in a very few minutes with Dr. Ford, whom everyone was glad to see. Chairs were pushed a little nearer together and Albert swiftly brought the necessary knives and forks and spoons, glasses and napery to the table. There ought to be one word to describe this collection of aids to feeding, but we cannot think of it and quite possibly it does not exist.

"Help yourself to wine, Ford," said Lord Stoke, and we think it was just as well that Albert had gone out of the room to collect what was necessary for Dr. Ford's lunch, or he might have taken umbrage at his employer's free and easy ways. "How's Mrs. Beeton's leg?"

"Don't blame me if it mortifies," said Dr. Ford cheerfully. "She has done every single thing I told her not to and left undone everything I told her to do."

"Well, you'd better tell me what she ought to do and I'll speak to her," said Lord Stoke.

"If you do that, she'll give notice," said Mrs. Morland. "She has a sister at Eastbourne who is always asking her to go and live with her."

"That is quite correct, my lord," said Albert who had come back and was hovering with dishes, the better to take part in whatever was going on.

"I've done all my first aid, and what's more, I've kept up with the Red Cross classes," said Sylvia. "Do you think I could help, Dr. Ford?"

At these words all were as silent as the beginning of the second book of the Aeneid. Then did Lord Stoke speak, from his seat of honour.

"That is very kind of you, Miss Gould," he said. "Very kind indeed. But you must finish your lunch. Tell Mrs. Beeton, Albert, that she is not to *touch* that leg and Miss Gould will come down after lunch with Dr. Ford."

Albert said: "Very good, my lord," and went away.

"Why is it," said Mrs. Morland, "that elderly women have legs but men don't?"

This question required some consideration owing to the vagueness of the wording, though everyone knew what she meant.

"I expect it's because no one knows about legs," said young Lady Bond. "If they did there wouldn't be so many. I don't mean like centipedes, but if doctors knew *anything*, they would do something about it. Oh—sorry, Dr. Ford."

But that hardened elderly practitioner had not taken her words amiss.

"I think," said Dr. Ford, considering his words slowly and carefully, "that there will always be some things, very simple things, that will not be known to us. By us I mean the body of surgeons and physicians. Very few of us have the magic."

"What *do* you mean, Dr. Ford?" said young Lady Bond. "There isn't any magic now—is there?"

"Lots and lots," said Dr. Ford. "It isn't called magic now. It's called psycho-therapy or names like that. But it's not for everyone."

Mrs. Morland asked who it *was* for then.

"For people who believe in it before they know anything about it," said Dr. Ford. "It's a rum thing, but belief still works miracles—small miracles."

"But not for us," said Mrs. Morland. "I can *believe* that I'm getting better every day in every way but I *know* that I'm not."

Everyone then began to speak at once, but luckily Albert came in with the last course, which was one of Mrs. Beeton's famed apple pies, which no lower servant was ever allowed to see her make lest the virtue should go from her. And as there was real cream from Lord Stoke's own cows and then real oatcake from Scotch friends with real butter (again from the estate cows) and some extremely good cheese of the hard and the soft variety, everyone felt comfortably replete.

Albert then came to Lord Stoke's side and asked whether his lordship would have coffee at the table or in the drawing-room, but before he could answer Mrs. Morland said in the drawing-room for the ladies, because the gentlemen would be much happier alone.

Albert looked to his employer for guidance.

"All right, all right," said Lord Stoke. "Can't you hear what Mrs. Morland says?" and he rose from his chair, as did the other men. Mrs. Morland then shepherded her ladies to the drawing-room, leaving the men to their own society. What they talked about we do not know, nor do we much care, but we are sure that Lord Stoke in Peacockian vein caused the bottle to be buzzed, while the latest news of Lord Aberfordbury, formerly known as Sir Ogilvy Hibberd, were eagerly and unkindly discussed, Dr. Ford going so far as to hint, *sub rosa,* that he had been asked to resign from The Club. We must explain to those who are not well acquainted with Barchester that The Club to Barcastrians was the best club in the city and therefore in the world and considered itself to be almost on a level with Dr. Johnson's Literary Club, if not having taken its place.

"If you don't mind," said Sylvia when the ladies were comfortably by themselves, "I'll go and have a look at that leg now. Not my business, of course, but as Dr. Ford said I could come with him, I'd like to go. And perhaps Mrs. Beeton will tell me what's really the matter."

This seemed quite reasonable to Mrs. Morland and Lady Bond, so Sylvia went away.

"Well, it is a very long time since we met," said Mrs. Morland to Lady Bond. "Was it at the Barsetshire Agricultural a few years ago?"

But Lady Bond couldn't remember either, though she was delighted to meet the well-known authoress again.

"I know where we met," said Mrs. Morland. "It has all come back to me suddenly. There was some kind of fête at Laverings and Mr. and Mrs. Middleton asked everyone to come in for tea or a drink and you were there, but you were Daphne Stonor then. And wait a moment—your father was a soldier, wasn't he, and your mother died in India leaving two children and then he married again so you were steps and then *he* died. All very confusing."

"But you've got it all right," said Lady Bond. "And sometimes I wonder why on earth I'm Lady Bond, except that I did love Cedric so much that I simply couldn't help marrying him. And our stepmother was most awfully kind and then she married a very nice man, Alistair Cameron, and they live in one of the inns."

Mrs. Morland said it sounded rather uncomfortable.

"Oh, not *that* sort of inn," said Lady Bond. "I mean the sort of inns where lawyers live, only a nice new one with an electric lift, and they are awfully happy."

"So everything is all right," said Mrs. Morland sympathetically. "I was married once, years and years ago, and I was quite happy and my husband died and I had quite enough to do with four boys on my hands. But thank goodness they all got married too."

"Then you are alone," said Lady Bond.

"Well, yes, if you can call it alone," said Mrs. Morland. "I mean it is almost impossible to be alone if you live in the country. Not that High Rising is exactly country, but when I first went there it almost was. Then it began to creep outwards and now it's a sort of town. But one knows most of the people. Do you know the George Knoxes, Lady Bond?"

"Do you mean THE George Knox?" said Lady Bond. "And I wish you'd call me Daphne if you don't mind, because two Lady Bonds does make rather a confusion sometimes."

Mrs. Morland said she would be delighted to call her Daphne, but did not add—as some older people are embarrassingly apt to do—that Lady Bond must call her Laura; not, we think, that Lady Bond would have been likely to do so. The question of Christian-naming for the first time can be a little awkward, especially to the older generation. As for the younger generation, a good many do call their elders and betters, and even mothers-in-law, by their given name (as our transatlantic cousins so prettily put it), while some, with equal affection, go on saying Mrs. Potts, or Mrs. Chips—which names we use as useful labels in memory of the names in Happy Families, that delightful game of our childhood. But young Lady Bond had been properly brought up and had no intention at all of using Mrs. Morland's Christian name unless pressed to, while Mrs. Morland had not the least intention of pressing her; so everything was very comfortable. And if one comes to think of it there are far more surnames than Christian names, as may be seen in the weighty tomes of the *Post Office Telephone Directory,* so it is easier to distinguish one's friends and acquaintances by their surnames.

While we are on this subject, we should like to pay tribute to those telephone encyclopaedias and the amount of information that can be gleaned from them, including the interesting and inexplicable fact that the B's have far more pages than any other letter of the alphabet—about three hundred, to be exact. We find the same preponderance of B's in our own address book.

Whether B also dominates the French or German tongues we have not bothered to enquire, but think it doesn't. If anyone can explain this, we shall be glad to hear the explanation.

Continuing their conversation, Mrs. Morland said that if Lady Bond would come to tea with her one day, she would get George Knox and his wife to come too, which appeared to give Lady Bond considerable pleasure, as she had not seen the Knoxes for some time.

"But I must warn you," said Mrs. Morland, "that he is still a quite indefatigable talker."

"Oh, that's all right," said Lady Bond, "because then I needn't talk myself. It's rather awful when you meet someone rather well known and you don't know what to say."

Mrs. Morland said that from her experience of people in general they mostly knew exactly what to say—or at least what they meant to say—and jolly well said it, and the great thing was to pretend you were listening.

"I suppose," said Lady Bond, "Miss Gould is good at that sort of thing. She looks awfully competent. I don't mean that nastily —I mean——"

"I know exactly what you mean," said Mrs. Morland. "She *is* competent. I don't know anyone who could deal with crises better. She has her parents under complete control and as far as I can make out—one does hear things, you know—she is practically top dog at Pomfret Towers, or will be; though what she does I haven't the faintest idea. There is something about the clergy that seems to make their children very competent."

"But aren't yours competent, Mrs. Morland?" said Lady Bond. "I thought I was the only person that couldn't really manage my family."

"I never thought about it," said Mrs. Morland. "All my four boys are married and their wives seem to do the managing extremely well and let me see the grandchildren as little as I like."

"As little . . . ?" said Lady Bond.

"Well, when you come to my age," said Mrs. Morland, "you adore your darling grandchildren, but they *can* be such bores, bless them. Of course as babies they are divine and can be *most* engaging for some years and then gradually they get ordinary. But I daresay it's because I am ordinary myself."

"Of *course* you aren't," said Lady Bond. "You are a very UN-ordinary person. I wish *I* could write novels."

"I believe," said Mrs. Morland, moving into her rather sibyllic vein, "that you could."

"But *why?*" said Lady Bond. "I mean it's most awfully kind of you to say that, but I know I couldn't. I wouldn't know what to write about, or how to write it."

"Well, you have to *start* some time," said Mrs. Morland. "It really doesn't much matter what you say—people will read *any-thing*. And do it your own way. Don't ask for advice; you'll get far too much. Writing's a JOB, like other jobs. And if you find you have written something that quite a lot of people like, it is a good thing to go on writing like that. The average subscriber to a circulating library mostly doesn't know what she wants—it's a very feminine affair. And if she has liked a book she will like to read another one by the same person, so long as it is like the book that she liked before."

Lady Bond said she would try to remember.

"Of course," said Mrs. Morland, "if you are really a great writer you don't need to think about that. Take Dickens. He wrote I don't know how many books—about fourteen or fifteen really good ones I think and a lot that were good but not his best. And every single one of them is different. And you don't meet the same people again in any other book—at least I don't think so. Of course Trollope *did* make people turn up in one book after another but then he was Trollope. So was Thack-eray."

"I don't quite understand," said Lady Bond. "I mean, do you

mean Trollope and Thackeray were really one person—like Currer Bell and Charlotte Brontë?"

"Not in the least," said Mrs. Morland. "I mean each of them brought the people from one book into other books. So no one can blame me if I do too. But I am not fit to loose the latches of their shoes—I mean Dickens and Thackeray. Of course there is Sir Walter, but he stands alone. I don't think anyone stands alone now though lots of people stick out for a bit."

"But, Mrs. Morland—" said Lady Bond, "what about *you?*"

"I haven't the faintest idea," said Mrs. Morland. "I mean I *had* to do something when my husband died—not but what I had to do a good deal *before* he died, but really I never think about him now. Some people die and you go on saying: 'I wish old So-and-So were here,' and other people just vanish and you forget them."

There was a short silence, during which we think that each of the ladies was reflecting upon friends who had vanished and were lost as it were—*spurlos versenkt*—and also upon the friends who still seemed to be hovering somewhere about, though no longer of this world.

"I don't want to be a bore," said Lady Bond, "but could you explain *why* people write books. I mean, I can't see how they find time, or enough things to write about. I suppose I ought to know but I don't."

"Nor does anyone else," said Mrs. Morland. "Of course you get those strange geniuses who are born as novelists—at least one can't account for it in any other way. People like the Brontës for instance who weren't well off and never went anywhere or met anyone and had a *most* trying and exhausting father and no mother. I don't mean like whoever it was in Greece whose real father was Zeus and her mother was either someone called Dione or else the sea-foam, I mean their mother died and really one can't blame her—Mrs. Brontë, I mean."

At this point she stopped talking and wondered—as she not infrequently did—what on earth she had been saying, and why; and whether what she had said meant anything at all. But Lady Bond appeared to be quite satisfied.

"Would you care to come to Staple Park one day, Mrs. Morland?" she said. "It isn't so awful as it was when C.W.'s father was alive. Cedric and I don't use that huge hall now. It had more draughts than any house in Barsetshire."

Mrs. Morland said Pomfret Towers must run it pretty close in the matter of draughts. Lady Bond said, with justifiable pride, that Pomfret Towers did have some windows in the big hall, but the Inner Hall at Staple Park had no light at all except from a lantern in the roof and whatever light could get through the great glass doors. "But we made it very comfortable for ourselves," said Lady Bond. "I do hope you will come and see us some day. My brother may be over from New York this year and it's the only time that the piano gets properly played."

Mrs. Morland said she would love to come over at any time that suited Lady Bond, and she remembered her brother Denis Stonor quite well and where was he now.

"Well, one hardly ever knows," said Lady Bond, "because he is always rushing between England and America about his music. He was in New York most of last year and luckily C.W. had to go there on business and I went too, and we heard Denis's newest music."

Mrs. Morland asked if that was the musical play that was coming to London in the autumn. Lady Bond said if it was *Starfall at Night*, that was the one.

"I'm afraid," she went on, "that it will be almost impossible to get tickets. That's what happens with all the plays with his music. The one that's running at the Cockspur now, with Aubrey Clover and Jessica Dean, is absolutely packed. Of course," she added, "he always sends tickets to us—a kind of permanent pass to the theatre and one box is *always* reserved for me, so per-haps you would come too. It holds four easily and if necessary four other people can sit just behind. Of course they don't see so well but they can boast to all their friends about it. But if you would come I would tell the manager to keep your date *very* specially."

Mrs. Morland was touched by this kind offer and said there was nothing she would like better.

"The box is right in the middle of the theatre," said Lady Bond. "I don't mean in the *middle* of course, but if you remem-ber the Cockspur Theatre it is rather like a French one with a lot of stalls that slope up towards the back and the boxes are a kind of semi-circle behind the stalls, so that you can see every-thing and nobody's head or shoulders gets in your way. And if you are bored, all you have to do is to go and sit at the back where there is a kind of small bar. That was Denis's idea."

Mrs. Morland expressed her gratitude for the offer and said she would love to come, only she had given up her little flat in Lon-don quite some time ago.

"But look here, Mrs. Morland," said Lady Bond. "We usually drive up to town for Denis's plays, so we'll pick you up and go straight to the theatre. Denis always has a kind of private repast served to us at the back of the box and then we drive home and we'll take you straight to High Rising. Unless you would come back to Staple Park with us for late supper and see some of the alterations."

But Mrs. Morland said much as she would like that, she did feel rather old and would rather be taken straight home if that wasn't a nuisance. To this Lady Bond was quite agreeable. With their new Lenz-Goblin car, she said, one really didn't notice the distance and it was *such* a bore to go back by train with a good chance of missing it and having to go to an hotel. She had a room more or less permanently reserved for her husband and herself at that new hotel near the Cockspur Theatre and this she sometimes lent to friends; but for herself she much preferred to get back to her own home and her own bed.

"So do I," said Mrs. Morland fervently, "and I am most grateful to you for making that plan. It's all very well to go to an hotel or one's aunt's house for the night, after a play, but it is so AWFUL to have all the bother of a small suitcase which is always too heavy and never has everything you want in it however carefully you pack it and having a nasty breakfast and the morning trains to Skeynes are so bad."

Lady Bond said that her husband and Mr. Middleton at Laverings were always trying to get the railway service improved, but with very little success.

"Still," she went on, "it's a kind of protection for us. If we had a good through service the whole country round here would burst into bungaloid growths. It's getting bad enough as it is and so I tell C.W. and he isn't going to sell any more land. I think he is beginning to see reason and will come to heel. Things don't get easier as one gets older," and she looked away towards the window. "The children will have to marry Money, though really I don't know how that is done. We have talked about it a good deal, but we don't get anywhere. If there were another war the Government would take over a lot of the house, as they did in the last war, and pay us well for it. But I don't see much chance of it now," and she fell silent, looking at the ruins of the old castle.

Mrs. Morland said the first well-meant words of comfort that came into her head, but without conviction.

"Thanks awfully," said Lady Bond. "I know I oughtn't to go on like this, but I do. And then I worry about the children, which is so silly, because there's a kind of Trust for them, so that they'll be more likely to marry the right people."

Mrs. Morland asked what on earth she meant.

"Well," said Lady Bond, "sometime or other our boy will

come into this property and with the trust money he will be able to live here—if he wants to, that is, and if his wife—if he marries—wants to. But I hope it won't be for a long time. I wish my brother Denis had married and had children—or at any rate a son to carry on. But he didn't and hadn't, so there we are. I wonder where on earth everyone has got to—the men I mean."

Mrs. Morland said she didn't think they had got anywhere and were still talking about things they didn't really understand in the dining-room.

"What kind of things?" said Lady Bond.

"Oh, whatever men *do* talk about when they are by themselves," said Mrs. Morland. "I don't see much of men except my boys."

"But," said Lady Bond, who had a very accurate mind, "boys aren't exactly *men*. Oh, I see what you mean—you mean your grown-up boys. One does get so addled with TIME."

"Time flies; you cannot," said Mrs. Morland, falling into what Adrian Coates called her sibyllic vein.

Lady Bond said she didn't quite understand.

"It's just a silly thing the boys brought from school, years ago," said Mrs. Morland. " 'Times flies; you cannot. They go too fast.' "

Lady Bond said she didn't quite understand; who was the they.

"Well, it's the sort of joke that seems very funny to schoolboys," said Mrs. Morland, "but really isn't. What it really means is: You cannot time flies—I mean time the time they take to get from one place to another—they go too fast."

"Oh, now I understand," said Lady Bond. "Like 'Which would you rather? Be a greater fool than you look, or look a greater fool than you are?' Denis and I used to giggle about it like anything. We still have giggles together and I suppose we always shall; unless, of course, he got married."

"But why?" said Mrs. Morland. *"You* got married and you still have giggles with Denis."

"Because C.W. understands," said Lady Bond. "And he likes to see us giggling and often nearly giggles himself. But I can't see Denis marrying anyone, ever. Heaps of girls—and women—have been in love with him, and he is charming to them all, but he doesn't care."

"Aren't artists often like that?" said Mrs. Morland. "I mean every kind of artist—not only the painting ones. I don't know why they are called artists and the other kind of artists usually get called arteests. English is *so* peculiar."

Lady Bond asked how, which seemed reasonable.

"Well, I don't exactly know what I meant," said Mrs. Morland, "which is a thing that often happens to me. It is extraordinary how one does think of something and just when you are going to say it, it suddenly fades—like the Cheshire cat's smile—and you are stuck."

"But," said Lady Bond, "I thought that Authors were—I mean——" and at this point she went off the air, as it were, and became dumb.

"There isn't really a set of people called Authors," said Mrs. Morland kindly. "Anyone can write a book if they can."

"But I thought one had to be sort of really brainy," said Lady Bond.

"Some intelligence is of course needed," said Mrs. Morland in a rather lecturing voice. "It isn't a bad plan to have a plot, but I can't make plots."

"But you *must,* Mrs. Morland," said Lady Bond.

"I may must, but I just can't," said Mrs. Morland.

"But how *do* you write a book, then?" said Lady Bond.

"It's quite simple," said Mrs. Morland. "There comes an Awful Moment when you *must* write another book."

"Couldn't you wait a bit—I mean have a holiday?" said Lady Bond.

"Not too long," said Mrs. Morland. "You see, people like to have another nice book like the last one and it's a help if you can get it published at about the same time every year. I shall go on writing another nice book like the last one till I die, I expect," she added cheerfully.

"I did meet an Author once," said Lady Bond. "I mean an Author that showed off about being an author. She kept on saying how many copies of her book were sold. She was some kind of relation of the Pomfrets and her books were all about women that weren't quite young and had got rather tired of their husbands and sort of had a lover, but they always thought better of it and their husbands were always quite pleased to see them come back."

"Oh, Mrs. Rivers," said Mrs. Morland. "Dreadful woman. She married a cousin of the Pomfrets which made her an Honourable and she's never got over it. Her husband was—and probably still is—living down in the Shires somewhere, but she doesn't and it seems to suit them both."

By the time both ladies had unpacked their bundles of county history, Sylvia Gould came to join them, full of Lord Stoke's cook's leg, which appeared to have given her great satisfaction.

"It'll have to be opened and properly treated," she said, "but she ought to be all right. Dr. Ford rang up the Barchester General and they're going to send an ambulance as soon as possible. Of course she began to cry, but I said she had better pack a suitcase—nightgowns and a few things—and I'd help her to do it. She had an awfully nice bedroom."

Both her hearers were temporarily silent. Each of them would willingly have helped as Sylvia had helped, but neither would have known exactly what to do; nor would it have occurred to them to inspect the cook's bedroom under pretext of helping her to pack.

"I've got a ghastly bed jacket," Sylvia went on, "that an old school friend I hadn't seen for ages sent me and I'll get someone to take it to the hospital—someone's always going to Barchester. It's a kind of mauve with some cheap lace and some awful art embroidery. I know the nurses will be impressed by it and I'll tell her she can keep it."

The men now joined the ladies, which was very agreeable because they could all talk about the cook's leg, which they did with such good-will that they were still talking when Albert came to say the amberlance was there and was he to show them in, which mixture of singular and plural rather perplexed such of the party as heard him, but Dr. Ford hustled him out of the room and went to collect the ambulancers—if there is such a word—who went quietly upstairs with their stretcher.

The party then said it must be getting home, though what they really meant was that they would like to be in the hall or the drive at the moment when the procession descended, and see Something being gently delivered into the ambulance. Then down the steps into the courtyard the ambulance people came and put their burden down for a moment to make some adjustment. One of the men was seen to lean over the patient and then went up to Lord Stoke, while the others gently slid the patient into the ambulance.

"Excuse me, my lord," said the attendant, "but the lady would like to have just a word with you," upon which Lord Stoke at once went down the steps and climbed into the ambulance, where his cook was lying, with warm blankets round her, ready for the journey.

"Sorry about this, cook," said Lord Stoke, "but you're in good hands. I'll come and see you as soon as the doctors let me."

"It's very good of your lordship," said the cook, who was sinking deeper into the quieting drug that had been given to her. "Here's the key of the store-cupboard," and she handed to him a large key with a label saying "Stores" on it. "And don't you let no one have it, your lordship. And there's another one under the mattress in my bedroom. I've locked the bedroom door and here's the key."

Lord Stoke, slightly embarrassed but always a father—even if rather a deaf one—to his staff, took the keys and promised to get the other key and keep them all safe till she came back. The ambulance men shut the door, the ambulance moved quietly down the drive, and Dr. Ford said good-bye and drove away.

"Here, don't *you* go yet," said his lordship to Mrs. Morland. "Come and have some tea—always does ladies good. You too, young lady; and you'll come, Daphne, won't you? Tea in the morning-room, Albert, as soon as you can."

So to the morning-room they all went and soothed themselves with very good hot tea.

"Well, Daphne, it's been a queer affair," said Lord Stoke. "Glad to have you here, though. Give your mother-in-law my love and tell her not to come over just yet as I haven't a cook. Tell her I don't know when I'll have one again. If you and C.W. want to come over, you come; any time."

"Thanks awfully, Uncle Stoke," said Daphne, who had after her marriage adopted him by this name. And then she and her husband went away, leaving Mrs. Morland and Sylvia.

"Well, did you enjoy yourself?" said his lordship as these last guests said good-bye.

"*Rather*," said Sylvia. "I say, Lord Stoke, I'll go and see your cook in hospital if she'd like it and take her some pink and blue ribbons for her hair. That always cheers them up."

Lord Stoke thanked her. Mrs. Morland and Sylvia drove away and he waved his hand to them from the doorstep.

"Sensible woman that," he said aloud to himself. "Woman like that wouldn't stand any nonsense from Lucasta. Well, well," and he went back into his house. Albert shut the front door and went back to his quarters, where the guests were discussed with great freedom, Sylvia being declared the pick of them and *hors concours*.

"Now a lady like that would liven his lordship up a bit," said
the head housemaid. "Proper brought up at the Vicarage. My
auntie's granddaughter goes there to oblige and she says Miss
Gould is a reel lady. We'll be seeing her here again, I dessay.
Anyone want another cuppa?"

As she had refilled the teapot with boiling water, everyone
had another cup.

CHAPTER 5

YOUNG Lady Bond, who was not one to forget a promise, nor to let the grass grow under her feet, at once rang up the Cockspur Theatre and secured her box for the following Saturday. She then rang up Mrs. Morland, who was delighted to accept and took it upon herself to pass on the invitation to Sylvia Gould; to which end she rang up the Vicarage. There was no answer, which meant that everyone was out and the staff probably turning a deaf ear, though as neither of them had ever succeeded in taking a message correctly it did not much matter. So she rang up the Pomfret Towers office at the time when she knew that the clerical staff were available, owing to elevenses, and was put through to Miss Gould by the nice girl at the switchboard, though not before she had paid the usual Danegeld in pretending to be interested in what the nice girl wanted to tell her about the film that was coming to the Barchester Odeon next week all about the love life of Anne Hathaway.

Then Sylvia was on the line and at once recognised Mrs. Morland's voice and greeted her by name.

"It *is* nice of you to remember voices," said Mrs. Morland. "I never can, even if it's people I've known for ever so long, and it sometimes offends them. I wonder why some people enjoy taking offence, especially when none is meant. If I *wanted* to offend people I would do it properly."

Sylvia's voice asked how she would do it properly.

"Well, I haven't really thought about it yet," said Mrs. Morland, "but I would try to do it on the grand scale. I mean I would simply shrug my shoulders, or shut my eyes, or look up till only the whites of them showed. Or perhaps say something in French or German."

"I wish my French and German were good enough for that," said Sylvia with a kind of admiring envy. "How *did* you learn them?"

"At school, of course," said Mrs. Morland. "What is school for? If we didn't pay attention to Mademoiselle Hamonet and Fräulein Kessler we were for it."

"Do you mean they *beat* you?" said Sylvia.

"Indeed not!" said Mrs. Morland indignantly. "They simply Petrified us. And the awful thing was that they hated each other. I suppose it was the Franco-Prussian war. If there had been any beating it would have been one of them beating the other. There was an Awful time when I was to act in a little French play at Breaking-up and Mademoiselle Hamonet said she must have me for some coaching and it was the same time as the German lesson and Fräulein Kessler turned quite white and went right off the deep end and I was terrified and then the headmistress came in and settled it."

Sylvia said How did she settle it.

"Well, when I was a girl—and that is a long time ago now—" said Mrs. Morland, "Headmistresses *were* Headmistresses."

Sylvia asked How exactly.

"Well, they were educated women who took up headmistressing because they liked it," said Mrs. Morland, "not university females who looked on headmistressing as a career. And there was no nonsense about uniforms; we all wore the frocks we wore at home—it was a day school in London—and most of us had two or three necklaces of beads. And the headmistress was rather fat and comfortable and we all liked her. But we respected her too, because if one of us had been particularly naughty she was sent for to the Headmistress's Room."

"Did she tell you off awfully?" said Sylvia.

"Not a bit," said Mrs. Morland. "She didn't say much, but she made one feel awfully small. And one never did whatever it was again."

"It sounds rather dull," said Sylvia.

"Not to us in the lower school," said Mrs. Morland. "The lessons weren't very long and in the middle of the morning our form-mistress marched us out into the corridor and we all went downstairs—three big flights of rather winding stone stairs—to the semi-basement where the kitchen lived and there was a hatch between the kitchen and the dining-room and we could buy a bun or a cake or two biscuits for a penny and get a glass of milk if we wanted it. And then we went out to the play-ground for ten minutes called Break."

"Did you play tennis?" said Sylvia.

"Well, some of the older girls did, but it was asphalt and the net mostly sagged in the middle and I could never hit a ball anyway, so we used to play at Princesses and Robbers."

"Not hockey, or tennis?" said Sylvia, rather shocked.

"Well, you can't play hockey on an asphalt ground very well, because it isn't big enough and it's bad for the hockey sticks and anyway it was marked with lines for tennis, but only the big girls played tennis and they couldn't get much of a game because the posts *would* lean over and the net was rather torn. But the morning interval was only a quarter of an hour including the milk and biscuits so it wasn't much use trying."

"*Do* tell me some more," said Sylvia. "All about your uniform and what the gym was like. Oh brother! The office telephone wants me. Could you hold on for a minute?" so Mrs. Morland held on and before long Sylvia's voice returned.

"It was only Amalgamated Vedge," said the voice. "We do a lot of business with them. It's rather a family affair."

Mrs. Morland asked how.

"Well, Mrs. Adams knows as much about vegetables as anyone in East Barsetshire," said Sylvia, "so Mr. Adams has pretty well handed that side over to her. I wish I knew only a quarter as much as she does."

"If you had been her you would," said Mrs. Morland and felt it might have been better put. "Oh, but I forgot why I rang you up. Lady Bond has got the tickets for next Saturday. We are going by train because there is such a jam of cars in London that you can't get into a parking area and even if you do, you can't get out. I'll fetch you and we'll meet her at Skeynes."

Sylvia expressed her thanks and Mrs. Morland put the receiver back.

"Nice girl," she said aloud to herself, at which moment Mrs. George Knox came in by the french window.

"Me?" she said.

"Certainly not," said Mrs. Morland. "Nice, but no girl. It was the Gould girl I was talking to—Sylvia. Not exactly a girl now either and her younger sisters are well into their thirties. But all women are girls now if they don't get married. I don't know why Sylvia hasn't married. She ought to have."

"I expect," said Mrs. Knox, "she doesn't particularly want to and no one has asked her. Rather like me, years ago."

"Nonsense, Anne," said Mrs. Morland. "George asked you to marry him and you did and well do I remember the evening with that dreadful woman Miss Grey creating all over my sitting-room and you as good as fainting in George's arms till I had to give you my emergency brandy and George carried you upstairs so that Stoker and I could get you to bed and Dr. Ford told George he would put arsenic in his toothpaste if he wasn't kind to you," which made Mrs. Knox laugh, and she said it was very kind of Dr. Ford to think of it, and then their talk went back comfortably to old times.

Saturday came, as it always does and so does every other day in its season—rather like the Defendant's song in *Trial by Jury*.

The weather was neither nice nor nasty, which it almost always is in our beloved country. As in "Ye Mariners of England" about "Britannia needs no bulwarks, No towers along the steep, Her march is o'er the mountain waves, Her home is on the deep." But we could often wish that her home were warmer and more cosy. Perhaps it was then. One remembers the summers of one's childhood as always warm. As a little girl at the turn of the century we remember being let loose in the holidays, when our parents took a house somewhere in Sussex, and we were allowed to wear just a pair of frilly drawers and a pinafore, and how blissful it was; for summers were really hot then. Barefoot always, whether in a valley with a streamlet, or on the Sussex downs where even the bravest feet could not always deal with those very flat thistles. *Écho du temps passé.* Bare feet for the young are heaven, but there comes a day when one looks down with horror, realising that one has Grown-up Feet. Then never again. Our generation will remember the dancer Isadora Duncan and her feet, unshod, untrammelled, and how one could see them grip the floor of the stage as she moved; almost pulling her along as a snake pulls itself. And they may also remember Trilby with her big loose shoes and how Little Billee drew an outline of her foot on the wall of the studio with a few perfect strokes. We are never quite sure if we believe in Little Billee, but if we began to discourse on this subject, this book would never get finished, thus bringing my publisher, his staff, and myself to toil, envy, want, the patron and the jail, as Dr. Johnson so well put it.

According to her word Mrs. Morland picked Sylvia up at the Vicarage and drove to Skeynes station, where they found Lady Bond; also her husband, who had no wish to come to Town himself but liked to drive his wife to the station and announced his intention of also coming to fetch her at her return, which pleased them both, for they were very fond of each other and were too often separated by their various county commitments. But the same can be said of the Pomfrets, the Mertons, and many other good citizens all over the county.

The London train puffed its way in. The engine, according to its usual custom, halted before coming into the station in order to refresh itself from a tank on four legs which supplied water to it through a leather hosepipe. The evening was warm. The little flower beds, beloved property of the stationmaster, who regularly whitewashed the stones surrounding them—chosen by him in his off-time and regularly watered by his own august hand—were crammed with flowers. When the engine had finished drinking, it gently puffed up to the platform and drew up in front of one of those advertisements, much valued by connoisseurs for its rarity in these degenerate days, enamelled on tin with a fine original example of the distich about the Pickwick, Owl, and Waverley pens. The party got in and the train puffed away towards Winter Overcotes, where they had to change for London.

As all lovers of Barsetshire know, Winter Overcotes is a junction with a high and a low level. Local travellers now change there for the London train, for gone are the days when one Up and one Down train would make a kind of circuit, or loop, so enabling passengers to go to London or return from it without changing. But the two trains are on very good terms and one will always wait for the other if necessary. There have been from time to time agitations or pogroms about reshaping the line, but as no one has put forward a really good scheme for it, nor does anyone want to have to contribute to the enormous sum of money it would cost, things stay much as they are; and the female porters Marlene Phipps and Sabrina Pollett, two very nice girls in dirty off-white sateen blouses, tight-seated bell-bottomed trousers, with a cigarette ever glued to their lips, are most kind and helpful and always find time to talk to the local passengers, from Lady Pomfret to Mrs. Pucken, who was always willing to come in and oblige and whose own family was probably far older than most of the local aristocracy, for they were Wambers, far-off descendants of Wamba the Witless, and just as easy-going as was the jester of Cedric the Saxon. At least all the antiquarians of the county had agreed that it was so. As for the Wamber family, they neither knew nor cared who their ancestors were, though always willing to oblige by telling any lie that they thought would please the gentry; unlike Edie Ochiltree, who so rudely disillusioned the Antiquary.

At Winter Overcotes they went up the stairs to the high-level platform, had the conversation with the stationmaster which was always expected of them, got the London train and so to Waterloo, where they were lucky in getting a taxi that skilfully took them by devious ways to the stage door of the Cockspur Theatre.

"My taxi," said Lady Bond, paying the man with a lavishness that impressed Sylvia. "Is Miss Dean in her dressing-room?" she said to the doorkeeper. "She's expecting me. Lady Bond and party."

"That's all right, my lady," said the man. "You've plenty of time. Miss Dean said to show you into her dressing-room. This way please," and he led them through a passage to a door behind which a good deal of noise including a piano could be heard. He knocked on it. From the inside came the famous voice of Jessica Dean mingling with other voices. The door was opened by a tall thin man whose large dark eyes were ringed with marks of suffering.

"Denis!" shrieked Lady Bond. "I thought you were in New York. Here's Mrs. Morland and this is Sylvia Gould. Mrs. Morland, you remember my brother Denis, don't you, when he was here years ago. Darling, *why* didn't I know you were here?"

"Because I wasn't," said Denis. "I only flew over today, be-

cause I wanted to see Jessica. Jessica darling, allow me to present
to you my sister Daphne Bond. Mrs. Morland I am sure you
know."

"Dear Mrs. Morland, of course I do," said Jessica. "How lovely
to see you again." And turning to Daphne, she added: "You
were Daphne Stonor, weren't you?" unblushingly drawing out
the *vox humana* stop from her own personal organ. "Denis has
so often told me about you."

"Enough to put anyone off for good," said Lady Bond.

"Well, it nearly did," said Jessica, at the same time favouring
her audience with the famous wink which, in the role of Mrs.
Carvel, had filled the Cockspur Theatre for more months than
we can remember. "But of course when he said you were his
sister, I *knew* I should adore you. Of course you aren't a *bit* like
him, which is perhaps just as well, but there is a *something* . . ."
and she assumed an expression of someone seeking the perfect
word—the *mot juste*.

"But of course what I am *longing* to hear," said Jessica, moving
quickly to the next scene, "is what Madame Koska is doing
now, Mrs. Morland. Your people are so *real*. You simply *must*
write a play for me and Aubrey. Where is Aubrey?"

Everyone looked vaguely round the rather crowded dressing-
room. With perfect timing Aubrey Clover opened the door, stood
in it for a moment, and walked in.

"Here!" he said, "and at your service, my good masters," which
made the company have the giggles; at least the ladies had them,
but as men are not as a rule gigglers, they contributed some
gentlemanly guffaws.

"I ought," said Aubrey Clover, quite unmoved by his success,
"to have said 'good, my masters,' but let that pass."

Then Sylvia was made known to Denis and the stars, and
after a few minutes of general conversation there was a knock
on the door, which was slightly pushed open. A Voice Off said
Ten Minutes Please and shut the door.

"I didn't know people *really* said that," said Mrs. Morland. "Come on, Sylvia—are you coming too, Daphne?" and she stood by the half-open door waiting.

"She is," said her brother, giving her a gentle push. The Voice Off was waiting for them and escorted them to their box, which was directly opposite the stage.

"It's more like a French theatre than an English one," said Lady Bond. "Enough seats in front and a nice background to retreat to if one wants to flirt. I wish Cedric could have come, because he hasn't flirted for ages and he is *so* good at it so long as he has the right setting," which made her hearers laugh, as indeed she had intended as she was extremely fond of her husband. Then the three ladies settled themselves in the very comfortable chairs. On the red velvet edge of the box lay three programmes, each with a gold border and printed in gold.

"Oh, look!" said Sylvia.

"I expect that was Denis," said Lady Bond. "He does like to do the right thing; and how well he does it. When I remember what a Misery he used to be! It was our stepmother who kept him alive, I think."

"You know Sylvia is not very well up in your part of the county," said Mrs. Morland.

"Oh, sorry," said Lady Bond. "It's so difficult to explain things when you know them and the other person doesn't."

"Well, do try," said Mrs. Morland. "We've got a few minutes before the play begins."

"You see, our stepmother Lilian, who is a darling," said Lady Bond to Sylvia, "is Mr. Middleton's sister—you know, the architect who lives at Laverings. Our father had been married before and Denis and I were the results. Then our mother died and later he married Lilian, who luckily had some money of her own and then *he* died and she was an angel to us. Ask Denis."

Sylvia said she would, but she didn't know when, because if Denis was acting (which we know he wasn't, only visiting), he would be too busy to talk and she felt rather shy of actors because she never knew if they liked to be talked to or not.

"Of course they do," said Lady Bond. "After all, talking is their trade and they need someone to talk with. I mean on the stage they always have someone to talk to or there wouldn't be a play at all and people don't have long soliloquies now, like Shakespeare."

"But *I* do," said Mrs. Morland. "I quite often talk to myself when I'm alone, because if you live alone you must talk to someone or you might forget how to talk. Of course, one *could* do soliloquies but I don't think reciting 'To be or not to be' would really help one. I say things like 'Oh, my goodness! if you haven't forgotten to post those letters, and you'd better hurry or you'll miss the last collection' aloud to myself; but that isn't a soliloquy."

"Well, if it isn't, I don't know what it is," said Lady Bond. "Oh! look!" and she pointed towards the curtain. "Denis always does that when I'm here. Can you see a kind of wiggling—just over where the 'cello is sitting?"

Mrs. Morland couldn't, but to save trouble said she did.

"It's Denis's own hole that he always looks through if I'm here," said Lady Bond. "And then if I am he tells them they can begin the play," which impressed Mrs. Morland a good deal.

"I saw the wiggling," said Sylvia, "but I didn't know it was Mr. Stonor."

"What he needs," said Mrs. Morland, "is to shine a little torch through it, only then I suppose everyone would see it."

"And they might supect something," said Lady Bond. "Anyway, the curtain's going up now," and up it went.

When we say up, we say so merely because that is the phrase one has been brought up on. But what the Cockspur did was to draw the heavy curtains aside and loop them at each side of the stage, showing an enchanting safety curtain with a picture of the old Cockspur as it might have been and probably never was, with Shakespeare and Dr. Johnson and Nelson discussing the drama—or a tableau much to that effect. This in its turn rose, disclosing Miss Jessica Dean and Mr. Aubrey Clover in a drawing-room, as they had been more times than anyone could count, saying what they had been saying, or much the same thing, for the how many-eth time we cannot guess. A play—we believe—can get stale, as can its players; but this was not allowed by Aubrey Clover, who never stopped gently altering a speech, a piece of furniture, a sentence, a turn of Jessica's pretty head, or a special timbre in her lovely voice—not to speak of such variations on a theme—namely his own part—that it took all Jessica's art and skill to keep up with him sometimes. But she loved it and Aubrey Clover was fascinated by it; spinning it out of his own entrails as it were, while remaining cool and word-perfect. And as often as not, one or other of them would suddenly improvise.

Those who were privileged to have been at the Red Cross Fête at Northbridge a few years after the end of the war will remember how Jessica Dean, who was playing the conventional *soubrette*, suddenly produced an entirely new reading of her part, putting into it a wealth of meaning that left the audience several bars behind with its laughs and even made Aubrey Clover fluff one of his entrances. And when at the end of the performance Aubrey Clover, in answer to the roars and applause of the audience, had led his little company to the footlights, to repeat the success of the evening, his "Argentina Tango," Jessica Dean with a perfectly imbecile face had sung right through the song on one note, never losing pitch; thus commanding the unwilling respect of all musicians in the audience.

This *tour de force* she had never repeated, but there was always a chance that she might for, as Aubrey Clover had so truly said, she was—like Voltaire's words about the prophet Habakkuk—*capable de tout*.

As we do not know which of Aubrey Clover's plays, with

Denis Stonor's music, was being acted, we shall not describe it. Everyone was enjoying it—a fair number of the audience for a second or third time; and as far as Sylvia was concerned it was pure escape and bliss and rapture. To crown all, a minion then appeared in their box, saying that Mr. Clover and Miss Dean weren't in a hurry and their car would take Lady Bond and her party to the station. The minion then led them to a side entrance, where the car was waiting, thanked Lady Bond for the piece of paper she pressed into his not unwilling hand, shut the door of the car, said Waterloo, Main Line, and disappeared.

So in great comfort they got to Waterloo, where the driver, who appeared to know everything, decanted them just at the right place, accepted graciously the piece of paper which Mrs. Morland offered as largesse, and drove away. Their train was already at the platform waiting for its turn, so they enquired from the guard if there was a through carriage to Skeynes, found that there was, and sank gratefully onto its cushions. For to sit for a long time is almost as tiring as to walk, if not more so, and the theatre seats though well cushioned had not got a nice solid padded back against which you could lean your head. Luckily the late evening train ran straight through without any change till Winter Overcotes, after which it would obligingly stop at local stations if required. A kind elderly guard who boarded it at Winter Overcotes promised to stop at Skeynes and all three ladies felt such confidence in him that they nearly went to sleep. Their confidence was well placed. As the train slowed down, he appeared at the door and said: "Skeynes in two minutes, my lady."

As the train drew up, he reappeared on the platform to open the door for them, nor was he disappointed, for Lady Bond pressed into his hand something which aroused almost grovelling subservience and gratitude. The ladies went through the quiet booking office to where Mrs. Morland's car was peacefully waiting, and even as they came out into the station yard Lord Bond drove up. Everyone was sleepy; good-byes and words of gratitude were exchanged and the Bonds drove away. Then Mrs. Morland drove Sylvia to the Vicarage, decanted her quickly—for she was tired and did not want to have to talk to the Vicar or his wife—and so back to her own home, where Stoker welcomed her and packed her off to bed.

"You go and have a nice bath," said the faithful handmaid. "I kept the water nice and hot for you and there's some nice hot milk in the Thermos in your room and some nice biscuits. Time we was all in our beds. And Lord Stoke rang up so I said Madam had gone to London and he could ring up tomorrow, not too early. Something about a sekertary, he said, but I said I didn't know nothing about sekertaries, so he said it didn't matter and he'd ring up again. There's an ever so good film on next week, all about Venice and someone called Cassie Nover—one of those new film stars, I expect. Anything else you want?"

Mrs. Morland thanked Stoker for remembering the bath and providing hot milk and biscuits; availed herself of all these simple pleasures, gladly got into her own dear bed, took up the novel she had been reading, and settled for the night. But so long and late an excursion had tired her more than she knew and before many moments the book fell out of her hand onto the floor, which roused her just enough to be able to turn off the bed lamp and then lose consciousness.

As for Sylvia, her homecoming was almost enough to make her walk out again and become an Orphan of the Storm, for her loving parents had decided to stay up till she came in, and were sitting in the Vicar's study. As was their custom when alone, they had been reading aloud to each other. Each was a good reader with a pleasant voice and enjoyed reading and being read to. But there is something of a narcotic nature in both. As a rule it was the Vicar who went to sleep first, while his wife read to him. She looked at him from time to time, with an occasional nod of her own head and a slight disposition to muddle the lines, till she saw him relaxed in a light comfortable slumber, looking, so she felt, even more handsome asleep than awake; in which she was not wholly wrong, for he had fine features and looked in his light doze not unlike a Crusader on a Tomb. If the Vicar was the first to read, he usually read himself to sleep pretty quickly, while his wife looked affectionately at him and went on quietly with her needlework, for they had a store of real linen sheets, tablecloths, and table napkins, which she patched and darned exquisitely.

From time to time both reader and listener went gently to sleep at the same time. Whichever woke first would look with affectionate tolerance at the other, ready when he—or she—awoke to tell a most whopping lie about having been awake all the time.

Sylvia, well-used to her parents' eccentricities, stood looking kindly at them. She was sleepy and would have been glad to go to bed. She could easily have slipped upstairs to her own room, but if she did she knew she would be in bed as quickly as possible and fast asleep and her father and mother wouldn't know she was back when they woke up and would certainly begin to worry. In such a case desperate remedies may be the best, so she went out of the room, leaving the door open, re-opened the front door, gave it a good slam, put the chain up, and came back to the study with a normal amount of noise.

Her parents—who, of course, had not been asleep at all, in their own estimation—were both looking a little mad, as people so often do if suddenly awoken, but pulled themselves together and asked if she had had a nice evening. This they had a perfect right to do, but we all know how annoying the question can be. One *has* had a nice evening, but somehow to be questioned about it by one's parents, who of course don't really understand things, is a jar to one's finer feelings. Sylvia, who was a good daughter, was prepared to give satisfaction to her parents,

when Rose and Dora, in dressing-gowns, came cascading down
the stairs and into the study to ask Sylvia all about her evening.
If Sylvia did feel that she would rather like to knock their heads
together we could not entirely blame her; but with real good
nature she choked back her annoyance and gave her family a
brief and quite entertaining account of the evening, from the
arrival at the stage door and the wonderful people in Jessica
Dean's dressing-room to the play itself and how wonderful Jessica was and how wonderful Aubrey Clover was and how they
had the royal box and programmes with golden borders. And
when she produced two programmes from her bag and gave one
to each of her sisters they were so overcome with gratitude and
sleepiness that they went back to bed at once.

Mrs. Gould, who had by now quite recovered from not really
being asleep, then pulled herself together, with great tact did
not ask Sylvia to talk about the play, and drove her straight up
to bed, for which Sylvia was truly thankful. Before going to
sleep she suddenly remembered Denis Stonor and how interest-
ingly pale he was with those dark shadows under his eyes and
vaguely felt that he was rather romantic, but before she had
really pursued this fascinating train of thought she was asleep.

What Denis Stonor may have thought, we do not know, but
think it extremely improbable that he ever thought of anything
except himself and the unreal world of his music in which he
lived and breathed. Such of us as were at Laverings some twenty
years ago may remember that during that warm summer when
his nice stepmother had taken a house near her brother and his
wife, the Middletons, Denis had been deeply attracted to Mrs.
Middleton, a quite happily married woman with no children
and a kind husband a good deal older than she was; and she had
been attracted by him. Both were honourable people. They
had felt too deeply, but kept their feelings well under control
and parted with a very few words; she to take up her own life
work of being a perfect wife to a husband for whom she had

real though quite unsentimental affection; Denis to go, through
the generous help of the late Lord Bond, to London and then
Manchester and finally America, always deep in his music and
now famous through it. On one of his later visits to England he
had met Mrs. Middleton again by chance. In each there had
been a quick heart-beat. Their eyes had met, they had spoken
kindly, but at that moment each knew that the old wounds
would not bleed anew: and better so. Romance had vanished
into thin air. Each was released from an imaginary chain, just as
the "I" of George Macdonald's *Phantastes,* imprisoned in the
magic tower, suddenly found that he only needed to open the
door and walk out to be completely free.

The one drawback to Pomfret Towers as a large business centre
was its distance from any station or bus route. As most of the
clerical staff employed there lived in Barchester, Mr. Adams had
organised a regular private coach service which took them to
and from the big bus station, built—we regret deeply to have to
say it—where some of the delightful, crooked, insanitary old
houses in Barley Street used to be. The affair of pulling down
the houses had of course roused strong feeling from all quarters.
The editor of the *Barchester Chronicle* had written a two-
column leader headed "The Hun Is at the Gate," but as very
few people knew the quotation what correspondence there was
in his columns languished and died. The editor of the *Barchester
News* had written half a column—for he believed in short
snappy articles—pointing out that the old order had changed,
giving place to new. The Society of Rodent Exterminators—
alias the few rat-catchers now left in a mechanised society—had
written to the third newspaper *The Barsetshire Courant* (a
publication which consisted of a front page with the latest news,
followed by five pages of small advertisements for houses, teeth,
neuter cats, young lady for hosiery department, etc.) pointing
out that the depopulation of Hamelin in Brunswick by a rodent

exterminator had been written up by somebody called Browning who was very well known and showed clearly that if there were no rats to catch there would be no rat-catchers. But no correspondence can go on for ever. The editors of all three papers agreed that rats were now dead as far as publicity was concerned and the world went on its way.

We regret the passing of Barley Street, even as we regret the death of the street in Kensington where we were born and had our early childhood. In it Thackeray had lived and Charlotte Brontë had visited it. Outside the Greyhound Inn, our next-door neighbour Esmond had spent the night before Queen Anne's death, hoping that the Old Pretender would be proclaimed, only to hear that George of Hanover was to be our king. The Greyhound in our childhood was much as Esmond saw it; a red brick house exactly like ours except that it had red twill curtains in the ground-floor windows as all good inns should have, while we had rather art-y bulls' eyes, unrelated to the old style.

In neither was there a bathroom, and not having one we did very well without, as England had done ever since Roman plumbing gradually disintegrated over the years. In fact it was still a civilisation supported—in many places literally—by hewers of wood and drawers of water. Electric light was as yet hardly known to us, gas was only for lighting, and scuttles of coal were carried up by the housemaid for drawing-room, dining-room, bedroom, and nursery fires. Though no one is likely to believe it, a stout newel post ran from the basement to the two attics on the top floor and the Jacobean staircase went winding round it. An echo of the past—all chewed and gobbled up by Big Business, which from two or three little shops has developed into a spreading grasping monster, always seeking whom it may devour.

But let us leave these nostalgic excursions and return to Mr. Adams and also to his delightful and masterful wife, formerly

Lucy Marling, who helped him to run his business with as much vehemence as she had formerly applied to her father's estate during the war years, and what is more had three very agreeable children. The eldest, now some nine or ten years old, is Miss Amabel Rose, but who the other two are we do not remember, and indeed are not quite sure if we have yet invented their sex, age, and names. Possibly the second child is a boy called William after his maternal grandfather, old Mr. Marling, and the third a girl called Leslie. This would be partly after the Leslie family at Rushwater, who were friends of long standing, and was also a useful name, being suitable for either sex.

As all friends of Barsetshire know, Mr. and Mrs. Samuel Adams now live in Edgewood, over Chaldicotes way, in the Old Bank House, so called because it used to be a private bank when such places still existed. Its last owner had been an elderly Miss Sowerby of good Barsetshire stock, connected with the Sowerbys who used to own Chaldicotes. The family had gently come down in the world, Miss Sowerby could not afford to keep up the house which had been her home and was glad to sell it to the wealthy industrialist who could give it all it needed in the way of repairs inside and out and modernising where it was needed, for Miss Sowerby had taken her bath in her bedroom all her life and would have been profoundly shocked if invited to walk in a dressing-gown and slippers to a bath used by other people. Being a practical woman with a very clear view of herself, she decided to move well away from her old home and live in Worthing with her widowed sister, who had a pleasant house in a Georgian terrace, not too near the sea, and her own pew at St. Praxed's, a very High Anglican church which was so full of dim religious light (filtering through some extremely bad modern stained glass) that the congregation were always stumbling over each other's umbrellas and hassocks.

Miss Sowerby had left her old home with a brave face and an aching heart, but we are certain that she has found agreeable

new friends in Worthing and will, together with her sister, give
and attend very pleasant tea parties and—rather dashingly—
equally pleasant sherry parties. She had also won the favour of
her sister's elderly cook and house parlour-maid, being recognised
in the kitchen as a lady who knows what's what, not like some of
those ladies—if they call themselves that—as try to be familiar.
For the good old servant knows the place of her mistress's friends
as well as she knows her own place and exudes an aura of protocol that makes it impossible for any of the gentry to consider themselves as her equals. We believe that Miss Sowerby, by simply
being herself, will win the approval of most people she meets in
Worthing, from the drawing-room to the kitchen. As for the few
houses where a butler is still kept, the social sense of that poten-
tate will at once tell him that this is a Lady. None of your being
affable and familiar to a butler who knows his place, but a certain condescension to a valuable supporter of society, spiced with
a touch of freemasonry as between two people each skilled in a
life and conduct handed down from the past.

Our reader may also be pleased to hear that Mr. Adams has
arranged to have sent to Worthing every Christmas a large case
from Fortnum & Mason containing food and drink of the best.
And as there is an excellent circulating library near by and a
cinema which has quite modern films as well as old favourites,
we think that Miss Sowerby's lines have fallen in pleasant places.
All of which is a great comfort to us, for the proud poor elderly
gentlewoman does not always find the comfort of friends
about her forlorn *hic jacet* (to use Mr. Wordsworth's words).
And although Miss Sowerby and her sister have not—like
Browning's bishop—already ordered their tomb in St. Praxed's
church, they often discuss with great interest the kind of memorial they would like and drive the rector nearly mad by changing
their minds every few weeks. But the rector has large charity for
his elderly flock and listens to them with an apparent interest
that can hardly be distinguished from the real article, so earning

merit. These divagations are not perhaps very relevant to the thread (if any) of this story, but Mr. Adams has a large number of friends who have nothing to do with his successful business life, so some of them may like to hear of one of his many acts of kindness.

Probably all mothers wish to see their daughters well married, and many must say to themselves ". . . were this wild thing but wedded, Much more love would I have and far less care . . ." though that is where Mr. George Meredith's toes turn in, for delightful as it is to be a Granny, it can be both expensive and exhausting. Mrs. Gould had thought of her Sylvia with a brood of babies who would come to the Vicarage for a treat, and how she would indulge in the Granny-habit of spoiling them. But those dreams had not come to pass. Sylvia had been a very good daughter, affectionate, efficient, and much liked by a large circle of friends, but there she still was, the useful daughter at home and not getting any younger, while her sisters Rose and Dora had got jobs in Barchester and appeared to like their work and enjoy the extra freedom and pocket money that it gave them as well as the amusement of the daily journey to and from Barchester, which they accomplished in a variety of ways; the bus which was not always punctual; the train which was, but didn't land one so near the centre of the city; and a certain amount of hitch-hiking—but only in the cars of friends, because their parents had a secret conviction that anyone who offered a lift might have fell designs upon their youth: though as a matter of fact they were extremely good at games, had learnt some ju-jitsu for fun, and were longing to practise it on a person or persons unknown.

Sylvia, as we know, had a daily job at Pomfret Towers, where the wealthy ironmaster Mr. Adams had taken a large part of the house for his clerical staff. A great many people had said how dreadful for those poor Pomfrets to give up the family home and live in the servants' wing; but, as Lady Pomfret most truthfully replied, she and her husband were far more comfortable in the old servants' wing where the rooms were a reasonable size and height and easily heated than they ever were in the main building with its huge hall and large reception rooms and a furnace that ate up coal and wood without really heating the great hall, the yellow drawing-room, the smaller green drawing-room, the library, the billiard-room, the estate room, and the huge staircase and the corridors on the first floor, not to speak of the servants' quarters. These were now sadly small and the resident staff was a minimum, reinforced by a few local women who still had a kind of feudal feeling, not to speak of the extra money they earned and the elevenses, which were practically a very good substantial lunch.

It was obvious to the Vicar and his wife that their younger daughters belonged to the Brave (and rather depressing) New World and would always find jobs and friends. When they considered their elder daughter they were less happy. Sylvia was a darling: intelligent, hard-working, liked in the village, well befriended by Mrs. Morland and the George Knoxes and Adrian Coates and his wife: but in none of these pleasant friendships did her parents see any future for her. By "future" we think they meant a husband. Rose and Dora had plenty of "dates" with various agreeable youngish men whom they had got to know in Barchester, but Sylvia, their elder by some years, didn't have dates; nor would her parents have known how to set about getting any for her.

This depressed them sometimes, for it was no good pretending that Sylvia was young. Of course all unmarried women are young in a manner of speaking, but quite often it is the married woman with a husband and children who looks younger. Visions of a nice elderly Admiral—perhaps a widower—flitted across their minds. Or perhaps the middle-aged rector of a very good living with private means—a kind of Mr. Arabin, whose name still lingered in the Close. But an Admiral on half-pay who has not private means needs a wife with some money, and as for the Close there was very little choice, nor were the Goulds particularly interested in the unmarried clergy there. Ever since the delightful Canon Fewling had married Margot Phelps, the daughter of Admiral Phelps (retired), there had been a kind of mild rejuvenescence in the Close, much encouraged when the Reverend the Lord William Harcourt married the youngest daughter of Sir Robert Graham, K.C.M.G., and Lady Graham, who had been a Leslie from Rushwater. But we do not know of any eligible curate at present.

Not having a daughter ourself—for she left us at a very tender age and is but a shadowy loved remembrance—we are a little vague as to how one marries one's daughters, except for a general impression that they now do it all themselves and are apt to turn up holding a pleasant, not to speak of sheepish-looking young man by the hand and uttering the words: "This is Bobbie that I told you about at that week-end with those people somewhere near Sonning"; after which there is a kind of embarrassed show of potential affection on both sides and much to your relief the young people go out together forgetting to slam the door, which reminds you that you must get the lock seen to and properly oiled, as on leaving the house for the last time the lovestruck swain has usually banged the front door behind him with such vigour that it has sprung open again and as his *innamorata* is not in a state to be really conscious of anything, you have to go down again yourself, shut it properly, and put the chain up. We believe that if a well-trained burglar wishes to come in, neither lock, bolt, bar, nor chain will keep him out and it is better and safer not to interfere if you are well insured, and to put your head under the bedclothes and hope for the best. But as our local council has caused the charming elegant Victorian gas lamps in our street to be dismantled and has put up in their place very powerful and hideous electric standards whose light shines ferociously into our front bedroom windows, we shall only be burgled from behind, where a number of small back yards with no light give the enterprising burglar the maximum of temptation with the maximum of opportunity. *Absit omen.*

As we have already hinted—and we have known it ourself for many years—that strange offspring of a military father, Denis Stonor, was a musician from the tips of his fingers to the ends of his toes. Why, nobody could explain. Just as nobody can explain music, or why some people are born with not only that immortal longing in them but also with the gift of being able to communicate it to the world, it remains to most of us a mystery, accepted and admired even if we do not altogether understand it. Why, as Browning says, God has allowed this gift to man, "that out of three sounds he frame, not a fourth sound but a star," we do not know. Again, to use Browning's words, ". . . God has a few of us whom he whispers in the ear; The rest may reason and welcome: tis we musicians know," and Denis Stonor, with no reason at all (for Erato alights in what seems to us at random on her chosen servants), was what a French fellow-musician had called *"de musique tout confit."*

The next excitement at High Rising was to be the Agricultural Show, which was on a small scale but much enjoyed by its patrons, who were able to meet there the people they met every day in the village—or little town as we ought perhaps to say now—and exchange news. It could not of course compare with the Show at Rushwater, or the Great Conservative Rally at Staple Park when the Barsetshire Pig Breeders' Association— known all over the county and farther as the B.P.B.A.— joined forces with the Conservative Association; and a Great Prime Minister, foursquare as a White Porkminster, commanding as a Cropbacked Cruncher, but unlike those intelligent quadrupeds smoking a large cigar, had driven through the park amid the applause of all present; but it would be a pleasant way of meeting the friends one saw every day and perhaps of making some new friends.

We need hardly say that George Knox—who knew nothing at all about animals (except as food, or to scratch one of his pigs' back with his walking stick to show how country-minded he was)—was foremost in the fray and a considerable nuisance to the organisers because he would talk at great length about things that he did not understand. His wife, who had taken his measure very accurately, kept an eye on him on these occasions and, in her own quiet way, deflated him in a manner that roused the admiration of all present.

It was Lord Stoke's habit to attend the Show, dressed admirably for the part in tweeds, gaiters, heavy boots, and a very shabby old felt hat with an artificial fly stuck on the brim. Not that he was or ever had been a fisherman, for although he had the little River Rising in the valley below his house, there were no fishable fish in it—if we make ourselves clear. The local small boys fished with an old can, or a bucket with a hole in it picked off the village rubbish dump, or even less successfully, with a bent pin hanging from a stick, but with little or no result. This hat was his greatest treasure and pleasure, and when he had a bad attack of bronchitis and was rather enjoying the fuss made over him, he asked Dr. Ford to promise, when the end came, to keep the hat, in his memory; which Dr. Ford promised to do, without the faintest intention of carrying out his promise of course, knowing well that short of a stroke his lordship has every prospect of living for ever—as most of his family had done, and as his rather trying sister Lucasta, Lady Bond, continued to do, on a very comfortable dowager's settlement. But as we are friends of young Lord Bond and his charming wife who was Daphne Stonor, we may say that they were not in the least anxious for his lordship's death, which would probably mean heavy death duties and the turning of the house into a school, or an Institution (whatever that is).

But everyone tried not to think about it, for though his lordship could, as we know, be very trying, partly from real deafness and even more from not trying to listen, he had become a county institution. The whole county knew his lordship's short grey top hat (we do not know the correct name) and his habit of going everywhere in his victoria or his brougham—for the doctor had forbidden him to climb the dog cart which had been his chief joy.

To cheer himself he had, early in the summer, paid a short visit to London, a town which he hated (but where luckily the rather old-fashioned hotel where his father used to go still knew a gentleman when it saw one), and there had bought himself a new grey hat almost exactly like the old one, saying in a loud voice to the staff who had assembled that his old governor and *his* old governor had always had a grey topper. The staff, rather sycophantically, made murmurs of appreciation and admiration, in joyful expectation of the generous largesse always bestowed by his lordship when he came to town —nor were they disappointed.

"I hope the hat will Give Satisfaction to your lordship," said the head of the firm, who always assisted—in the French sense—at everything that happened in the shop. Lord Stoke said if it didn't fit after all the trying-on he would eat it.

"For Ascot, my lord?" said the manager.

Lord Stoke said an old feller like himself didn't go racing now, received the bowings and scrapings of the assistants, and went away.

CHAPTER 6

ONE morning, about a fortnight before the Agricultural, Stoker came in to clear the breakfast things and found her employer shaking her head over the letter she was reading.

"Oh dear, oh dear," said Mrs. Morland.

"Nothing wrong, I hope and trust?" said Stoker quite untruthfully, for like most of us she was always ready to enjoy a nice bit of not-too-bad bad news.

"Oh, nothing really *wrong*," said Mrs. Morland. "It's just come as a bit of a shock, that's all."

"I expect it's the coal gone up again," said Stoker, "though how they have the imperence to call it coal I'm sure I don't know. Last lot we had was nothing only dust, and the big pieces they're slate, like, and spit out in your face. My auntie's cousin's daughter, she was sitting by the fire watching the television, and one of them nasty slatey pieces come out and hit her in the eye. She had to go to hospital and have an operation, and she's never felt the same about the telly since."

"It's not the coal," said Mrs. Morland, "it's my grandson Robin. He's at a boarding-school and breaking up this week. And Tony writes to say that one of the younger children has just started measles, so of course both the others are in quarantine, and can I have Robin for the holidays. Oh Stoker, can we manage it? You know how exhausting Robin is, and what a tremendous appetite he's got. Not that I don't adore him, because I do, I adore all my grandchildren, but it means such a terrible upset of everything, and I'm not as young as I used to be."

"Now don't you commence to worry," said Stoker calmly, stacking the plates and tea things on a vast tin tray. "You haven't eaten hardly any breakfast. There's another piece of toast gone wasted and I'll have to give it to the birds, though goodness knows they don't need it, greedy things, particularly them starlings. You didn't ought to worry on an empty stomach and you don't eat enough to keep a cat alive. I've got a nice bit of grilled sole for your lunch, with garden peas and summer pudding to follow. Master Robin, he won't be no trouble, and if he is, I'll soon sort him out. You leave him to me. He's just the spit and image of his father afore him. No vice in him at all, if you know what I mean, just mischievous he is. Like when Master Tony and his friend Master Donkey——"

"Wesendonck," murmured Mrs. Morland, slightly overwhelmed by this flood of conversation.

"That's as may be," answered Stoker darkly. "I never could get round to that boy's heathen name. As I was saying, like them summer holidays when Master Donkey come to stay with Master Tony, and they shelled the peas in Master Tony's bedroom, because he was in bed with a ricked ankle, and let them all go down the drain and had to open the U joint with a spanner."

"They only meant to soak them in the bathroom basin," said Mrs. Morland, feebly defending her now middle-aged young. "Only Wesendonck forgot to put the plug in."

"That's what I mean," said Stoker. "It wasn't vice as you might say, just mischievousness. And Master Robin, he's another of the kind, and we can put him in Master Tony's old bedroom if I give it a good turnout, and as for food there's plenty of tins in the larder and any amount of fruit and veg. and poultry, and if the worst comes to the worst we can always fall back on eggs."

Mrs. Morland was just conjuring up an inner vision of the massive Stoker falling back on eggs when the door opened and in came Sylvia Gould, dressed in her going-to-work clothes, which consisted of a mackintosh over her suit and a plastic hood; for the morning, after deciding to be nice, had changed its mind, just as the Weather Men had said it wouldn't.

Ripping off her hood and pulling it shut by the ends in concertina fashion (for in no other way can we describe the method, familiar to all our female readers, of reducing this head-contraption to a narrow ribbon), she put a pile of envelopes on the table and said they were all ready for the post, and if Mrs. Morland would just sign the letters she would pop them in the pillar-box on her way to Pomfret Towers.

"Don't bother about that, Sylvia," said Mrs. Morland. "I've got another letter to write and Stoker will take them all down to the post office on her bicycle. Oh dear," she added, with another sigh.

"There's been Disturbing News from London, miss," said Stoker with some relish, "but I've told Mrs. Morland not to commence to worry."

"Not from the publishers, I hope," said Sylvia, "asking for early delivery of the Madame Koska book?"

"No, though I expect that will be the next thing," said Mrs. Morland. "It's about my grandson Robin, Tony's eldest boy. You remember Tony, don't you, Sylvia?" to which Sylvia replied: "Who could forget?" in a heartfelt, almost reverent voice, for the young Tony Morland had never been backward in putting himself forward.

"Well, Robin's school is breaking up this week," went on Mrs. Morland, "and Tony writes to say that one of the younger children is measling and the others are almost sure to catch it and can we have Robin for the holidays, the first part at least, until the measling's over. I don't think you've met Robin, Sylvia, but he's exactly like Tony at his age, which is about eleven, I *think*, but I can't be certain because I've got so many grandchildren of different kinds that I never quite remember how old they are. I remember their birthdays, of course, but not always *which* birthday."

"Well, if this one's like Tony we can cope all right," said Sylvia cheerfully.

"That's what I say, miss," observed Stoker, picking up her tray and moving to the door. "Just mischievous and high-spirited that's all. And it'll be nice for Mrs. Morland to have someone lively about the house. Take her mind off all that writing and a good thing too. Ring when you're ready for me to take the letters to the post," she added to her employer as she departed, with a nice bit of news to impart to the gardener and Annie's niece, who obliged in the mornings three days a week, when they came in for their elevenses.

"You're not really worried, are you?" asked Sylvia, left alone with Mrs. Morland. "Tony was no trouble really, if you used a firm hand."

"I'm afraid that's what I never did," said Mrs. Morland. "*You* did, I know. Do you remember the summer when Tony boasted so dreadfully about his diving, and then he sploshed into the water all anyhow, and you made him come out and held his arms and legs in the right positions until he got the hang of it? He was so cross. No, I'm not really worried, Sylvia. In fact, now that I've recovered from the first shock, I'm beginning to look forward to it. Robin's a darling, only he is lively, as Stoker so politely put it, and he does have such a hearty appetite and he *will* talk so much."

"Like father, like son," said Sylvia, who had once been acclaimed by Dr. Ford as the only person in the world who could talk Tony Morland down. "You can't be games mistress at a big school without learning the knack of handling them. Tony was all right, only he'd never make a swimmer, not like that friend of his who didn't say a word, and kept a mouth-organ in his bathing cap. I remember I ragged him about boys wearing caps, and then he swam across the lake in half a tick and sat on a rock and played the mouth-organ at us. He had a name like Moke. I don't think I ever knew what he was really called."

"Wesendonck," said Mrs. Morland. "Tony always called him Donk. He was a brilliant boy all round, and afterwards he swam in the Olympic team. I'd forgotten you were games mistress at a big girls' school. Why did you give it up? You must have been quite young that summer."

"I was twenty-three," said Sylvia, "and a very silly girl. I got a chance to go abroad and thought it would be fun to teach in a school in Switzerland. It wasn't, not for long, and anyway, there was a complication." She paused. "I was sort of half-engaged to Dr. Ford, but I thought he'd only asked me on the rebound from Anne Knox, because I knew he'd been in love with her before she married George. So I wrote and told him that it wouldn't work. And after that I got a lot of jobs in other schools, and took a secretarial course when I grew too old for games, and then there was the war and the Red Cross, and then I drifted back to look after the parents and do secretary for Mr. Adams on the side. It's all been quite nice really, but sometimes I can't help feeling that I've missed the boat. Sorry to bore you with all this," she added, getting up and unfurling her concertina hood, "only I started thinking about old days, which was really very stupid of me."

"Not stupid at all," said Mrs. Morland. "Quite natural. We are what we are *because* of the old days, and it's one of the blessings of increasing years that we learn to see them in proportion as time goes on. Now what *is* really stupid is to look back in anger, because that isn't proper looking back at all, just squinting back and seeing things the way you want to see them, and blaming someone else for our mistakes. I sometimes think psychiatry, or what passes for psychiatry, is one of the greatest curses of the modern world. Well, never mind, Sylvia, you're a good girl, and there's plenty of time still for things to change. And somehow I Have a Feeling that they will."

With which sibylline utterance she put on her writing spectacles and began a letter of cordial invitation to her grandson, while Sylvia went off in the rain to her day's work with Mr. Adams at Pomfret Towers.

Those who have followed with concern the declining fortunes of the House of Pomfret, since we paid our first visit to the Towers in the old Earl's day, will be glad to know that the arrangement made some years ago between the present Earl and the wealthy Hogglestock ironmaster had worked out to the satisfaction of all parties. The family was now able to live in reasonable warmth and comfort in what used to be the servants' wing, retaining the stables and as much of the garden and grounds as could be kept in order by the few elderly men who still worked about the place and were always ready to do a bit of digging or lopping, or to mow the winding grass path known as the Green River, which led up a gentle slope shaded by ancient beech trees and carpeted in the spring by wild daffodils, primroses, and bluebells, to the stream and the pool.

The main block of Pomfret Towers, conceded with modest pride by the best local authorities to be the most repellent pile in all East Barsetshire, only excelled in hideousity by the Duke of Towers's family seat in West Barsetshire, a triumph of mixed architecture which combined the worst features of a French seventeenth-century chateau, a mid-Victorian railway station, and the Natural History Museum, had been taken on long-term lease by Mr. Adams and his associates Mr. Pilward of Pilward's Entire and Mr. Macfadyen of Amalgamated Vedge, who were going in for business together in a big way and needed large permanent quarters for their clerical staff, dealing mostly with overseas trade; as well as a good bit of well-watered land to use as an experimental station for producing first-class root crops and green vegetables.

Mr. Macfadyen, we are sorry to say because we liked and

respected that honest Scotsman, was now dead, but a worthy successor had been found among his staff, and Amalgamated Vedge was still supplying most of the canteens in Hogglestock and doing an increasing business overseas, watched with a maternal eye by Mrs. Samuel Adams, she who was once Lucy Marling and knew as much about the ways of vegetables, not to mention pigs and hens, as almost anyone in Barsetshire.

Sylvia Gould's office at Pomfret Towers was on the first floor, a part of what in old Lady Pomfret's day had been a drawing-room, with a sash window looking out onto the sweep of semi-circular drive, the trimly formal flower beds, now bright with geraniums, salvia, and lobelia, and the elegant little fountain, fed from the spring above, throwing up its fine jet of spray. Mr. Adams's own office next door, which might fairly be described as the master-office at the Towers, since its owner had a controlling finger in almost every pie, comprised the rest of the old drawing-room, and although equipped with all the latest aids to business, had not entirely lost its character, for Sam Adams, as he himself would be the first to say, was always a one to learn something from his betters. Accordingly he had cut his own requirements to the minimum, and with the cordial approval of his wife Lucy, had given his old friend Mrs. Belton a free hand with the furnishings. The result was a very pleasant room indeed, with few of the formalities of an office, and Mr. Adams's natural, though untutored taste, had kept it singularly clear of knick-knacks.

Sylvia often thought it was a pity that the room was left so much to itself. The rich ironmaster's main work lay in the rolling mills at Hogglestock, where the redoubtable Miss Pickthorn was his secretary-in-chief. About three days a week he drove over to Pomfret Towers, to attend to the joint concerns of the companies he controlled, and in these concerns Miss Gould had become an important secretarial factor, a lesser figure than Miss Pickthorn, with whom she was on the best of terms, but treated with respect by all the staff, with a private telephone to her employer's office, and special biscuits with her cup of tea.

On the morning when she had seen and talked to Mrs. Morland after breakfast, Sylvia went up in the lift to the first floor with a divided heart. It was one of Mr. Adams's In days, and as she took the cover off her typewriter she knew she ought to be alert. But somehow her mind was squirreling round a number of other things, which worried her, for she was a conscientious worker. She kept thinking about the various, unaccustomed events of the past few weeks, the visit to Rising Castle and Lord Stoke's old-fashioned kindness, the treat of sharing a box with young Lady Bond and Mrs. Morland at the Cockspur Theatre, the thrill of going backstage to meet the stars and Denis Stonor's deep-sunk, melancholy eyes; the satisfaction of helping Dr. Ford with the emergency of Mrs. Beeton's leg, and Mrs. Morland's news this morning about her grandson's visit and reminders of the golden summer when she, Sylvia, was twenty-three and discontented because she had the whole of life before her.

Automatically she slit open and sorted Mr. Adams's mail, took the letters which he would have to deal with personally into his office and laid them neatly on the desk, came back to her own room and did a bit of desultory filing, sharpened half a dozen pencils which were sharp enough already, and tried to settle down to type the minutes of a company meeting. But somehow her mind refused to concentrate. By the time her employer's step was heard in the passage, followed by the sounds of his key in the outer door, the creak of a chair and the faint rustling of papers, Sylvia had only typed half a page, and was beginning to tell herself angrily that she had chosen the wrong profession. "A job is a *job*, my girl, and don't you go and forget it," she said crossly to herself out loud, rubbing out a typing error with unnecessary zeal, so that she made a hole in

the paper, and almost jumping when the buzzer at her elbow
sounded and Mr. Adams's voice over what is known, we believe,
as the inter-com, asked if she could spare him a few minutes
for dictation.

Samuel Adams, now father of three young children by his
second marriage, and twice a grandfather through his married
daughter Heather Pilward, had greyed a little but otherwise
scarcely changed since we met him last. His instincts, as he
would once have called them, were uncommonly sound, and
he gave his secretary a sharp look as she came into the room,
but made no comment other than his usual cheerful greeting
and a remark that the rain looked like letting up, until Sylvia
had a dozen shorthand letters in her notebook and a number of
reports to file and classify. Then he leant back massively in his
swivel chair, put his blunt fingertips together, and said: "That's
the lot for today, thank you, Miss Gould. I've got a conference
at Hogglestock this afternoon, so you'd better cut off early,
those reports can keep. You're looking a bit peaky, anything
wrong?"

Sylvia, feeling a flush mounting to her cheeks, said no, really
nothing, and she'd rather stay and get the work done, if Mr.
Adams didn't mind. "Because she knows when she gets home
there'll be nothing else to do but wait hand and foot on those
old parents of hers," thought Mr. Adams to himself, in which
he was not entirely right, but we believe he had the root of the
matter in him. Aloud he said: "Well, do exactly as you please.
Ask the canteen to send me some lunch upon a tray, and have
any important calls put through to Hogglestock this afternoon.
There won't be anything this morning except Mr. Roote of
Amalgamated Vedge, about that consignment to the West
Indies. By the way, Miss Gould, aren't you about due for a
holiday? or leave, as they call it in those government depart-
ments, though I've never had a fancy for the word myself. Nor
I don't like vacation neither. Now with a good old-fashioned

word like holiday you know just what people are talking about."

Sylvia said yes, she was down for a fortnight in August, but it didn't really matter when she took it, as she wasn't planning to go away anywhere.

"More's the pity," said Mr. Adams. "Not that I hold with going away myself, my home's my holiday, but a Mediterranean cruise or a fortnight on the Riviera would do you a power of good. Still, everybody kills himself in his own way, and mind you take that fortnight and no nonsense, or I'll be up creating at the Vicarage myself."

Alarmed, but strangely reassured by this ultimatum, Sylvia went back to her own room and put in a useful hour with the typewriter. She was just finishing a tactful letter to a customer in Peru, who wanted to know the distinctive merits of Washington's Vimphos and Corbett's Bono-Vitasang and Holman's Phospho-Manuro, which were all controlled by the Holman Fertiliser Group in which Mr. Adams held the majority of shares and we don't think there was a penny to choose between them, when the Reception Desk rang up to say Miss Adams with another young lady, to see Mr. Adams, and was he in?

"Send them up to my office," said Sylvia, "I can cope. Mr. Adams is tied up for the moment with Mr. Roote of Amalgamated Vedge, but I don't suppose he'll be long now."

Presently there was the sound of loud whispers and some scuffling outside the door and in came two little girls, one about ten and the other slightly older, wearing the uniform of Barchester High School, which as we know was a grey silk blouse, a blue gym tunic, and a blue blazer with brass buttons, topped by a hat of blue felt with a grey hatband bearing the school symbol, a tree with three leaves and two pieces of fruit of no identifiable variety. Each little girl was carrying a mackintosh and slung about or laden with numerous bags and satchels, as well as a tennis racket with tennis shoes attached and other pieces of impedimenta which reminded Sylvia of the White Knight.

She smiled at the children and said good morning, adding kindly: "You look a bit top-heavy. Wouldn't you like to dump all that stuff there in the corner?"

"Ouf!" said Amabel Adams, the younger and solider of the two, as with many puffs and heavy breathings she banged her burden down on the floor. "Thanks awfully, Miss Gould. We've just broken up and it's a ghastly lot to carry. This is Eleanor Leslie, who goes to my school, and we've come over in the bus from Barchester because there's something special she wants to talk to Dad about. Is he in?"

Sylvia said he was and he would soon be free, she thought, and would they like some biscuits while they were waiting? Assured by Miss Adams that they were absolutely famished, she opened a drawer of her desk and brought out a tin of very nice mixed biscuits, telling the visitors to help themselves. Miss Adams she knew well of course, for she not infrequently turned up at the office with her mother, but Miss Leslie she had never seen before, and Sylvia looked with interest at the fair-skinned face with dark eyes under long dark lashes and thought that in a few years' time the child would be a beauty.

Presently the unmistakable sounds of departure were heard from the next room and Mr. Adams, who had been apprised by Sylvia of his daughter's visit, opened the communicating door and said to come in now.

"Well, girlie," he remarked as Amabel banged her way into his office, almost dislodging a pile of papers from the desk and followed by the dark-eyed, silent Eleanor, "what's the trouble and who's your friend?"

Amabel said it was Eleanor Leslie that went to school with her and she had something awfully important to tell Dad.

"Leslie, eh?" said Mr. Adams, extending a friendly but we must say large and rather hairy hand. "Pleased to meet you. I think I know your parents. Farm over Rushwater way, don't they? Mrs. Adams meets them when she goes over to talk cows with her cousin Emmy Grantly. Fine man, your father. Got a game leg in the war, didn't he? But he's done a grand job with the place, neatest bit of mixed farming in West Barsetshire. Now what can I do for you, young lady?" and he motioned the little girls to comfortable chairs and sat down in the swivel chair himself.

As Eleanor hesitated, slightly overpowered by the wealthy ironmaster, Amabel rushed into the breach.

"You know Wiple Terrace, Dad?" she said.

"Can't say as I do offhand," replied her father.

"Well, you do really, if you stop to think about it. It's the place that all the houses are called after girls' names and it sort of half belongs to Southbridge School. Eleanor's brother goes to school at Southbridge, and there's an awful flap on because Wiple Terrace is going to be pulled down and Lord Somebody I don't know what he's called is going to build a factory instead, and Georgy, that's the one that's Eleanor's brother, says——"

"Now hold your horses, girlie," interrupted her father, kindly but firmly, "and let your friend get in a word edgeways. What is all this about Wiple Terrace, young lady, and what can Sam Adams do to help you?"

"I'm awfully sorry to bother you, Mr. Adams," said Eleanor shyly, flushing a most becoming wild-rose pink, "but they really are upset at Southbridge, and Amabel said you were the right person to come to. You see, Wiple Terrace doesn't *belong* to the school exactly, but some of the masters live there, and it's such a nice little terrace, it's ghastly to think of pulling it down for a horrid factory. I *hate* having old things destroyed, like dogs and horses," she added almost inaudibly, fishing in her blazer pocket for a handkerchief.

"So do I," said Mr. Adams warmly. "There's too much getting rid of things these days, without stopping to think more often than not, and stands to reason you can't put back what's gone. Who is this Lord Somebody and what's the factory for?"

"I think he's called Lord Aberfordbury," said Eleanor, "and I don't know much about the factory, but it's something to do with picture postcards."

"Aberfordbury, eh?" said Mr. Adams, in what his friends would at once have recognised as his Business Voice. "Well, if it's Aberfordbury, we'd better look into this. I wouldn't put anything past him. Don't you fret now, Miss Eleanor, and leave it all to me. Shall I get my chauffeur to drive you back to Barchester?" he asked his daughter. "Looked like you had a tidy lot of stuff out there."

"That's all right, Dad," said Amabel. "I rang up Mother and she's coming here to fetch us. Matter of fact," she added, looking at the handsome wrist-watch which her half-sister Heather Pilward had given her for Christmas, "she ought to be here now. I said we'd wait for her at the front, so she didn't have to park the car. I'll tell you what, Dad, you will do something about Wiple Terrace, won't you? It's like Guy Fawkes and blowing up the House of Commons. We did Guy Fawkes last term in history."

"Run along now, girlie," said Mr. Adams, "and don't keep Mother waiting. I can't promise anything except I'll look into it and do the best I can."

When the little girls had gone away with their impedimenta, Mr. Adams sat for a few minutes drumming his square fingers on the desk and thinking. Then he buzzed for his secretary, who came in with her pad and pencil.

"What do we know about Wiple Terrace, Miss Gould?" he said. "Wiple Terrace at Southbridge."

"Not much, I'm afraid," said Sylvia, "but I can soon find out."

After a little telephoning she came back to say that Wiple

Terrace was the property of Paul's College, which also owned the Vicarage and the living, but there was some talk that the new Bursar, who had Labour leanings, was planning to make a number of changes in the investments.

"Paul's College, Oxford?" said Mr. Adams. "Then it shouldn't be too hard to get at the facts of the matter. I've got a couple of good friends there, who're certain to be in the know. There's Fanshawe, who married the Deans' eldest girl, and there's Carton who married Miss Sparling, Heather's old headmistress. He's retired now, but he still has a lot of influence. See if you can get Dean on the phone for me, will you? And remind me to drop a line to Carton. Aberfordbury's a member of my old party, I'm sorry to say, but he's about as straight as a corkscrew and no gentleman, even if he did get himself made a Lord. We can't let him go mucking up the countryside with factories, though I says it as shouldn't, but Hogglestock's one thing and Southbridge is another."

After a brief but illuminating talk on the telephone with his fellow-industrialist Mr. Dean, the wealthy consulting engineer at Winter Overcotes, he sat down to his canteen lunch of milk and sandwiches with a good deal of thought.

Wiple Terrace, as all friends of Southbridge will remember, is a little block of four mellow, red-brick, two-storey cottages lying back from the road with a strip of grass in front of them. They are surmounted by a stucco pediment on which the name and the date 1820 can be read, though with some difficulty. Their creator Mr. Wiple, whose monument is to be seen in Southbridge Church, was a small master builder who elected to name the cottages after his four daughters, Adelina, Maria, Louisa, and Editha. Adelina and Editha had a slight advantage over the others, in that each could be approached by a small lane running alongside the garden, whereas at Maria and Louisa, in the middle of the block, the coal and dust and all kitchen visitors had to go in and out through the front door; for the long, narrow gardens of the terrace were bounded by a field to which there was no exit.

At the moment of writing, and indeed ever since we paid our first visit to Southbridge, Adelina Cottage was occupied by Miss Hampton and Miss Bent, two spinster ladies of uncertain age and masterful habits, to whom a sort of honorary rank was conceded as tenants of the longest standing. Maria and Louisa were occupied respectively by Mr. Traill and Mr. Feeder, two masters from Southbridge School, while Mr. Feeder's mother, a dashing and formidable old lady, lived at Editha. The same gardener worked for all the cottages, and Mrs. Dingle, a respectable widow who really understood the art of turning out a room, "did" for Miss Hampton and Miss Bent three days a week, and was always ready to oblige the other tenants of a morning.

On the evening of the day on which Eleanor and Amabel had brought their shocking news to Mr. Adams, an informal indignation meeting was taking place at Adelina Cottage, assisted by Miss Hampton's lavish hospitality in the way of drinks. Fortified by brimming glasses of gin and French, gin and It, gin and white Cinzano, or in Mrs. Feeder's case a Bloody Mary, an innovation to which Barsetshire as a whole had not yet quite lent countenance, partly because of the name, partly because it was difficult to get, and partly, we think, because the natives felt it was in some way unpatriotic to be drinking vodka, the ladies of Adelina and Editha and the gentlemen of Maria and Louisa were discussing the burning topic of the day.

"Any further news?" asked Miss Hampton, who was dressed in an extremely well-cut coat and skirt, with a gentlemanly silk shirt and tie, and was smoking a cigarette in a long ebony holder.

"Nothing you could call hard news," said Mr. Feeder, "but of course the whole school's buzzing with it. I shouldn't be a bit surprised if all the boys had heard of it by now. Not that they'll care, of course," he added, in which, as we know, he did less than justice to these small, eager beings. "Blood-thirsty little devils, I expect they'd like to see the whole of Southbridge blown up by a bomb, and think they could have a holiday for ever."

"All the same, Feeder," said his co-master, Mr. Traill, "you must admit there's some substantiation of the rumour. This man Aberfordbury is stinking rich and quite a menace, according to what they tell me, and he seems to have squared the Bursar of Lazarus with some bribe or other, and now he's got his claws fast into the new Bursar of Paul's."

"He's a Vandal," fiercely proclaimed Miss Bent, whose dim, floppy dresses and rows of supernumerary beads were apt to delude strangers into underestimating the forcefulness of her character. "Hampton and I can remember the time when he tried to buy Pooker's Piece near Skeynes, and put up a teashop and a garage there."

"What happened?" asked Mr. Feeder. "That was before my day."

"Old Lord Pomfret bought it over his head and made it over to the National Trust. Aberfordbury tried to run the price up by a hundred, but he didn't get a penny out of it."

"To do him justice," broke in Miss Hampton, in a voice that said she meant to do nothing of the kind, "he was only a Liberal then; he hadn't gone the Whole Hog. He was one of those Lloyd George knights, something to do with shipping, and was called Sir Ogilvy Hibberd. No real vice, I think," she added reluctantly, for Vice was her subject. "Just plain fool."

"But a knave *in posse*," announced a new voice at the door, and in came Mr. Wickham, the Mertons' agent, his pockets bulging with bottles of various shapes which he skilfully disgorged and set out on the side, or what is known in stage directions as the Drinks Table. "A spot of real Navy rum and some Aquavit sent me by a friend in Sweden, guaranteed to burn the chill out of any summer evening."

"Mix yourself a drink and join us, Wicks," said Miss Hampton heartily, for Mr. Wickham was a welcome guest at Wiple Terrace, as indeed he was at almost every house in Barsetshire. "You always have the latest news. Tell us the worst and let's get it over."

Pouring himself a stiff tot of Navy rum and cradling it in his capable hands, Mr. Wickham sat down on the window-seat and said: "Well, it's not good news, I'm afraid. I've got it hard that Aberfordbury has put in a bid for Wiple Terrace, and the Bursar of Paul's is ready to sell. He's a new chap and a pal of those people at Lazarus, and Aberfordbury's got Lazarus in his pocket."

"What's the idea?" said Mr. Traill. "What are they going to do with Wiple Terrace?"

"Pull it down, I'm afraid," said Mr. Wickham, "and put up a streamlined factory for the son, young Hibberd, who's never been any good at anything, so he's going in for what he calls commercial art in a big way."

"I know exactly what you mean," said Mrs. Feeder, savagely tossing back the last of her bloody Mary. "Glossy picture post-cards with All the Beauty Spots of Barsetshire sideways across the corners and the Cathedral all out of proportion in the middle."

"That's about the size of it," said Mr. Wickham. "They call the stuff Rotochrome Polychrome pictures or something, and personally I wouldn't be seen dead with one of the things in my pocket, but Aberfordbury's prepared to pour any amount of money into it. It's a damn scandal, but it looks as though the whole thing's in the bag and I'm afraid we've had it."

"A *fait accompli*," said Miss Hampton, getting up to recharge her glass of gin and French, and looking round for any other takers, of which we must say there were several.

"Where is your courage, Hampton?" cried her friend Miss Bent, her necklaces jangling with emotion. "This is no time for Paltering, this is something we must Fight to the Last Ditch."

"I'm all with you in theory," said Mr. Feeder. "But what in practice can we do?"

"Couldn't we appeal to the present Lord Pomfret?" asked his mother. "After all, he *is* Lord Lieutenant of the county."

"Not a hope, I'm afraid," said Mr. Wickham. "Pomfret's one of the best fellows in the world, but he wouldn't cut much ice with the Hibberd lot, and he's hardly got two beans to rub together."

"We might write to the *Barchester Chronicle*," suggested Mr. Traill.

"Or to *The Times*," said Mr. Feeder.

"Wouldn't do a jot of good," observed Miss Hampton, who by virtue of her calling as a novelist, though of what some held to be a rather curious order, was accepted by all present as a natural literary authority. "If I know Aberfordbury and his lot, they're well in with the *Chronicle* already, telling them a factory would add to the amenities of Southbridge and provide labour for the starving proletariat. As for *The Times*, my dear man," she added, fixing a stern eye on Mr. Feeder, "we're simply not in their class at all. It might be a different thing if we wanted to get in a letter about cricket or the Congo or the choice of a national British bird. But all we've got to write about is a nineteenth-century terrace in a small country town, which we happen to be very fond of, and They want to pull it down, and who outside Barsetshire is likely to be interested in that?"

We do not think Miss Hampton, that fearless author of outspoken novels, of which perhaps the most celebrated were the Banned Book of the Month Club choice, *Temptation at St. Anthony's,* and *Chariots of Desire,* a powerful exposure of the sex life of lorry drivers, had ever delivered herself of such a feeling speech in public, and the result was momentary silence.

Then Mr. Wickham, raising his glass to her and saying: "Cheers, Hampton, that's the boy!" suggested they might call a public meeting, to try out the temperature of Southbridge. A committee was elected, consisting of all those present, and it was unanimously agreed that Colonel the Reverend Edward Crofts, vicar of Southbridge, and his wife who had been F. E. Arbuthnot and was a fellow bird-watcher of Mr. Wickham's, should be co-opted. A date was tentatively fixed, and both Mr. Feeder and Mr. Traill were confident there wouldn't be much trouble about borrowing a room at Southbridge School, seeing that it was holidays and the school staff, though not personally affected by the threat to Wiple Terrace, which really had no connection with the school at all, were a very decent crowd. Miss Bent offered to type out the invitations, which, as she said, would be child's play after typing Hampton's books, and after another drink for the road all round, although Mr. Wickham was the only one who was taking to the road, the gathering broke up.

With a slight but definite sinking of the heart, of which she felt curiously ashamed, Mrs. Morland drove to the station at Stoke Dry to meet her grandson. She was normally a very careful driver, but that afternoon her mind was distracted. Half of it was occupied with the ordeal in front of her, for deny it who may, the irruption of a small, lively boy, however much beloved, into the household of an elderly lady, is something of a disturbance; the other half toying with an improvement in the plot of her latest Madame Koska novel, which would have to be finished and delivered to her publisher Adrian Coates in a few weeks' time if it was to get into the Spring list. So at the crossroads she was forced to pull up with a jerk to avoid collision with Dr. Ford's shabby old car, which was coming from the direction of the Cottage Hospital.

"I'm dreadfully sorry, Dr. Ford," she said, as he parked

quite illegally on what is called The Verge and walked across to speak to her. "I know you're thinking Women Drivers and all that, but really I'm a bit distracted, what with one thing and another. I'm going to Stoke Dry to collect my grandson; you know, Tony's eldest boy. He's staying with me for the holidays because the younger children are measling."

"That young limb," said Dr. Ford. "I remember him, spitting image of his father, or was a couple of years ago when he came here last. Don't let him get on top of you, or mark my words, you'll be sorry. Little devils they can be at that age, though I'm speaking without personal experience, mind you, for thank the Lord I've stayed a bachelor."

Strongly resisting a desire to say: "But not for want of trying," Mrs. Morland asked after her old friend Lord Stoke and his invalid cook Mrs. Beeton, to which Dr. Ford, who was an inveterate gossip except over really serious things, replied that the one was deafer and the other better. "That girl from the Vicarage, Sylvia Gould, has done wonders for Mrs. B. Brought her hair-ribbons and bits of nonsense from Sheepshanks', and made her feel Queen of the Ward. And when she saw the way the other patients were looking at her, she brought them all bits of nonsense too. Sound girl, that. Must lead the hell of a life at home with those old parents."

Mrs. Morland said with reservations, for she remembered the conversation at the breakfast table, that she didn't think Sylvia really minded, only it would be nice if she could get out sometimes and meet more people. "The Goulds are very kind, but they *are* rather dull, and Rose and Dora have always been so much together that they're not much help to Sylvia." She then added that she must be getting along, or she'd be late for meeting Robin.

"No need to panic," said Dr. Ford, pulling out the large turnip watch he had inherited from his father, "plenty of time still and no point in standing about on a draughty platform.

Besides, Mallow at the station will see to it the lad's all right. Have you heard about the to-do over at Wiple Terrace?"

Mrs. Morland replied that she hadn't and what sort of to-do? "Nothing bad, I hope," she said. "I'm very fond of Wiple Terrace. I've often been to parties there with Miss Hampton and Miss Bent. And I remember when I went to stay with the Birketts at the beginning of the war, to help them with the evacuation of a London school, no, I don't mean that exactly, I mean help them with a London school that was unloaded on them, there was a very nice master and his wife, Bissell their name was, who took a furnished house in Wiple Terrace, and they were very happy there. Oh yes, it's all coming back to me now. They had an imbecile adopted child and were so pleased because there was a print of the Van Gogh sunflowers in their bedroom. They said it made them feel like home. What is the trouble at Wiple Terrace?"

"Plenty," said Dr. Ford grimly. "They say it's going to be pulled down, and Lord Aberfordbury's going to build a factory there."

"A *factory* at Southbridge?" cried out Mrs. Morland, who was not easily aroused, except when anyone spoke in what she called a beastly, traitorous way about Sir Winston Churchill or the Royal Family. "But that's impossible. It's downright wicked. It makes me want to go out and kill somebody, I don't care who. Isn't there anything we can do to stop it?"

Dr. Ford said he didn't know, but he had heard some talk about a public meeting. "Then I'll most certainly be there," said Mrs. Morland, running her hands fiercely through her hair and pushing her hat quite crooked with the force of her emotions. "And I shall Speak My Mind. And for a start I shall ring up the Birketts and the Everard Carters and Lord Stoke too. Not that he has much to do with West Barsetshire these days, but he's very good at getting angry. And angry is exactly what I am," she added, restarting her car with a ferocious grinding of gears. And so she continued on her journey to Stoke Dry, with a new sort of thinking in her mind, which we believe is always a good thing for writers.

At Stoke Dry the elderly stationmaster, Mr. Mallow, nephew by marriage of the redoubtable Mrs. Mallow, who had kept house for Dr. Ford as long as we can remember, was standing on the down platform, gloomily contemplating a bed of asters.

"Never do no good, them asters won't," he said. "Evening, Mrs. Morland. Sickly is what they are, eel-worm or something of the kind. Plants aren't what they used to be in our young days, nor nothing else neither. Look at British Railways. When I first come to Stoke Dry, Our Line was something to take a pride in. Now it's not even Our Line any more, belongs to the Government in London, and a fat lot they cares about it. When I look at the rolling stock sometimes I feel downright sorry for the engines, having to pull that trash. I give you my word, Mrs. Morland, I do. And it's the same with seeds. When I was a lad you could buy a penny packet anywhere and they come up fine. Now you pay six times as much for a measly packet at Sheepshanks' with coloured pictures on the back, and what's the result, I ask you? This here is," he said, prodding with a malevolent boot at a particularly jaundiced seedling. "Well, I don't care to grumble," he added quite mendaciously. "The down express, she's just about due, and for once she's running up to time. I reckon you're here to meet your young gentleman?"

Mrs. Morland said yes she was, and how did Mr. Mallow know?

"Ah well, your Mrs. Stoker she gets talking to my old auntie along of the Women's Institute, and she let fall the other night you was expecting Master Tony's boy to stop the holidays. Proper young limb, Master Tony was. Remember when he put a thrupenny bit on the up rail, to see if the engine would flatten it into a sixpence?"

Mrs. Morland replied that she remembered it only too well, and she had seldom been more angry with her offspring in her life. Then the sounds of the approaching train were heard, and Mr. Mallow went off to attend to his official duties, which mostly consisted of a long and interesting chat about late peas and runner beans with the engine driver, who was the nephew of a Pollett cousin on his mother's side.

Mrs. Morland waited while a scattering of passengers emerged, mostly London business men who were being met at the station by their wives and cars, and several crates of assorted livestock were hauled out of the guard's van by Bert Margett, the porter, their occupants protesting vigorously. She was looking up and down the platform in a mounting panic, assailed by the certainty that Something Had Happened to her grandson, either he had missed his connection and was stranded alone in some strange, alien town, or else there had been an accident and he was tossing feverishly in a hospital bed, when she became aware of a small boy in grey flannel shorts and jacket and a sky-blue school cap, who was making a rearward exit from a carriage, dragging a number of pieces of luggage onto the platform with a great deal of grunting and groaning.

Angry with herself for her own worry, and pierced in the moment of relief by the thought that the backs and particularly the necks of little boys all looked pathetically alike, she hurried up to the burdened traveller and said could she land a hand?

"No, I don't think so, thanks," replied the small boy. "Oh hullo, Gran, it's you. I can manage all right if someone gets my bike out of the van. I had to bring my bike because of breaking up, besides I thought you mightn't have a bike and I rather need one."

Mrs. Morland said she saw Bert Margett getting the bike out of the guard's van, and she was sure he would take it out to the car along with all his other stuff. "You seem to have brought an awful lot of stuff," she added, eyeing the miscellaneous pile with some anxiety and wondering what Stoker would say. In which she showed less than her usual common sense, for the formidable Stoker could cope with almost any situation, and liked above all things to have a small boy about the house whom she could boss and fuss over.

"I know," said Robin, and sounded so exactly like his father at the same age that Mrs. Morland almost hugged him, but resisted the temptation, for as the mother of four sons she knew that demonstrations of this kind were but ill received. "You see, I had to bring all my clobber, and all my shoes and cricket bat and things, because of coming straight from school. I hope they'll squash into your house all right. It's awful what they burden you with at school."

"I daresay we shall manage," said Mrs. Morland, taking a firm grip on an attaché case whose contents seemed to be breaking loose from their moorings, and at that moment up came the porter, Bert Margett, wheeling a bicycle with one hand and pushing a small hand-truck with the other.

"I'll see to the young gentleman's things," he said. "No need to commence to worry, Mrs. Morland. 'Tisn't fitting for a lady to carry such as that." And so saying, he twitched the battered case out of her hands, swung it onto the truck as if it were a feather-weight, added all the other bits and pieces, and went out with them to the station yard, whistling cheerfully.

Mrs. Morland paused long enough to wave a friendly good-bye to Mr. Mallow, who had finished his dissertation on peas and beans and was now flagging the down train on its further journey, and went out with Robin to her shabby little car, into and onto which Bert Margett was busy stacking all the luggage.

We shall not attempt to describe Robin Morland, who looked exactly like hundreds of other little boys, except in the eyes of their doting parents and relations, with a deceptively candid face, a freckled, slightly turned-up nose, wrists so thin that you felt you could break them at a touch, and a dreadful habit of boasting.

"Oh I say, Gran," he said, watching Bert Margett prepare to lash the bicycle to the back of the car, "can't I ride the bike back to High Rising? It's a very fast bike and I can whizz past you like anything, and it'll give Stoker such a nice surprise to see me come whizzing up the drive."

"More likely whizz into a ditch," replied his heartless grandmother, "and that wouldn't be a nice surprise for anybody. No, Robin, you can ride the bike tomorrow, but we've got to get home now as fast as possible. Stoker will be waiting with the supper."

So with only the lightest frown of discontent on his round, young face, Robin climbed into the car beside his grandmother; some pieces of money changed hands, Bert Margett touched his cap, and they were off on the home journey to High Rising.

"Did you have a nice term?" asked Mrs. Morland presently, as in duty bound.

"Well, you can't call school ezzackly *nice*, can you?" replied Robin. "But this term wasn't bad. I got into the junior eleven, at least I got into the reserves, and I expect I should have won the junior diving, only my dives went rather flat. I can swim two lengths easily and almost do the crawl. I have a kind of natural gift for swimming."

Mrs. Morland, the greater part of her mind concentrated on driving, said that was very nice.

"Can I get some swimming these hols?" pursued her grandson. "I was too little to swim the last time I was here, but I've brought my swimming things in case."

Mrs. Morland said she thought it might be arranged.

"And can I get some riding? I'm jolly good at riding. We've got a pony club at school and my pony's miles the fastest. Only I can't always have him, because he sort of belongs to another boy called Donald. D'you think I could get some riding, Gran? A bike's all right for getting to places, but a pony's sort of more companionly."

"We'll see what we can do about it, but I can't promise."

As they took the turning into High Rising, they met a vintage brougham approaching in sedate fashion from the opposite direction. It was driven by an elderly groom and had a single occupant, to whom Mrs. Morland waved a cheery hand of greeting.

Robin, who had been watching a combine harvester at work on his side of the road, swung round as they passed and said: "Who was that you were waving at, Gran?"

"Lord Stoke," said Mrs. Morland. "He lives at Rising Castle and used to know your father when he was a little boy. I mean when your father was a little boy, not Lord Stoke."

"I know," said Robin. "Is it a real castle?"

"Quite real, only a lot of it's in ruins now."

"Can I explore the ruins? Are they haunted?"

"I daresay you can, and I shouldn't think they are. You'll have to ask Lord Stoke."

"I don't mind if they are haunted," said Robin loftily. "You see, I'm not supersistious. There's a boy in my form called Simpson who's frightfully supersistious. When he spills salt on the tablecloth at dinner he always throws it over his left shoulder. One day he threw it whang at Matron, when she was going behind him with a jug of water. You see he didn't know she was there, because she was going *behind* him. I don't suppose Simpson would like to explore the ruins, do you, Gran?" Without waiting for an answer to a question that obviously did not expect one, he rattled on cheerfully: "Are there any dungeons?"

"I don't think so, but there's a place called the Stokey Hole," said Mrs. Morland. "But you can't get into it now, because Lord Stoke put a gate across to stop the trippers. It's a very deep cave under the castle, with a passage that people used to think led to the Tower of London."

"And did it?" asked Robin, jigging up and down in his excitement.

"I shouldn't think so for a minute. Do be careful, Robin, or all the things on the back seat will come toppling down."

"I and Mother saw a film in London last hols," said Robin, "about some people who dug a tunnel right into the vaults of a bank. Of course they knew ezzackly where to tunnel because they'd all been in the Army."

Mrs. Morland rashly remarked that she didn't see how that would help them.

"Oh, Gran," said Robin reproachfully, "you must have heard of sappers in the Army. Everybody knows about sappers. I say, Gran, is this the right way to your house? It looks quite different somehow."

"It is different," replied Mrs. Morland, turning the car into the home stretch. "They've built quite a lot of new houses and resurfaced the road since you were here."

"I daresay it needed it," said her grandson, with a grave air of authority. "Traffic can do a lot of harm to road surfaces. They're always pulling up the roads in London because there's so much traffic. I don't suppose there's as much traffic in High Rising as there is in London. I say, Gran, did you know macadam was a person?"

"I did," said Mrs. Morland.

"He invented road surfaces," went on her grandson, persistently if somewhat inaccurately. "He found out about using bits of broken stone, and making them convex instead of concave. We learnt that at school in General Knowledge. General Knowledge is a jolly interesting lesson. I don't suppose Macadam really liked being called after a road surface, do you?"

"He wasn't," said Mrs. Morland. "The road surface was called after him. And anyway, they call it tarmac now."

"I know," said Robin. "Just like Mackintosh. I say, isn't this your house? The trees have grown whopping big. Shall I get out and open the gate for you?"

"Thank you, that would be very kind," said his grandmother, touched by this act of courtesy, and thinking with gratitude that in a slapdash world Tony's children, however exhausting and boastful they might be, had been very well brought up.

As Robin struggled with the gate, which had warped during the winter and made a horrid scrapping noise against the gravel unless it was eased up by a shoulder, a description which our reader will readily understand, a bare-headed boy of sixteen or seventeen rode past slowly on a neat little chestnut mare.

Mrs. Morland stuck her head out of the car window, thereby dislodging her hat so that it nearly fell off, and called a greeting.

"Hullo Giles, how's the Pony Club?"

"Pretty busy," said the Honourable Giles Foster, pulling up his mare and sketching a kind of token salute. "Good evening, Mrs. Morland. My Uncle Roddy is a first-class teacher, and all the kids in these parts seem to want to join. The next thing we'll need is some more stabling, and though Father's being frightfully decent about it, I don't suppose he'll want to cough up much more money."

Mrs. Morland, who was well acquainted with the hard-working, hard-pinched Earl of Pomfret, privately agreed with this opinion, but contented herself with saying that you never knew when something might turn up.

"By the way, Giles," she added, "I was meaning to ask you. Do you think it would be possible to find a pony for my grandson," she jerked her head towards the gate, "who's staying with me for the holidays? He tells me he can ride, though it's safer to take everything he says with a grain of salt. I should be tremendously grateful if you could fix up something."

Giles ran an expert's eye over the small figure at the gate, measured him up in hands and ounces, and said he'd see what could be done. Then he shook up the reins of the chestnut mare, who had stood still like a perfect lady during this conversation, and trotted off. Mrs. Morland, forestalling Robin's inevitable: "Who's that?" turned the car into the little drive and pulled up at the front door, where Stoker was waiting to receive them.

We shall not attempt to describe the confusion of arrival and unloading, Robin's heartfelt groans as he shouldered the lighter luggage, and Stoker's tart comments on the Stuff that young gentlemen brought back from school nowadays. All parents amongst our readers will be able to supply the dialogue for themselves, and understand how things were dumped down anywhere for the time being and we'll find a proper place for them tomorrow.

"You're in your old room, Master Robin," Stoker said, as she unlashed the bicycle from the back of the car. "Now don't you come meddling here. I'll put the bike in the hall for tonight and bring up your attachy case. Supper's in twenty minutes sharp, and mind you give yourself a good wash first."

"What's for supper, Stokes?" said Robin. "I hope there's a lot, because I'm absolutely famished."

"There's sausage and mash and treacle tart and some raspberries and cream left over from lunch."

"Good for you, Stokes," said Robin, plunging upstairs with a good deal of unnecessary noise, and turning round at the half landing to add: "You *will* be sure and make the sausages extra brown, won't you, Stokes, with lots of little frizzled burnt bits? They never give us enough burnt bits at school."

With which encomium of the school cooking he temporarily vanished, although frequent noises were heard off, as it says in stage directions, leaving his grandmother to take off her hat, run her fingers wildly through her hair, and wonder, over a grateful glass of sherry, whether she would manage to survive the holidays and how.

CHAPTER 7

THE Honourable Giles Foster was as good as his word, as indeed
the Pomfrets always were, and early next morning he rang up to
say that they had found a very nice, quiet pony for Mrs. Morland's grandson, as its usual rider had gone off with her family
for a month at Etretat.

"Send him over any time you like," said Giles, "and if my
Uncle Roddy's busy with estate work, Emily or I can see to
him. Hold the line a sec., Mrs. Morland, Mother wants to
speak to you."

The voice of Lady Pomfret then said good-morning, and
wouldn't Mrs. Morland drive her grandson over to the Towers,
and have tea with her while the children did their riding? If it
wasn't too short notice, what about this afternoon, as Gillie
had a committee meeting at Barchester and she was quite
alone? To which Mrs. Morland replied that she would like it of
all things, and was half-past three too early? which it wasn't.

So after a very good lunch of steak-and-kidney pudding, with
lemon meringue pie for afters, she and Robin set out for Pomfret Towers and drove up, not to the main pile, for that as we
know was occupied by Mr. Adams and his associates, but to the
side entrance in the old servants' wing. Here they were met by
the Honourable Emily Foster, a tall girl with a pony-tail, dressed
in riding kit. Having greeted Mrs. Morland with very nice manners, for she was not Girl of Honour at Barchester High School
for nothing (that being the elegant title bestowed on her head
prefect or monitor by the headmistress Miss Pettinger, more
often referred to as Beast Pettinger), she measured Robin with

a practised eye and said she thought they had some riding breeches that would fit him nicely. Whereupon she handed Mrs. Morland over to the charge of an ancient servitor who was hovering in the doorway, and conducted Robin to the stable yard, whence came loud sounds of jingling, stamping, neighing, and shrill childish voices.

We shall not attempt to describe Robin's exploits that afternoon, as we know regrettably little about horsemanship or even ponymanship, but we believe he thoroughly enjoyed himself, fell off his pony several times, mounted again with a few grunts and groans to which nobody paid any attention at all, and was none the worse for finding himself in the company of his betters.

Meanwhile Mrs. Morland had been escorted by the ancient servitor, who wore a kind of butler's apron, more common in the pantry than the gentry quarters, and had in his time worked as odd-job man for the late Sir Harry Waring at Beliers Priory, to Lady Pomfret's sitting-room on the first floor, where as it was July there was a bright fire burning.

Sally Pomfret, although she was no longer the ardent horse-woman with the best hands in the county; the carefree, brisk young thing who had rescued the reluctant heir to the title, Gillie Foster, from his sense of impending doom by encouraging him to propose to her in the estate room so many years ago (though we believe she will go on rescuing him for life), was still crisp and tireless in her middle years and had kept the trimness of her youthful figure.

"How *very* nice to see you, Mrs. Morland," she said. "It is so kind of you to come. Gillie has been dragged off to another of those tiresome meetings, where they'll do nothing except argue and get nowhere in the end. I often wish he wasn't Lord Lieutenant of the County. He always comes back from the meetings with a splitting headache, but he insists on going to every one of them. He says it's his duty. Oh, well. Would you like to have tea now, or wait until some of the others get back? My brother Roddy's out on the rounds of the estate, but he usually drops in for tea at about four."

Mrs. Morland said she would much rather wait, and how kind it was of Lady Pomfret's young people to take charge of her grandson. "He's a dear boy and I'm very fond of him," she added, "but he *is* rather a handful when you've grown unaccustomed to having small boys about the place. And I'm afraid he does boast most frightfully."

Lady Pomfret said comfortably that they always did at that age, at least in her experience, and she was certain Giles and Emily could cope. "I've never seen them rattled by anything in their lives," she said. "Now if it were Ludo it might be a different matter."

Whereupon Mrs. Morland asked warmly after the Pomfret's shy elder son, Lord Mellings, who had followed his Graham cousins into the Brigade of Guards.

"He's been out in West Germany for months," said Lady Pomfret, "but we're expecting him back on leave at any moment. And I hope, at least we've heard a rumour, that he's likely to be posted to London from now on, which would be simply wonderful, because, though he *has* come out a lot in the last few years, he's really a home-bird like Gillie. What he needs is a wife who'll give him confidence in himself, some nice girl who's strong and sympathetic and can make him laugh. We thought at one time there might be something between him and Edith Graham, but now she's Lady William Harcourt and in any case it wouldn't really have done. They were too much of an age, apart from being cousins, which meant she was too old for Ludo. Now perhaps——" She broke off suddenly and her eyes took on what Mrs. Morland described to herself afterwards as a Matchmaking Look.

However, the sentence remained unfinished and the guest, although as full of curiosity as any nice, normal woman would be, was far too sensitive to atmosphere to press the point. Instead she asked Lady Pomfret about the younger children, and whether there were any plans yet for their future.

"I thought your Emily looked remarkably handsome when I saw her just now," she said. "And how tall she's grown, almost as tall as Ludovic as I remember him."

"Well, not quite, thank heaven," said Lady Pomfret, "that would be too dreadful for a girl. But she's grown up a lot lately, in a number of ways. She's leaving school next Easter, and going to spend the summer in France and Holland with some nice friends of Margot Fewling's, you know, the one who was married to Mr. Macfadyen of Amalgamated Vedge. Margot's been the greatest help to Emily, because of course she knows almost everybody in the agricultural world through her late husband's connections."

Mrs. Morland asked if Emily meant to go in for farming.

"Strangely enough, no," said Sally Pomfret. "She's very much the outdoor type, of course, and for a time we thought she'd grow up cow-minded like her cousin Emmy Grantly. But she seems to have set her heart on market gardening. She wants to grow strawberries and peaches and tomatoes and all sorts of soft fruit, and the plan is to send her to a horticultural college when she comes back from Holland. And after that she'd like to get a job as assistant gardener on some big estate where they've got lots of glass. But all that's a long way off and anything might happen."

Mrs. Morland said she understood the feeling very well, because she'd once been to the Chelsea Flower Show and absolutely *gloated* over the smell of strawberries. "There were exhibits at each end of the big tent," she said. "One lot came from the Duke of Norfolk's estate and the other was from Reading, I think, and as soon as you got near them the air was so thick with scent you couldn't even smell the flowers.

If I knew how to grow strawberries like that, I'd never want
to write a book again."

Lady Pomfret laughed and said it was a good thing for a
great many people that Mrs. Morland had never learnt how
to grow strawberries, to which her guest replied that she kept
on keeping on, and what was Giles planning to do?

"Oh, Giles never *plans*," said his devoted mother, "he just
bangs along happily from day to day and enjoys every minute
of it. By rights he ought to stay at school for another year
at least, but he's not really a school type, and would never
pass his exams. So Gillie and I are arranging to let him go
for a time as a trainee to a pony-breeding stables in the New
Forest. He's really at his best with horses. After that he'll go
to Barchester and take a course in estate management. My
brother Roddy says his bookwork isn't nearly up to standard
yet, but he'll make a splendid estate agent in the end. I expect
he'll become Roddy's assistant and take over The Towers
when Roddy gets too old, for heaven knows Ludo will need
somebody to run the place for him."

At this point in the adumbration of years to come, tea was
brought in, almost simultaneously with the arrival of Lady
Pomfret's brother Roddy Wicklow, agent to the estate, and
conversation became general. Roddy asked if they'd heard
about that shocking business over at Southbridge? He'd just
run into Wickham, the Mertons' agent, who was full of it.
Sally said no, she hadn't, but Mrs. Morland said if it was
Wiple Terrace yes, she had.

"Lord Aberfordbury and his lot," she explained, turning to
her hostess, "want to pull down a very pleasant little terrace
of nineteenth-century cottages at Southbridge and put up a
horrid factory for hideous picture postcards. The BEASTS,"
she added vehemently. "If they had their way they'd get rid
of everything that's left in England, and fill the county full

of factories and skyscrapers. And what makes me so downright Furious is that somebody is certain to appear on television and call it Progress. I wouldn't put it past them to pull
down the Cathedral spire, because it interfered with the view
from Hogglestock New Town."

"The Bishop would be able to put a stop to that, wouldn't
he?" said Roddy Wicklow. "After all, he's hand in glove with
Them."

"But the Cathedral doesn't belong to the Bishop," protested
Mrs. Morland stoutly. "I know he's got his throne there and
a private room for robing, or whatever they call it, where they
put on their vestments and take off their gaiters, or *do* they
take off their gaiters for a service? I've never really noticed. I
must ask somebody. Octavia Needham would be sure to know,
the one that married the clergyman at Lambton with only one
arm, he lost the other somewhere in the war, but he manages
quite splendidly with just the one, though I've always thought it
must be difficult at christenings. Octavia knows everything
about the Church; she's the Dean's youngest daughter, you
know. And that reminds me of what I meant to say. The
Cathedral really belongs to the Dean, doesn't it? But if They
decided to pull down the spire, and the Bishop backed Them
up, the Dean wouldn't have a chance to get a word in edgeways."

After which outburst a very interesting and ill-informed discussion took place about the exact hierarchy of the Close and
the provenance of episcopal authority.

Presently the young people came roaring in, Emily and
Giles clamouring for tea, and Robin, very pink of face and
no whit the worse for his afternoon's adventures, insisting that
the pony, Skylark, had distinctly told him he must come
again. "He said he'd like some Cox's orange pippins next
time, Gran," Robin whispered, tugging at Mrs. Morland's

hand. "Do you think Stoker could have some Cox's orange pippins for Skylark?"

"I expect so. We'll see when the times comes," said Mrs. Morland. "Say good afternoon to Lady Pomfret, Robin." Which her grandson, recalled from the world of horsemanship, did very nicely. Lady Pomfret smiled at Robin and told her young people they must all be ravenously hungry, she'd ring for a fresh pot of tea and cook had better send up the other cake and an extra plate of sandwiches, as she was sure they would get through these in no time. After which they legged their chairs up to the table, an expression which our reader will readily understand, and fell to with a hearty appetite.

Roddy Wicklow asked Mrs. Morland if she was interested in horses, to which she replied that she always had two shillings or even half-a-crown each way on the Derby.

"But if you mean have I ever ridden, the answer is no. They did try to teach me when I was a little girl, but I never had much head for horses, like not having a head for heights, and I soon gave it up and rode a bicycle. And at my great age I find motoring *much* more satisfactory, although I did once know an old gentleman, several years older than I am now, who bicycled to his college every day. He was a Professor of Philosophy and had a white forked beard that streamed out into the wind. He always reminded me of Blake."

We are afraid this allusion was somewhat lost on Sally Pomfret and her brother, although Roddy's nice wife Alice, who was no mean artist in her own quiet way, would have taken it at once. But they were kind people, and if Mrs. Morland's snipe-flights sometimes eluded them, as indeed they did most members of her circle, they were determined not to show it.

So Lady Pomfret tactfully changed the subject and asked her guest if she was going to the Agricultural at High Rising. Mrs. Morland said she felt she had to go, or her old friend

Lord Stoke would be so dreadfully put out. Besides, she added, Robin would enjoy it.

"They've booked Packer's Universal Derby," said the Hon. Giles through a mouthful of cake, referring to the famous roundabout which had been a feature of Barsetshire life and a source of rapture to children for several generations. "I ran across old Packer at Winter Overcotes the other day, and he said he'd had to get a new cock and a couple of new gondolas, because the kids did so much damage to the old ones when they were over at Hogglestock last Whitsun."

"Little brutes," observed his mother. "They'll damage anything these days. I caught a bunch of them pulling up the annuals in front of the Red Cross Library last week, and they said teacher told them to bring a lot of different flowers for Nature Study."

"I'll tell you what," said Emily, who had caught this expression, we think, from her cousin Lucy Adams, whom she much admired. "It's about time old Packer got some new tunes for the Derby. I'm sick to death of 'Handhold in the Twilight.' It's a sloppy tune anyway, and there's a place towards the end where it's so worn out it sounds like a gramophone running down."

Roddy Wicklow said he'd often wondered why Packer hadn't cottoned on to that thing from *La Ronde* or whatever it was called, because after all it was about a roundabout, wasn't it?

"I think it's such a pity," observed Mrs. Morland, "that nobody says merry-go-round nowadays."

"Oh, but Mrs. Morland," Emily protested, though in a very polite way, "you couldn't possibly say what you gain on the swings you lose on the merry-go-rounds, could you?"

Her Uncle Roddy said that personally he didn't intend to lose anything on the merry-go-rounds or the roundabouts either, because he abominated the things, and now he must be pushing home to Nutfield, or Alice would be waiting at the gate with the look on her face that meant she hadn't been worrying in the least, no, not a bit really.

Soon after that the party broke up, with expressions of thanks from Mrs. Morland and renewed promises from the young Fosters that Skylark would be available for Robin any time he cared to come and ride him.

On the journey home, Mrs. Morland found her grandson unnaturally quiet. "Didn't you enjoy yourself?" she asked him anxiously, and forbore to say did you fall off and hurt yourself? although she had her own suspicions.

"Of course I did, Gran," said Robin. "It was awfully decent, and Emily and Giles are awfully decent too, though I like Emily the best, Giles does boss you about a bit. I did fall off several times," he added with a rush of confidence, "but it wasn't really Skylark's fault. I expect he's been used to girls not boys. If I take some Cox's orange pippins to Skylark next time, I expect I won't fall off."

Mrs. Morland waited, for she felt sure that there was more to come, in which her grandmotherly instincts were in no wise at a loss.

"I say Gran," added Robin, after a good deal of preliminary wriggling and squirming, "are you really terribly old? I heard what you said to Lady Pomfret and that man about your great age, and I know grandmothers have to be fairly old, but you're not a bit discrepid so I just wondered."

Mrs. Morland, who believed in truth, told him she would be seventy next birthday.

"When is your birthday, Gran?" Robin pursued, and Mrs. Morland said pretty soon, and gave him the date.

"Are you going to have a party?" Robin asked, and Mrs. Morland said no, she didn't think so, because when you got old you didn't bother so much about birthdays, and in any case there were very few people left who would really want to come.

For the rest of the way to High Rising Robin pursued his

unnatural silence, thereby leading his grandmother to believe
that he had really hurt himself in one of his falls from Skylark,
and she'd have to send for Dr. Ford if he wasn't any better in
the morning.

But Robin was following a train of thought, and as soon as
he had washed his hands in a somewhat perfunctory way, he
betook himself to the kitchen, where Stoker was frying rissoles.

"What's that?" he said. "It smells jolly good, and I'm terribly hungry, Stokes."

"Them's rissles," said Stoker imperturbably, "and I'll thank
you to change your muddy shoes before you come messing up
my kitchen. There'll be plenty of rissles for you along of supper-
time."

"I know," said Robin, fiddling most tiresomely with the minc-
ing machine and standing on one leg like a stork. "I say, Stokes,
isn't seventy most terribly old?"

"As old as your tongue and a little older than your teeth,"
replied Stoker. "And if you don't leave go of that mincer, Master
Robin, you'll chop your fingers off."

"I know," said Robin, picking a shred of meat out of the
mincer and eating it. "But what I mean is, seventy's a Great
Age, isn't it, a sort of record?"

"Not so far as I've heard tell of," answered Stoker. "It's the
age they give us in the Bible, threescore years and ten, but
that's not to say you can't grow older in the Bible, look at
Methuselah. My old auntie over Plaistow way she's rising
ninety, and she still goes to the public every evening for her
drop of stout and does all her own shopping. You're as old as
what you feel, that's what I always say, and I'll trouble you to
take your muddy feet off my nice clean linoleum."

"Do you suppose Gran feels terribly old, Stokes?" persisted
Robin, rubbing out a mudstain on the linoleum with one foot
and adding another and much bigger one.

"Sometimes, when she's wore herself out writing those rubbishy books to pay for you and your schooling," said Stoker quite unfairly, for Tony Morland earned a comfortable income from whatever job he had in London, and since we don't know exactly what it was we won't trouble to invent it, and never asked his mother for a penny. "Now go upstairs and wash your dirty self, with plenty of soap mind, and let me have your shoes, I'll wipe them off with a damp cloth while the mud's still fresh. And don't you go disturbing of your poor grandma. She needs a good set-down and a nice glass of sherry before her supper."

So Robin, sighing heavily, scuffed off his shoes by the simple expedient of scraping one foot against another, and ploughed his way upstairs in stockinged feet with a look of secret purpose on his round young face.

The morning of the Agricultural dawned bright and fair. Naturally there were wisebeards who shook their heads over this and said Ar, that were a bad sign for certain sure, rain before seven, fine before eleven, and stands to reason the contrairy holds. But we are glad to be able to reassure our readers that they were utterly discomfited, for the weather stayed on its best behaviour all day long, and the people who had come out with mackintoshes and umbrellas wished they hadn't.

It had been arranged that Mrs. Morland and Robin should set off for Rising Castle soon after breakfast, taking a picnic lunch packed by Stoker and collecting Sylvia at the Vicarage on the way. For both ladies had volunteered their services in such things as Seeing to the Flowers in the tea-tent, the supervision of the toilet arrangements, and the discreet disposal of clear placards saying: "Out of Bounds" "Teas One Shilling" "NO LITTER PLEASE. KINDLY PUT ALL YOUR RUBBISH HERE."

Mrs. Morland had been briefly exercised over the problem of how to occupy Robin during the morning, but as soon as they drove into the grounds of Rising Castle it became evident that her worry was for nothing. The whole place was seething with activity. Animal and vegetable contestants for the various prizes had long ago arrived in trucks, Ford vans, and station wagons, accompanied by ancillary humans, and the judges were already busy on their rounds, testing the weight of vegetable marrows, prodding protesting piglings in the ribs and sampling milk yield as if it were vintage champagne.

Meanwhile the minions of Messrs. Scatcherd and Tozer, the well-known firm of Barchester caterers, were unloading crates and cardboard boxes from a van, whipping up trestle tables, disentangling Laocoön-like groups of chairs, and setting out glass, chinaware, and cutlery; all under the watchful eye of Mr. Tozer himself, who had not missed a major Event in Barsetshire for nearly forty years; even attending, with the proper hint of respectful reproach, the Bishop's annual garden-party, with, as Mr. Tozer confided later to a few selected friends, sandwiches and gatto on Our Lowest Tariff.

A little farther down the drive, an immense beer-dray had pulled up, drawn by a team of the magnificent grey Percherons who belonged to Messrs. Pilward and Son's Entire; their coats burnished and glossy, their brasses shining, all of them bearing names beginning with the syllable Pil; although, as their owner Mr. Pilward observed to his colleague and co-father-in-law Samuel Adams, it was getting a bit awkward now and he really couldn't hardly think which way to turn when it came to making up new names, but Chee Serra Serra, as they sang it in some film or other.

Like all small boys, Robin was entranced by these activities, and his grandmother lost all track of him for the next two hours. However, she was of a naturally confident disposition, particularly in the ability of small boys to keep themselves out of any serious trouble, and she went on with her job of sticking labels on what looked like toothpicks into piles of sandwiches, bearing the beautiful words "Ham" "Sardine" "Egg and Cheese"

"Cheese and Tomato," and perhaps the most beautiful words of all "Gentleman's Relish"; asking any passing friend who was likely to know her grandson to see what he was doing and tell him not to.

"I think I know where he is, Mrs. Morland," said Lucy Adams, who had come early with her husband to watch the judging of root-crops and fertilisers. "If it's the boy that's the one in the blue school cap, only he's stuck it in his pocket now, he's watching Packer put up the Universal Derby. I say, Mrs. Morland, is he Tony's son? He looks exactly like him."

"He does and he is," somewhat grimly replied his doting grandmother. "I hope he isn't making a nuisance of himself. I'll just finish this lot of sandwiches and then I'll go and see."

"Now there's no cause for you to worry, Mrs. Morland," said Mr. Adams reassuringly. "Our Amabel's down there too if I know my girlie, and I'll just pop along and have a look-see what they're up to. I want a word with Packer anyway."

"That means Sam's going to tip him," observed Lucy, watching her husband's departing back with a look of deep affection. "I know. He's worried about the damage those little devils over at Hogglestock did to Packer's Derby, though they had nothing whatever to do with the Rolling Mills, they weren't even children of employees, but Sam's awfully softhearted that way. He's got an awful conscience about Hogglestock, I suppose it was because he was born there. I'll tell you what, Mrs. Morland, Amabel's growing up most awfully like him. I mean, she seems awfully tough and businesslike on the outside but inside she's awfully soft. I've said too many awfullys, but you do know what I mean?"

Mrs. Morland said she knew *exactly* what Lucy meant, and when Tony was ten or eleven there were times when she would have gladly killed him, only when she went upstairs to say goodnight to him he looked so touching that she felt a brute. "And he had a *very* soft heart under that boastful man-

ner. I remember him in tears over a foxhound that got run over
by an engine, not killed, I don't mean, but its leg was broken,
and when it was convalescent Tony used to take it out to look
at things for treats, like some men dragging a car out of a ditch.
It was my publisher's car and *entirely* his own fault." To which
Lucy replied that Sam was quite marvellous with cars, only he
didn't often drive himself now, he had so much to think about
what with the works and Adamsfield and Pomfret Towers.

"You're a lucky woman, Lucy," said Mrs. Morland. "You've
got a real treasure of a husband." And even if she added to
herself quite privately, for after all she was a writer who lived
in a world of words: "Though he may be a bit of a rough diamond," her compliment was none the less sincere.

Mr. Adams, as he had expected, found his daughter Amabel
and her friend Eleanor Leslie assisting in the French sense at
the final assembly of Packer's Universal Royal Derby. The
roundabout and its organ had arrived the night before, the re-
volving platform with its shining brass poles had been erected,
and two oily men in overalls were now rounding up the various mounts, a cock, an ostrich, a swan, a number of horses,
and several boats, on which and in which the customers would
take their rides, as tenderly as if they had been real stable-lads
at Epsom.

Both little girls were dressed in flowery summer frocks, and
looked a great deal nicer than the last time we met them, in
the functional but hideous uniform of Barchester High School.
A few yards away from them a small boy of about their own age
was standing, hands thrust into the pockets of his grey flannel
shorts, from one of which protruded the peak of a blue school
cap. From time to time he eyed the little girls with the combined mistrust and interest with which all children survey other
and strange children.

Mr. Adams, who was no mean diplomat in his own rough

way, cocked a beckoning finger at his daughter Amabel, approached the small boy and said: "Hullo, young feller-me-lad, I think your grandma is a friend of mine. You're young Morland, aren't you?"

Robin looked with nervous curiosity at the large stranger, replied: "Yes, sir," and made to touch the brim of the cap that wasn't there.

"Well, my name's Samuel Adams, and this is my girlie Amabel, and this is her friend Eleanor Leslie." At which the children regarded each other guardedly and said hullo.

"Your parents here, young lady?" Mr. Adams said to Eleanor, thereby as it were, sealing the party circle. Eleanor said yes they were here somewhere, but she didn't quite know where, they'd come over to show Cowslip, who was a champion milker, at least they hoped she would be. "I daresay they're looking at Uncle George's little pigs," she added, referring to her mother's brother George Halliday, who farmed over at Hatch End with his very nice and country-minded wife, she who had been Jane Crawley.

"I say, Dad," broke in Amabel, "have you got any news yet about You Know What?" and her lips formed the words Wiple Terrace with her back turned to Robin. "Eleanor's still frightfully worried."

"So's half Barsetshire," said her father, though not at all unkindly. "Between you and I and the gatepost, girlie, I think things are moving in the right direction. But it doesn't do to say anything until you're certain. When I was younger and knew less than what I do now, I lost a lot of business deals that way. Just leave it to your old Dad, girlie, and keep your fingers crossed."

At this moment a head, followed by a distinctly oily body, emerged from the intestines of the roundabout, and revealed itself as Mr. Packer in person.

"Hi, Packer, I want a word with you," called Mr. Adams,

drawing the proprietor of the Royal Derby aside, and since we did not listen to their conversation we shall not trouble to invent it. We are reasonably certain, however, that a number of bits of paper passed from hand to hand, as Lucy had already adumbrated, and that Mr. Packer and his two oily companions drank Samuel Adams's health that night in quite a lot of tankards at the Wheatsheaf.

As activities at the Royal Derby seemed temporarily suspended, until the roundabout burst into full clamour at two o'clock, Robin and the little girls strolled away, at Eleanor's suggestion, to look at Uncle George's piglets.

"What did you mean just now, when you said You Know What?" Robin asked Amabel.

"That's a secret," she replied.

"All right then," countered Robin, "I've got a secret too."

"Ours is a secret plan," said Amabel.

"So's mine a secret plan," said Robin. "I expect it's just about the most important secret plan in Barsetshire."

"It can't be, because ours is," said Amabel. "Tell us yours."

"Certainly not," replied Robin with dignity. "You don't tell secret plans until they're ready."

"Well, ours is nearly ready, isn't it, Eleanor?"

"Yes," said the quiet Eleanor, contributing her only mite to the discussion. Robin shot her a quick glance, thought she was on the whole a better sort than Amabel, who seemed a bit too bossy for a girl, and decided that perhaps he would let Eleanor into his secret sometime. Aloud he spoke the words: "I know," which had made his father, Tony Morland, almost insufferable to the inhabitants of High and Low Rising some twenty years earlier.

Eleanor's mother, Sylvia Leslie, was leaning over the edge of a pig-pen, scratching a piglet's back with a bit of stick and talking

to her brother George Halliday. The subject was the absorbing
one of George's infant son, a lusty boy almost a fortnight old,
and answering, in his parents' optimistic view, to the name of
Martin, after Sylvia's husband Martin Leslie.

"Do you know, Sylvia, he weighs more than nine pounds
now?" George told her proudly. "And jove, the little blighter's
got a grip like iron! Jane wanted to come over this afternoon,
just between his feeds you know, but Sister Chiffinch said better not, you never know with cars how long they're going to
take. I believe she thinks they've got a will of their own or
something."

"Well, so they have in a way," said Sylvia, "I know our land-
rover always sulks if I take her by the low road into Barchester;
she likes to go over the downs and see the view. Hullo, here's
Eleanor. And Amabel. And who's your other friend, darling?"
she asked her daughter.

"That's Robin Morland, Mother, and he really lives in London, only he's staying with his grandmother at High Rising for
the holidays, and he wants to look at Uncle George's pigs."

"Are you interested in farming, Robin?" asked Sylvia, looking at the small boy with quiet amusement, and liking what she
saw.

"Well, I'm sort of *studying*," said Robin gravely. "Because
we're going to do part of the Georgics next term in Latin, and I
think it's always best to know. I say, sir, those are pretty decent
piglings, aren't they? Can I scratch one of their backs, sir?"

"You can and they are," replied George, obligingly handing
him a piece of stick. "How come you know pigs like to have
their backs scratched?"

"I read it in a book by P. G. Wodehouse," Robin said. "I
think he's an awfully good writer. I say, sir, are you bothered
much with tension?"

"With *what?*" said George, completely taken aback.

"Oh, you must know about tension, sir, it comes from Yugo-slavia, and it makes the pigs go all paralysed. I saw about it in an article on foot-and-mouth disease."

"Oh, you mean *teschen*," said George Halliday, a great light dawning. "No, I'm thankful to say it hasn't reached Barset-shire yet, and I hope and trust it never will. You seem to have been studying farming to some purposes, young man."

"What a pity Emmy isn't here," said Sylvia. "She'd love to tell you about foot-and-mouth disease, and all sorts of diseases that you've never heard of. She had to stay at Rushwater with Tom," she added, turning to her brother, "because there's a cow due to calve at any moment, and Emmy said she wouldn't leave her to old Herdman. Yes, what is it, Eleanor?" for her daughter was tugging, very gently, at her hand.

"I only thought, Mother, that it would be rather nice if Robin could come to Rushwater some time. Then he could talk to Cousin Emmy about foot-and-mouth disease, and see the bulls, and study lots more about farming."

Sylvia looked down at her usually shy daughter with amused approval, and told Robin it would be very nice indeed if he could come and stay at Rushwater, and she would ring up his grandmother and make a plan.

The Agricultural Show was formally opened at two o'clock sharp by Lord Stoke, wearing his celebrated flat-topped hat, by which time all the exhibitors, helpers, and their various han-gers-on had partaken of some sort of light repast; Robin and his two friends doing extremely well out of the contents of their respective picnic baskets, augmented, by courtesy of Mr. Adams, by liberal supplies of lemonade, orange squash, and ice-cream.

At this point we are glad to be able to tell our readers that the Martin Leslies' Rushwater Cowslip duly took first prize for quantity and quality of milk yield, and that George Halliday's piglings were by no means disgraced, winning a silver medal and a very honourable mention. The *victor ludorum,* however, was generally conceded to be Mr. Marling's Marling Magister, a fifty score White Porkminster with an evil little eye and barely enough room between his undercarriage and the ground to put a finger through, if anyone had cared to make the experiment.

It is also satisfactory to know that Mr. Marling's daughter, Lucy Adams, was awarded a first for outdoor tomatoes and vegetable marrows, although we rather think that one of the Thatchers from Grumpers' End would have beaten her on marrows, if his wicked little boy had not carved the words "Teechers A Fule" on the most promising exhibit.

After a number of enquiries and reassurances as to her grandson's well-being, Mrs. Morland was just coming out of the tea-tent, where she had been relieved by Anne Knox, when she was hailed by a familiar voice and there was Lydia Merton, accompanied by an extremely pretty girl of about twenty, in a devastatingly simple dress of Paisley silk, whom Mrs. Morland at first glance didn't recognise.

"Hullo, Mrs. Morland," said Lydia, "you remember my daughter Lavinia, don't you? She's just back after six months in Paris, living with a family we know."

Lavinia Merton greeted Mrs. Morland very nicely, and said she had picked up one of her Madame Koska books in Paris in a French translation. "It seemed awfully funny reading it in French," she added, "although of course a lot of the dressmaking words are the same in both languages, like *couturière* and mannequin."

"Or like cooking," said Mrs. Morland, leaving her hearers momentarily at a loss. "Not everywhere, of course, though even at the White Hart they do talk about sauté potatoes, that is when they have them, but those long menus you know, with

extra things written in blue ink that you can't read if you
haven't got the proper spectacles, and not always then, because
all the handwriting is foreign."

There followed an interesting conversation about the ghastly
prices they charged you in London restaurants if the names of
the dishes were in French, but Mrs. Morland noticed that
Lavinia's eye was wandering. Presently she heard the distant
sound of a small car pulling up, and a very tall young man
came striding towards them across the grass.

"Here's Ludo," said Lavinia, in a too deliberately offhand
way.

And Lord Mellings it was, who greeted the older ladies very
charmingly, with a confidence that would have been impossible
to him a few years ago, before the Army and that enchanting
actress Jessica Dean had taken him in hand, and then he turned
to Lavinia with a special smile, which made her whole face
light up with an inner radiance. "Just like one of those con-
cealed electric lamps, the kind you don't notice till you switch
them on. Rose colour," thought Mrs. Morland.

After some polite but desultory talk about the Show, and
how the Car Park was nearly full, and Lord Stoke had kindly
told Lord Mellings he could park his little bus on the gravel
sweep outside the Castle, Ludo asked Lavinia if she'd like to
come and have a look at Packer's Universal Derby. She replied
with alacrity that she would, and the two young people strolled
away across the grass, although not, we may say, by the direct
route to the roundabout.

Mrs. Morland looked at Lydia and raised an eyebrow.

"We think so, yes," said Lydia. "We hope so. He's been writing to Lavinia all the time she was in France, and when he got
home on leave yesterday, almost the first thing he did was ring
her up. It would be very nice," she added. "Ludo's a dear boy
and we've known him such a long time now."

Mrs. Morland remembered Sally Pomfret's half-finished,

heart-felt sentence, and said she thought it would be perfect and certain to please everybody. Then she enquired after Lydia's other children, Harry and the youngest, Jessica, who had started life in the perambulator as Miss Kate Merton but decided early in her schooldays to be called by her second name, after her godmother Jessica Dean, star of the Cockspur Theatre.

Lydia, who was always thoughtful for the comfort of older people, said: "Let's sit down, shall we? These look like fairly decent chairs," a suggestion which Mrs. Morland gratefully accepted, for she was growing very conscious of her feet after a morning of duty in the tea-tent. Accordingly they disposed themselves in two of the folding canvas chairs which Mr. Tozer, with an experienced eye on His Ladies, had set out in strategical positions, and Lydia said how happy they both were about Harry, who had grown into such a sensible boy, and knew exactly what he wanted.

"Next term he goes up to Cambridge to take a Science degree, and he's determined to become President of the Union. I daresay he will too, because he's got an extraordinarily clear mind, and he can speak almost as well as Noel," referring to her husband Sir Noel Merton, Q.C., who was already mentioned as a likely Law Lord.

"Jessica," her mother added frankly, "is going through a rather tiresome stage just now. She was sixteen last birthday, and she thinks she's frightfully modern, and all of us are just old fogeys. The last time I took her up to London, I wanted to go and see Jessica and Aubrey's new play at the Cockspur, but *our* Jessica said the Cockspur plays were old-fashioned and had had it, and couldn't we go to the Royal Court and see one of those dustbin dramas."

"So what did you do?" asked Mrs. Morland with lively curiosity.

"Oh, we compromised and went to *My Fair Lady*," said Lydia. "I was lucky enough to get a couple of returns and Jessica was enchanted by it. I was a bit worried about the Cockspur at first, because Aubrey had offered us the stage box, but when I explained what our Jessica felt, he simply roared with laughter and said she was absolutely right, it was just because the Cockspur plays were so old-fashioned that they went on for ever and ever."

At this point they were joined by Sylvia Gould and young Lady Bond, almost immediately followed by Lord Stoke, in his redoubtable grey hat, leading a slightly bewildered Robin by the arm.

"Found this young man looking for you in the tea-tent, Laura," said Lord Stoke. "Don't know who he is or what he wants. Never set eyes on him in my life."

"This is my grandson," replied Mrs. Morland.

"Eh, what's that? Your son?" said Lord Stoke. "Couldn't have a son that age, Laura. Don't talk nonsense."

"I said: This. Is. My. Grandson." Mrs. Morland patiently repeated, adding the word GRANDSON in capitals.

"Grandson, eh?" said Lord Stoke. "Didn't know you had one. Why didn't you say so at first? Well, the lad wants something, don't know what, he mumbles so."

Robin, in a voice suddenly become piercingly shrill to prove that he didn't mumble, said Please Gran, could he have some extra sixpences for taking Eleanor on the roundabout? The extra sixpences were provided, mostly in the form of shillings and half-crowns, and Robin hurried away towards the intoxicating sounds of Packer's Universal Derby, which was now in full swing and grinding out, as Roddy Wicklow had said it should, the strains of "Love's Roundabout."

"Nice boy," observed Lord Stoke. "Good manners. Credit to you, Laura. Not like some of the young barbarians you see about these days."

Mrs. Morland, who was a very fair-minded person, was about to explain that the credit was not due to her, but to Robin's parents who had brought him up and the masters at his boarding-school who had broken him in, but decided to abandon the attempt in view of her old friend's increasing deafness. Whereupon Lord Stoke turned to his half-niece by marriage, Daphne Bond, and asked where her brother Denis Toner was, feller that wrote the music.

"S-S-Stonor," said Mrs. Morland under her breath, but nobody heard her except Lydia Merton.

"Oh, Denis had to go back to the States, Uncle Stoke," replied Daphne in the clear ringing voice her uncle never failed to hear. "He got a telephone call from Nat Blumenfeld in New York, something about a film offer for his new show, and he was off by the first plane next day. He's never really *happy* now in England," she explained to the ladies. "He says America is his spiritual home. I expect he'll become a U.S. citizen in the end."

If Sylvia Gould felt a slight sinking of the heart at this news, remembering a face with hollow cheeks and a pair of sad, slightly romantic eyes, she knew the feeling was quite unreasonable, and would certainly not keep her awake at nights. In any case she had no time to brood, for Lord Stoke cut her neatly out of the party and took her away, on the pretext of showing her those parts of Rising Castle that were Out of Bounds.

Daphne cocked her eyebrows at Mrs. Morland and observed that the servants' hall said It Was A Case. Mrs. Morland said she was pretty sure it wasn't a Case on Sylvia's part, though goodness knew the poor girl had a dull enough life at home, after which she was stricken with contrition, felt she had been unfair, and added that Mr. and Mrs. Gould were very nice people really.

At this point Lydia, who hardly knew the Goulds at all, said she was sure they were and she thought she'd stroll over to the Derby and see how the young people were getting on, and Mrs. Morland and Daphne went back into the tea-tent, upon which the ravening hordes were now descending, to lend a hand in case Anne Knox was in need of extra helpers.

At Packer's Universal Royal Derby business was fast and furious. A long queue of customers was lining up for rides, now we regret to say priced at sixpence a go and even at that, according to the oily man at the ticket office, a dead loss to the proprietor.

A few perspicacious or experienced clients, who had wrenched enough money out of their parents and relations to put down a substantial lump sum at the beginning, were enjoying their fifth or sixth round. Among these were Amabel Adams, who had attached herself resolutely to the cock, Robin Morland astride the ostrich, and Eleanor Leslie, who was mounted very elegantly side-saddle on the old Derby winner Persimmon.

Giles and Emily Foster, who had ridden over from Pomfret Towers, were straddling a horse apiece, and Lydia observed that her daughter Lavinia and young Lord Mellings were sharing a boat shaped like a swan. And we can't help feeling ourselves that this was a noble sacrifice in the cause of love, and that to Lord Mellings the circular journey backwards was almost as daunting an experience as it had once been to Sir Noel Merton, Q.C., the eminent barrister.

"Feel like a ride yourself, miss? Or I should rightly say My Lady," remarked a well-known voice behind Lydia, and there was Mr. Packer, the proprietor, in person, whom she had known since she was a bouncing schoolgirl, dressed in something that looked like a sack with holes cut in it for the arms and head.

"Oh! hullo, Packer," said Lady Merton, "no fear, thanks all the same. I'm far too old now for that sort of thing. I say, you've got a new cock, haven't you?"

"Had to get a new one, miss," said Mr. Packer, "on account of the damage them little devils over at Hogglestock done at

Whitsun. Smashed up the old cock proper *and* a couple of gondolas. But I will say for Mr. Adams he's a gentleman. He paid up for what they done and plenty over."

"That's his daughter on the cock now, isn't it?" said Lydia, to which Mr. Packer answered that it was, she was a rare one for a roundabout was Miss Amabel, and she'd booked up solid for the afternoon. Lydia, having decided that her own daughter was in safe hands, and having settled her old nostalgia for roundabouts once and for all, turned back towards the tea-tent and the society of older people. Robin and Eleanor, who had used up all their sixpences by now, moved off in the same direction.

"I'm ravenously hungry," declared Robin. "I've hardly had a thing to eat all day. Let's go and see if there's some food left in the tea-tent. I say, Eleanor, I was thinking, why don't you tell me a bit about your secret plan and then I'll tell you a bit about my secret plan?"

Eleanor, who had fallen under the spell of Robin's attentions, but still remained loyal to her school friend, said she could only tell him just a little bit, because it was really Amabel's secret as much as hers. It was something about a lot of old houses called Wiple Terrace at Southbridge where her brother's school was, she said, and some horrid people were trying to pull them down.

"I know," said Robin. "Delomition. There's always a lot of delomition going on in London. My secret's about grandmothers. Have you got any?" To which Eleanor replied that she had two, but she didn't see them very often, because one of them spent most of the time in the south of France and the other one lived in America. For as we know, Martin Leslie's mother had married again, after Martin's father was killed in the First World War, and had for many years been happily settled in the United States, surrounded by a large brood of American children and grandchildren.

"My grandmother lives at High Rising," Robin said. "She's rather a famous person who writes books and she's frightfully old. She's going to be seventy in September and she doesn't want to have a birthday party, but I'm planning to make one for her. That's my secret."

Eleanor looked at him with adoration and said how lovely.

"Oh, I don't know," said Robin in a consciously offhand way. "I feel it's a kind of family responsibility. I don't mind telling *you,* but I don't think Amabel's quite old enough to understand family responsibility yet. You see, Gran's rather like an Ancient Monument. You know about the Prevention of Ancient Monuments?"

"Isn't it Protection?" asked Eleanor timidly, who, for all her hero-worship, was at least a year older than her new friend, and had come out top of her form in English.

"I know. That's what I said. Well, Ancient Monuments have got to be Prevented or they crumble. I feel a family responsibility not to let Gran crumble at High Rising."

"Oh, Robin, you are wonderful," said Eleanor in rapture. "*Do* come and stay with us at Rushwater and we'll make a splendid plan about the Protection of Ancient Monuments."

"Then that makes two secret plans," said Robin. "Gran and Wiple Terrace. I expect they are about the same age really," which would have been a considerable surprise to Laura Morland, since Wiple Terrace, as we know, was built in 1820. By this time the two children had reached the tent, and Robin, ploughing his way with Eleanor in tow towards the table where his grandmother was enjoying a nice quiet talk with Daphne Bond and Lydia, boasted most fearfully of his exploits on the ostrich and vociferously demanded tea.

Dr. Ford, of whose movements we cannot always keep account, since he was an extremely hard-working G.P. with a large and scattered country practice, dropped in at the Agricultural a few minutes later, and detaching Sylvia Gould from what he privately considered the distinctly senile gallantries of Lord Stoke, asked her if she'd care to come for a ride to Barchester.

"I've got to see a couple of patients at the Barchester General," he said, "and you could look in and enquire after Mrs. Beeton's leg. And then, what about a spot of dinner at the White Hart? It's not the Ritz, but the food could be much worse. I've not got any surgery tonight, because it's Saturday. How about it?"

Sylvia, who had found it quite a strain shouting at Lord Stoke for more than half an hour, and who, to tell the truth, felt a little out of things in this gathering of Barsetshire old friends, few of whom she knew really well, said she'd love to, only she must ring up home first and make sure that Rose or Dora could look after the parents. "They're really quite responsible and not nearly as keen on the pictures as they used to be, so I don't suppose they'll be going out tonight."

So Dr. Ford gave her four pennies for the telephone, which she gratefully accepted because she had no change in her bag except one penny and a threepenny bit, and she rang up the Vicarage and found that Dora was going out but Rose wasn't, and it was only casserole for supper so everything was under control. Dr. Ford told Mrs. Morland, who had brought Syliva to the Show, that he would see her safely home; so the vicar's daughter climbed into the doctor's rattle-trap of a car and they set off on their way to Barchester.

CHAPTER 8

DINNER at the White Hart was never a very exciting affair, although the food was excellently cooked, served with quiet efficiency, and the best that Barchester could offer. But to Sylvia Gould, the hard-working daughter of the Vicarage, it was sheer bliss to sit down to a meal that she had not herself helped to prepare, and would presently have to wash up, and she would have enjoyed it even if it had been a cut off the joint and two veg., with stewed plums and custard to follow. (Which it most certainly was not, for the White Hart, though of modest size, was a four-star hotel, with a long and enviable reputation.)

We do not think that Dr. Ford was a regular customer, but he was well known everywhere in Barsetshire, and Burden, the old head waiter, had kept a nice table for him in a corner.

"Evening, Burden," said Dr. Ford, as the old waiter flicked a few imaginary crumbs off the spotless tablecloth with a napkin. "How's the leg, eh?"

"Up and down, sir," replied Burden. "But I was never one to grumble." Which was a manifest lie, as his long-suffering wife could have testified. "Nobody seems to understand my leg, sir, and that's about the size of it."

"Well, that's your own fault," said Dr. Ford unsympathetically. "You wouldn't let us X-ray it at the hospital."

"I don't hold with them inside photographs," said Burden. "Never have done. And now they say it's mostly young ladies as takes the pictures. Hardly seems decent for a gentleman."

"Have it your own way," grunted the doctor. "Now what are you going to give us to eat? What's good tonight?"

"If I might suggest, the consommay for a start. That's the clear soup, miss," Burden kindly explained to Sylvia, "made with real chicken stock. Then what about some fresh Dover sole, with Our special sauce? We always find ladies are partial to the taste of sauces."

"Well, don't overdo the sauce for me," said Dr. Ford. "I'm partial to the taste of sole, myself. Have you any decent fillet steak?"

"Oh yes, sir," replied the old waiter reproachfully. "Beautifully tender you'll find it cuts. I don't suppose it'll be on the menu long, this being Saturday night and several American gentlemen driving over from the airfield. Will the lady take the steak as well, or would you fancy a nice omelette, miss? The cook we've got now is a foreigner, and I must say for him he does understand an omelette, though I wouldn't trust him with a steak-and-kidney pudding."

Sylvia said she'd love an omelette, upon which Dr. Ford told Burden that was that and to get on with it, as they hadn't all evening to spare, and he'd leave the choice of wine to him. "You might bring us some sherry while we're waiting," he added.

"Certainly, sir," said Burden. "If I might suggest, we have some very fine dry Manzanilla."

Dr. Ford said perhaps Miss Gould didn't like her sherry dry, upon which she promptly replied that it couldn't be too dry for her, and Burden went away to fetch the Manzanilla.

"Admirable woman," remarked Dr. Ford. "I wish there were more like you."

Over sherry, the conversation turned to Mrs. Morland and her approaching birthday. "It worries me a bit," said Sylvia. "She says she doesn't want a party, but I think that's just her *humbleness*, if you know what I mean. She feels she isn't important somehow, at least not important to Barsetshire, though how she can think *that* when everybody loves her books so much I simply do not know."

"Laura Morland is one of the most unselfish women I have ever met," declared Dr. Ford. "She never stops working, never complains of aches and pains, though heaven knows she must have had her fair share of them by seventy odd. Quite remarkable woman. Spent her whole life writing to bring up those sons of hers. Now they're all grown-up and married, I suppose she's working for her grandchildren. Got one on her hands now, Tony's eldest."

"Robin," said Sylvia. "He's rather a nice boy."

"He may be," agreed Dr. Ford, "but he's a boy, all the same. Bound to be an upset in an old lady's house. Don't suppose he ever stops to consider his grandmother. Kids don't." In which sweeping generalisation the good doctor was unfair, for Robin, as we know, did consider his grandmother and her great age quite a lot, often for as much as ten minutes a day.

Through the clear soup and the fish, both of which, we may add, lived up to Burden's commendations, the talk about Mrs. Morland and her birthday continued, Sylvia maintaining that *something* ought to be done by way of a party, even if she thought she didn't want it.

"Something to make her feel she's part of Barsetshire, and not what they call an offcome any longer. I know she's lived at High Rising for nearly forty years, and she's got hundreds of friends and everybody's always glad to see her, but somehow she gives you the impression of being rather a lonely person really. As if she didn't quite *belong*, I don't mean only in Barsetshire but anywhere. Oh, am I talking frightful nonsense?"

"Not in the least," said Dr. Ford, as the steak and a foamy golden omelette arrived. "Thanks Burden, that looks splendid. You're talking hard common sense and what's more you're right, which doesn't always follow. Laura Morland *is* a lonely person, partly by nature and partly from force of habit. Not much you can do about it, though. Wouldn't be a kindness.

You've got to allow old people the right to enjoy loneliness in
their own way. But keep an eye on 'em."

Which precept, we may add, Dr. Ford carried out in practice,
visiting his old patients regularly and often without fee, on
some such pretext as borrowing a book or passing on a bit of
county news, which goes a long way to explain why he was
still the best-loved and most-trusted G.P. in all Barsetshire.
Some day, we think, young Dr. Gus Perry from Harefield will
be qualified to fill his place, but these things are of the future.

By the time coffee was reached, they had agreed to sound the
county tactfully on the subject of Mrs. Morland's party, and the
talk had turned pleasantly to other things, when suddenly there
was a small commotion at the door, and Dr. Ford looked up
and groaned: "Oh my God, we've had it."

Bearing down upon them was a tall, handsome, not-so-young
woman, with just a touch of grey in her fair hair, followed by
an abundant personage in purple, crowned with what we can
only describe as an inverted coalscuttle covered with violets.

"Good gracious," whispered Sylvia, "she *is* a bit overpowering,
isn't she? Somebody ought to tell her she's not really the right
shape for purple."

"What?" grunted Dr. Ford. "Oh, I don't mean *that* one.
She's comical but harmless. Rather jolly when you get to know
her. No, it's the other one, dreadful woman called Frances
Harvey, from the Ministry of General Interference."

He rose to his feet as the two ladies approached their table,
and was greeted by Miss Harvey with her bright official smile.

"How very nice to see you, Dr. Ford," she said. "May I
present you to her Excellency the Mixo-Lydian Ambassadress?"

"Evening, Gradka," said the doctor, holding out his hand.
"Good to have you back in these parts. Put on a bit of weight,
I see, but you're looking blooming. How are the chilblains?"

We must admit that this is the first time we have heard that the Ambassadress suffered from chilblains in the winter, but those were the doctor's exact words, and who are we to dispute them?

"Ha! Dr. Ford! Ollways the roguey-poguey!" said Gradka, giving him a slight poke in the ribs. "Which joy, which pleasure, to be seeink an old friend again. Be introducink this Prodshkina, which is new of me."

So Dr. Ford introduced Sylvia to the Ambassadress, whom he had known when she was acting as cook to Sir Robert and Lady Fielding at Hallbury, and had pursued her studies so diligently under the tuition of the Fieldings' old governess, Miss Bunting, that she had passed the examination of the Society for the Propagation of English by correspondence course, in due time become head of Mixo-Lydia's only educational institution, known as Bunting College, then a member of the Mixo-Lydian Trade Delegation, and finally Ambassadress. Somewhat as an afterthought, he introduced Miss Gould to Frances Harvey, who accorded her the less bright smile reserved for minor employees.

"I do hope," she said with a faint touch of malice, "that we are not intruding on your little party, but that rather futile old man Burden insisted that all the tables were taken, and I felt sure you wouldn't mind our sharing yours."

"Unfortunately," said Dr. Ford, "we are on the point of leaving, but do sit down and have a drink with us before we go, and then you can take over our table. Burden!" he called out, "just pull up another couple of chairs, will you? and bring a snifter for these ladies. What'll it be, Grad?"

"Vröj," replied the Ambassadress, "that is what we ollways be drinkink before eatink in Mixo-Lydia. So are you not tastink it at the time, but it strokes you later."

Dr. Ford said he doubted if the White Hart would run to Vröj, and perhaps a spot of vodka would be the nearest. Frances

Harvey observed with a light laugh that she would be very English and just stick to sherry. "And not too dry, I beg of you, my dear man," she added. "It is an affectation of the English to pretend they enjoy dry sherry." At which remark Sylvia felt, as so many others had felt before her, that she would gladly murder Miss Harvey on the spot.

The drinks were brought and Dr. Ford, who had ordered a brandy for himself and Sylvia, to keep the other ladies company, asked Gradka what she was doing in this part of the world.

Before she had time to answer, Frances Harvey broke in to say that Her Excellency had come to make enquiries about an absurd little *contretemps* at Gatherum. "You know," she said, "or perhaps you may not know, since Ministerial affairs are probably a closed book to you, that I was temporarily posted by Our Government, I mean of course, the late Labour Government, to the local branch of the M.G.I. at Gatherum, to take charge of cuts in *personnel*. It seems now that one of the minor clerks discharged as redundant happened to be a Mixo-Lydian subject. Our present Government is not prepared to accept my very simple explanation of this trivial incident. That is all."

"Oll, my feet!" exclaimed the Mixo-Lydian Ambassadress. "Hark you of this type which is sayink me a Mixo-Lydian subject is trivial. I would have you know, Prodshkina Ministry of General Interference, that this young lady you have socked——"

"Sacked," said Frances Harvey automatically.

"So, I thank you, sacked, is a graduate of Bunting College and a pupil of high excellency. So will we pursuit this matter to the end."

Whereupon she turned to Dr. Ford, lifted her glass of vodka, and said: "*Zwe Bog*," to which he replied with what seemed to him the nearest English equivalent: "God bless." "Ha! see me this doctor which onderstands Mixo-Lydian," said Her Excellency. "So am I tellink you, Dr. Ford, and you too Prodshkina

Gould, why for another cause I comm to Barsetshire. My Government, she is wantink to set up a tabloid, how you say memory stone, to Prodshkina Bunting, she who is Patroness of Education in Mixo-Lydia."

"But I say, Your Excellency," said Sylvia, at once confused and fascinated by this conversation, "she can't be a patroness of anything, can she, if she's dead? There's a tabloid, I mean a tablet, up to her already in Rushwater Church."

"So is she dead," replied the Ambassadress calmly. "So does she comm to life again. You spik of patron saints, is it not? which they are oll dead. So is Prodshkina Bunting our patron saint of education. The Mixo-Lydian people has roused a fond of lydions———"

"Raised," interrupted Frances Harvey, in her insufferably superior manner. "I think Her Excellency is trying to explain that her Government is anxious to erect some sort of memorial to Miss Bunting, preferably at Southbridge, where so many Mixo-Lydian refugees were billeted during the war. A quaint idea, one thinks, to perpetuate the memory of a Victorian governess in these days of state education."

"Wish we had some of 'em today," grunted Dr. Ford. "People they taught *got* taught and stayed taught."

"Ah, I can see you are a reactionary, Dr. Ford," said Miss Harvey with her irritating laugh. "I daresay you are one of those people who object to the demolition of Wiple Terrace. We have heard rumours of disaffection."

"Disaffection's not the word," said Dr. Ford. "There's very strong feeling in the county over Wiple Terrace."

"You will be tellink me, pliss," said the Ambassadress. "What is this Wiple Terrace?"

"A dreadful little row of cottages at Southbridge," replied Miss Harvey, "occupied, I believe, by masters from the school and their connections. Quite an eyesore, and really most unsuitable for modern living. The cottages are going to be pulled

down, and a friend of mine, Lord Aberfordbury, a most enterprising and far-sighted business man, is planning to erect a factory."

"A factory at Southbridge? *Czy provkà, provkà, provkà,*" cried
out the Ambassadress, which Dr. Ford, who had heard the
phrase repeatedly during the reign, we might almost say the
tyranny, of Mixo-Lydian refugees, rightly interpreted as: "No,
never, never, never." "What is this you do to Barsetshire, which
is belovved of Prodshkina Bunting?"

"One must move with the times, Your Excellency," said
Frances Harvey, with her tolerant smile. "The new wave has
reached us even in this remote corner of the world."

"New wave!" cried the Ambassadress. "That is oll I hear today, new wave! And what is it, this new wave? A bit of dirty
wotter which is carrying feelth, what you coll in English fletsam
and jotsam. I say pouf me of this new wave. It is robbish, and
those which spik of it are robbishers."

Sylvia told Dr. Ford afterwards that she felt at this point
she wanted to stand up and cheer. Instead, she turned to the
Ambassadress with great daring, and said that if she was really
interested in Wiple Terrace she might care to have a word
with Mr. Adams, her employer.

"Adams?" said Her Excellency. "That is beink the father of
Heather Adams, which was the friend of Prodshkina Anne
Fielding, the pupil of Prodshkina Bunting? Yes?"

Sylvia, although a little awed by Her Excellency's grasp of
Barsetshire relationships, assured her this was so, and very practically jotted down Mr. Adams's business address and telephone
number on the back of an old envelope, which she passed
across the table.

"So, I spik with this Mr. Adams, yes?" said Gradka, stuffing
the envelope into her capacious handbag, which was covered
with a rough kind of Mixo-Lydian embroidery and completely
hideous, but had the merit of a shapelessness that would ac-

commodate anything. "So do we discover to offwit these schwenk, how you say vermin that is died and becomm eaten by maggots, which is wantink to despile the home-place of Prodshkina Bunting."

Frances Harvey, with a light laugh, remarked that all this enthusiasm was quite delicious, but she was afraid it would prove wasted effort, as the matter of Wiple Terrace was already settled.

"So can it ollso be onsettled," said the formidable Ambassadress, at which point Dr. Ford detected Burden hovering, paid his bill, and took Sylvia away.

On the Monday after the Agricultural, George and Anne Knox drove the short distance from Low Rising to High Rising, to have tea with Mrs. Morland, as was their frequent custom. Over cups of the fragrant China tea, sent on regular order from a famous London store, which was one of Mrs. Morland's few luxuries, and plates of Stoker's really admirable scones and cake, made with real butter, they discussed the Show, and agreed how nice it was that the Martin Leslies should have won a prize for milk and how pleased old Mr. Marling must be about the success of Marling Magister. At least, when we say discussed, it must be understood that the term applies to Mrs. Knox and Mrs. Morland, for whenever George Knox lent the authority of his powerful mind and voice to table-talk, all lesser voices were hushed and conversation became soliloquy.

Both his devoted wife and his old friend Laura Morland, however, were accustomed to George Knox's particular form of bulldozing, and paid no attention to it whatsoever. Robin, who was also present and never as a rule backward in putting himself forward, preserved an unnatural silence which made his grandmother glance at him anxiously, convinced he must be sickening for measles, although a moment's thought would have reassured her, had she stopped to think, that no prospective invalid could have made such a hearty tea, and in any case he had not been within a hundred miles of his measling family.

Robin, in fact, was preoccupied by his own secret plans, and as soon as tea was over he withdrew with unmarked ostentation to a table by the window, pulled out of his pocket a very leaky fountain pen and a grimy sheet of paper, and fortified by a light rere-meal of chocolate biscuits, began to write.

Meanwhile the grown-up conversation veered from the Agricultural Show to literature. Anne Knox asked Mrs. Morland how the latest Madame Koska thriller was getting on, to which that gifted authoress made reply that it wasn't getting on at all, she had come to a dead stop, and she sometimes wished that someone else would write all her books for her in future.

"Because then at least they would be *new*," she said, "I don't mean *old* new, I mean *new* new. I've written the same story so many times that I'm never quite sure now which book I'm in, and I find I'm always making people the wrong age, or mixing up their names, or forgetting whether they know each other or not. You see, *I* know them all of course, and that's what makes it much more difficult. And then I get such dreadful letters sometimes, and I do hate getting dreadful letters, though it's not so bad when they are anonymous, because you don't have to answer them. But they make me feel quite sick inside all the same."

Anne Knox said she felt quite certain that Mrs. Morland's readers didn't want to read anything new, and what kind of dreadful letters?

"Well, the other day I had one from a woman who signed herself 'Professional,' and it said something like: 'Dear Miss Morland, you must have one foot in the grave or you would know that models are not called mannequins any more. Seeing as you live in London and pretend to be all up in fashion I thought I ought just to drop you the hint. It makes you look no end silly to we young people.' And the trouble is," concluded Mrs. Morland, "that she's right up to a point, and it makes me look no end silly to *me*."

"Laura," declared George Knox in his mighty voice, "you are too frail, too vulnerable. You must mettle yourself with steel against the slings and arrows of youthful arrogance. The young have supped too much of life, too little of wisdom, they have plunged too recklessly into the wave that will engulf them———"

"George," broke in his wife, "you are mixing your metaphors, and if you'd ever had a letter in your life from anyone who signed herself 'Professional,' you'd know you were a best-selling author and not just a distinguished one. Now do stop worrying, Laura, and tell us what the new Madame Koska is about."

"Well," said Mrs. Morland, "I started with a good idea about a traveller in silks who is really an enemy agent with a book of samples that has microdots on some of the patterns, showing the position of our nuclear defences. Only then I found I knew nothing really about microdots, and whether they would work on silk, and I can't help thinking about it at night. I mean when I'm not sleeping."

"Sleep!" boomed George Knox, "O, magic sleep! O, comfortable bird! *Somne, quies rerum, placidissime, somne, Deorum!* Sleep that knits up———"

"No, George, no," interrupted his wife firmly. "That's quite enough. We simply cannot have the ravelled sleeve of care. If you can't go to sleep, Laura, why don't you try hot milk and whisky?"

"Sometimes I do," confessed Mrs. Morland. "And sometimes Navy rum with boiling water and a lot of sugar. Wicks—you know the Mertons' agent, Mr. Wickham—put me on to it, and he often brings a bottle over when he's round this way. I can't persuade him to take a penny for it, he always says it's a present from a pal of his, I wouldn't know him. *Such* a kind creature, Wicks. I can't think why he never married."

"Alas, Laura," pronounced George Knox, "merit is no cer-

tain aid to matrimony. Would that it were so, but fate decrees
it otherwise. Even I myself, I must remind you, my dear Laura,
I who have always striven to walk the strait and narrow path
and render unto each human being that which belongs to him;
even I myself, I must repeat, would have been left a half-soul,
a mere drifting thing, widowed and aging, had you not been
inspired, for no lesser word than inspiration will serve, to cherish and bring to me my dear wife Anne, the solace and happiness of my declining years." To which Anne Knox, who had
been Mrs. Morland's secretary before her marriage, felt tempted
to say: "Oh come off it, George," but didn't.

"And then," said Mrs. Morland, calmly sweeping on, "there
was that charming young American called Lee Sumter, who is
some kind of cousin to the Duchess of Towers. He told me how
to make hot buttered rum, which sounds delicious, and he said
it was sure-fire to put anyone to sleep. Only it seems so extravagant to use real butter in a drink, and I'm certain that marge
wouldn't work. The real trouble isn't so much *going* to sleep.
It's waking up at about two o'clock and feeling that you'll never
go to sleep again. Of course," she added, "it's all right once you
get the people."

"Pray expound, my dear Laura," said George Knox. "What
people do you get, and how do you get them?"

"Oh, it's nothing that *I* do," said Mrs. Morland. "They
simply come. Faces of people you've never seen in your life,
quite fascinating some of them, and then you know you're going
off to sleep."

"Thronging through the cloud-rifts," quoted George Knox,
who for all his pomposity sometimes came up with an astonishing bit of percipience.

"That's *exactly* what I mean, George," said Mrs. Morland.
"How very clever of you. Though of course none of them are
Heroes, at least so far as one knows at present. A great many of
them are children, and there are some really lovely girls, with

their heads tilted at just the right angle for a portrait. Though why girls I can't imagine, when all my own are boys."

She paused a moment for reflection and then ran on: "And I can't imagine either where they come from, it's got nothing to do with me at all. At least in a way I suppose it has, because it *is* such an effort to make one's mind a blank, when you are deliberately trying to remember to forget about writing to your publisher or taking an extra pint of milk, or sending that tweed skirt to the cleaners. And why," she added, "it takes so much longer to get things cleaned nowadays, when there are so many new things to clean them *with*, I simply cannot think. But anything you want done now is about a week, which means at least a fortnight."

These sudden snipe-flights of Mrs. Morland's were apt to bewilder even her oldest friends, and Anne Knox, whose mind was never of the darting type, said what on earth did Laura mean, if anything?

"I don't think I can explain," began Mrs. Morland, but Robin, who had left his corner table and was hovering about the group with a very nasty wet pen in his hand, was in no wise at a loss.

"Oh, Mrs. Knox," he said, "it's quite easy really. It's what they call stream of conscienceness thinking. Oh, Mr. Knox, you must know about stream of conscienceness thinking."

"Not by that name, boy," observed George Knox, who was a precise man of words. "If you mean consciousness, I do."

"I know," said Robin imperturbably. "Stream of conscienceness is like that game where you think of one thing and that reminds you of another thing, and you say it all round and then you have to remember which was the thing that reminded you of the other thing backwards. I say, Gran, please can I have another piece of paper?"

"You'll find plenty of paper in the drawer of my desk," said

Mrs. Morland, "and do stop waving that horrid pen about. Haven't you got a pencil you can write with?"

Robin magnanimously conceded that he *had* a pencil, but the point was broken, and anyway what he was doing was far too important for pencil writing. "It's got to be permanent," he added. "I expect I'll have it published."

"Is it a story?" asked Anne Knox.

"Oh, *no,* Mrs. Knox," said Robin reproachfully. "You can easily write a *story* with a pencil. Gran writes all her stories with a pencil. This is a List, and its ackcherly Top Secret."

"Actually," said Mrs. Morland mechanically.

"I know. Don't you ever play the stream of conscienceness game, Mrs. Knox? We play it lots of times at school, only it's called the Remembering Game. I'm specially good at the Remembering Game, even when some of the chaps are cheating."

George Knox remarked that to his simple mind it was impossible to conceive how anyone could cheat at such a game, to which Robin patiently replied that it was cheating when you didn't say the first word that a word reminded you of, but the next one. "For showing off really," he added.

We are afraid this subtlety was somewhat lost upon his audience. If young Lady Lufton, she who was Grace Grantly, had been present, she would readily have understood, remembering the time when Ruby Alcock of the Barchester High School said at Miss Pettinger's party that mouthwash reminded her of *Paradise Lost,* because of Milton. But Grace, more handsome now than ever, and happy in her marriage to the tall, shy Lord Lufton, was miles away at Framley Court, devoted to the care of her increasing brood of children.

"Of course," Robin went on relentlessly, standing on one leg and threatening all the elders with splashes from his fountain pen, "when you say a word that isn't the first word, it usually means you've murdered somebody. That's the way psychitrists catch criminals, did you know that, Mr. Knox? I bet I could catch heaps of criminals with the Remembering Game."

Luckily at this point, when the Knoxes felt they were on the point of going mad, the door opened and Dr. Ford came in. After a personal exchange of greetings, for the Knoxes were old friends, indeed there was a time before her marriage when Anne Knox might have become Mrs. Ford, the doctor said he was going over to Rushwater the next day and were there any messages?

"Oh dear," said Mrs. Morland, "I do hope there's nothing wrong with any of the children?"

"All fit as fleas," said Dr. Ford. "But the Leslies' cowman has a couple of nasty boils, and I've got to lance them."

"Oh, can I come and watch you lance them?" said Robin.

"Certainly not."

"Well, can I come to Rushwater with you, Dr. Ford? I've got a terribly important secret to discuss with Eleanor, and I must show her my List before it's published. Please, Gran, can I go to Rushwater with Dr. Ford?"

"But you haven't been invited," said Mrs. Morland feebly.

"Oh, but I *have*," said Robin. "Eleanor invited me at the Agricultural, and Eleanor's mother invited me too."

And at this moment, as so often happens, though whether by mere chance or some sort of telepathy or remote control it is not for us to say, the telephone rang and it was Sylvia Leslie, asking whether Mrs. Morland would allow her grandson to come and stay for a few days at Rushwater. Permission was given, gratitude expressed, and Mrs. Morland came back and told Robin that he seemed to have been quite right about the invitation.

"Mrs. Leslie says any time and stay for a few days. And bring your oldest clothes," she added, "not that any of your clothes are new."

"Oh good-oh!" exclaimed Robin ecstatically. "So can I go tomorrow, Gran? Can I go with you tomorrow, Dr. Ford?"

"I can drive you over," said Dr. Ford. "But I can't promise to fetch you back. I'm not often over Rushwater way."

"It doesn't matter," said Robin loftily. "I can easily walk back."

"Thirty miles?" said Dr. Ford drily.

"That's all right, Dr. Ford," said Robin. "I have a tremendous power of walking. Somehow other chaps get tiredness in their legs, but I never seem to get tiredness in my legs. I bet I could walk for days on end without getting tiredness."

"Shut up," said Dr. Ford. "Do you want me to take him, Laura?"

"Well, if you wouldn't really mind," said Mrs. Morland. "And if you can put up with his chatter on the way. It's really too far for him to bicycle, and I can't take him myself, as I simply must get another chapter of Madame Koska done tomorrow. I'll see that he gets back all right, when the Leslies have had enough of him."

"Oh, Dr. Ford," said Robin reproachfully, "I don't chatter. And I can be a great help to you on the way, because I can tell you all about how to make road signals."

"*Shut up!*" said Dr. Ford. "I don't want any passenger-drivers in my car. That's how accidents happen. And I knew all about road signals long before you were born."

"I know," said Robin. "But I bet you didn't have Road Safety lessons at your school, Dr. Ford. At our school we have Road Safety lessons twice a week, and we have to answer papers. I came out top in my last Road Safety paper. Of course it's really meant for bicyclers. Our headmaster's very strict about Road Safety for bicyclers. Last term I and another chap——"

"SHUT UP," said Dr. Ford.

And so it was arranged that Robin, with his oldest clothes, should be collected tomorrow after lunch, and Dr. Ford went back to his evening surgery.

It is some years since we visited Rushwater, now the home of Martin Leslie and his wife Sylvia, also of Tom Grantly and his wife Emmy, who lived in the delightful little Regency house just up the slope which Macpherson, the old agent, had asked Martin Leslie to pass on to Emmy after his death, partly as a token of a lifelong devotion to Emmy's grandmother, Lady Emily Leslie, and partly we think as a tribute to her own devoted and extremely practical cow-mindedness. But Rushwater is one of those happy, timeless places that never really change, and except that some of the larger rooms were now dust-sheeted and unused, and that the servants' hall had been turned into a kind of furniture depository, since in these do-it-yourself-or-die days there is far more furniture than there are servants, it looked very much the same as when we first spent a summer there, with the maddening but enchanting Lady Emily Leslie as our hostess, at the beginning of these Barsetshire chronicles.

The sun had broken through the clouds and settled for a golden afternoon when Dr. Ford with Robin took the short cut through the park and along the back drive into the stableyard, which seemed to Robin to be entirely populated by children and pigeons.

Young Leslies and Grantlys of all ages and sizes, including one in a push-cart firmly held by Nurse, and a schoolboy of about Robin's own age leaning on a bicycle, were clustered in a group, in animated talk, which turned into shouts of "Dr. Ford! Dr. Ford!" as the doctor's disgraceful rattle-trap of a car pulled up.

"Hullo, young 'uns," he called back cheerfully and clambered out, bag in hand. "Keep your paws off my Rolls-Royce, understand? Afternoon, Nurse, you're looking bonnier than ever." At which Nurse, who would never see fifty again, was pleased to bridle.

Sylvia Leslie, who had been talking estate business with her husband and the Noel Mertons' agent, Mr. Wickham, now joined the group, and very kindly welcomed Robin, who was, for once in his young life, feeling a little shy and almost bereft of words.

"Children," she said to the assorted small fry, "this is Robin Morland, who has come to stay here for a few days. Nurse, this is Mrs. Morland's grandson from High Rising and a friend of Eleanor's. I've promised to send him back in good condition, so perhaps you'll kindly keep an eye on his clothes. Eleanor, you'd better take Robin upstairs and show him his bedroom and where to wash his hands before tea. He's sleeping in Cousin Tom's old room, you know."

"Yes, Mother," said Eleanor, coming forward and looking at Robin from under her dark lashes. We think she sensed his shyness, being shy herself and very kind by nature, and we think too that Robin, who was accustomed to be cock-of-the-walk both at home and at school, although in neither place was this attitude encouraged, felt an unwonted comfort in putting himself into her sympathetic hands among this gathering of strangers.

Whether he also noticed that Eleanor was extremely pretty we cannot say, never ourself (or ourselves) having experienced the emotions of a schoolboy ten or eleven years old. But we rather fancy not. Had she been what he would ungallantly have described as a blot or a super-ghastly kid he might have paid more attention to her looks, if our reader can understand our meaning.

"Come along, Ford," said Martin Leslie, limping rather heavily on the leg which had been injured during the war in Italy. "I'll take you over to old Herdman and you can have a go at those boils. He complains about them all day long, but he won't be a bit pleased to see you. He's one of those obstinate old devils who believe that doctors delight in carving up their patients. And he won't go near a hospital. He says that nobody doesn't go to hospital except to die."

"And then you will come back to tea, won't you, Dr. Ford?" said Sylvia. "Wicks is staying. He's just dropped in from a preview, or whatever it's called, of a farm sale at Allington, with a catalogue of agricultural machinery. Tom's somewhere about the stables and Emmy will be over presently. And Georgy," she added to the schoolboy with the bicycle, "if you're going to tea with Nicholson Minor it's quite time you were off. Tell Mrs. Nicholson I won't forget about the honey."

"Okay, Mother," replied Georgy, and with a kind of all-embracing salute wobbled away across the cobbles. Dr. Ford, having regretfully said he couldn't stop for tea because of surgery hours, went off with Martin to inspect the boil-sufferer. Robin, carrying the small suitcase which Stoker had packed, as requested, with his oldest clothes, and for the honour of High Rising, a reserve of others, followed Eleanor through the kitchen passages, reputed to be the haunt of innumerable beetles, and so into the house itself.

"I say, Eleanor," he observed, his tongue loosened at last by her friendly presence, as she led him upstairs to a sunny bedroom with a faded wallpaper of large roses, intermingled with sprays of some rampant but highly improbable foliage, which it would have taxed the combined brains of the Royal Horticultural Society and the National Rose Society to identify. "I say, Eleanor, are all those children yours?"

"Not all of them," said Eleanor. "Some of them belong to Cousin Emmy. This is your bedroom. Be careful of that step. Most people don't notice it at first, and then they fall up it or fall down it. And look out for the window too. The sashcord's wonky, only it's all right if you don't touch it."

"I know," said Robin. "We've got a wonky sashcord in our dormitory at school. It nearly came down and guillotined a chap called Simpson, when he was fishing for his gym-shoe in the ivy."

Eleanor asked with interest how the gym-shoe had got into the ivy.

"Oh, it just got there," replied Robin airily. "I say, Eleanor,

I've been writing some awfully important Lists. Would you like to read them?" So saying, he pulled out of his pocket two rather crumpled sheets of paper, liberally spattered with ink-blots, and handed them to his new friend, who sat down on the foot of the bed, smoothed them out with clever, tidy fingers, and began to read.

Both lists were headed, in bold capitals, MRS. MORLAND'S CLXX BIRTHDAY. TOP SECRET. Below this came a sub-heading; on one sheet of paper PEOPLE; on the other FOOD.

The PEOPLE list was comparatively short. It ran:

> *Mrs. Morland*
> *R. Morland*
> *Stoker*
> *Stoke*
> *Doctor Ford*
> *Silvia*
> *Knoxs*
> *Elliner*
> *Emilly*
> *Ammerbell*
> *Gils?*

"It isn't really finished yet," said Robin. "I expect I shall think of hundreds of other people."

"Who's Gils?" asked Eleanor with interest.

"Oh, that's Giles at Pomfret Towers," said Robin. "The one that's Lady Pomfret's son and lets me ride Skylark. I put a question mark because I don't like him quite as much as Emily, he's rather bossy. But I daresay I shall let him come. You need a lot of people for a party."

"You've written Stoke down twice over," said Eleanor, politely refraining from the comment that her own name (if she were indeed the Elliner referred to) was not spelt that way.

"Oh *no*, I haven't," said Robin reproachfully. "You just haven't read the List properly. There's Stoker and Stoke, that's Lord

Stoke at Rising Castle. They're not any relation. At least, I don't think they are."

Eleanor said it was a very nice list, and took up the sheet of paper headed FOOD.

"That's what I plan to give them for the party," said Robin. "For tea, I mean. I haven't put in any wines, because I don't know much about wines yet. But I daresay there'll be wines *ad lib*. That means *ad* liberty," he added kindly.

The FOOD list ran as follows:

> *Sossages*
> *Chips*
> *Fride eggs and bacon*
> *Chocolat cake*
> *Strawberries*
> CREEM
> *Merangs*
> *Jam*
> *Honey*
> *Sirup*
> *Stake and kidney pudd*
> *Pancakes*
> *Kippers*
> *Bisciuts*
> *Bread and driping*
> *Sooplay*

"What's Sooplay?" enquired Eleanor.

Robin looked puzzled for a moment, then his face cleared and he said oh, that was where the ink had splodged. "Of course it's really soufflé," he explained. "You know soufflé, Eleanor, the one that it squelches when you put your spoon in, all soft on the inside and all crispy on the outside. Stoker makes jolly good soufflés, and she lets me scrape the brown bits off the edges of the dish when she takes it back into the kitchen."

Eleanor said doubtfully she didn't think people had soufflé for tea.

"I shall," said Robin.

There was a moment's silence while the lists went back into their author's pocket, and then Eleanor, with great courage, made the shy suggestion, "You know what, Robin, I think we ought to tell some grown-ups about your secret plan."

Robin looked doubtful. "They wouldn't help," he objected. "Grown-ups don't do anything. That's because their minds are affotrid."

"What's affotrid?" said Eleanor, in whose vocabulary, in spite of being top in English, the word "atrophied" had not yet found a place.

"I don't exactly know," said Robin candidly, "but I *think* it means gone wonky. My father always says about people that their minds are affotrid when he doesn't like them. My father has great power over language," he added, with which anyone who had ever known Tony Morland would agree.

Eleanor said she didn't think that Mr. Adam's mind was affotrid, look at how he was helping over Wiple Terrace. "I wish," she added, plucking up more courage, "you'd let us tell Mother and Daddy. And perhaps Cousin Emmy. And perhaps Mr. Adams. I'm sure they'd help us make a plan."

While this conspiratorial talk was going on upstairs, Sylvia Leslie had taken Mr. Wickham round the side of the house to the terrace, which was bathed in grateful sunshine but also infested by ungrateful midges. To add to the discomfort of this perfect summer day, what appeared to be millions of winged ants were swarming out between the cracks in the stones, some of them taking off in reckless flight, others dragged back into the Air Raid shelters by their A.R.P. wardens.

"No," said Sylvia firmly. "I think we will NOT stay here to be devoured. Let's go into my sitting-room until tea's ready." And she led the way into a very pleasant room, slightly shabby, but the sort of room that says to you at once that it is accustomed to be loved and lived in.

"I always have liked Rushwater," said Mr. Wickham. "Feels like home, somehow."

"I know," said Sylvia. "Martin and I are tremendously lucky. This is a happy place. Just shove those toys off that chair, Wicks, and do sit down."

So Mr. Wickham very tenderly removed a rubber giraffe, a model fire-engine, and a battered copy of Andrew Lang's *Blue Fairy Book*, which fell open at the enchanting picture of Snow White and Rose Red brushing the snow off the bear, coloured by childish hands. He looked at each of them with interest and then sat down.

"You know you ought to have been married, Wicks," said Sylvia, in whom the motherly instinct was dominant. "Didn't you ever want to be, or is it rude to ask?"

"It isn't a bit rude," said Mr. Wickham, "and to be quite truthful, no. I did have a couple of shots at a proposal, and they quite rightly turned me down. I was never more thankful in my life. But I do like a house that's got a bit of everything. You know, the past, the present, and the future all together."

"I know exactly what you mean," said Sylvia. "So do I. Well, for the moment, mercifully for the running of the estate, there's no hint of the future here at Rushwater. But there's plenty of the present, what with all our children and Tom's and Emmy's. I really don't know how we should have coped if Eleanor's nurse hadn't decided that she liked it here, and wanted to stay on, even when Eleanor and Georgy went to school. Luckily she gets on well with Mrs. Siddon, our old housekeeper you know, and she feels that all the Rushwater children are *her* children. The more there are about the place the better she likes it."

At this point the sitting-room door was kicked open by a bronzed Amazon in breeches and blue cotton shirt, carrying a toddler over her shoulder, rather as if it were a sack of potatoes, and Emmy Grantly came in.

We have hardly met Emmy Graham (as she used to be) since her marriage, but we have always cherished an affection for her, from the days when she fell into the goldfish pond at Rushwater and was rescued by that gallant young Frenchman M. Pierre Boulle, at the expense of his nice white flannel trousers. This escapade was later falsely attributed to Emmy's youngest sister Edith, for so is history made.

Lady Graham had once described her eldest daughter, in all affection, as "the silliest of a clever family," but in this we think her ladyship showed less than her usual judgment. For Emmy was by no means silly, and although no master-mind on other subjects, she had grown up with a knowledge and a practical grasp of cowmanship which was conceded to be unequalled in the county.

It has been said, and not disputed in West Barsetshire, that the first word distinctly spoken by the Grantly's eldest child, a boy, was "cow." This young gentleman, whose name we haven't yet invented, although at the moment of writing it comes to us quite suddenly that it was James, after his eldest Graham uncle, had been followed by several lusty brothers or sisters, of whom the reigning baby was the afore-mentioned toddler, called Agnes after her grandmother Lady Graham.

Miss Agnes Grantly could manage pretty well now on her own feet, but did not always find it worth the trouble. Dumped on the sitting-room floor by her mother, dressed in blue dungarees, white socks, and sandals, she proceeded at high speed across the room by the simple method of sitting on her behind and punting herself along. When she reached Mr. Wickham she hugged him by the leg, gave him an adoring look, and said: "Dad-da."

"Not on your life, my girl," said Mr. Wickham, very kindly.

"None of that, Agnes," said her mother. "Into the pen with you." Upon which she heaved her offspring into the light pen or corral which was standing in the corner, flung in a few assorted soft toys, and dropped into a chair with a long "Whew!"

"Heavy," she said. "And she won't stay put. Give me potatoes every time. They don't wriggle. I say, Sylvia, have you seen the flying ants? There are simply masses of them down by the stables. I say, Wicks, have you looked at Rushwater Randolph? He's putting on tons of weight, and his lines are marvellous. He's going to be a champion bull, all right."

"So you've gone back to the names beginning with R for the Rushwater bulls," said Mr. Wickham. "Why Randolph?"

"Because his sire was Rushwater Churchill," said Emmy simply.

At this point there was an interruption, as Deanna, the village girl who had unaccountably preferred to stay on as general help at Rushwater to going into a factory or serving behind the counter at Sheepshanks', stuck her head round the door.

"Please, Mrs. Leslie," she said, "Mrs. Siddon says to ask you how many to lay for tea?"

"Tell Mrs. Siddon just ourselves and Mr. Wickham. Dr. Ford isn't staying," said Sylvia. "Oh, and Miss Eleanor and her friend Robin Morland. Nurse is giving the other children tea upstairs."

"And be a sport, Deanna," added Emmy, "and put up the high chair for Agnes. And lay her special milk, will you? It's Cowslip's. Siddy knows."

"Okeydoke," said Deanna cheerfully, and was gone.

"Amazing girl, Deanna," said Mr. Wickham. "Never seems to get a day older, though to my certain knowledge she's been walking out with Ted Higden at the radio shop for the last ten years. I saw them outside the Barchester Odeon the other Saturday, and Lord! what a hat the girl was wearing! It looked like a beehive covered with canary creeper. Never saw anything like it in my life."

"You don't keep up to date with women's fashions, Wicks," said Sylvia. "It's what's known as a Margaret hat. There's a whole window stuffed with them at Bostock and Plummer's. 'As supplied to her Royal Highness Princess Margaret for Her Honeymoon,' that's what they say. You can get them with any sort of flowers and in any colour. Deanna bought hers in the summer sales."

"Good God!" murmured Mr. Wickham in a tone of reverence.

"You haven't heard the worst yet, Sylvia," said Emmy. "The Bishopess has got one, only hers is geraniums. Lucy Adams saw her wearing it in Barley Street the other day."

"I suppose it'll be Miss Pettinger next," said Sylvia.

"Oh, *she* got one ages ago," said Emmy. "So did the Mixo-Lydian Ambassadress."

"Bless that woman, I can't help liking her," said Mr. Wickham. "She's somehow *real*. I don't mean as an Ambassadress, but as a person. Though I daresay she's a pretty good Ambassadress too, as Mixo-Lydians go. She certainly wouldn't stand for any nonsense."

"She's the only person that's ever been able to put that ghastly Geoffrey Harvey in his place," said Emmy. "You know, the one that was so hateful to poor Tom when he was at the Red Tape and Sealing Wax."

"And his even ghastlier sister," added Sylvia, "the one that almost bullied Oliver Marling into marrying her."

"A fate worse than death," said Mr. Wickham.

"You've said a mouthful, Wicks," said Emmy warmly. "Stop that AT ONCE, Agnes," she added to her youngest daughter, who had grown bored with being left alone, and was methodically hurling all the toys out of her pen, scoring a good hit on Mr. Wickham's stomach with the rubber giraffe. "If there's any more of that nonsense, I'll take you straight upstairs to Nurse. Here's your silly old giraffe. Sorry, Wicks."

"Sijaff," said Miss Agnes Grantly, smacking the toy which her mother had tossed back into the pen, with great affection.

"You see, she really can talk now," said Emmy proudly. "I say, Wicks, what's the latest news about Wiple Terrace?"

"Scandalous business," said Mr. Wickham. "If it does come off. I've been worried about Miss Hampton and Miss Bent. Southbridge School is pretty sure to look after the others, but Hampton and Bent, they're different. They'd be lost without Adelina, though I daresay Brown would let them have a room at the Red Lion *pro tem*. He damn well ought to, after all the cash they've put into his till. And I must say for them, they pay regular as clockwork. They're a couple of real gentlemen."

"I *hate* Lord Aberfordbury," said Emmy violently.

"You're not the only one, my girl," said Mr. Wickham. "There's a protest meeting at the school next week, and I've promised to lend a hand. But, well, I get about a lot, you know, and hear a bit, and I've got a fancy that there's something brewing."

"So have I, Wicks," said Sylvia, looking up from the sock that she was darning. "Eleanor and Georgy have been full of it for weeks, and then Amabel Adams took Eleanor to Pomfret Towers to see her father. Mr. Adams said he wouldn't make any promises, but he'd do the best he could."

"And Sam Adams's word is as good as his bond," said Mr. Wickham, quoting one of the wealthy ironmaster's more familiar sayings. "Well, that's the buzz that I've got too. I hope it's true, because Adams is a good fellow and can pull a lot of strings. I didn't know your youngsters were involved in it."

"Well, you know what children are," said Sylvia. "They do have a capacity for *starting* things. And they are so dreadfully transparent, especially when they're being secretive. Eleanor thinks she has another secret now, with Robin Morland, something about a party for Mrs. Morland's seventieth birthday. It's all terribly hush-hush, and Eleanor hasn't actually said a thing.

But of course I can't help knowing, and I expect she'll come and tell me any time now."

"Why has it got to be a secret?" said Mr. Wickham. "Everyone in Baretshire likes Mrs. Morland, even if she's only lived here forty years. Marvellous woman, the way she keeps on working. I'd be the first to jump at a chance to celebrate her birthday. Come to think of it, I know where to lay hands on some first-rate liqueur brandy, guaranteed to bowl you over with one sniff."

"I know, Wicks," said Sylvia. "That's what I feel too. But Robin's got the idea that his grandmother mustn't know about it, because she says she doesn't want a party."

"But if she's going to be *at* the party," said Emmy practically, "she's got to know about it some time, hasn't she?"

"Of course she has," said Sylvia, "and if I know Barsetshire, she soon will. You can't keep these things quiet for long. But at the moment it's the children's secret, and we've got to pretend we haven't heard anything about it."

At this point a tremendous tumult broke out in the hall, which was Deanna sounding the gong for tea.

"Gong, Agnes," said Emmy to her offspring, who was excitedly banging the giraffe on the railings of her pen. "Say GONG. She can say it beautifully, can't you, Baby? Say gong for Wicks."

"Whskzs," said Miss Grantly obediently.

"Clever girl," said her mother, scooping her up in a capable arm, giraffe and all. "She's saying Wicks, aren't you, Agnes?"

"Whskzs-z-z-z," repeated Miss Grantly, pleased with her performance.

"First time I've heard my name in Mixo-Lydian," said Mr. Wickham. "But it's gratifying to be recognised."

And then they all went in to tea, which had been laid in the dining-room, with the high chair used by generations of young Leslies pulled up beside Emmy's. On its tray was a feeder, a plate of thin, cut-up bread-and-butter, and a plastic mug of curious shape, containing milk. And when we say curious, we mean it wasn't straight, but slanted forwards or backwards from its base, according to which way you turned it.

"Rather like the funnel of a liner," observed Mr. Wickham, regarding this object with nautical interest.

"Martin's mother sent it from America," said Sylvia. "I believe you can get them easily here now, but at the time it was a tremendous novelty. Here are the children," she added, as Eleanor came in with Robin. "Sit anywhere you like, darling. We won't wait for Daddy and Cousin Tom. I expect Robin is ravenously hungry."

"I am, rather," admitted Robin. "It's a long way from High Rising, and Dr. Ford's car doesn't go very quickly. I expect I'd have gone much quicker on my bicycle."

"Hullo," said Emmy, who was trying to restrain her daughter from cramming her mouth much too full of bread-and-butter. "You're Robin Morland, aren't you? The one that your grandmother's Mrs. Morland and writes books? This is Agnes."

"She's rather small, isn't she?" asked Robin, surveying the gourmand dubiously. "I mean, I suppose she doesn't talk much yet?"

"Phoo-oo-oo," said Agnes, gulping a mouthful of milk and at the same time blowing out the bread-and-butter in a most unladylike manner.

Robin laughed, and Miss Grantly, delighted with the impression she had made, repeated the performance.

"Small pig," said Emmy, mopping up the pieces with the feeder. "I say, you mustn't laugh at her, it only makes her worse."

"Mother," said Eleanor, "will it be all right if I take Robin up to the Temple after tea?" referring to the Palladian folly, part pyramid and part pagoda, which a Leslie ancestor had caused to be erected in the grounds of Rushwater, and which the hands of generations of Leslie children had embellished with *grafitti*. "It's nice and quiet up there, and we've got some rather important plans to talk about. They're still a secret, but I expect we'll be able to tell you about them soon."

Permission was given, and almost at once Martin came into the room with Dr. Ford, who reported that the boils operation had been successful and the patient was ungrateful but fairly comfortable.

"I think he'll do all right now," he said. "I'll drop in and have another look at him next time I'm round this way. Now I must be off, or I'll be late for surgery. I'll tell your grandmother that you were safely delivered, young man, and don't fall off the roof of the Temple and break your neck, or chop your hand off in the sawmill. It would spoil her birthday."

Turning to the others, he continued: "Mrs. Morland's got an anniversary coming up. Doesn't do to say which anniversary, a lot of the ladies don't care for it. But I was discussing it with somebody the other night, and we both thought Barsetshire ought to give her some kind of party. Do her a power of good and she deserves it. I said I'd find out what the county felt about it. Well, I mustn't stay here gossiping all night. Good-bye, all."

And with this bombshell he went away.

CHAPTER 9

A few days later, at Northbridge Manor, Lydia Merton and her husband Sir Noel Merton, the eminent Q.C., were sitting in front of a bright fire in the horrid, lingering twilight of summertime, finishing their after-dinner coffee.

For once they were alone, as Lavinia had said rather vaguely that she would be out for dinner, Harry was up in the old schoolroom listening to a dreadfully dull wireless talk on "The Uses of Atomic Power in Industry," and Jessica had retired to her bedroom with a book of John Betjeman's poems, for which she had lately developed a violent passion. ("And a damn sight better for her than all that Sartre and Ionesco," her father said.)

"Do you know, Noel," observed Lydia suddenly, "I have the queerest feeling tonight that Things are going to happen."

"What sort of things, my love?" asked Noel.

"Nice things," said Lydia. "As Tony Morland might have said, I seem to have a strange power of feeling when Things are going to happen."

Noel, who knew his Lydia very well, looked at her in silence for a moment and then asked, with apparent irrelevance, exactly where was Lavinia this evening?

"I don't know *exactly* where," replied Lydia the truthful. "But wherever it is, she's out with Ludo. She told me they were going for a drive over the downs, and they'd pick up something to eat on the way. I don't suppose for a minute that they will," she added.

"I see," said Noel, who was no fool, nor a squanderer of words, since words were the tools of his profession.

After that, Palmer came in to clear away the coffee things, and for about half an hour Lydia and Noel made a pretence of reading; Noel the Law Reports in *The Times,* Lydia a highly acclaimed novel by one of the Young Angries, which she subsequently returned to the library, having failed to get beyond page 55 or take in any of it at all.

As the little clock on the mantelpiece was striking ten, the french windows suddenly burst open and in came Lavinia, closely followed by Lord Mellings. "Darling," Noel murmured to his Lydia, noticing the Look on the young people's faces, "that was certainly one of your more sibylline utterances."

Lavinia was becomingly flushed, and sparkling with that inner radiance which can only mean one thing to those who have eyes to see it.

"Mother," she said, "Father—I've brought Ludo. We've got something terribly important to tell you. We—he—I—well, we've just got engaged and it's all absolutely heaven."

"I hope you don't mind us bursting in like this," said Ludo, whose training and natural good manners never failed him, even in moments of high emotion. "But we felt we had to come to you at once. I know Lavinia is still under age, sir, but we're very much in love, and we'd like to have your consent to our marriage."

"I *do* hope you're pleased, darlings," said Lavinia to her parents, "because we are. And anyway I'll be twenty-one next year. You *are* pleased, aren't you?"

At which Lydia hugged her daughter and said she couldn't be happier, and Noel told Lord Mellings that he was delighted to give his consent to the marriage, and there was no one he would more warmly welcome as a son-in-law.

"And that, I think, calls for a drink all round," he added, moving to the side-table where bottles and glasses were set out on a tray. "I can't offer you champagne, I'm afraid, but this is a very decent brandy. Spot of brandy, Ludo? And you, my dear?" to

Lydia, who said she would be very dashing and have a large one for a change. "What about you, Lavinia?"

His daughter, still in a daze of happiness, said she didn't care what she drank, anything would do, and how soon could they get married? Could they get a special licence and do it all in a rush, like Clarissa Graham and Charles Belton?

"Well, hardly that, Lavinia," said Noel. "This is a slightly different case. For one thing, there will be a number of legal formalities to settle, and they take time."

"I know, sir," said Lord Mellings. "It's a hell of a job—sorry, Lady Merton, I'm afraid I'm a bit excited—it's a terribly complicated job when a chap with an entail and a title hanging over him asks a girl to marry him. And specially a girl with means," he added a little ruefully.

"What do you mean, *means*, Ludo?" said Lavinia. "I'm not a millionairess."

"You have quite enough money," said her father drily, "to make settlements a fairly complicated job, as Ludo quite rightly appreciates. I daresay it will take the lawyers at least a couple of months to sort them out."

"I'll ask my father's solicitors to get in touch with yours, sir, as soon as possible," said Lord Mellings.

"But *our* solicitors are only Uncle Robert," Lavinia objected. "I know they're called Keith and Keith, but it's only Uncle Robert really. I'm sure he'd rush things through if we asked him to."

Lord Mellings, who shared his Lavinia's eagerness for an early marriage, but understood the responsibilities involved more clearly than she ever would, looked rather desperately towards Lydia for guidance. Lydia, who had never failed anyone in her life, did not fail now.

"Lavinia, darling," she said, "you mustn't make things difficult for Ludo. Of course it would be much better if he were Mr. Smith or Mr. Jones, and you were just a goosegirl—which you

are, in a way. But he isn't Mr. Smith or Mr. Jones. Some day
he'll have to be Lord Pomfret, and take over the Towers." And
even as she spoke the words, her heart was smitten with solici-
tude for Ludo's father, the tired, hard-working, present Earl of
Pomfret, and she remembered the haunted look in his eyes,
which were so like his son's, and went on hastily. "You simply
can't rush into these things, my darling, and when you're Lady
Mellings you'll understand. Doesn't that sound rather nice,
'Lady Mellings'?"

"It sounds quite marvellous—with Ludo," said Lavinia, turning a radiant face to her betrothed, who took her hand and gave
it a gentle squeeze.

"Well, then," said Lydia, thankful to find that she had made
her point, "let's leave all the tiresome business details to the
lawyers, and get on with our own plans for the wedding. Dresses
and bridesmaids and flowers, there's such a lot to think about. I
think a spring wedding would be rather nice, don't you? About
Easter, when the cherry blossom's out. 'Loveliest of trees, the
cherry now——

> "Is hung with bloom along the bough,
> And stands about the woodland ride
> Wearing white for Eastertide."

"And for *my* wedding," added Lavinia, flinging herself upon
her mother, with a bearlike hug, from which tears were not far
distant. "Oh Mother, you do *understand*."

In which we think she had discovered the *mot juste,* and as
we feel sure they have a great many things to talk over, and are
entirely happy by themselves, we shall say good night to them
and leave them.

Even before the formal announcement in *The Times,* the news
of the engagement had spread rapidly through Barsetshire, with
the assistance of the Milk, the Fish, the Bread, the Shop, and

Miss Palmyra Phipps at the telephone exchange, ably seconded by Miss Norma Pollett, the Other Girl who relieved her.

We may say at once that the news was very well received. Lord Pomfret's quiet and patient work for the county, although he had only come into the title sideways, as a distant cousin of old Lord Pomfret's whose only son had been killed long ago in an Indian frontier skirmish, had earned him general liking and respect. His heir, Lord Mellings, although not so well known to the gypsies and the bodgers and other ancients of the soil as his younger brother Giles, was regarded as a proper gentleman and a bit of a dark horse; for nobody who was present had forgotten his appearance, with Aubrey Clover and Jessica Dean at the Northbridge Coronation Do, in a sketch entitled *Two-Step for Three*, singing that heart-breaking little Clover number "Though I am Not Twenty, Sweet, Here is my Heart," which was later to go round the world and break all disc records.

As for the Mertons, even if Sir Noel Merton, who was London born and divided his time between the Law Courts and Northbridge Manor, was still regarded somewhat as a foreigner, his wife Lydia had been fully accepted by all ranks of the county. She was a Keith by birth, and the Keiths were good, sound Barsetshire stock; moreover, Mrs. Merton, as she was then, had shown what she could do when the responsibility for the Coronation festivities at Northbrige had fallen into her astonished hands.

And as we are aware, the Mertons' agent, Mr. Wickham, was known and welcomed everywhere he went; and as he had been born and bred over Chaldicotes way, with ancestors who stemmed from the days before the Norman Conquest, it was felt that if he approved the match he must have the root of the matter in him.

Between the friends and connections of the engaged couple, telephone communication was fast and furious. And when we say "fast" we do not mean to imply that the calls were brief, for most of them were extremely long, and it was a source of great satisfaction to Palmyra Phipps to be able to tell the Palace for the fourth time that she was sorry she couldn't put Her through to Pomfret Towers, as the line was still engaged. This she did with the greater pleasure in that she knew, from an earlier conversation she had overheard between the Palace and old Lady Norton, who was back from Cheltenham for a brief visit, that the Bishopess was proposing to bully Lady Pomfret into taking the chair at a lecture given by Miss Frances Harvey, under the auspices of the Ministry of General Interference, on "How to Direct Our Mothers into Industry."

We cannot say to whom Lavinia telephoned, as we have never been introduced to her circle of Barsetshire contemporaries, and it is far too late to think about them now, when she is on the point of leaving them. But we are certain that she sent a telegram in her best French to kind M. and Mme Pierre Boulle, with whom she had spent such pleasant months in Paris, and that they responded with their compliments the most sincere, and cordial expressions of esteem and friendship.

One of the first calls that Lord Mellings made was to the Aubrey Clovers in London, at a time when he guessed they would be back from the theatre. The telephone was answered as usual by their faithful Miss M., who had a name, and it was Mowbray, but hardly anybody used it.

"Good evening, Miss M.," said Ludo. "It's Lord Mellings from Pomfret Towers. Do you think, please, I could speak to Jessica?" And the next minute Jessica Dean's celebrated and enchanting voice was on the line, saying: "Ludo, my lamb, no need to tell me, for I *know*; Aubrey says we players always know. My sweet, it's heaven, and your Lavinia's such a darling girl. When is the wedding to be? In the spring? Lilac time or cherry-blossom time? I'm all for cherry-blossom time myself. Who is the best man?"

Ludo said it would be one of his Graham cousins, whichever

could get leave at the right time. "And Jessica," he added, with a sudden burst of his old shyness, "it isn't really my affair, I know, and Lavinia's mother will be asking you, but we did think—we did hope—I mean Lavinia and I felt it would be most awfully nice if Sarah Siddons could be one of the bridesmaids. The others will be my sister Emily and Lavinia's sister Jessica, and Angela Carter perhaps to make it four. Oh bother, no; they wouldn't match a bit, in size I mean. We'll have to scrounge round for someone else."

Jessica laughed her lovely, modulated laugh and told him not to worry, she and Aubrey and Lydia would stage-manage everything. "Sarah Siddons would adore to be a bridesmaid, and—just a minute, Ludo, what?—Aubrey says is there a chance for him to be an usher? He can ush most beautifully, and you'll never notice him. He just melts into the background. Well, good night my sweet and happy dreams. My love to your Lavinia. Good night, good night."

Robin returned from his visit to Rushwater (and in the end it was Dr. Ford who brought him) full of ill-assimilated information about foot-and-mouth disease and contagious abortion. His grandmother welcomed him with great affection and a certain sinking of the heart, for as every mother and grandmother knows, life is a good deal easier when the Little Darlings are away for the time being, safe in someone else's trusted hands.

"I've had a letter from your mother," she said, after listening patiently to a long and exceedingly boring dissertation on the breeding points of Rushwater Randolph, the astonishing milk yield of Rushwater Cowslip, and the chances as an expectant mother of Rushwater Primrose. "She says the measling's all over and they are out of quarantine."

Robin's face fell.

"Do you mean I've got to go back to London, Gran?" he said

in tones of horror. "Oh, Gran, I simply can't go back to London."

"Well, it's not London, it's Littlehampton," said Mrs. Morland. "Your mother is taking the children there for two or three
weeks, to blow away the measles. She thought you might like a
bit of seaside too," and with a true grandmother's devotion she
made no reference to the sentence in her daughter-in-law's letter which ran: "Besides, I'm certain you've had quite enough
of him."

"Oh Gran, *must* I go to Littlehampton?" said Robin desperately. "Couldn't I stay here with you and Stoker? I think I've
grown a bit old for the seaside. It's all right when you're by yourself, but children do spoil things rather. Children are so *young*,
somehow. *Please*, Gran, can't I stay here?"

"Of course you can stay here, Robin, if you want to," said
Mrs. Morland, touched against her will by this vehement appeal. "I only thought it might be a bit dull for you, with only
two old ladies in the house."

"Oh, Gran, it isn't dull for me at all," said Robin. "And it's
terribly important that you *are* so old. That's why I've simply
got to stay at High Rising and not go to Littlehampton. Besides,"
he added artfully, changing the subject as he realised he had almost let out a Top Secret, "I do *need* Stoker to build up my
strength. They starve us at school, Gran, we never really get a
decent meal. They don't know how to constitrute a balanced
diet."

"What on earth do you know about a balanced diet?" asked
Mrs. Morland, well aware that she was beaten.

"It's what they give the cows at Rushwater," said Robin. "It's
quite easy, really. All you have to do is——"

"All right, Robin, you can tell me about it later," said Mrs.
Morland. "I must get this letter to your mother finished if I'm
going to catch the post. Go and ask Stoker to give you a special

tea, something that constitutes a balanced diet. There's some summer pudding left over from lunch, and a bit of cream, and I know she's frying fish and chips. And do have a bath and change your shirt. That one's quite filthy."

"I know," said Robin. "Eleanor's Nurse wanted to wash it, but I wouldn't let her. I didn't want to spoil the dirtiness for Stoker. There's something rather splendid about getting things really dirty. It seems to make it worth while washing them. If they're not *really* dirty, it's only half worth while."

In the doorway he hovered, then rushed back to his grandmother and hugged her in careless rapture with young arms as thin as celery sticks. "Thanks for letting me stay, Gran," he said. "Thanks most awfully. It really *is* important."

Then he hurried away in search of Stoker and the balanced diet. Mrs. Morland turned back to the letter she had started to her daughter-in-law, read it through, tore it up, and started quite another, wondering what quality it was in little boys that made them so maddening and appealing at the same time.

As we know, it was the custom for the Palace and the Deanery to entertain one another to dinner twice a year, and it had now come round to the turn of the Deanery. A date had long been fixed, arrangements for provisions made, and invitations had been accepted not only by the Palace, but by Dr. and Mrs. Joram and Canon and Mrs. Fewling, who were now firmly established in the Close.

At almost the last hour, however, a message was delivered through His Lordship's secretary, saying that the Palace expressed its deep regret and would be unable to keep the engagement. Her Ladyship, it appeared, had expressed a desire to pay a ceremonial visit to Ghana, where Christianity, she understood, was becoming manifest in a new form under the auspices of that enlightened Premier, Dr. Nkrumah.

We cannot pretend that the Deanery was completely stricken

by this news, but coming at such short notice it was, to say the
least of it, annoying. Dr. Crawley was all for cancelling the arrangements and putting off the other guests, but Mrs. Crawley
said why not have a party for themselves for once?

"We could ask Mrs. Morland," she said, "and Tommy Needham would fill in as extra man," referring to her son-in-law, the
incumbent at Lambton, who had lost an arm in the war, but
was doing very well without it. "Octavia won't want to come.
She's expecting the baby at any moment."

The Dean said yes indeed, Laura would be delighted, and
one could always count on Tommy.

"And I was thinking," pursued Mrs. Crawley, "wouldn't it be
a kind act to invite old Lady Lufton? I always feel she must
be so lonely over there at Framley Parsonage, now that the
children are all married. But oh dear me," she added, "that
leaves us one man short again. I can't think of any really *suitable*
unattached men, though I suppose one could ask Lord Stoke or
Sir Edmund Pridham."

In the end, the matter was quite easily settled, since it appeared that Lady Lufton's son-in-law, Oliver Marling, would be
free on that date and delighted to escort the Dowager; since his
wife, the Hon. Marie Marling, was committed to go to Cardiff
and judge the spaniel class in a South Wales dog show.

The evening of the party was uncommonly kind for that repellent season, and most of the ladies were wearing summer
frocks, some of the guests bringing a mackintosh just in case.
Mrs. Morland, who always felt the cold, had providently stuck
to a light woollen dress, telling her hostess that it had been so
nice all day that she was certain it would turn nasty before
evening, on the principle of rain before seven, fine before
eleven, or rather the other way round.

"And when one thinks," she added, sipping the gin and Du-
bonnet which had been provided to supplement the sherry in
the awful expectation of a Palace visit, "of the glorious summer

that we had last year, with hardly a drop of rain between May and October and it almost felt like central heating, it makes one really want to cry."

"But people grumbled about *that*," said Mrs. Joram, she who had been Mrs. Brandon. "They said that in a few days it would be an official drought, or else it *was* an official drought. I never can remember what makes a drought official."

"When you are not allowed to use the garden hose," said Lady Lufton, "and have to water the hydrangeas and the rhododendrons by hand, to make their leaves stand up again."

"People are always grumbling about something," said Margot Fewling. "They wouldn't be happy if they didn't." To which her husband added almost under his breath:

> *"And isn't your life extremely flat*
> *With nothing whatever to grumble at!"*

"What on earth's that, Fewling?" said Tommy Needham. "It rings a bell in my mind, but somehow I can't place it."

"*Princess Ida*, act three," said Canon Fewling. "Not the best act, I'm afraid. The second act is the real vintage stuff. I once played King Gama in a Mess show when I was in the Navy, and it was a source of great mortification to me that all the best music came in the act where I wasn't on. I still think that *Princess Ida* is underrated," he added, whereupon a fierce and largely uninformed discussion broke out as to the relative merits of Sir William Gilbert's words and Sir Arthur Sullivan's music and what would happen to the operas now that the Gilbert copyright was so soon to expire?

Since most of the guests were old friends of the Deanery, there was no formal seating arrangement at the dinner table, except that Dr. Crawley was careful to place the Dowager Lady Lufton, who was not really an intimate of the Close, on his right hand, and Mrs. Crawley almost dashingly invited Oliver Marling, the odd-man-out among this company of clergy, to squire

her. And we must say at once that Oliver did this very hand-
somely, for although we grew a little bored with him at the
time when he was mooning after Jessica Dean, star of the Cockspur Theatre, and composing his opuscule on the Reverend
Thomas Bohun, Canon of Barchester from 1657 to 1665 and
author of some metaphysical and highly erotic poems, we think
that marriage to the Hon. Maria Lufton, and the somewhat
belated experience of fatherhood, had done a world of good to
him, and turned him into a different and much nicer man.

The conversation at table naturally veered towards the main
Barsetshire topic of the moment, the engagement between Lord
Mellings and Lavinia Merton, and general opinion was that it
would Do very well, although not all the guests were familiar
with both the contracting parties. The Dean, turning to Lady
Lufton, asked her if she would be able to attend the wedding,
which had been fixed for just after Easter in the Cathedral.

"Unfortunately," he added in a dry voice, "His Lordship will
be attending a Diocesan Conference at that time, and so will
not be able to conduct the ceremony. Lady Merton, who is a
very old friend of ours, having been at school with our daughter
Octavia, has done me the honour to ask if I would officiate.
Naturally I am delighted to fall in with her wishes, and Canon
Joram has consented to assist me."

Lady Lufton, while privately admiring the craftsmanship of
the timing, said that she very much hoped to come; that is, she
added, for she was an extremely modest woman, if she received
an invitation.

"I don't know Lady Merton and her daughter very well,"
she added, "but what I have seen of them I admire immensely.
The girl is charming, and seems to have a good deal of character. I think she should be just the right wife for Ludo, who always reminds me so much of my own Ludovic, so shy and *un-
confident*, poor lamb, but such a stickler for duty. I shall never
be thankful enough for all the things my dear daughter-in-law

Grace has done for Ludovic. She really is a tower of strength to him."

At the other end of the table Mrs. Crawley was discussing marriage rites in many lands with her left-hand neighbour, Dr. Joram. As one-time Bishop of Mngangaland, he had a store of curious anecdotes to tell, and Mrs. Crawley listened to him fascinated, saving up the best stories to pass on to her husband later, and observing with the serene command of every situation which had made her such an admirable Close wife and mother, that there would appear to be marked differences between the nuptial ceremony as practised in the mud huts of Mngangaland and the altogether simpler ritual of a wedding in Barchester Cathedral, but that the sanctification of the union was all.

Meanwhile Mrs. Morland, on Dr. Joram's left, was getting on very well indeed with her other neighbour, Canon Fewling, whom she had known since the long-ago days when he was priest-in-charge of St. Sycorax under Mr. Villars, the rector of Northbridge, and darkly referred to as A Bit Too High by people who didn't care for incense and were unable to appreciate his sterling worth of character. But we hasten to assure our reader that Tubby Fewling, in his next cure of souls at Greshamsbury, before he was promoted to the Close, had abandoned the incense in deference to his parishioners' feelings; albeit reluctantly, for he was really rather fond of it, and had quite a struggle to persuade himself that his addiction to the censer might be a form of selfishness and spiritual pride.

Across the table his wife Margot, to whom, as Margot Phelps, he had never told his love, so that she was swept into a brief but very happy marriage with the late Mr. Macfadyen of Amalgamated Vedge, was doing her duty nobly by Oliver Marling; asking him after his wife and family, that helpful word which can cover a great deal of ignorance as to the sex and number of the children. Also she asked sympathetically about Oliver's eyes, which was both kind and clever of her, for few people either knew or remembered the constant headaches from which he used to suffer in the war years, when the only man who really understood his eyes was abroad somewhere with the Forces. And how Margot Fewling happened to have heard about them we cannot say, we only know she had.

The Reverend Thomas Needham, on Mrs. Fewling's right, expressed to his other neighbour, Mrs. Joram, his delight in the news of The Engagement. Lydia Merton, he said, Lady Merton he really ought to say, but he was so accustomed to hearing her referred to by her Christian name, and indeed she was in the charming habit of addressing him as Tommy, was a very old friend of his wife Octavia. Indeed, he added, had it not been for Lydia's kind offices, he might never have summoned up courage to propose to his dear wife, thus gaining many happy years of comradeship and the blessings of their large brood of children.

Mrs. Joram, with an appearance of lively interest that did her great credit, since her mind was really occupied with the choice of new curtains for her drawing-room, asked how many children? To which Mr. Needham replied, with a slight touch of embarrassment, six at the present time to the best of his knowledge, but they were expecting a seventh at almost any moment.

With the arrival of the saddle of mutton, accompanied by mint sauce, red currant jelly, and all the proper trimmings, host, hostess, and guests set to other partners. We shall not attempt to record the rest of the table-talk, which was not particularly interesting, although unconstrained and friendly.

Nor shall we linger in the dining-room after the remains of the excellent ice-pudding had been removed, and a decanter of the Deanery's famed port placed upon the table by the reverent hands of Verger, the butler, for we have no idea whatsoever of the kind of talk likely to pass amongst four gentlemen in Holy Orders and a fifth gentleman who, although a layman, was deeply versed, through his researches into the career of the Rev. Thomas Bohun, in Cathedral history. Let us rather follow Mrs.

Crawley and her ladies to the drawing-room, where a small fire had been built up with wood and fir-cones and was burning brightly.

Mrs. Morland, who was a very old friend of the Crawleys, said how lovely it was to sit down by a *proper* fire, she meant one that really crackled and had such a delicious smell. "Of course I *could* have one at High Rising if I wanted," she added truthfully, "but it hardly seems worth while lighting it just for me."

"But that, Laura, is ridiculous when you feel the cold so much," said Mrs. Crawley.

"I know," said Mrs. Morland, "it is one of my bits of parsimony, like hoarding string, when I could quite easily go out and buy a ball or even some of that repellent cellophane or tape that sticks all over your fingers and nobody can ever undo it."

Margot Fewling said that the world seemed to have gone cellophane-crazy, and it took twice as long to open packets now as it used to in the good old days.

"And plastic tops to jars," added Mrs. Joram. "It was ever so much easier when you could simply screw them off. Now you have to Press Down in Centre of Lid to Open, but they hardly ever do open, at least not for me, and putting them on again is even worse. You're supposed to Squeeze Edges Gently and I do, but the lid stays squatting on the top quite loose and makes me feel a fool."

"All labour-saving devices," pronounced Mrs. Morland in her deepest and most impressive voice, "are designed to create the labour they are devised to save. What could be better than a hot potato?"

"What *do* you mean, Laura?" asked Mrs. Crawley, to the intense relief of all her hearers, who were dying to ask the same question, but hardly liked to.

"In your muff," said Mrs. Morland. "I remember my mother, when she went to the Opera, or for a drive in the victoria, or for a railway journey, though you could get fresh, hot footwarmers in first-class carriages at most of the big stations, and lunch and tea hampers too, with really *excellent* cold meat and cakes and sandwiches, so much nicer than banging your way along swaying corridors to the restaurant car, and the food is hardly ever worth it when you get there and so expensive, my mother always carried a hot potato in her muff, so cheap and simple. It wasn't peeled, of course," she added.

Lady Lufton broke the slightly awed silence by observing: "Rather like a hot brick wrapped in flannel at the bottom of your bed."

Mrs. Crawley said that one of the nicest things about growing old was that there was so much to remember, and every year the earlier impressions, which were almost always happy ones, at least they seemed happy seen in retrospect, probably because the mind refused to retain with any sharpness experiences that it had not enjoyed, unless of course you belonged to the professional look-back-in-anger group, grew vivider and vivider.

Every lady present was moved by this remark to recapture, for a moment, the halcyon days of childhood; even Margot Fewling, by far the youngest of the party, who had not really reached the age of retrospection, and whose youth had been a strangely vagrant one, spent in all manner of foreign ports, wherever her father, the Admiral, had been stationed.

"But one of the *worst* parts of growing old," said Mrs. Morland, recovering from a dream of childhood in an old house in Kensington, "is that there are so many things you know better than ever how to do, only you can't do them any more."

"Like darning and mending," said Mrs. Joram. "Because of your eyes."

"Or spring cleaning," added Margot, "because of your back."

"Or keeping up with your children on a walk," said Mrs. Crawley. "When the children are little you have to slow down for them, and when they're big they have to slow down for you."

"I understand exactly what you mean," said Lady Lufton to

Mrs. Morland. "It's what I always feel about the garden. I *know*
I could fork the rose beds better than old Podgens, who doesn't
look what he's doing and breaks the new shoots and just says:
'Oops-a-Daisy, sorry about that, ma'am.' But when I've done
about a yard I give up in despair, or rather my bones give up. It's
horribly frustrating."

During this conversation, the ladies had been aware of the
ringing of a telephone bell, and the sound of voices in the hall,
but Mrs. Crawley, like a good hostess, had made no move, and
we think that only Mrs. Joram, remembering the conversation
at the dinner table, was conscious of the tension in the air.

Presently the drawing-room door opened and the gentlemen
came in, Mr. Needham looking as pale as a ghost, the Dean's
face lit up by a beaming smile. "Well, my dear," he said to his
wife, "that was a call from Lambton. Octavia has twins, one of
each kind, all doing well."

"Twins!" cried Mrs. Crawley, and warmly embraced her son-
in-law. "Dear Tommy, this is wonderful news. Now it makes
eight, *such* an economy having two at once. Octavia will be delighted. She always set her heart on having eight children," she
told the rest of the party, "because she was the eighth child herself, but at her age she was running it a bit fine," a statement
which all the ladies present understood. "This really is a merci-
ful dispensation of providence."

The warmest congratulations were offered to Mr. Needham,
who was beginning to recover from the shock; the health of the
twins was drunk in Armagnac; and Mrs. Crawley began to count
up how many children, grandchildren, and great-grandchildren
she had now, making the sum total about sixty.

Dr. Joram, finding himself next to Mrs. Morland on a sofa
for two, remarked that this proliferation of families put him in
mind of the old days in Mngangaland, where hardly a week
passed without the celebration of the birth of a boy-child in the
Chief's family, for of course the daughters didn't count. "I left

my diocese a good many years ago now," he added, "but I still
hear from my successor, who is doing excellent work there. And
of course I saw a great deal of the Chief's favourite son, when he
was at Balliol." And even as he spoke the words a faint cloud
crossed his face.

Mrs. Morland, who was very sensitive to atmosphere, asked
which son that was, and why was Dr. Joram worried?

"Alas, alas," said the ex-Bishop of Mngangaland, "I sometimes fear I was remiss in my charge. He was the eightieth son,
and a highly promising young man. He took a third in P.P.E.,
and read a bit of law before he went home. And there, I regret
to say, he ritually slaughtered most of his relations, including his
father, and seized the Chiefhood from his elder brothers, pro-
claiming himself King."

Mrs. Morland said how *awful*, in a voice of deep enjoyment.

"What saddens me most," went on Dr. Joram, "is to learn
from my successor that the slaughter was conducted to the tune
of the Eton Boating Song, with an accompaniment of native
drums. The foolish fellow had been persuaded to believe that it
was a great song of triumph, applicable to all occasions. I fear his
sense of humour was always slightly primitive, and he had made
bad friends at Lazarus, who delighted to pull his leg."

Mrs. Morland enquired with unfeigned interest what happened afterwards.

"Everything settled down very nicely," said Dr. Joram, bright-
ening visibly, "and now that Mngangaland is to become a Re-
public, I daresay the King's knowledge of P.P.E. will come in
handy. He should make an admirable President, for of course
he will be elected automatically. He is a charming fellow really,
when he can curb his atavistic instincts. He sends me a Christmas card each year, and when he read the announcement of
our marriage in *The Times* he sent us the most delightful wedding present."

"*What* was it?" asked Mrs. Morland eagerly, expecting to

hear at least of a shrunken human head made into a paper-weight.

"Nothing at all extravagant," said Dr. Joram. "He understood my simple tastes, you see. Just a large bowl carved out of a tree-stump with wifestooth decorations round the rim."

"Wifestooth?" asked Mrs. Morland, who had seldom enjoyed a dinner-party conversation more.

"It is the Mngangaland equivalent of dogstooth," said Dr. Joram. "The women have their teeth filed to a sharp point, and use them for the most elaborate needlework on wood and bark and leather. The bowl was of course intended for ceremonial purposes, hardly of a Christian kind, I fear, but we find that it does very well for oranges. Or apples, of course, when there are no oranges."

We feel that Mrs. Morland would have been happy to pursue this fascinating topic all the evening, but by now the conversation had become general, or perhaps it would be more correct to say that the Dean had the floor to the exclusion of all others. Margot Fewling, it appeared, had been describing some incident during her frequent visits to Scotland with her late husband, Mr. Macfadyen the master market-gardener, and a dispute had arisen as to the correct usage of the terms Scotch, Scots, and Scottish, with a passing reference to the observance of the Sabbath in that proud and splendid country.

At this point Dr. Crawley was heard to remark that indeed, indeed, he was second to no man in his admiration of the Scotch, or Scots, or Scottish, but there were times when he felt that their zeal had outrun their discretion. If he were asked to give an instance, he added (which we may say he had not been, for nobody, except perhaps his wife, who was thinking of other things, was bold enough to interrupt the Dean's flow of words in full spate), he would remind his hearers of the metrical psalm or adaptation of the Scriptures which ran:

> *"How blessed shall that warrior be*
> *Who riding on his naggie,*
> *Shall take their little children up*
> *And dash them on the craggie."*

Which truly dreadful words, recalled by us but imperfectly we fear from our own childhood, and uttered in the Dean's best pulpit voice, struck awe into all his hearers; even Mrs. Morland, who had been tempted to wonder on occasions, such as the wilful damage to Packer's Universal Royal Derby, whether a touch of Herodry in Hogglestock might not be an admirable thing.

After this the conversation languished, and since it was perfectly clear to all the ladies present that Mr. Needham, though in the most polite way, was straining to get back to Lambton and see his wife and the new additions to his family, several people glanced at the clock and said they really must be going now, and the party very soon broke up.

The residents of Wiple Terrace were gentlemen of their word, in which term we include Miss Hampton and Miss Bent of Adelina Cottage and Mrs. Feeder of Editha. The committee, as promised, had called a Public Protest Meeting over the threatened demolition of the Terrace. Handbills and what we believe are known as throwaways had been printed by the Barchester Press in remarkably short order and at considerably cut rates, through the kind offices of Colonel the Rev. Edward Crofts, Vicar of Southbridge, who was known to Have Influence; an influence by no means weakened by the friendly drinking relationship between the Colonel's ex-batman, Bateman, and the foreman printer.

Miss Bent, who, to most people's surprise, was an expert with the typewriter and indeed with almost any form of machine, had sent out a number of special invitations to people she deemed likely to be helpful and interested. She and Miss Hamp-

ton, moreover, had introduced a bold poster into all the bars of
the Red Lion, and Mr. Brown, the proprietor, had undertaken
to Pass the Word to all his Pals.

The enterprising Mr. Wickham, with the help of some excellent Navy rum, had managed to inspire a paragraph in the cur-
rent issue of the *Barchester Chronicle,* headed "Threat to Noted
Barsetshire Beauty Spot," with a sub-head "Must We Sacrifice
Our Ancient Monuments?" and a note that All Were Welcome,
and admission to the meeting would be free.

A room had been secured at Southbridge School, which had
of course broken up for the holidays, through the intromission
of Mr. Feeder and Mr. Traill, with the willing consent of the
headmaster. And at this point we must ask leave to divagate (although our faithful reader knows that nothing would prevent
our divagations, with or without leave) and explain that a great
many changes have occurred at Southbridge School since our
last visit there.

We are not so much referring to the addition of a new wing,
which provided several extra classrooms and a splendid modern
library, opened by Professor Hacker of Redbrick University in
1958, as to changes in *personnel.* The late headmaster, Everard
Carter, whose wife Kate was Lydia Merton's elder sister, had retired some couple of years ago; too soon, in the opinion of many
people, for the Carters were much liked, and kind Kate, in par
ticular, had a way with boys that gave confidence to many an
anxious mother.

The gap had been by no means easy to fill. Southbridge, although a minor public school, was a public school with high
standards and a considerable reputation in the West. What was
clearly needed was a scholar, with experience in the handling of
boys, and a wife who could get on with Matron, keep a motherly eye on all her charges, and talk to parents and prospective
parents in the terms they understood.

For a time Mr. Shergold, the Senior Housemaster, had been

considered, but Mr. Shergold was a bachelor, and in any case too useful where he was to be removed. The appointment might have gone to Robin Dale, a good housemaster with a very nice wife Anne (she who had been Anne Fielding), but the Dales, with a growing family of children, had moved away to Allington, there to start a highly successful pre-preparatory school for little boys.

In the end, the Governors had approached Eric Swan, who, as we know, was a resident master at Philip Winter's preparatory school at Harefield. Swan was a Southbridge Old Boy; his academic qualifications were unimpeachable; he had the experience of many, but not too many, years of teaching; and his wife Justinia, younger daughter of the Dowager Lady Lufton, seemed exactly the right helpmate (or helpmeet) for a relatively young, progressive headmaster.

This unexpected offer involved Swan in racking days and nights of doubt, in which his wife was far too wise to interfere. It was an honour, no doubt about that; but he was happy in his work at Harefield, he liked his colleagues and the little boys, and his home in one of the elegant wings of Harefield House was both comfortable and charming. After several talks with Philip Winter, who told him not to be a ruddy young fool but take the gifts the Gods offered while he had the chance, he finally decided to accept the post. And, we may say at once, the Governors never had cause to regret their choice nor Swan his decision.

There had been a good deal of discussion at Wiple Terrace about a chairman for the meeting. By this time it was fairly common knowledge that Lord Aberfordbury was the villain of the piece, or the nigger in the woodpile, and the Dean was suggested on the grounds of certain strong comments he had been heard to make on the character of that gentleman in the past ("A pestilent fellow. I had the pleasure of blackballing him for the Polyanthus"). However, this idea was dropped on the advice of the Rev. Edward Crofts, who reminded everybody very kindly that it would be difficult for Dr. Crawley to associate himself publicly with a demonstration against a known friend of the Palace; although he was certain that the Dean's heart, he would almost venture to say his prayers, would be wholly with them in their cause.

Eric Swan declined the offer on the grounds that, as headmaster, he could hardly commit the school to such a course without the consent of the Governors, most of whom were away in Switzerland, or Bermuda, or the Aegean, or taking a golfing holiday in Scotland. As an individual, he added, he was only too pleased to lend a room in what amounted to his private house, and afterwards there would be tea for everybody.

Mr. Adams, who was next approached, gave a strangely enigmatic answer. They could count on his attendance at the meeting, he said, and he might have something to tell them before the conclusion of the proceedings, but things being what they were, he felt it was not his place to take the chair.

Upon hearing this news from Miss Hampton and Miss Bent, whom he had met by accident in the bar of the Red Lion, Mr. Wickham gave a long, low whistle. "Bet you a dollar that there's something in the wind," he said. "With Adams a wink is as good as a nod." Miss Hampton, who was usually game for any bet, said sorry no takers, and it was agreed that the odds against Lord Aberfordbury had shortened considerably.

Finally, on the suggestion of young Lady Bond, who had been an active participant in the pre-war scandal in which Lord Aberfordbury, then Sir Ogilvy Hibberd, had bought and proposed to build a garage and road-house upon Pooker's Piece, and had been so signally routed by old Lord Pomfret, Lord Stoke was unanimously elected to take the chair. Although old, absentminded, and extremely deaf, as his niece by marriage readily admitted, he was still an outstanding figure in the county and *capable de tout*. As a precaution it had been arranged that young

Lord Bond, whom we shall always think of as C.W., should stand by in case of emergency. "Because with Uncle Stoke," Daphne Bond added, "you really never know."

It was obvious from the large numbers of people who arrived at Southbridge School that afternoon by car, or foot, or bus, or bicycle, that the meeting was of far more than local interest. Emissaries such as Mr. Wickham, Dr. Ford, and Mr. Brown of the Red Lion had done their duty well; few of Miss Bent's invitations had fallen on stony soil; and the heinousness of Lord Aberfordbury's crime had closed the ranks of all men and women of ill will against him.

Apart from the friends and connections of Wiple Terrace and the School, Southbridge residents generally, and the people who are always ready to oppose anything on any grounds, there was a strong stiffening of Vidlers, Panters, Bunces, Hubbacks, Caxtons, Puckens, Gobles, Margetts, and other natives of the soil, some of whom had come from quite long distances to see what it was all about.

When Mrs. Morland arrived with Sylvia Gould and Robin, a good ten minutes before the time advertised for the meeting, she found the corridor as crowded as Barley Street on market day, and the room already full. And when we say full, we mean that three-quarters of it were much too full, and the other quarter comparatively empty; for there was the usual reluctance on the part of those not specifically invited to sit in the front rows, lest all should think that they were proud, and the usual consequence of a dreadful huddle of sitters and standers at the back and in the middle.

Mrs. Morland, who was far too modest to suffer from self-consciousness of any kind, and who liked to be as close to the speaker as she could because of her eyes, made her way deliberately to the front, where she was hailed by young Lady Bond and given a seat in the front row. Here she found herself among all her old Southbridge friends; the contingent from Wiple Terrace, the vicar and his wife, Kate Carter who had come over from Northbridge with her sister Lydia Merton, and, to her great delight, Mrs. Birkett, wife of the last headmaster but one of Southbridge School, who had long since retired to Worsted to write his massive work on the Analects of Procrastinator.

Next to Mrs. Birkett was a plump, grey-haired woman of vaguely familiar appearance, who turned to her and said: "I daresay you won't remember me, Mrs. Morland, but the name is Bissell. Mr. Bissell and I spent several happy years at Wiple Terrace, when the Hosiers' Boys' School was evacuated to Southbridge early in the war, and when our friends Miss Hampton and Miss Bent wrote and told us about this dreadful business of Lord Aberfordbury, Mr. Bissell remarked that it was only right and proper I should come down and lend what help I could. Mrs. Birkett very kindly offered hospitality, so here I am."

Mrs. Morland, who had always liked the hard-working headmaster of the Hosiers' Boys' School and his wife, although their images had somewhat faded from her memory, greeted Mrs. Bissell warmly, introduced Sylvia Gould, and looked round for Robin. But Robin, with the elusiveness of all small boys, had slipped away, and was engaged in animated conversation with Eleanor Leslie and Amabel Adams, who had deserted their respective mothers and withdrawn into a secret huddle, wearing the smug looks of those who could say plenty and they would.

By this time it was after three o'clock, and there was no sign anywhere of Lord Stoke, the Chairman, although his brougham had been observed in the drive by several people. "I think you'd really better start things going," said young Lady Bond to her husband. "Uncle Stoke seems to have gone adrift. We'll have to send out a search party."

"He's probably in the kitchen talking to Cook," said C.W.

"If there were any animals here——" began Daphne.

"The boys do keep some pigs," said Mr. Feeder, who had overheard her.

"Then that's where he'll be," said Daphne triumphantly, and turning to the first boy she saw, who happened to be Robin, said to him: "Do you know where the pigsties are?"

For once in his young life Robin would have had to confess his ignorance, but fortunately Eleanor came quickly to the rescue. "I do, Lady Bond," she said. "I've often been there with my brother."

"Then cut along and see if you can find Lord Stoke," said Daphne. "And if he's not there try the kitchen. And when you find him tell him that the meeting's started and he must come AT ONCE! You'll have to shout at him pretty loud, I expect, but anyway don't come back without him."

So the three children sped away on their allotted task, and C.W., mounting the platform, told the audience that Lord Stoke was unavoidably delayed, and he thought they might as well start the proceedings. As they all knew, he said, this meeting had been convened to discuss the threat to Wiple Terrace, which had long been the property of Paul's College, Oxford, but which had now been sold, or was on the point of being sold, and likely to be demolished to provide the site for a factory. If any members of the audience had anything to say on the subject, or if they had any helpful suggestion to make, would they please do so, as no formal speeches had been arranged and the floor was open to all.

After the usual silence which follows such a request, a local bank manager got up and said the facts were substantially as stated by Lord Bond. Paul's College did indeed intend to sell, and he had it on the best authority (though whose he was not at liberty to divulge) that the directors of the National Rotochrome Polychrome Universal Picture Postcard Company had made a substantial offer for the property. After which he sat down rather smugly, with the air of a man whose mission is accomplished. We do not know the name of this bank manager, nor shall we trouble to invent it, since we have taken a violent dislike to him at first sight, and have decided that he is pompous, self-opinionated, far too ready to speak of the Bank's private concerns in public, and probably in the pocket of Lord Aberford-bury.

As a result of his speech there were loud murmurings in the audience, to the effect that "So Lord Aberwhatsisname's up to his old tricks again," and "Remember what he done that time over Pooker's Piece?" and "Ar, didn't I tell you he was at the bottom of it?" Calling the meeting to order, Lord Bond said that perhaps Miss Hampton, as the resident of longest standing in Wiple Terrace, would care to say a few words.

Miss Hampton's speech was brief, lucid, and unexpectedly moving to a number of her hearers, who had not realised that the author of those daring novels, *Chariots of Desire, Temptation at St. Anthony's,* and *Crooked Insect,* had so much of the root of simplicity in her. She mentioned the close ties that had always existed between Wiple Terrace and the village, now really the little town of Southbridge, as well as with the School. She said that in leaving Wiple Terrace, where she had lived for more than thirty years, she would feel that she had lost a real home; and added that to her mind the far more important thing was that with the building of a factory Southbridge would lose its character.

As she sat down, to quiet but very genuine applause, there rose to his feet in one of the middle rows an elderly man wearing a Norfolk jacket with a belt, knickerbockers buttoning below the knee, and a faded silk scarf passed through a kind of flat ring.

"Who on earth is that?" whispered Sylvia Gould to Mrs. Morland, who replied: "Mr. Scatcherd, he's a local artist, brother of Scatcherd's Stores at Northbridge. His sketches are quite dreadful but he means well."

Mr. Scatcherd, finding himself in possession of the floor, said that nobody had yet reluded to the Crux of the matter, which was the *purpose* of this here intended factory. "Art is Art," he said, "and commercial photos is commercial photos. It stands to reason that anyone can take photos of what he sees from *outside*, but it's what the Artist sees in the Mind's Eye as matters. I've said it before and I'll say it again, if Art dies in this dear old country of ours, it will be the likes of Lord Aberfordbury and his son as done it. Easy enough for Mr. Hibberd and his commercial photos to come up and take a snap, but *they* don't stop to see the Inner Meaning of a bulrush, like what Darvinchy and Renwar and all the rest, they would have done."

Lord Bond hastily thanked Mr. Scatcherd for his contribution, which seemed likely to go on for ever, and was looking rather desperately round the room for other speakers, when Mr. Brown of the Red Lion, who was heavily supported by a number of cronies in the back rows, got suddenly to his feet.

"I don't know whether it's right, sir," he said, "for a man to speak out a personal view, but I'd like to tell my mates in every sort of trade that if they're expecting a factory in Southbridge to do them good they're wrong. You've got to look at things in proportion like, I say, and though there's no denying that a factory would bring us all a lot of custom for the time being, it wouldn't be of no use in the long run. Next thing you know, after a factory they'll build a Housing Estate, and next thing after that there'll be a Southbridge New Town, with its own pubs and shops and cinemas and everything. And what does that get us, I ask you? Nothing but ruination." After this valiant speech, which was greeted by loud applause in all sections of the audience, Mr. Brown grew rather redder in the face than usual and sat down.

At this point there was a stir as the children ushered in Lord Stoke, who mounted the platform remarking in a voice clearly audible to almost everybody in the room: "Nice little lot of pigs they've got here." (And if any reader wonders how a room in a private house came to have a platform, it was because

Snow, the school carpenter, had caused one to be erected for the occasion.)

"What's all this about, Bond?" added His Lordship as he took the chair. "You did tell me, but it's slipped my mind. Something about Lord Aberfordbury, eh? Want me to move a vote of censure, eh? I'll move a vote of censure against Aberfordbury any time you like. Abominable fellow. His ties are disgusting. And he's a friend of the Palace lot. Trying to get a motor mower into the Close, I hear. Says the old pony mower's out of date. Preposterous. I've driven a dog-cart all my life, and what's good enough for me should be good enough for him."

By this time young Lord Bond was going quietly mad, but fortunately there was a fresh interruption in the form of Mr. Adams, who came in with the headmaster, moved purposefully to the foot of the platform, handed a sheet of paper to C.W., and then sat down next to his wife Lucy in the front row.

C.W. passed the paper to Lord Stoke, who put on his glasses, saying: "What's this? What's this? Confound it all, these are my wrong glasses. You'd better read it, Bond." Lord Bond glanced at the contents of the paper, with difficulty stifled a long, low whistle, and got quickly to his feet.

"Ladies and gentlemen," he said, "there has been a most startling and happy development. I am authorised to tell you that Wiple Terrace has been bought from Paul's College by a Syndicate, and presented as a free gift to Southbridge School, in recognition of all that Southbridge School has done for Barsetshire."

There was a moment of stunned silence; then a hum ran through the audience, broken by the young man from the *Barchester Chronicle,* who, seeing himself with the local scoop of the century, asked with great daring if we might know of who the Syndicate consists?

After consulting Mr. Adams with his eyebrows, C.W. replied that he would be glad to read out the names, with Lord Stoke's

permission. "They are," he went on, "Sir Robert Fielding, Sir
Robert Graham, Mr. Adams, Mr. Pilward, Mr. Dean, and Her
Excellency the Mixo-Lydian Ambassadress, whom we have the
honour to have with us this afternoon."

At these words everyone became suddenly aware of a personage in purple, who sprang to her feet from the seat next to
Lucy Adams.

"Bog, yes," she said, turning to address the audience, "it is oll
true which that paper is sayink. The Mixo-Lydian Government
is requirink to honour the home-place of Prodshkina Bunting,
which is patroness of education in our country. So will we put
up a tabloid in the front of Wiple Terrace, and we will make an
exchangement of students between Southbridge and Mixo-
Lydia. So will the young men and maidens of our countries become familiarated. As for this Lord Aberfordbury, if that *is* his
name," she added darkly, "who has once ollready made a shoddy
business deal with Mixo-Lydia, and is an unfriend to oll good
people and the home-place of Prodshkina Bunting, so will he
be pilfered and becomm the laughing-stick of Barsetshire. Bog
be thanked."

This speech by the Ambassadress was greeted with wild applause, and since it was amply clear that the audience was growing out of hand, and could hardly get away fast enough to discuss the events of the afternoon, young Lord Bond proposed a
vote of thanks to the chairman, Lord Stoke, which was promptly
seconded by the Vicar and passed with enthusiasm, and said the
proceedings were now terminated and he was grateful to everyone for coming.

After that the meeting broke up into excited groups and presently went away, the better to tell the world of what had happened; or repaired either to the School dining-hall or (by
special invitation) the headmaster's drawing-room, in both of
which the headmaster's wife, the Hon. Justinia Swan, had provided a most hospitable and lavish tea.

CHAPTER 10

WE NEED hardly say that the rout of Lord Aberfordbury and his minions, and the last-minute reprieve of Wiple Terrace ("Quite like the pictures it was really," as the Matron of Southbridge School wrote in a letter to her eldest nephew, he who was chief wireless operator in a large Atlantic liner), caused great satisfaction in West Barsetshire.

Almost everybody was delighted, with the exception of the local bank manager, who had been rash enough to invest quite heavily in shares of the National Rotochrome Polychrome Universal Picture Postcard Company, and Miss Frances Harvey, of the Ministry of General Interference, who had devised a scheme for directing all the married women near Gatherum to work in the new factory at Southbridge, travelling thereto daily in a fleet of coaches, leaving their husbands to get their own lunches, teas, and often suppers, and their children to be looked after in a crèche provided at the expense of the ratepayers. As for the views of the Palace, we are in no position to give them, since the Bishop and Bishopess, as we have said already, were paying an official visit to Ghana, to find out if the principles of Nkrumahism could be liberally adapted to the Close.

At the Red Lion business was so brisk that Eileen, the ex-barmaid, who had retired to marry Colonel the Reverend Edward Crofts's ex-batman, Bateman, and become cook at the Vicarage, asked her employer's leave to oblige in the Saloon on her evening off, which leave was readily granted.

At Wiple Terrace, where the glad news had been received from Southbridge School that the lease of all present tenants

would be indefinitely extended, there was a celebration party
which started at six o'clock in the evening and went on into the
small hours. Soon after which the dashing Mrs. Feeder decided
on a quick trip to Monte Carlo, where she gambled more heavily than ever and did, we are happy to say, extremely well.

The young man from the *Barsetshire Chronicle* achieved his
heart's desire, a two-column spread with banner headlines:
"Beauty Spot Saved In Nick of Time," and a sub-head "Local
Patriots Thwart Threat to Wiple Terrace," over his own by-line.
The *Barsetshire Evening News,* not to be outdone (which it
was), printed an Exclusive Interview with Mr. Samuel Adams,
one of Our Southbridge Benefactors, in which Benefactor Adams answered "No Comment" to every question.

The tabloid to Miss Bunting, to everyone's relief, turned out
to be no worse than a small metal plaque, of the kind one sees
in public parks bearing the legend "Keep Off the Grass" or "No
Dogs Allowed," with prongs (if we make our meaning clear) so
that it could be removed for mowing. And if it happened to be
removed for other purposes, such as wicked little boys from Hogglestock having a bit of fun like, it is doubtful whether the
Mixo-Lydian Government would notice or anybody be a whit
the worse.

Not the least delighted person was the artist, Mr. Scatcherd,
who might be observed day after day in his Norfolk jacket,
knickerbockers that fastened below the knee, and deerstalker,
seated on a camp-stool on the verge, as he liked to call it, opposite the Terrace, adding a new item to his repertwaw (his
phrase, not ours).

There he was discovered one morning by Mr. Wickham and
Mr. Feeder, on their way back from the Red Lion. His calculated start of surprise struck both gentlemen as more calculated
than usual, and so they stopped and asked him how he did.

"Ar, that's as may be," replied Mr. Scatcherd darkly. "That's
in the lap of the gods, as you might say. But I don't deny as I'm

attempting a piece of nouvo art in this here picture. If you care to look at it, you're welcome."

Both gentlemen accepted the invitation, though not, we fear, with any great alacrity.

"By Jove," said Mr. Feeder, "it's Wiple Terrace."

"Ar," said Mr. Scatcherd, with smug satisfaction, "that's what most people will say, likely as not. But look at it more close and you'll get the Crux."

Obediently they did so, and suddenly Mr. Wickham gave a thundering exclamation. "Great Jumping Jupiter! It's The Girls!"

"There," said Mr. Scatcherd, delighted with the effect he had created. "There speaks the eye of the connoozer."

Mr. Feeder looked puzzled. "But there aren't any girls in Wiple Terrace," he objected. "Now that you mention it, Wicks, I can see there's somebody in every garden. I suppose that's my mother at one end, and it could be Bent or Hampton at the other end, though I wouldn't call any of them girls exactly. And I haven't a clue about the two chaps in the middle. Traill and I don't wear bags like that."

"You're on the wrong track, old man," said Mr. Wickham, thoroughly enjoying himself. "You're not up in your local history. Those are *The* Girls, the original Wiple Terrace Girls, Adelina, Maria, Louisa, and Editha. The ones the cottages were named after. Isn't that right, Scatcherd?"

"That is perfickly correct," said Mr. Scatcherd. "This small work is what is known to we artists as an Abstrack Conception. When I look at Wiple Terrace with the inner eye, I sees them there old-fashioned girls as clear as I see the cottages. They was the inspiration of the Terrace, if you take my meaning, and in Ars all time and place is one."

"It's terrific, Scatcherd," said Mr. Wickham, hastily cutting short the disquisition which was bound to follow. "I'm sure the copies will sell like hot cakes in Barsetshire. Beat all the Hibberd picture postcards hollow. What would you take for the original sketch, if it's for sale? I'd like to present it to Wiple Terrace."

"Well," said Mr. Scatcherd, immensely flattered by this tribute from the gentry, "seeing as if I live, this here is the work I'll live by, I couldn't hardly take less than a pound or thereabouts."

"Done," said Mr. Wickham, pressing a green note into the artist's hand. "And here's a shilling to seal the bargain." And considering the amount of interest and entertainment that Mr. Scatcherd's Abstrack Conception later provided for all visitors to Wiple Terrace, bargain we believe it was.

A few days after these stirring events at Southbridge, the Pomfrets gave a small, informal dinner party to the Mertons and their Lavinia. It was to be a strictly family affair. The only other guests were Lady Pomfret's brother Roddy Wicklow with his nice wife Alice, and Mr. Choyce, Vicar of Hatch End, and his wife, formerly Miss Merriman, who might almost be regarded as a member of the family.

Miss Merriman, as we know, had married late in life; partly because her long years of service as secretary and companion, first to the late Lady Pomfret, and then to the exasperating and enchanting Lady Emily Leslie, had kept her more or less *adscripta glebae*; and partly, we think, because of a sentimental memory from long ago, when a foolish secretary had spent a sleepless night after young Mr. Foster, the present Earl of Pomfret, had told her that he was engaged to Sally Wicklow, the young agent's sister. This memory Mrs. Choyce had confided to her husband and to no one else. They had laughed about it together, gently and kindly, and the ghost was laid. The Choyce marriage turned out to be a quietly happy one, and the ties with Pomfret Towers remained unbroken.

On the evening of the party, which could not make up its mind whether to be nice or nasty, and had finally settled on nasty as the easiest way, the Mertons were the last guests to arrive. Young Lord Mellings died a thousand deaths, imagining his beloved Lavinia lying broken and bleeding by the roadside, carried by stretcher-bearers to an ambulance, cut about by soulless surgeons, pallid and inanimate in a hospital bed. But when the door opened and Lavinia followed her parents into the room, all these fears were swept away in a great gush of love and wonder, not for the first time, as to what he had done to deserve this exquisite creature.

Lavinia was certainly looking her best this evening, in a simply-cut summer frock, which to the eye of every woman present said Paris, in a soft and subtle shade of green. "Undine," murmured Mr. Choyce, almost under his breath, to which his wife, overhearing him, replied she hoped not *quite* for Ludo's sake. And whether we prefer Undine or Ondine, we take her meaning, for as a wife to a landowner with roots in native soil, a Lady from the Sea is never wholly satisfactory.

While Lydia Merton was apologising to her hostess for their late arrival, due to roads blocked by cows, sheep, Packer's Universal Royal Derby, and a fleet of coaches belonging to the Southbridge United Viator Passenger Company, which were bringing back the Barsetshire Mothers' Union from a day at the seaside, Lavinia found herself gently led by her betrothed to talk to Alice Wicklow, for whom her nephew had a deep and quiet affection.

"Lavinia would like to show you something, Aunt Alice," said Lord Mellings. "We hope you like it. Look after her for me, will you, while I circulate and do the doings? I've brought you both some sherry to be going on with. Lavinia doesn't like it very much, but I tell her she's got to learn to take it like a lady. *Noblesse oblige* and all that. Back in a few minutes, darling." With which he went off to attend to the older guests, Lavinia following him with adoring eyes.

Presently she became aware of Alice Wicklow's quiet voice

saying: "I don't much care for sherry either, so we'll just pretend and sip it, shall we? Now what was it that Ludo wanted you to show me?"

"Oh, it was *this*," said Lavinia, suddenly recalled to her surroundings. "My engagement ring. Ludo took me up to town to choose it, and he gave it to me yesterday. Isn't it lovely, Mrs. Wicklow?" And indeed it was, a very fine clear emerald in an open claw setting. "The ring was really very old, but Ludo had the stone reset. He said it would be easier to clean this way. I do love green, I think it's quite my favourite colour."

"It is your colour," said Alice Wicklow, "and the most restful colour in the world. That's a very lovely ring, Lavinia. And you really mustn't call me Mrs. Wicklow. I'm going to be your Aunt Alice next year, so you might as well get used to it."

"Oh, thank you very much, Aunt Alice," said Lavinia, with modern youth's complete absence of embarrassment, and then the talk turned naturally to Ludo, his needs, his accomplishments, his shyness, his charming, untrained singing voice, and Lavinia felt that in this new family she had really found a friend.

We shall not attempt to record the conversation at dinner, since it was of no particular interest to anyone outside the family. At one end (if you can speak of the end of a round table) Lord Pomfret had Lady Merton and Mrs. Choyce on either side of him, while Lady Pomfret at the other end had Sir Noel Merton and Mr. Choyce as neighbours. In the middle the young people, who included Emily and Giles, were making a good deal of noise, while the kind Wicklows, who were never great talkers at the best of times, were content to hold their peace and put in a word anywhere when needed.

Just once, while Mrs. Choyce was asking Roddy about some of the old tenants on the estate, Lord Pomfret found a chance for a quiet word with Lydia. He said how delightful her Lavinia was, and how happy he and his wife were about the engagement. "She is just what Ludo needs," he said, "exactly what I found in Sally. It takes fortitude," he added with his tired look, "to be a real wife to a Foster. Ludo is a Foster through and through. Emily and Giles are Pomfrets. They know exactly what they want, and they'll bang and bash their way through life to get it. But Ludo's different. I've worried about him again and again, seeing my own weaknesses repeated in him. But thank heaven, the boy's chosen the right wife. Your Lavinia has fortitude. She'll do for him what Sally did for me. I can't tell you what a relief it is to us, how deeply we are thankful."

After dinner, Lady Pomfret took her ladies to the sitting-room, where there was a nice fire burning. Emily and Giles had asked to be excused, and gone off to the stables to make sure that the Pony Club had left everything in order. Lavinia, suddenly bereft of all young company, might have felt a little ill at ease, had not Lady Pomfret, who had not been chairman of half the committees in Barsetshire for nothing, invited her to come and show Mrs. Choyce her ring.

Meanwhile Lydia and Alice Wicklow were talking about the arrangements for the wedding, which as we know was to be just after Easter in the Cathedral, at a time when the Bishop was most fortunately engaged to attend a Diocesan Conference.

"Dr. and Mrs. Joram," said Lydia, "have very kindly offered to lend us their home in the Close for the reception. It is a lovely house with an enormous drawing-room on the first floor, and two staircases. That makes it so much easier for getting people in and out, as there are doors at each end of the room and everyone can circulate."

Alice Wicklow asked who were to be bridesmaids, and Lydia said Emily for Ludo's side of the family, and Jessica for Lavinia's, with Sarah Siddons Clover as a friend of both sides. "We haven't found anyone to match her yet," she added. "Lady Graham has several grandchildren who would do, and so has Mrs. Crawley.

But I'm rather in favour of leaving Sarah Siddons by herself. She's a dramatic little person, like her mother, and if she carries the train and holds Lavinia's bouquet, she'll manage beautifully and the press photographers will adore her."

Then Lydia, who felt she had talked quite enough about her own affairs, asked after Alice Wicklow's children, who were not really children any more, but almost young grown-ups (for teenagers we will not say).

Alice replied that Young Alice was still at Barchester High School, and in two minds whether to become a ballet dancer or a veterinary surgeon. Their boy, Guy, was spending the summer with friends in Sweden, learning about forestry, and their elder daughter, Phoebe, was going to an art school in London in the autumn.

"She is quite a pretty water-colourist, with a good sense of line," her mother added, "and all she wants to do is draw and paint. I can quite understand it. I used to do a little water-colour drawing myself."

"*Used?*" said Lavinia, who had overheard these last words. "What about that heavenly thing you did of Harefield House a few years ago? They showed it to us in art class when I was at school, and I absolutely fell in love with it. And then I got a book out of the library, and it was one of Mrs. Barton's novels about Popes and Cardinals and people; and you had done the illustrations, Mrs. Wicklow, I mean Aunt Alice. They were absolutely marvellous. You *must* remember, Mother, I showed you that darling picture of the Cardinal's children who oughtn't to have been his children but they were. *You* remember, don't you, Lady Pomfret?" she added, turning to Sally, for whom she had not yet found a sobriquet.

"Indeed I do remember," said Lady Pomfret. "It was the winter when Gillie and I got engaged, and we were all staying at the Towers. That dreadful Julian Rivers," she added to the others, "dragged poor Alice up to a freezing cold attic and painted her portrait in purple and green triangles, to show at an exhibition of the Set of Five."

"I remember too," said Mrs. Choyce in her quiet voice. "Indeed I had the pleasure of telling Mr. Rivers that if he wanted to do any more painting, it was to be in the racket-court and not in the north attic."

"You were quite splendid, Merry," said Lady Pomfret. "If anyone could put Julian in his place, you could. And then there was that awful scene on the front steps, when Julian was trying to get into Alice's car so that he could go into Nutfield and have his hair cut, and Roddy dragged him out, and there was a young footman who almost winked at Peters."

"Peters was the butler," Mrs. Choyce kindly explained to Lavinia. "He is over in East Barsetshire now with Lord Crosse. He ought to have retired, of course, but when Grace Crawley married young Mr. Crosse it gave him a new lease on life. I saw him a few weeks ago, and he said it was a treat to work for a young mistress who really understood silver and the shammy."

"Good old Peters," said Lady Pomfret. "Do give him my regards next time you see him, Merry. I'm sure he was as pleased as Punch when Roddy pulled Julian out of the car, but of course he wouldn't show it. I've often thought about that week-end, Alice, and wondered how on earth you managed to put up with a third-rate artist like Julian, when you were a first-rate artist yourself."

"I'm afraid," said Alice, "I was a bit silly about him. He looked so Byronic, and he was so rude that it was almost fascinating. I couldn't understand his pictures, of course, but he talked as if he were a famous painter, and I was only muddling along with sketches and water-colour drawings in my own way. I thought Heaven had fallen when Mr. Johns, the publisher, offered me five pounds for the jacket and end-papers for Moth-

coming the Grand-Nanny who will stand no nonsense from the
new babies' nannies.

At High Rising, it was becoming increasingly apparent that the
plan for the proposed birthday party could not be kept from
Mrs. Morland much longer. For one thing Robin, despite his
self-imposed vows of secrecy, was obviously excited and a bit
above himself; and for another there was a tendency for conversation to stop when Laura came into a room, or for somebody to say: "Well, I must be going now," which made her
feel, she said, just like a leper.

"Like the wicked uncle in *The Black Arrow* who goes about
ringing a bell and saying: 'Unclean, Unclean,'" she remarked
to Anne Knox, "and why Stevenson thought so poorly of that
book I shall never understand. All my boys loved it. They liked
it much better than *Treasure Island* and *Kidnapped,* except for
Alan Breck of course. And it was the only thing that made me
really interested in Richard Crookback, until I read the book by
that clever woman with three names, who proved that Richard
didn't murder the little Princes in the Tower, and was a hero
all the time and not a villain."

In the end it was decided that somebody must break the news
to Mrs. Morland that there was to be "a small party" on her
birthday, and that Anne Knox was the proper person to break
it. Accordingly, the gifted authoress went to tea by invitation at
Low Rising, accompanied by Sylvia Gould. Robin was not with
them, as it was one of his days for riding Skylark at Pomfret
Towers, and he had gone off early on his bicycle.

Anne Knox told her guests that they would find her husband
at work somewhere in the garden. "It is one of his Celebrated
Author Exchanges Pen for Spade days," she said. "The gardener
has gone over to Stoke Dry about some winter broccoli, so
George is interfering with the vegetables."

She led the way down to the kitchen garden, where George

Knox was indeed manifest, looking larger than life in baggy brown plus-fours, a gigantic pair of what seemed to be decayed football boots, a scarlet handkerchief knotted round his neck, and a tweed shooting coat with half its buttons off and all its pockets flapping.

He was leaning on his spade, wiping the sweat from his brow, with the exhausted air of a man who has done all that man can do. In front of him the earth was freshly turned ("The gardener did that this morning," Anne Knox whispered to Mrs. Morland), and he was ably assisted by a robin, who every now and then took time off from his digging to perch on the handle of the wheelbarrow and scribble a postcard to all his relations: "Having wonderful time, wish you were here." Which was manifestly untrue, for if any of his brothers or uncles or cousins had ventured to turn up in his territory, he would have engaged them at once in savage battle. For such is the nature of the robin redbreast, the friend of man.

As it came to the point, Anne Knox found it increasingly difficult to broach the subject of the party. Over tea she made several false starts, and was really thankful when at last Mrs. Morland looked at her sharply and said: "Anne, you've got something up your sleeve. There's something that you want to say to me, and you don't know how to begin. I've felt it in the air for a long time, and I shall go mad if someone doesn't tell me what it is. Has Adrian told you that he doesn't want to publish any more Madame Koska books, and asked you to break it to me gently? Mind you," she added, "I wouldn't blame him."

"No, *no,* Laura," said Anne Knox hastily. "It's nothing of that kind at all. Really the opposite, if anything."

"You don't mean that he wants me to write *two* books a year?" said Mrs. Morland in dismay.

"It's nothing to do with Adrian," said Mrs. Knox, "although I'm certain he'd agree if he knew about it. It's just that some of us, your old friends, feel that we'd like to give you a little party on your birthday."

"A poor reward, a moiety, a mere token payment," boomed George Knox, "for the pleasure, nay the joy, the relaxation, that your books have so long given us, dear Laura."

"Rubbish, George," said Mrs. Morland. "You know you have never read one of the Madame Koska books right through in all your life."

"Touché," said George Knox, "but I have sipped the nectar, I have sipped. And when I survey these serried ranks," he added, waving his hand towards the bookshelf where stood all Mrs. Morland's novels, "though why the word serried, a noble word, should have become so debased in modern English usage I do not know, when I survey these serried ranks, I repeat, I am aware of the deep debt we owe to your indomitable application, my dear Laura, and feel that any tribute, however slight, is due to you from those who cherish you."

"I don't know," said Laura thoughtfully, "whether anybody really *cherishes* me. Except Adrian, of course, in a business way, and perhaps the boys, because they can always send the children to High Rising in the holidays."

"And your fans, Mrs. Morland," said Sylvia. "Just think of the dozens of people who write and tell you how much they love the Madame Koska books, and how they've got the last one beside their bed now, and how they can hardly wait for the next one."

"Oh, *going-to-sleep* books," said Mrs. Morland. "Yes, I suppose I can write *them*. If I'm in bed with a nice hot bottle, and Stoker brings me up a glass of hot milk, with perhaps a drop of rum when I can get it, I only need to pick up *any* Madame Koska book and read a couple of paragraphs, and I'm asleep at once. Usually with the light on," she added.

Anne Knox brought the conversation back to the point by

saying that she was sure Laura's friends would be extremely hurt if they were not allowed to give her a little birthday party.

"Well, if it's only going to be my *friends*——" began Mrs. Morland.

"I promise it will only be your friends," said Mrs. Knox, privately asking heaven to forgive her for a white lie, or at least a barely misleading statement.

"Then, I must say, a birthday party would be rather nice," said Mrs. Morland. "I haven't had one since I was a child, and there were ginger snaps with cream inside and éclairs, we used to call them Othellos and Desdemonas. The Othellos were chocolate with white spots, and the cream was custardy and simply *oozed* out of them. And the birthday cake had red candles and hundreds and thousands on top."

"Ah, those gluttonous and happy days of youth," said George Knox. "Memory brings back the richness of the pastry, the succulence of the fruit cake, the sponge fingers that were really sponge, not strips of cardboard sugared in a vain similitude."

"Well, George," his wife observed, "I'm afraid memory is about the only thing that *will* bring them back. But Stoker has asked if she can make the birthday cake, Laura, and I'm sure she'll do it very well. We can still manage the hundreds and thousands, although Stoker despises the ones at the village shop. She says they are only tens and twenties nowadays. I can't promise about the éclairs, because of course you *can* get them, but the inside doesn't taste the same. All that the young people seem to care about today is cheese-straws and cocktail sausages and snacks."

"Well, don't put seventy candles on the cake," said Laura, "because I couldn't possibly blow them out in one go, and I don't particularly want to think about my threescore years and ten."

"You might have three big candles for the scores," suggested Sylvia, "and a half-size candle for the ten."

"And how could you possibly arrange them?" said Mrs. Morland, who had occasional wild streaks of practicality. "You couldn't put a little one in the middle of three big ones, or you wouldn't see it, and there is no other way. And don't, Anne, please don't let anyone sing Happy Birthday, dear Laura, Happy Birthday To You. Fond though I am of our American cousins, I simply could not bear it."

So Anne Knox promised that there would be only one candle on the cake, if any, and absolutely no Happy Birthday to You. At this point a diversion was caused by the arrival of Lord Stoke, all dressed up for driving. He included everybody in a general greeting, refused a cup of tea, looked round the table, and said "Ha!" as his glance lighted on Sylvia.

"I came to look for you, young lady," he said. "Went to the Vicarage and they said you might be here. It's a pleasant evening, thought you might care for a drive. My brougham's outside. Not allowed to use the dog-cart now, doctor's orders. Ford's a good enough chap, but he's like all these doctors, think they know better than their patients. Never been fitter in my life, though my hearing isn't what it used to be. But I can hear anyone who doesn't shout, and a great deal more than certain people think."

Mrs. Morland afterwards declared that at this point Lord Stoke winked at her, and the names "Aberfordbury" and "The Palace" rose unbidden to her mind. Aloud she said: "If you would like to go for a drive, Sylvia, I can leave a message at the Vicarage on my way home."

Sylvia looked in a slightly distraught way from one lady to another, then said it *was* a nice evening and if Lord Stoke really wanted her——

"Shouldn't have asked you if I didn't," said Lord Stoke. "Always know my own mind. Drive over the downs, back to Rising Castle for a glass of sherry, see that you get home all right. Fetch your bonnet, or whatever you girls wear nowadays. Doesn't do to keep the mare waiting."

"Actually it's a handkerchief, Lord Stoke," said Sylvia, and Mrs. Morland gave her full marks for not saying ackcherly. "Please, will you tell Mother that I'll be back in time to get the supper, Mrs. Morland? Thank you for the nice tea, Mrs. Knox. Good-bye, Mr. Knox." And with a glance that nobody could quite interpret she tied a silk square round her head, picked up her handbag, and was gone.

"So *that's* the way the wind blows, is it?" said Anne Knox after a moment's silence.

"I think it blows one way and not the other," said Mrs. Morland rather carefully. "Sylvia has been several times to Rising Castle lately, which is entirely her own affair, and she was very kind and helpful when the old cook, Mrs. Beeton, hurt her leg. But I have felt for several weeks that Lord Stoke was working up to a proposal. I think Sylvia has realised it's inevitable, and I suppose she's flattered in a way, but I don't think she'll accept it."

"But it wouldn't do at *all*," said Anne, "just look at the difference in their ages."

"Difference in age, my dear Anne," said George Knox, "as you should know full well, is not a fatal bar to happy marriage. I hope, I trust," he added, in a slightly injured voice, "that I am not deceived in this belief."

"Oh, don't be silly, George," said his devoted wife. "You aren't well over eighty, or nearly deaf, except when you choose to be, and you haven't the sort of heart that makes a doctor say you mustn't use the dog-cart any more. Not that you ever did, of course," she added.

"True, Anne," said George Knox, "your rebuke is just. I should be thankful that even at my advanced age I am still sound in wind and limb."

"You are one of the healthiest men I ever knew, George,"

said Mrs. Morland, "that's what makes you fuss so much when you get an ache in your little toe."

"*Et tu*, Laura," murmured her old friend, lowering his head in abasement, and impressing neither of his hearers in the least.

"It doesn't seem a proper marriage somehow," went on Anne Knox, returning to her point. "I don't mean that it's *im*proper, but it doesn't make much sense. I know that Sylvia's no chicken, but she's still a good-looking and very active woman, and she can't be really fond of old Lord Stoke."

"I think that in a certain way she is," said Mrs. Morland, "and I'm quite sure that she is sorry for him. He is rather a touching person when you get to know him."

"Stranger marriages have taken place," observed George Knox, "and often proved rewarding to both parties. Lord Stoke is a reasonably rich man and a gentleman in the best sense. I have no doubt that any arrangement which he might propose— for I feel certain, Anne, that you are thinking of the nuptial bed—would be scrupulously observed and entirely honourable."

"Separate rooms, you mean," said Mrs. Morland, who was not one to mince her words.

"Moreover," George Knox went on, "I have gained the impression, as a mere onlooker, a casual observer only, so pray correct me if I am wrong, that the young woman does not lead a happy life at home. With due respect for his cloth, you must admit, my dear Anne, my dear Laura, that Gould is but a dull stick, and his wife is not much better."

"You are quite right, George," said Mrs. Morland, "the Goulds are very nice but *very* dull, and the younger girls don't seem to be much help."

"What happened to the other sister, Ruth?" asked Mrs. Knox. "It's so long since I saw her that I quite forget."

"She runs a chicken-farm with The-Friend-That-I-Live-With," said Mrs. Morland darkly. "And more I could not say. Sylvia never managed to escape somehow. She had her chance once but she didn't take it. Now I hope that luck is turning her way at last. And I don't mean that she is necessarily going to marry Lord Stoke."

"Our Laura is in one of her more sibylline moods," said George Knox to his wife. "And by the way, why did I call my only daughter Sybil?" (For George Knox, as we know, had been married once before.) "Why did I cast such a heavy mantle of responsibility upon an innocent, a hapless child?"

"I expect," said Anne Knox with her usual calm good sense, "it was because you and your wife just thought it a nice name. And so it is, and what is more it has gone gracefully out of fashion, which makes it nicer still. Now let's get back to where we were before Lord Stoke arrived."

"Where were we?" said Mrs. Morland. "It's like that terrible Remembering game. I never can do it backwards, because my mind is going forwards much too fast. I know I was eating another scone and honey, and how lovely it is to have real honey-comb, with all the crunch and juice together."

"We were saying, Laura," said Anne Knox firmly, "that your friends wanted to give you a birthday party, and you had agreed to come."

"Come?" said Mrs. Morland. "Come where? Why can't we have the party at High Rising? There's plenty of room there for all my friends."

"It might," said Anne Knox, with the sudden inspiration of despair, "be asking rather much of Stoker. I'll talk to her and then we'll see. Another house might be more suitable."

"And my dear Laura," added George Knox, blundering to his wife's rescue, "who—I speak as a mere man, not conversant with such affairs—but who, I repeat who, ever gave a birthday party to herself? Gone is the mystery, gone the magic, gone, I should almost say, the ritual."

"They might do it in one of those modern French plays," said Mrs. Morland thoughtfully. "Cocteau or Anouilh or some-

body. Like the beginning of *The Eagle Has Two Heads*, only
that wasn't a birthday of course. All very ghostly, with candles
and a table laid for two. Still, I admit it isn't very cheerful.
Have it your own way, Anne, but don't, I beg of you, turn it
into a Laura Morland Benefit, with all the guests contributing
towards a silver rose-bowl for the poor old lady."

"That," said Anne Knox, who was so relieved by this happy
issue out of all her troubles that she felt she would agree to
anything, "is something I can promise that we will not do."

Within a few hours the news had sped round Barsetshire that
the Mrs. Morland Do was On. Anne Knox rang up Dr. Ford,
who rang up Mr. Wickhmam, who rang up Roddy Wicklow,
who told the Pomfrets, who told the Leslies and the Grahams
and their cousin Lucy Adams, who had the wit to tell Palmyra
Phipps at the telephone exchange (not that she didn't know
already) and ask her to pass on the news to anyone who might
be interested. For this was Barsetshire, and so, in Barsetshire,
are such things done.

The main problem, of course, was to decide where the party
was to be held. Offers of hospitality poured in from Rushwater
to Rising Castle, from Pomfret Towers to Wiple Terrace, from
Framley Court to Beliers Priory. The Close was strongly represented, with tenders from The Deanery (the Crawleys), Number Seventeen (the Fieldings), The Vinery (the Jorams), and
Acacia House (the Fewlings).

It was Lucy Adams who had, as she so often had, the last
word. "I'll tell you what," she said to her husband one evening
at the Old Bank House, while they were drinking coffee in the
long drawing-room which ran from front to back of the house,
with its elegant Chippendale furniture and faded Chinese
wallpaper. "We really ought to have the party here."

"You take the words right out of my mouth, Lucy," said Mr.
Adams, who had never quite lost his first sense of wonder and

delight at becoming the owner of so beautiful a home, "but Mrs. Morland has so many friends that I didn't hardly like to mention it."

"Friends are one thing and houses are another," said Lucy firmly. "Pomfret Towers and the Priory and Wiple Terrace aren't really *houses,* and the Close isn't safe at all—it's far too near the Palace and you don't know what might happen. I wouldn't put it past the Bishopess to turn up in the middle, and ask why she hadn't been invited."

"Like the wicked fairy at the christening," observed Amabel, who was toying with some problems in Advanced Mathematics in an armchair by the window.

"Of course," Lucy went on, "Rushwater is different. It *is* a house, and there have been some marvellous parties there, but it's a bit off the track for people without cars. No, Sam, I'm certain that we ought to have it here. It's a friendly sort of house, and this room will hold a lot of people. And if there are too many we can always spill out into the garden."

"There are going to be *hundreds* of people, Mother," said Amabel. "Sylvia Gould, you know the one that she's Dad's secretary at Pomfret Towers, showed me the list of people who have asked to come, and she said we really ought to take the Albert Hall."

"And that's where Mrs. Morland's party ought to be," said Mr. Adams. "By rights she ought to be a Dame of the British Empire. Nothing's too good for that lady, in my opinion. We'll have the party at the Old Bank House, and show her that she's a Dame of Barsetshire at least. I'll get on to Scatcherd and Tozer in the morning, when Miss Gould has roughed out an estimate of the number of guests. Then I'll put through a rush order for printed invitations."

"Don't you think," said Lucy, with a tact which we doubt whether she would have displayed as Lucy Marling, "that it would be best if I wrote myself to Mrs. Morland, and explained that it is only going to be a friendly sort of party?"

"I'll tell you what, Mother," said Amabel. "You ought to talk to Mrs. Knox at Low Rising. Robin says she's the only person who can do anything with Mrs. Morland, except Stoker, that's the cook." And so it was arranged.

A couple of mornings later, Laura Morland opened the envelope, addressed in Lucy Adams's powerful hand, and read that she was invited to a Birthday Tea at the Old Bank House, Edgewood, with the addendum that Lucy had talked to Mrs. Knox and asked "just a few other friends" to drop in.

If Mrs. Morland was a trifle surprised by the place chosen for the party, she had not much time to think about it, for Madame Koska was demanding all her attention at the moment. The last chapters of *Death by Microdot* were due for delivery by the middle of September, and their gifted authoress had not yet discovered how to rescue the beautiful mannequin from the clutches of the villainous salesman, who was fleeing from the police in a stolen motor car with his captive and the incriminating book of samples. After making certain that her grandson was happily and harmlessly occupied with young Leslies and Fosters and Amabel Adams, and was, in Stoker's words, eating his meals a treat, she wrote to thank Lucy for the invitation, said she would be glad to come, and concentrated on the affairs of Madame Koska, without much further thought about her birthday, which seemed to her just a day like other days.

In the meantime, Robin sat down and with many groans and splutterings of the pen composed an important letter to his parents.

DEAR MOTHER AND DADDY,
   I hope you are quite well as I am now. This Letter is to tell you that Gran (Mrs. Morland) is having her CLXX birthday next Saturday. I and Elliner and Ammabel and some other

people are giving her a secret birthday party at the old bank house from 4 to 7 p.m. (post mortem), dress optoinal. It will be quite a small party not more than 100, and Stoker is making all the things to eat except champaign and some other things which are to come from Scacherd and Tozers, which is a shop in Barchester. I hope you are quite well but I said that before. I have to stop now as I am needed at a jimkana.

Lots of love from your affec. son

R. Morland

p.s.—Please will you send me another shirt because I am growing so fast the last one split.

p.p.s.—I know everything about contajious abortion it is very interesting
R.M.

The Gymkhana at which Robin was needed took place at Nutfield, and was a mixed sporting event of considerable local interest. As well as the jumping and what we can only describe as various games with horses, in which their riders had to pick things up or pull things down, or put their mounts through the most complicated movements, there was a Dog Show and a Children's Pet Show, with a special prize for the Pet With the Most Soulful Eyes.

Alice Wicklow and her daughter Young Alice, who, as we know, had not yet decided whether to take up ballet or become a veterinary surgeon (although we think ourself that she will be a vet., and an extremely good one too), were showing a couple of cocker spaniels and had entered their golden labrador Rex in the Obedience Class.

Since Young Alice was riding in several of the events, her mother had asked Robin if he would like to come and help to hold the dogs, an invitation which he accepted with alacrity. Although London-born and bred, he had a sensible and kindly way with animals, as Roddy had noticed with approval at the Pony Club, and he fell in love at first sight with the two cockers, Sheila and her daughter Penny, who was really too young and silly to display herself to advantage in the show ring, but as her young mistress said, it is never too soon to learn.

We shall not attempt to describe the events of the Gymkhana, which seemed to take an inordinately long time, except to say that everyone was very hot and very happy, the ice-cream and soft drinks stalls did a roaring trade, and the amount of litter left behind on the grass broke all records in the history of Nutfield.

The Hon. Giles Foster, who, as we know, could ride anything on four legs, won the Blue Ribbon in the Junior Class for his dashing displays on a number of different mounts, but the Silver Challenge Cup went to a young Thorne, who farmed with his father over Chaldicotes way. "That boy," said Roddy Wicklow to his wife, "is going to turn up at the White City before long. I shouldn't wonder if he got into the Olympic team. Best hands in the county, sound judgment, and tremendous patience. Wicks knows his people, sound old Barsetshire stock. It's a pleasure to watch him ride. Giles is good, but he'll never be in Thorne's class. How are the dogs doing?"

Alice was able to report that Sheila had tied for first place in the cocker spaniel class (judged by the Hon. Maria Marling, who bred spaniels herself, and had told Mrs. Wicklow that she would like to have a word with her afterwards about a spot of mating), and that Rex had won the Obedience Test paws down.

Penny, she added, had utterly disgraced herself, sat down and refused to budge when she was led into the show ring. "Do you think, Roddy," she said anxiously, "that she ought to be sent to a dogs' Borstal?"

"Not on your life, my girl," said Roddy. "There's nothing wrong with Penny that Young Alice can't cure. Two wins out of three entries isn't such bad going. You wouldn't have liked it, would you, if they'd chosen Penny as the Pet with the Most Soulful Eyes?" Which made Alice laugh and say no, she would have hated it, and she was going back now with the dogs and

Robin Morland, and there would be something waiting in the
oven for Roddy's and Young Alice's supper or high tea.

The only other incident which need concern our reader took
place during the preparations for the final jumping event,
when an exceedingly naughty little boy, who had no business
there at all, crawled underneath the ropes into the ring and got
his hand trodden on by a horse. The horse's rider, a fair schoolgirl with a pony-tail, dismounted in a panic and felt certain
she was going to be lynched.

A small crowd gathered. There were mutters of "It's a
shame," "Tommy's got kicked by a horse," "Serves him right
too, see what he been and done?" "Horses is vicious brutes,"
and "Why don't somebody do something?" The fair schoolgirl,
who was dreadfully impeded by the horse's reins, and knew
nothing whatsoever about first aid, was looking round desperately for help when Sylvia Gould, who had arrived late at the
Gymkhana with Dr. Ford, thrust her way between the on-
lookers and knelt down beside the bawling victim.

"I can deal with this," she said in a voice of quiet authority.
"Just move aside, please, and let me take him to the First Aid
post. You," she added to a Boy Scout who had suddenly materialised beside her, "go and find Dr. Ford. You know him?
Good. He's having tea in the judges' tent. Bring him to the
First Aid post and stand by in case you're wanted. And you," she
said reassuringly to the fair schoolgirl, "stop worrying and go
back to your jumping. I don't think there's much harm done,
and it wasn't your fault anyway. I saw everything that happened."

With that she led the bawling Tommy in the direction of
the First Aid post, gave him a peppermint cream and a nice
clean handkerchief to wipe his face with, delivered him into
the hands of a St. John's Ambulance man, and asked if somebody would go and find his mother.

"Please miss," said a pasty-faced girl who was sucking a lollipop outside the tent, "Tommy hasn't got no mother. It's his auntie as looks after him."

Resisting a strong desire to retort that she didn't do it very well, Sylvia said all right then, go and find his auntie.

"Please miss," said the pasty-faced girl, "she isn't here."

"Well, fetch whoever brought him," said Sylvia with grim patience.

"Nobody didn't bring him," said the pasty-faced girl. "He come here of hisself, and he won't half get a leathering when his dad finds out."

At these words, heard through the open flap of the First Aid tent, the victim set up such a renewed bellowing that Sylvia was profoundly thankful for the arrival of Dr. Ford, preceded by the Boy Scout and followed at a respectful distance by P. C. Haig Brown of Southbridge, nephew of Mr. Brown of the Red Lion, who was off duty and out of his own manor, but could not resist the professional instinct to find out what was going on here.

Dr. Ford gave the patient a quick but thorough examination, did whatever was necessary at the moment, and turned to find the policeman's large form looming.

"Oh, it's you, Brown," he said. "Good. You can do something for me. Ring up the Barchester General and tell Matron that I'm bringing in a casualty, boy suffering from shock and possible hand fracture. I'll want an X-ray and a bed. By the way, who is the boy, do you know?"

"He's one of the Margetts over to Grumper's End," said P. C. Haig Brown. "His dad works with the bodgers, but like as not he's on the way to the Three Tuns by now. His auntie, she looks after Tommy, but she's got nine kids of her own like, so I dessay she won't have noticed this one's missing."

"All right, Brown," said Dr. Ford. "Get somebody to let the Margetts know. Say Tommy's gone into Barchester General for observation, and they'll keep him there tonight. Won't do any harm to put the fear of God into them. Tell Margett to get in touch with the hospital tomorrow."

So P. C. Haig Brown went off to telephone, while Dr. Ford and Sylvia, with assistance from the Boy Scout, got Tommy into the doctor's little car, his arm neatly bound up in a sling by the St. John's Ambulance man. "Care to come along?" Dr. Ford asked Sylvia, who said Rather, and without more ado tucked a rug around Tommy's legs and sat down in the back seat beside him.

We are happy to inform our reader that an X-ray of the trampled hand disclosed no serious damage. After a few words with Matron, who undertook to tackle Margett Senior firmly on the morrow, and tell him what Tommy needed was more care and less leathering, Dr. Ford left his patient comfortably tucked up in bed, with a hot bottle and a nice hot drink, and went off to the car where Sylvia was waiting.

On the drive back to High Rising, not much was said at first, although a good deal seemed to be hovering in the air. Then Dr. Ford observed, in a curiously gruff voice: "You know, Sylvia, you're the sort of assistant any doctor would be proud to have."

Blushing furiously, although she could not imagine why, Sylvia replied that she hadn't forgotten her first aid.

"I don't mean only that," said Dr. Ford. "I mean that you can keep your head. You know how to handle things and people. I told you once that you were a woman in a thousand——"

"That was a long time ago," said Sylvia, in a voice she hardly recognised as her own. "Beside the Rushmore Pool, and it was only because I'd managed to talk Tony Morland down."

"Well, this is now," said Dr. Ford, "beside the Gas Works, and it's still true. I offered you my homage then, and I offer it again."

"What exactly do you mean?" said Sylvia feebly.

"I mean that you haven't grown any younger and I've

grown a good deal older, but you're still a woman in a thousand, and if you would consider marrying me and helping to look after the practice of an aging G.P., I should be both honoured and delighted."

There was a long moment of silence. Then Sylvia gave a curious little laugh and said: "There's something that I think you ought to know."

"Meaning that you won't consider it," said Dr. Ford.

"Meaning nothing of the kind," said Sylvia, suddenly finding herself mistress of the situation. "It's just that a few days ago Lord Stoke asked me to marry him. I haven't told anyone before. Oh, it was all going to be most discreet, separate bedrooms and a wonderful settlement. He's a dear old thing, and I couldn't help feeling flattered. But I said no."

"Any special reason?" asked Dr. Ford. "Stoke's a good man and he'd look after you."

"Yes, James," said Sylvia, "there is a special reason."

Dr. Ford pulled his little car up at the side of the road, and turned to look straight at her. "You've never called me James before," he said.

"Well, it is your name, isn't it?" said Sylvia. "I'll have to learn to use it if I'm going to marry you. Thank you very much indeed, James. I'd like to be a country doctor's wife more than anything in the world. If I hadn't been a silly little idiot I'd have said yes twenty years ago.

"There's only one thing that worries me," she added a few minutes later. "What is Mrs. Mallow going to say?" For that redoubtable woman had cooked and kept house for Dr. Ford as long as anyone could remember.

"If I know Mrs. Mallow," said her employer, "she'll say that she can't keep on for ever and the house needs a mistress. Just wait and see."

They drove up to the house and Mrs. Mallow opened the door before its owner had time to get out his latchkey. "Shock for you, Mrs. Mallow," said Dr. Ford without preamble. "Miss Gould has promised to marry me."

"And a good thing too," said Mrs. Mallow imperturbably. "I'm sure I'm very glad to hear it. This house needs a mistress, and I can't keep on for ever. I'd like to see you settled before I'm Taken. My best wishes to you, miss, and you too doctor, and there's been no calls, except for P. C. Haig Brown, who rung up to say as he'd located that Mr. Margett. There's a nice piece of liver and onion hotting up in the oven for your supper, and if Miss Gould fancies an apple turnover I'm sure she's very welcome. There's a nice fire in the sitting-room and Mr. Wickham just come by and left a bottle of burgundy. He said he thought you'd find it rather special. Seems," she added, with enormous relish, "as if it was Almost Meant."

CHAPTER 11

LAURA MORLAND woke on the morning of her seventieth birthday, which was a Saturday, with an uneasy feeling that this was not like other Saturdays, although she had forgotten why. When she remembered what it was she had forgotten, she experienced a slight sinking of the heart. Of course, it was her birthday, and although she wasn't really expecting anything, she felt certain that she would be disappointed.

Birthdays when you are old, she thought, were like the Christmas Days of later years, when all your children had grown up and gone away, and everything was over after breakfast; the parcels opened, wrapping paper neatly folded, tinsel tape put by for another year. And after that, church, with a lot of solo singing from the choir and most of the hymns pitched far too high, a much too filling lunch, the wireless, no appetite for tea, and an evening that seemed to drag on for ever.

She snuggled down under her nice warm blankets, and between sleeping and waking thought idly of the Christmases of childhood. Those *were* Christmases. They began on Christmas Eve, with the putting up of decorations—holly, ivy, mistletoe, and evergreens of every sort—and the mysterious sound of carol-singers in the dark; the thick woollen stocking hung at the foot of the bed and a child's desperate certainty that she would never go to sleep.

Then there was the wakening on Christmas morning to the sound of early church bells, the excitement of groping for her stocking with its satisfying bulge, the crackers at the top, the tangerine in the toe, and all the toys and little books between;

Gems from Sir Walter Scott, Gems from Tennyson in limp
suède covers, and sometimes a Beatrix Potter to keep a child
happy until breakfast time. After that the morning service,
with all the dear, familiar Christmas hymns, the Christmas dinner that was never too much for a young appetite, and when
dusk fell, the Christmas tree with its coloured candles gleaming.
Christmas Day then was much too short for all the joys it held.

> *Bliss was it that dawn to be alive*
> *And to be young was very heaven.*

Ah well, thought Mrs. Morland, giving herself a mental
shake, she never would be young again, and if you were seventy, as she was today, you might as well make the best of it,
treasure your memories and enjoy what was left of life.

At any rate, she had sent off her Madame Koska book in
time for publication in the spring. Tomorrow, perhaps, she
would start thinking about the next one. Her maddening but
adorable grandson would soon be back at school or with his
parents, and life at High Rising would settle into its quiet
course again. There was, she remembered with a touch of
alarm, that birthday party at the Old Bank House to be got
through this afternoon, but Anne Knox had promised it would
only be a party of her friends, and Mrs. Morland, who was a
modest creature, felt that they could not be so very many.

At this point her reflections were interrupted by Stoker, who
came in with the morning tea, wished her employer a happy
birthday and drew the curtains with a clatter. "Bit of fog about,"
she said, "but that's only to be expected in September. The
wireless says it's going to clear by midday. Not that I hold with
the wireless," she added darkly, "more often wrong than right
they are, and stands to reason, they can't be everywhere at
once. I go by my back. When it commences to open and shut,
I know it's going to rain. What I say is, backs was made before
the wireless and they ought to know best. Would you like your

breakfast on a tray, seeing as it's a special day, and scrambled eggs?"

Mrs. Morland replied firmly that she wouldn't like her breakfast on a tray at all, even if she was a year older than she was yesterday. She would be down in half an hour, and if Robin was frightfully hungry, don't let him wait for her.

"No cause to worry about Master Robin," said Stoker. "He come into the kitchen an hour ago and asks as bold as brass for bread and dripping. I sent him up to wash and brush his hair and change his shirt. His old one's all in rags and tatters. I'm sure I don't know what his poor ma will say when she sees the wreckage he brings home with him. There's a nice lot of parcels and letters waiting for you downstairs, and a brace of partridge come over from the Towers, and two dozen eggs from Rushwater with some cream and butter, and there's a dozen port from Rising Castle."

"Oh, dear," said Mrs. Morland feebly, "how *very* kind people are. But what shall we *do* with two dozen eggs and a brace of partridge and a dozen port? I mean, how can we use them all?"

"Don't you commence to worry," replied Stoker darkly, "there's ways for everything."

Mrs. Morland was as good as her word, as indeed she always was, and half an hour later she came down to breakfast, to a room comfortably warmed by a nice bright fire, appropriate to the last days of an English summer.

Her grandson, freshly washed and brushed, wearing a shirt that was unnaturally clean, with a rather dreadful gaudy tie bought with his own money at Sheepshanks', was already seated at the table, dealing with a heaped plate of sausage, fried egg, fried bread, and a rissole left from last night's supper.

"Good morning, darling," said Mrs. Morland as she went to her own place.

"Morning, Gran," said Robin through a mouthful of sausage.

"Happy Birthday. I was ravenously hungry, so I thought I'd better start. I've been up for simply *hours*. I say, Gran, how do you like my tie? I put it on specially for your birthday. Sheepshanks' say they'll never have another one like it."

"I'm sure they won't, darling," said Mrs. Morland, looking with horror at the diagonal stripes of gold and puce, with a recurrent motif of red and blue horses. "And it's very nice of you to keep it as a surprise for my birthday. Oh, thank you, Stoker," she added, as that massive Hebe came in bearing a plate of golden scrambled eggs, which she set down in front of her employer with an almost minatory air. "That looks lovely."

"Eat them while they're hot," said Stoker, "I had an extra yolk left over from the meringue pie, and a drop of cream from yesterday. Don't you start opening your letters and let them spoil. Scrambled eggs is never the same again once they get cold."

Mrs. Morland gave her solemn word, and obediently finished the delicious scrambled eggs and drank a cup of tea before she turned to the pile of letters, flanked by parcels of all shapes and sizes, which were set out beside her plate.

With the wisdom of long experience as a mother of sons, she opened first the ones without stamps, because she knew they would be tokens from her nearest and dearest. Guided by the almost mesmeric stare of her grandson, who had finished what restaurants describe as "the main dish" and proceeded to toast and golden syrup, which dripped on to the tablecloth as he watched, she picked up a rather grubby parcel of brown paper fastened with an indiarubber band.

Inside it were five HB pencils and a pencil sharpener, rolled in a sheet of paper from an exercise book, again fastened with a rubber band. Smoothing out the sheet of paper, she read: "To Gran on her CLXX birthday, with love from Robin. P.S. The pensil sharperner is because you have to sharpen pensils and I thought a sharperner would be more easy than a penknife as you may not be used to using penknifes. The sharperner makes it an extra present. Your sincere grandson R. Morland."

"Oh Robin, that's a lovely present," said Mrs. Morland, hugging the little boy. "Just what I wanted, and you're quite right, I'm not very good at using penknives. I seem either to break my nails or break the pencil."

"I know," said Robin. "I thought the pencil sharpener was less tiring. I did mean to give you an exercise book as well, but I rather need my money for going back to school. I have to buy some food for going back to school, because they starve us rather badly on the first days of term. I think they use up all the food at the end of one term and haven't bought enough to start another."

"Well, Robin, it's very kind of you indeed," said Mrs. Morland, "and I don't need the exercise book at all. I dare say we could find a tin of biscuits for you to take back to school. And if you want to go now, do go," she added as she felt him hovering. "I shall be a long time working through these parcels and letters, and I'm sure you've got important things to do."

"Well, there *are* some pretty important things," said Robin. "I've got to make a lot of arrangements, and people depend on me about arrangements. I don't know how it is, but I seem to have a sort of power for arranging things. I *can* help you to open your parcels first if you really need me, but I do have an important engagement pretty soon."

"Run away and keep it then," said Mrs. Morland. "I can manage to open my parcels by myself quite well. And mind you don't tear your new shirt, whatever your engagements are, or there won't be anything fit to send you home in."

"I didn't tear my old shirt," said Robin reproachfully. "Not on purpose. It just tore of itself, because I'm growing. Stoker says growing boys need lots of room for expansion, and you wouldn't like me to stop expanding, would you, Gran?"

With this he left the room, not quite shutting the door, which immediately sprang open, and banged gently back and forth, idly but persistently. Mrs. Morland was trying to bring herself to get up and shut it properly ("Though it's not as bad as in the middle of the night," she thought aloud to herself, "when it goes on and on, and you can't decide whether it's better to be annoyed or get out of bed"), when Stoker saved her the trouble by entering forcefully to clear away the breakfast things.

"I thought I'd better bring this now," she said, producing a small parcel from the capacious pocket of her apron. "It's not much of a present, but they do say as it's the thought that counts."

Unwrapping it, Mrs. Morland discovered a heavy gunmetal brooch, with the word "Mizpah" picked out in gilt lettering, surmounted by what seemed to be a pair of clasped hands, amorphous in outline and tinted a horrid flesh colour.

"It belonged to my old Auntie in Plaistow," said Stoker proudly. "She give it me just before she died, and said to pass it on to someone in remembrance. She always wore it with her Sunday blacks. The word that's wrote across it comes out of the Bible."

Almost overwhelmed with emotion and embarrassment, and wondering what in the world she could do with the hideous gift without hurting the giver's feelings, Mrs. Morland warmly but untruthfully thanked Stoker for a lovely present. "Mizpah," she said. "The Lord watch between me and thee when we are absent one from another. But I do hope and trust, Stoker, that we *shan't* be absent one from another."

"That's as may be," said Stoker, with a gruffness which we think hid her own emotions. "I'm sure I'm very satisfied at High Rising and I hadn't thought to move, not while there's nothing but these flyaway girls to look after you, with their heads full of rock 'n' roll or whatever they call it and dirty cochineal on their finger-nails. But what I say, it's always best to be on the safe side." With which sibylline utterance she scooped the breakfast dishes onto her tray, opened the door with her foot, and shut it firmly and reasonably quietly, with that small extra tug, which everyone familiar with a recalcitrant door knows how to give after it has pretended to be closed.

Left to herself, Mrs. Morland started to unwrap her other presents, folding the paper neatly, and patiently unknotting the string, with gratitude to people who were old-fashioned enough to cling to that rapidly disappearing commodity.

There was a pair of fleece-lined bedroom slippers from Sylvia Gould, and from Lydia Merton a pair of fleece-lined gloves. A bulky parcel addressed in the familiar handwriting of Anne Knox disclosed a light, warm travelling rug with the message: "Much love from George and Anne, dear Laura, and Many Happy Returns of the Day. This is to put across your knees when you are writing, as a protection against draughts in winter and midges in summer."

By post from her son Tony and his wife had come the softest Shetland bed-jacket, in an enchanting shade of misty blue, which made Mrs. Morland almost want to go back to bed at once. And there were letters or cables from her three other sons, and birthday cards, in varying degrees of exuberance and art-lessness, including a spirited chalk drawing of a birthday cake, with seventy kisses (not quite accurately counted), from her large brood of grandchildren.

From her old friend Amy Birkett, wife of the ex-headmaster of Southbridge School, where all the young Morlands had received and healthily resisted their education, came the imagina-tive gift of a couple of extra-large and fluffy bath sheets, "be-cause," as Mrs. Birkett wrote, "most of the towels that they call bath sheets now are so skimpy that they barely cover you."

Mr. Wickham had contributed a bottle of Navy rum, a bottle of cherry brandy, and one of very special green chartreuse. Her fellow authors, Miss Hampton of Adelina Cottage and Lady Silverbridge, who had been Isabel Dale before her marriage and wrote highly successful thrillers under the name of Lisa Bedale, had sent advance copies of their new books, a thought which touched Mrs. Morland very much indeed, as did the friendly inscriptions on the flyleaf.

Her friend Lord Crosse in East Barsetshire had sent a basket full of hothouse grapes and peaches, while a prosperous-looking hamper in the corner proved to be the gift of Jessica and Aubrey Clover. It came from a celebrated London store and was filled with delicacies for the table, from game cooked in wine sauce and strawberries in brandy, to calves' foot jelly, a jar of Stilton cheese, and an assortment of delicious sweet or cheesy biscuits which, thought Mrs. Morland, who was by no means greedy, really made your mouth water.

We don't know what the other presents were, nor shall we trouble to invent them, lest we become as verbose, though not alas as noble, as Homer with his catalogue of ships. Enough to say that so many people had remembered Mrs. Morland's birthday that it was nearly half-past eleven before she had opened all the parcels and read her cards and letters. At which point there was the sound of a car pulling up on the little gravel drive, and Stoker announced: "It's Mr. Coates and Miss Sybil," for such was her artless way of referring to the publisher's wife, George Knox's daughter, whom she had known since girlhood.

"Dear Laura," said Sybil, hugging her affectionately, "we just ran down for a moment to wish you the happiest of birthdays and to bring our present. It's a bit bulky, I'm afraid, and rather complicated, and we thought we'd better show you how it works. Put it up, will you, darling?" she said to Adrian, who thereupon tore open the large package he was carrying, with a sacrifice of paper that made Mrs. Morland wince, and proceeded to assemble the various parts of an immense Heath Robinson contraption, which combined a folding-table with a goose-necked lamp and tilting book-rest, and seemed to be entangled, Laocoön fashion, with yards of flex.

"It's for having breakfast in bed," said Sybil, "so that you can read at the same time."

"Or supper in bed," added her publisher, looking with veneration upon his expensive and complicated gift.

"You see it goes right across your bed," said Sybil, "so that you can't knock it over, and the lamp plugs into the wall, and the pockets at the sides are for your glasses, or newspapers or the book you aren't actually reading."

"There now," declared Stoker, who was hovering as usual, "I was saying to Mrs. Morland only this morning would she like her breakfast brought up in bed, seeing as this was a special day and everything, and she said she couldn't do with trays."

This gross distortion of the truth was well received by the Coateses, and Mrs. Morland thanked them warmly for their gift, saying with equal divagation from the truth that she was sure it was exactly what she needed. Privately she resolved never in any circumstances to allow herself to be imprisoned by this terrifying contraption. But her gratitude for the kind thought was genuine, and she begged Adrian and Sybil to stay for lunch, disregarding Stoker's emphatic No-face, which said clearly that there were only cutlets for three, and half the blackberry-and-apple tart left over.

Luckily Sybil said they had promised to go to lunch at Daddy's, and Adrian had to be back in town by six for a literary cocktail party. So the visitors embraced Mrs. Morland again and went away, leaving that pleasing, anxious creature with the feeling that kindness could sometimes be too kind, and gazing with a sort of wild despair at the apparatus which Adrian had put up and neglected to take down.

Stoker, who knew her employer very well, solved the problem by dismantling the structure in one fell swoop, bundling the various pieces under her massive arm, and remarking: "I'll put them in the broom cupboard in case you want them. There's a salmon come by post with the compliments of Sir Edmund Pridham. I've put it in the fridge, and it'll be tasty with peas for your lunch tomorrow. Just you leave all that rubbish be," she added, with a dark look at the torn discards of brown paper. "I'll soon sort it out."

Mrs. Morland knew when she was beaten. Gratefully and a little cravenly she told Stoker that she was going to her room to write some letters, and a few minutes later was deep in the opening chapters of Lisa Bedale's new thriller, *Don't Spare the Hearses,* which she had meant to keep for bedtime, but suddenly felt she needed in a bad way.

It had been arranged that Mrs. Morland, after a nice lay-down after lunch (Stoker's words, not ours), should be driven to the Old Bank House by Anne Knox. ("Though why I can't be trusted to drive myself, I don't know," said Laura.) By this means, it was considered, she would be certain to arrive at the party at the proper time, with some of the circumstance befitting a guest of honour, although there were those who held that the sight of the distinguished novelist drawing up in front of the Old Bank House in her familiar rattletrap of a car would add just the needed touch of drama.

"I'll tell you what," said Lucy Adams in her powerful voice, "it wouldn't work. If she comes here by herself she wouldn't come at all. I mean she'd see all those cars and things and go straight back home. That's what Wicks says anyhow, and he knows her pretty well."

So it was settled that Anne Knox, with her husband George as extra guard ("Because he'll talk so much about motoring in the olden days and how ghastly all this building is that Mrs. Morland won't have a chance to think about the party until she gets there"), should call for Laura in their car, in time to deliver her at the Old Bank House by half-past four. All unconscious of her doom, the victim ate a hearty lunch of cutlet, peas, and blackberry-and-apple tart, followed by a dashing glass of Lord Stoke's admirable port. Then she lay down for a few minutes on her bed with *Don't Spare the Hearses,* and had almost reached the second murder before she fell asleep.

Robin, who had spent the morning studying train and bus time-tables, set out for Edgewood immediately after lunch by a complicated itinerary of his own devising. His grandmother had wondered for an anxious moment whether it was her duty, *in loco parentis,* to forbid this, but decided that small boys with common sense could usually be trusted to mind their own affairs, and compromised with some extra pocket-money and the telephone number of the Old Bank House, just in case.

Stoker, an important figure in the catering department although she had delegated to Messrs. Scatcherd and Tozer the supreme honour of creating the Birthday Cake, which was designed, as Anne Dale would probably have said, for forty feeding as one, had made her own arrangements for transport. After seeing her employer comfortably settled for a nice lay-down with a hot bottle and That Book Something About Horses, she said that Annie's niece was obliging in the kitchen if she wanted anything, and she'd told Palmyra Phipps at the exchange not to ring the telephone if she could help it. After which she put on her best blacks, protected by an enormous apron, collected various laden baskets, and made her way to the trysting-place at the pillar-box, where she was picked up by Panter, George Halliday's carter, who was going over Edgewood way to collect some fertiliser and deliver a couple of young pigs.

The overcast morning had broken up, just as the weather experts, professional and amateur, had prophesied, and by three o'clock Barsetshire was basking in a mellow September sun, not strong but sweet, and it was one of those tender, golden afternoons which come so often and so gratefully with the first fall of the leaf.

The Old Bank House at Edgewood, always gracious, was looking at its best in the warm, slanting light. Our reader who was present at the garden party given by Samuel Adams, the wealthy Hogglestock ironmaster, to celebrate his housewarming some dozen years ago, will be glad to know that Timon Tide, as Mr. Adams used to call it in his less couth days, had left the charming Regency house in the High Street virtually untouched.

Although Progress was rapidly invading Edgewood, and there was a supermarket at one end of the High Street and a public car park at the other, not to mention an espresso bar and a cinema with neon lighting and posters of outstanding hideousness, the Old Bank House was still a pleasure to the eye. Three storeys high, with well-proportioned windows, it stood flush on the street with a few steps leading up to the white front door with its elegant shell canopy. This door, in pleasant country fashion, was left unlocked all day in summer, and friends of the family had only to turn the brass handle and walk in. For the benefit of others, there was an old but handsome brass door-knocker, which we are glad to say the present owner had stubbornly refused to change for a bell with chimes, although urged to do so by several of his Hogglestock colleagues, who considered it would add a Touch of Tone.

On the afternoon of the birthday party the weather, as we have said, was on its best behaviour, and from the windows of the long drawing-room, which ran from front to back of the house, the garden looked, as several helpers said, A Picture. The drawing-room and hall were filled with flowers, arranged by the clever fingers of Clarissa Belton, who had come over from Harefield very early in the morning, cut them while the dew was on them, and plunged them up to their necks in water.

Soon after lunch, which was cold, to save the staff (although we must say that they enjoyed a very hearty meal of fried fish and chips themselves), the various helpers and arrangers went to work, under the able command of Lucy, her stepdaughter Heather Pilward, and Miss Hoggett, the Adams's quite hideous but faithful housekeeper. Mr. Adams, who knew as well as any man when he was in the way, had thoughtfully arranged to have lunch at the Club, and we are happy to say that this act of kindness was rewarded, for there he met a very rich man from the Argentine, with whom he made a satisfactory deal for a big casting.

At the Old Bank House, Messrs. Scatcherd and Tozer's well-trained staff were already busy. Deftly and quietly they erected tables, assembled chairs, unpacked glasses, silverware, plates, and snowy tablecloths, and set up a small marquee in the garden and a buffet bar at the far end of the drawing-room, over which Mr. Tozer himself proposed to preside, assisted by Dr. Joram's butler, Simnet.

Mr. Adams had ordered six dozen bottles of champagne, with more in reserve, to be opened at Mr. Tozer's discretion. This was not, he said, a garden party at the Palace. No expense was to be spared, and he wanted the best of everything on the firm's highest tariff. He did not add, as he would have done some years ago, that Sam Adams's word was as good as his bond, and indeed this would have been a work of supererogation, for everybody knew it was.

In the kitchen the mobled birthday cake was unveiled before an admiring audience, and Miss Hoggett's niece Ireen, who had come over from Hogglestock to help Auntie with the washing-up, observed that Margaret and Tony couldn't have had no better for their wedding. Cocktail delicacies and thin sandwiches of smoked salmon, pâté, and chicken breast were unpacked and reverently set out on plates with doyleys (Mr. Tozer's word, not ours), covered with napkins to keep them moist. Chipolata sausages on sticks and delicious little *vol-au-vents* were popped into the oven (again Mr. Tozer's phrase) for last-minute heating; ice-cream blocks went into the deep fridge, and Miss Hoggett had shone up the silver tea-urn, quite a treat for those guests who felt that a tea-party should *be* a tea-party.

Stoker, arriving in the middle of the afternoon by courtesy of George Halliday's carter, went to work with a will as Miss Hoggett's aide, after agreeing that she wouldn't say no to a nice cup of tea, and added her amateur gifts to the professional collation. To her credit it must be said that these, although numerically slight, were extremely good, as Mr. Tozer was the first to testify when he accepted one of her home-made sponge fingers with his cup of tea.

"Madam," he said, raising his cup to her and sketching the motions of a bow, "I drink to a fellow artist of the quizzeen. I haven't tasted nothing like these fingers since I was a lad. Nowadays it's savouries *ad nauseous,* as they say, but I've always had a sweet tooth myself and everyone to his fancy. I'll take two lumps in the next cup, Miss Hoggett, if you please, and another finger, Mrs. Stoker, if you can spare it."

While these activities were taking place downstairs, the younger Adams children were whisked out for a walk and later to their own quarters by a strong-minded Hogglestock Nannie. Amabel, freed from the shackles of the nursery at the advanced age of ten, decided that now was the time for all good women to come to the aid of the party. She carried out this programme with such zest, telling everybody what, getting under the feet of Scatcherd and Tozer's men, and interfering with the helpers with such hearty good-will, that even her gentle friend Eleanor Leslie, who had been invited to spend the previous night at the Old Bank House, was moved to mild expostulation.

"I say, Amabel," she suggested, "don't you think we'd better go up to the bus stop and look for Robin? That man in the white coat with the sandwiches is getting awfully waxy. He's said Pardon at least four times, and last time I think he said something else as well."

"All right," said Amabel good-humouredly, "but I'll tell you what, when Robin gets here lets all go to the kitchen and see if Hoggs has anything to eat. There might be some dishes that we could scrape the bits round the edges of them. I'm frightfully hungry."

This plan, however, was ably forestalled by Lucy, who, when Robin arrived in plenty of time to be a nuisance, packed all three children off into the garden, with a light repast of apples, greengages, chocolate bars, and biscuits to fill the aching void between lunch and tea-time.

"Let's go and sit on the well," said Amabel. "We can hear the people coming from there."

Accordingly the two little girls and Robin, munching as they went, made their way down the garden path and through a door in a brick wall into a kind of courtyard behind the old stables, paved with moss-covered cobblestones, in the middle of which was a well with a little wooden penthouse and an iron handle to raise or lower the buckets.

"I say," said Robin, as they perched on the brick coping, "this *is* a decent well. Can I throw down a greengage stone and hear it go plop?"

A distant and very feeble splash rewarded his efforts. "I expect it hit a dead rat or something," said Amabel carelessly. "You never know what you'll find in wells. A man jumped down one of Lord Pomfret's wells once, his name was Horace Tidden."

"Is he still there?" asked Robin with interest.

"Oh no," said Amabel. "Percy Bodger helped to get him up. He said he looked *ghastly*. But if he hadn't drowned they would have hung him anyhow. He'd bonked his old aunt and uncle on the head with a mallet or something."

"Don't, Amabel," said Eleanor, shuddering, "it's horrid." And rather quickly she slid off the coping and perched herself on a convenient horse-block. "I can hear cars," she said, "in the stableyard and outside in the road. That's the Rushwater land-rover, I know the sound of the engine."

"I heard Dad's car come home a long time ago," said Amabel. "And that's Mr. Wickham's in the stableyard. I know the rattle."

"The horsemen and the footmen are pouring in amain," said Robin, as the noise of car doors banging and voices raised in greeting came to their ears.

"What do you mean, A Main?" asked Amabel.

"I don't know *exackly,"* said Robin with unusual modesty, "but anyway that's what it says in the poem."

"I expect it's just a word put in to rhyme with plain," suggested Eleanor, and then, seeing that the intellectual level of the conversation was beyond her hostess's grasp, she added quickly that she didn't suppose Amabel had done Horatius yet, but she was top of her form in maths last term.

"But Horatius isn't a thing you *do,"* said Robin, in his turn frankly puzzled, "it's something that you *read."*

Unable to explain the fine distinction between people who read poetry for pleasure and people who do it because they have to, Eleanor went on to say that anyway there weren't any footmen at the Old Bank House unless you counted Simnet, and you could hardly say he was pouring in amain because he'd been there for hours. "I suppose," she added, "you *could* count Mr. and Mrs. Grantly, because they're only walking down the High Street from the Rectory. But I can't think of any horsemen, unless Mr. Wicklow rides over from Nutfield, or Lord Stoke drives his dogcart, because they're all coming in their cars."

"Horsepower men," suggested Robin, which witticism sent both little girls into a fit of the giggles. After this they played a very entertaining game of discovering how many people were arriving at the Old Bank House from north and south and east and west and intermediate points of the compass, in which Robin, through his ignorance of Barsetshire topography, found himself hopelessly outclassed, until he had the bright idea of saying somebody might come by helicopter.

"That would be north, wouldn't it?" said Eleanor doubtfully, "I mean north's always at the top of the map." Amabel said it didn't follow, because up and down were in a different dimension, and Robin said what fun it would be to see old Stoker landing in a helicopter.

"Or Miss Pettinger," said Eleanor.

"Or the Bishop," said Amabel. "I'll tell you what, if the Bishop landed in a helicopter with his gaiters, everyone would say he'd come down from heaven."

With such pleasing fancies did the children divert themselves, until the last apple core and greengage stone had been tossed down the well, and Amabel decided that it was time for tea. So they pushed open the wooden door in the brick wall, and made their way across the garden, where waiters with trays were circulating amongst the groups of guests, to join the birthday party, which was already in full swing.

As anticipated, Mrs. Morland had quite enjoyed her drive from High Rising in the Knoxes' car, listening to George's diatribes against ribbon development, hideous hoardings, arterial roads, and the supreme abomination of bungalows and caravans which appeared to have been thrown together for the sole purpose of supporting television masts or perhaps he should say aerials, the just word for these monstrosities having escaped him. But as they turned into the High Street of Edgewood and drew up in front of the Old Bank House, she gave one look of horror at the serried ranks of parked cars and shied like a startled horse.

"Oh, *Anne*," she said reproachfully, "you promised that this was just a *little* party."

"I promised it would be a party of your friends," said Anne. "And so it is."

"*Du courage,*" murmured George Knox. "*Noblesse oblige.*"

"Deceivers, both of you, this is a conspiracy," said Mrs. Morland, climbing out of the car with a sinking heart and feeling with Touchstone that when she was at home she was in a better place. We think she might have turned and fled even on the doorstep, had not the watchful Mr. Adams flung the door open wide, and putting a comforting though unexpected arm round her reluctant shoulders, urged her towards the hall where Lucy was waiting to greet her. "Welcome to the Old Bank House," he said. "Not for the first time nor yet I hope the last time, but it's a fine old house and friendly, though I say it as shouldn't, and it's never had a prouder day than this."

Before she had time to think how terrified she was, Mrs. Morland found herself engulfed by Adamses and Marlings, amongst whom she noticed her own grandson with Amabel and Eleanor, hopping on one leg in his excitement. Stoker, materialising suddenly, disengaged her employer from the various winter wrappings which it was her custom to wear for summer warmth, and Lucy led her straight into the drawing-room and to the handsome Chinese-Chippendale sofa with its golden brocade cushions, on which Mrs. Dean had slept so powerfully throughout the housewarming so many years ago.

"Nobody will bother you here," she said. "I'll head them off for a bit. And most of them are at the bar or in the garden anyway. I say, Mrs. Morland, do you like the flowers? Clarissa did them. I'm no good at flowers, only vegetables, but I'll tell you what, Clarissa ought to be with Constance Spry."

Her mind thus artfully distracted, Mrs. Morland looked at the low bowls of late roses, and the jars with their elegant tall spires of autumn flowers and foliage, and said she was no good at flower arrangement either, but Clarissa was a genius, she thought she got it from her grandmother, the late Lady Emily Leslie.

At this point she became aware of a waiter hovering beside her with a tray, suggesting in a smooth, low voice: "A glass of champagne for Madame?" Still in a daze, she accepted and sipped the heart-warming champagne, then coming to her senses, did what is known in entertainment circles as a double-take and nearly dropped her glass.

"Aubrey Clover!" she exclaimed. "It's you—but I thought ——"

"Darling Mrs. Morland," cooed Jessica Dean, sliding in beside her on the sofa, "yours not to think today. Yours not to reason why. I know exactly how you're feeling, like a first night at the Cockspur, with butterflies in your stomach. But there aren't any critics here, only your friends. Aubrey makes a good waiter, doesn't he? I want him to play the waiter in a musical version of *You Never Can Tell*. Denis Stonor is madly keen on the idea, and I'd like to do the *soubrette* part, Dolly, if I'm not too old. But we can't think of a good title. What do you suggest?"

The professional writer in Mrs. Morland at once rose to meet the challenge. Sipping her champagne in an absent-minded way, and feeling easier each minute, she gave her attention seriously to the proposal of a fitting title for a musical version of *You Never Can Tell*. "Although," she said with vehemence, "you can't really beat Shaw's own." Jessica favoured her husband with the famous Mrs. Carvel wink, and listened with rapt attention. Aubrey Clover, palming his tray, if one can palm a tray, moved away with Lucy Adams, saying: "Don't worry, Jessica's doing her stuff."

By the time Mrs. Morland had nearly finished her glass of champagne, and nibbled a minute square of caviar on biscuit, proffered by a real waiter, while various friends came up to give her greeting, she found to her surprise that she was almost enjoying herself. When Mr. Adams arrived with a small table for her glass and plate, she thanked him warmly for allowing her to see his lovely home again.

"I've never forgotten this exquisite Chinese wallpaper," she said. "I noticed it at your housewarming party and I do admire it so much." At which Mr. Adams, delighted with this praise, told her the story of how old Miss Sowerby, his predecessor, had given the extra rolls of wallpaper as a parting present to the house, before she went to live with her widowed sister in Worthing.

"Wonderful old lady that," he added, "straight as a ramrod she still is and never misses a visit to see the garden in spring and autumn when I send a car over to fetch her."

"And yet," said the voice of Mrs. Grantly, who had walked down the High Street from the Vicarage with her husband, "she thought she wouldn't be alive when Palafox Borealis came into flower in 1955. Do you remember Palafox, Mr. Adams, and how Miss Sowerby gave it to us when she went away, because she was certain that old Lady Norton would come and take it?"

Mr. Adams replied that he didn't like to use harsh words about any lady, but Lucy always said that the Dreadful Dowager, which is what she called her, was a pain in the neck, and he wasn't going to contradict her. By this time Jessica Dean, her mission accomplished, had slipped away to join the other guests, and the Vicar's wife sat down by Mrs. Morland.

"I cannot begin to tell you," she said, "how utterly revolting Palafox Borealis is, but dear Miss Sowerby set great store by it. She said it was the only specimen of its kind in England, and the Royal Horticultural Society would give their eyes to have one like it."

"What does it look like?" asked Mrs. Morland with interest.

"Well," said Mrs. Grantly judicially, "you'd really have to see it in flower to appreciate the full horror, but it has hairy grey leaves and a stalk with a kind of sticky knob on top, and the petals, if petals they are, look like three strips of pink house-maid's flannel. It's only supposed to flower once in seven years and personally I think that's once too often. But our nice girls at the Vicarage, Edna and Doris Thatcher, put it on the kitchen window-sill, and Doris's boy Sid took a tremendous fancy to it and really looked after it splendidly. He said it liked the wire-less, particularly the comic bits, so they kept the Light Pro-gramme on at full blast, from first thing in the morning until last thing at night."

Mrs. Morland, fascinated by this scene from clerical life, asked what happened to the plant?

"It flowered years before its time," said Mrs. Grantly. "Miss Sowerby was delighted. She told me I ought to write to the Secretary of the R.H.S. and not let them have the seeds for less than fifty pounds, and Sid was to be sure and keep a seed for himself. We got the money without any trouble, and I put it into Sid's post office account. He has a real gift with plants, and wants to be a gardener."

"Sam's had his eye on young Sid for a long time," said Lucy, coming up with a plate of tiny *vol-au-vents,* which she set down on the table beside Mrs. Morland. "I think he'll take him on at Adamsfield. I say, do eat these while they're hot. Some are chicken and some are lobster, and they're awfully nice, but you've got to be careful because they squish. It's funny how these kids with no fathers often turn out to be the best."

"No fathers that we *know* of," said Mrs. Grantly darkly. "I sometimes have a dreadful thought that Sid's father and the other children's fathers will suddenly turn up, and claim all their earnings and their post office accounts."

"Not likely," said Lucy, with difficulty resisting the Shavian adjective. "Just think of all the back maintenance they'd have to pay. Anyway, Sam wouldn't stand for anything like that with Sid. I say, Mrs. Morland, will you see Sister Chiffinch for a moment? She can't stop, because she has to get back to Harefield."

"Of course, I'd love to see Sister Chiffinch," said Mrs. Morland, looking round. "Oh, *there* you are, Sister. I didn't recognise you in your ordinary, I mean your plain, I mean your off-duty clothes," and she thought, as so many of us have thought before, how much better nurses look in uniform.

"I'm afraid it's only hail and farewell," said Sister Chiffinch, "but I had a couple of hours to spare, and I said to myself: Well, Chiffy, that's what my friends Heathy and Wardy call me, you've just got time to pop over to Edgewood and say Many Happy Returns to Mrs. Morland and give her your tiny present. It will go into your bag quite easily," she added, producing from her own bag a small tissue-paper packet exuding a powerful scent of lavender.

Mrs. Morland received it with the warmest thanks and stuffed it down among her various spectacle cases, saying that she looked forward to opening it when she got home, and could she guess that it was lavender?

"Well, I never," exclaimed Sister Chiffinch. "However did you know? It's just a wee sashay that I made while I was waiting for Mrs. Freddy Belton's baby. I always think they're nice to pop in among your hankies. Well, I must be wending my way back to Harefield, to relieve poor Granny, and give our young gentleman his bath and put him to by-byes. I often say to my friends Heathy and Wardy, nobody knows what Grannies mean to we nurses. Of course *you* do, Mrs. Morland, because you're a Granny yourself, and you too, Mrs. Grantly, and if the Vicar wouldn't mind the word, I'd call them a Godsend."

Mrs. Grantly said she was sure the Vicar wouldn't mind the word a bit, and Grannies thought that nurses were a Godsend too, which remark pleased kind Sister Chiffinch very much, and so she pattered away.

At this point Mr. Wickham materialised with a fresh tray of full glasses, accompanied by his employer Lydia Merton and Emmy Grantly, who after warmly greeting Mrs. Morland fell into family talk with her mother-in-law.

"I say, Wicks," said Lucy, "you oughtn't to be doing that. Simnet will be livid, and so will Mr. Tozer."

"Livid is as livid does," said Mr. Wickham. "Tozer and Simnet and I have come to a very proper understanding on certain matters."

"What you mean, Wicks," said Lucy, "is that you bribe them with bottles of something or other."

"Mrs. Adams," said Mr. Wickham, "you have a dark, suspicious mind. The result of our understanding is that I am sometimes allowed the honour of carrying a tray to a distinguished guest. I wanted to say many happy returns of the day to Mrs. Morland, and this is the first chance I've had."

"But you said it this morning, Wicks," said Mrs. Morland. "Three times over, bless you. Do tell me, have you seen George Knox about and is he all right? I feel a bit responsible for him somehow."

"Not to worry," said Mr. Wickham, "he's at the top of his form, sitting in the best chair on the lawn, with a long, cool drink beside him, telling Aubrey Clover about his lonely childhood in a big house in Rutland Gate. You never heard such a heart-rending tale so powerfully delivered. Clover is the perfect stooge and audience. He keeps feeding him lines, and I swear he is memorising every word of it for his next play."

"Poor George," said Mrs. Morland, "he never knows how boring he can be, except when he comes up against Mr. Middleton from Laverings, and then he gets a kind of mirror image."

Mr. Wickham went off with his empty tray, and Mrs. Morland turned to Lydia Merton, with whom she had already exchanged greetings. "Do pull up your chair and sit beside me, Lydia," she said, "and help to dispose of some of this champagne. I *am* so very glad you came. They told me you were in London for the week-end."

"So I am really," said Lydia, "at least Noel is and I was supposed to be. A lot of legal engagements, and the men are so much happier talking shop without their wives. I managed to escape after lunch, only the Saturday afternoon trains are terribly slow. I tried to ring up from Barchester Central to say I should be late, but when I got into the kiosk I found I hadn't enough pennies."

"I know," said Lucy, "one of those nasty threepenny bits with square edges and two halfpennies. It's always happening to me."

"Well, actually I had *one* penny," said Lydia, "and two threepenny bits and a sixpence."

"And of course nobody could give you change," said Mrs. Morland, stating a grim fact of life.

"They never can," said Lucy. "It's even stuck up on the station booking office: 'Sorry, No Coppers For The Telephone.'"

"This time," said Lydia, "it wasn't even Sorry. Just 'No Coppers.'"

"But I'll tell you what," said Lucy. "It doesn't always help much if you do get them. They're usually too thin and just fall through."

"Or else they won't go in," said Margot Fewling, who had joined the group, "because the box is full."

"I don't know how it is," said Mrs. Morland, "that pennies seem to have disappeared. You can't do *anything* with a threepenny bit that you couldn't do much better with three pennies. I suppose they didn't change the slots because they knew they were going to put it up to fourpence," she added darkly.

"I expect it will be sixpence soon," said Margot.

"I say," broke in Emmy, "Palmyra Phipps told me we're going on the dial in a year or so. That means that all our num-

bers will be changed to make four figures, or else we'll all be
O Something Something Something."

"O Naughty Naughty One Mayfair," murmured Mrs. Morland, but we doubt whether any of her hearers, except possibly
Mrs. Grantly, recognised this echo of *The Arcadians.*

"There's one very peculiar thing about the dialling system,"
said Margot. "It makes you think of numbers in quite a different way."

"What do you mean, a different way?" asked Emmy, who
liked to have all her facts clear.

"Well," said Margot, "you know how you think of people's
numbers as Barchester Double Two Six One, or something like
that? When we go onto the dial, we'll have to think of it as
BAR Two, Two, Six, One, which is quite a different thing."

The others agreed that it certainly was, and a lively discussion broke out as to the various ways of dialling, whether
you used your finger or a pencil, and how long you ought to
wait between each turn, and how difficult it was to find the
letters when there were three of them to each hole, but probably it would grow on you like touch-typing.

"What I shall miss so much," said Mrs. Grantly, "is being
able to give Palmyra or Norma or whoever it is at the exchange a message, or say not to be rung up after ten o'clock
because you're going to bed."

"Or, if my son rings up when I'm out, tell him I'm having
dinner at the Deanery," said Mrs. Morland, who was by this
time the centre of a large and eagerly chattering group and
found, to her great surprise, that she was enjoying it immensely.

A few minutes later, everyone was startled out of his or her
wits by a tremendous booming noise.

"Good heavens," said Mrs. Morland. "Whatever is that?"

"I'm afraid it's Amabel," said Lucy. "She can be awfully St.
Trinian's at times."

And Amabel indeed it was, pounding with vigour on the big

hall gong, an activity which gave her vast delight, and which might have gone on until everyone was deafened, had not her father said: "That's quite enough for now, girlie," and kindly but firmly removed the gong-stick from her hand.

The din, however, had produced results. Guests came flocking in from the garden and from the other rooms. Waiters went round quietly re-charging glasses. Mr. Adams mounted a small platform or podium which he had caused to be erected near the bar and lifted a large hand for silence.

"May I calm your attention for one minute, all?" he said. "As you know, we are here today to honour a certain lady who is very well-known hereabouts, and I may say we love her as much as we respect her. This is her seventieth birthday, and we felt we couldn't let the occasion pass without some token of our esteem. Lord Pomfret, the Lord Lieutenant of the county, is here with us today, and has kindly consented to say a few words. My wife and girlie have tipped me the wink that I mustn't talk too much, so I'll just say that the Old Bank House is honoured by your presence, and ask you to raise your glasses and drink a birthday toast to Mrs. Morland, and long may she go on writing books for us."

The toast was drunk with wild enthusiasm, and Mrs. Morland scarcely had time to wish that the earth would open suddenly and swallow her up before Lord Pomfret was on the platform.

His speech was admirably brief and simple. He spoke of the affection which the whole of Barsetshire felt for Mrs. Morland, although she, like himself, was a native by adoption and not by birth, and of the pleasure her books had given over so many years to so very many people. Her friends were anxious, he said, to give her some tangible proof of their regard, and he hoped she would find it in this birthday present "from us all."

Without more ado, he produced a folio volume which Aubrey Clover, suddenly materialising at his elbow, carried across the room and offered to Mrs. Morland, saying: "Mrs. Laura Morland, This Is Your Life," with the hint of an Irish accent and the merest adumbration of a bow.

Everybody crowded round to look, there was a great deal of handshaking and kissing from people who had never kissed Mrs. Morland before, and that gifted authoress, fumbling for her handkerchief and spectacles, could hardly see the pages of the book for tears.

"Too, too B.B.C., my dear," murmured Clarissa Belton to Mr. Wickham, who was standing by.

"Too, too critical, my girl," said Mr. Wickham. "Clover is a showman and he gives the public what it wants. Wait until you hear his Richard Dimbleby." Then seeing Clarissa's pretty face cloud over and knowing, for he was a kind creature, how often she regretted her impulses to mockery, he gave her elbow a gentle squeeze and added: "Come and see the book now that it's finished. It's really rather a nice job."

It was indeed. A large tome, beautifully bound in dark red leather, with the name "Laura Morland" stamped in gold letters on the cover, it contained sheet after sheet of signatures from well-wishers in all parts of Barsetshire, from the stiff upright hand of Lord Stoke, the dashing schoolgirl scrawl of Rose Fairweather, and the minute scholar's hieroglyphs of Mr. Carton and Mr. Downing, to the touching mark of Ed Pollett, who could do almost everything with his hands but write.

Alice Wicklow had interleaved the pages with the most charming water-colour drawings of Barsetshire scenes and characters. Here was Packer's Universal Royal Derby in full swing. Here was the elegant front of Harefield House and the far from elegant but familiar front of Pomfret Towers. Here was a lovely drawing in cool colours of the Cathedral Close, and a sunny picture of a school playing field, with tiny flannelled fools engaged in cricket.

There too was Lord Stoke driving his dog-cart, Dr. Ford

carrying his little black bag, Leslie Minor climbing a monkey-puzzle tree, Lady Graham in a pony carriage full of children, the Warings' half-gypsy keeper Jasper with his poacher's pockets bulging, Mr. Scatcherd with his easel beside the River Rising, and Goble in his Sunday best scratching the back of an enormous pig.

It was a book which anyone who loved Barsetshire and its people would treasure, and we don't think that the county could have given Mrs. Morland a more welcome present. How all the signatures were obtained in time we don't quite know, but we have given a lot of consideration to the matter and have decided that it could only be done by a kind of zoning arrangement, under which the various clergy, estate agents, doctors, and other willing organisers took responsibility for their special sections, using loose sheets which could later be collated. And if our reader can think of a better way, let him or her imagine it for his or her self.

"We've left a blank page at the end," said Lucy to Mrs. Morland, who was turning the pages in a daze of rapture. "That's for the other people to sign, the ones that they're away on holiday. Like Sir Edmund Pridham, he's in Scotland salmon-fishing."

"And the Bishop," added Mrs. Crawley, without a trace of colour in her voice. "As you know, he is detained in Ghana."

"Can I be the first to use the empty page?" said a familiar voice behind Mrs. Morland, and a hand came round her shoulder with a fountain pen and neatly jotted down the signature "A. Morland."

"Tony!" cried Mrs. Morland, whirling round.

"Myself in person," said her youngest son, "come all the way from London to wish you many happy returns of the day. And please observe with what modesty I have signed my name a long way from the top, so that the Bishop, when he returns from Ghana, can head the page."

"But how did you get *here?*" said Mrs. Morland. "How did you know there was going to be a party?"

"Answering your first question," said her son, "I drove here in my speedy motor car. Answering your second, I knew there was to be a party because Robin wrote to tell me so, in curiously elliptic terms. And by the way, Mama, allow me to congratulate you upon looking so blooming on your hundred and seventieth birthday."

"Oh, Tony, I know," said Mrs. Morland. "It's Robin's Roman numerals. He's so proud of them, poor lamb, so don't say anything to him, will you? It would hurt his feelings dreadfully, and he's been such a good, kind boy."

"Not a word shall pass these lips," said Tony. "Word of a Morland. Now I must circulate and meet some of my old friends. Why, there's my darling Lydia, and if my eyes don't deceive me, that's Ma Birky. I can hardly wait to talk to them." And he began to drift away.

"Tony!" his mother called after him anxiously, "you're not going back to London tonight, are you?"

"Staying till Monday," he called back, "if you can bear with me. I've seen Stoker in the kitchen and everything's arranged. I'll bring Robin home, so don't you wait for us." He waved his hand nonchalantly and vanished in the crowd.

After the various excitements of the day, Mrs. Morland suddenly began to feel extremely tired. She looked round rather wildly for Anne Knox, but before she had time to panic, Mr. Adams, who was a great deal more observant than most people realised, was at her side.

"Mrs. Morland," he said, "I don't want to hurry you, but if you'll pardon me for saying so, I think you've had enough. I know what it feels like after one of our big castings, nothing like home and bed and call it a day. Mrs. Knox is ready with the car whenever you say the word."

"Sam sent Mr. Knox home some time ago in one of the office

cars," said Lucy. "He was getting a bit fractious, the old pet. Stoker's coming with you and she's all packed up and ready. Let me carry that thing," she added, picking up the birthday book, "and have you got your specs?"

Mrs. Morland fumbled in her bag and said she had, and to a chorus of good-byes she went into the hall, where Stoker was waiting with her various wraps. The car was at the door, and with the warmest thanks to her kind hosts she tumbled, rather than climbed in beside Anne Knox. Stoker got in at the back with her baskets, and took the birthday book onto her capacious lap. Anne started the engine, and Lucy and Mr. Adams stood on the steps of the Old Bank House until they were out of sight. Then they turned and went in to join the remains of the party.

The drive to High Rising passed in a not uncompanionable silence, and when she reached home Mrs. Morland gladly accepted Stoker's suggestion of a nice hot bath and bed with a nice hot water bottle. When, some time later, Stoker came up with a nice hot supper on a tray, she found her employer vastly recovered, and gloating over the drawings and signatures in her birthday book.

"Do you know, Stoker," she said, "I am really quite hungry, and hardly a bit tired now."

"You will be in the morning," observed her handmaid darkly. "I've brought you some nice nourishing soup, and there's roast chicken under the cover, and some of Lord Crosse's fruit, and a glass of Lord Stoke's port. He just rung up to say he was sorry he didn't get to the party, but he fell asleep. Is there anything else you want?"

"If you'll just take away this book," said Mrs. Morland. "It's too big for eating with, and give me the one on the side table."

"You mean the one about the Horses, what you were reading this morning?" said Stoker.

"That's the one," said Mrs. Morland cravenly. "And please

tell Tony to look in and see me when he gets back, if my light's still on. I do hope he won't keep Robin out too late. Oh, Stoker, what bliss it is to be in bed, but everyone has been so kind. It's been a wonderful day."

The bright golden afternoon melted into a pale golden evening. At the Old Bank House, Messrs. Scatcherd and Tozer's men packed up their properties and departed, with a generous recognition of their services. In the kitchen Miss Hoggett entertained Mr. Simnet at a light collation, assisted by a bottle of champagne provided by her employer. In the long drawing-room Mr. and Mrs. Samuel Adams, with the few guests, including Heather Pilward, Clarissa Belton, and Mr. Wickham, who were staying on for supper, agreed that it had been a very successful party.

At Harefield, Sister Chiffinch was tucking into his cot the youngest Master Belton, replete with food, rosy from his bath, and yawning prodigiously. At Rushwater, Emmy had arrived home just in time to assist at the birth of a sturdy little heifer calf, who by common consent was to be named Laura.

At Southbridge School, Eric Swan and his staff were working on time-tables for the new term, and down at Wiple Terrace Miss Hampton and Miss Bent were drinking Mrs. Morland's health in gin and something and no heel-taps.

At Low Rising, George Knox was telling his wife Anne how all his contemporaries were growing very old, but that young fellow Clover, he didn't know what the fellow did but he seemed intelligent and listened to his elders, might write a book some day about his experiences. Meanwhile that celebrated actor-manager was speeding back to London with his wife Jessica, in time for the evening performance at the Cockspur Theatre. (And in case our reader wonders how the Clovers had managed to get to the party at all, we hasten to say that their understudies had taken over for the matinee.)

At Pomfret Towers Lavinia Merton and Lord Mellings were strolling along Golden Valley hand-in-hand, stopping every now and then to look at the changing colours of the trees, the first evening star, or any other romantic thing that caught their fancy.

"It is a beauteous evening, calm and free," said Lavinia gently.

"Darling," said Lord Mellings, "you surprise me. I never knew that you read Wordsworth."

"I do sometimes," said his Lavinia. "Not very often. But I like him when he says the ordinary things that I can't say myself."

"When we are married," said Ludo, "I can play you music that does just the same thing. Some of the old German *lieder,* some of the old folk-songs."

"We'll let the children play the piano *very* young," said Lavinia, "and they shall have all the books they want to read, real books I mean, not like the Fairy Joybell and the Goblin Hobo-Gobo. Oh Ludo, I wish we could be married *now,* and not wait until next Easter. It's so long to wait."

"Darling Lavinia," said Lord Mellings, "so do I, with all my heart, but we can't. Are you sure you really want to marry me?" To which foolish question he neither expected nor received anything but a silent answer. And so they lingered in Golden Valley for a short, precious time, while from faraway Barchester came the chime of bells, and the setting sun struck a last glint of light from the most beautiful cathedral spire in England.

ANGELA THIRKELL was born in London, where she lived until she went to Melbourne, Australia, in 1918. She was the granddaughter of Edward Burne-Jones, the daughter of Professor J. W. Mackail, and the sister of Denis Mackail. (And she was, of course, the spiritual daughter of Anthony Trollope.) While living "down under," she did some broadcasting and began to contribute to British periodicals. Her first book was completed after her return to Britain in 1930, and during the rest of her lifetime she wrote nearly thirty novels. Mrs. Thirkell died on the eve of her seventy-first birthday, leaving unfinished her twenty-ninth Barsetshire story. Anxious that no fragment of these county chronicles should be lost, C. A. Lejeune, who had often discussed the various characters with their creator, picked up the broken threads and completed the novel. C. A. Lejeune (Mrs. E. Roffe Thompson) was for many years, until 1960, the film critic for *The Observer* in London; she has also been a broadcaster, a television script-writer, and a feature writer for magazines.

January 1962

A NOTE ON THE TYPE

THE TEXT of this book was set on the Linotype in
FAIRFIELD, a type face designed by the distinguished
American artist and engraver, *Rudolph Ruzicka*. This
type displays the sober and sane qualities of a master
craftsman whose talent has long been dedicated
to clarity. Rudolph Ruzicka was born in Bohemia
in 1883 and came to America in 1894. He has designed and illustrated many books and has created a
considerable list of individual prints in a variety of
techniques.

Composed, printed, and bound by
H. Wolff, New York.